W9-BTT-515

AVALON,

TIN MEN,

DINER

AVALON,

Three Screenplays

TIN MEN,

by Barry Levinson

DINER

With an Introduction by Jesse Kornbluth

A MORGAN ENTREKIN BOOK
THE ATLANTIC MONTHLY PRESS
NEW YORK

Published simultaneously in Canada
Printed in the United States of America
FIRST EDITION

Library of Congress Cataloging-in-Publication Data

Levinson, Barry
Avalon; Tin men; Diner: three screenplays / by Barry Levinson; with an introduction by Jesse Kornbluth.
"A Morgan Entrekin book."
ISBN 0-87113-435-7
1. Motion picture plays. I. Title II. Title: Avalon. III. Title: Tin men. IV. Title: Diner.
PS3562.E9213A95 1990 791.43'75—dc20 90-41929

The Atlantic Monthly Press
19 Union Square West
New York, NY 10003

FIRST PRINTING

Contents

Introduction

Barry Levinson was just starting his sophomore year at Forest Park High School in Baltimore when he noticed a particularly striking classmate. "I'm going to take her out," he told a friend. "No, you're not," his friend said. "She's going with a guy in college." Levinson wasn't upset. "When they break up, I'll take her out," he said. His friend bet him five bucks. Levinson took the bet. Six months later, his friend announced that the girl was no longer seeing the college guy. The bet was activated. And Levinson made a phone call.

"Barbara, this is Barry Levinson," he began.

"Who?" she asked.

Undaunted, Levinson invited her to the junior prom. "I was hoping that someone else would ask me," she replied, "but . . . okay." Levinson was furious. There was, however, the matter of the bet. He took the girl to the prom. Then he collected the five bucks.

Twenty years later, Barry Levinson was living in Los Angeles. He had won two Emmys for the comedy sketches he had written for Carol Burnett's television show and was being nominated for an Oscar for *. . . And Justice for All,* an original screenplay he had co-authored. But he was also—and this was of equal, if not greater, importance—in contact with many of the Baltimore people he'd grown up with, which is why, that year, he found himself at a gathering with the woman he'd taken to the prom in 1958.

"I reminded her of our conversation," he recalls, "and she went, 'I remember saying that—there *was* someone else. But I meant what I said: It was okay to go with you.' See, it was a put-down for *me,* not for *her.* I carried something around for twenty years that had no meaning for the other person. And that's life. It's all about misunderstandings."

That anecdote holds the key to Barry Levinson's Baltimore trilogy. *Diner, Tin Men,* and *Avalon* are films driven by misunderstandings—a misspoken phrase, a wrongly taken word, an ambiguous gesture. Though these movies were written in Los Angeles, they have almost nothing in common with conventional studio-financed films. Indeed, with the possible exception of the work of Woody Allen and Eric Rohmer, Levinson's Baltimore films have no antecedents in cinema; if anything, they are literary creations. In these films there are few big events. Mostly, people just talk. The resolutions are often as open-ended as everything that has occurred in the preceding hundred minutes. And, taken together, they create a world that's credible and consistent from one film to the next—films that have more in common with the novels of William Faulkner than the predictable sequels of Hollywood's blockbuster action movies.

The unlikelihood of efficient communication, the myriad possibilities of misinterpretation, and the absence of clearly defined patterns in life are also the threads that bind Levinson's career. He didn't grow up collecting experiences that he intended to use in a trio of movies about his hometown—he didn't intend to write or direct movies at all. *Diner* got made, he says, because his very powerful executive producer seemed to think it was about something else; when the movie was finally released by a studio that also expected a very different film, it was in cities where it had minimal chances of succeeding. If a few passionate critics and some equally passionate audiences hadn't taken it to heart, Levinson would have had great difficulty making more films about Baltimore. "It's all so crazy, it's hard to talk about," he says, trying to analyze the mechanics of the film business almost a decade after *Diner.*

It's not, however, hard for him to talk about writing these movies. This isn't because he is egotistical—he's too shy and too much of a perfectionist for that—but because the pride of authorship doesn't loom large for him. Unlike many writer-directors, Levinson doesn't go to a studio, tell the story, and get a contract to "develop" the screenplay; not only does he loathe meetings and the collaborative creativity that they are intended to foster, he doesn't have a clue what the screenplay is about until he writes it. Once he gets an idea, he makes no outlines. He bulls his way through the screenplay in a state of constant curiosity and excitement, usually finishing it in less than a month. Then—and this will infuriate almost everyone who's ever written anything—he doesn't rewrite. When it's time to make the movie, he tries to accommodate his actors' suggestions and is always willing to improvise on the set, but the movie tends to be filmed almost exactly as written.

And so, although this too will probably be misunderstood, Levinson never fails to tell interviewers, "I don't think of myself as a writer."

Barry Levinson's résumé couldn't be more impressive. *The Natural,* which he directed but didn't write, was the first film released by Tri-Star Pictures.

Good Morning, Vietnam, again from another writer's script, is one of the most successful comedies ever made. *Rain Man,* which wouldn't have been made if Levinson hadn't signed on as its director, swept the Oscars. These films, like his Baltimore movies, have been completed on time and, more often than not, under budget. For Levinson is that rare director—steady but inventive, intensely private but immensely responsible.

And, as a young man, 460th in a high school class of 460.

"I was a *terrible* student," Levinson says, "and what's more, my bad performance never made me nervous. I used to fail most of my courses, then I'd have to work harder to make them up. I didn't want to fail, but it meant nothing for me to get an A. All I wanted was to get out." The problem wasn't an inability to concentrate on subjects that didn't interest him—Levinson was a terrible student in every area. "I used to fail English, too, so I was really hesitant to write. I was always failing the English themes. We'd be assigned certain topics to write about, and if I didn't like the topic, I'd pick my own. And they'd always fail me."

Levinson wasn't indolent, merely busy elsewhere. His base of operations at Forest Park High School was the Hilltop Diner, with forays to Colts and Orioles games, and, on weekends, the movies. "I was in the tenth grade when we started going to the Hilltop," Levinson recalls. "Some of the guys had been kicked out of Mandel's, the deli across the street. The diner became the place to go after you took your date home. Sometimes you didn't have a good date, and then you couldn't wait to drop her off and get back to the action. You'd make these little excursions out with the girls and then run back to the guys. That's when the night really started. You'd get there at two in the morning, and you stayed until daybreak."

"The guys" are now legend, and, as Levinson drily notes, almost everyone who grew up in Baltimore in the fifties and sixties claims to have been a regular at the Hilltop. In reality there were perhaps a dozen young men, all bright, verbal, and shockingly indolent. "It was a different time," Levinson explains. "It was hanging around, wasting your life. But that was okay. No one was really making plans back then. You knew you'd ultimately grow up, but no one got that serious about it. I look back now and wonder what we talked about, and I can't tell you. I don't remember myself as the funny one in the sense of being outgoing funny. All I remember is that it was big, big laughs."

Levinson didn't intend to go to the senior prom: "I didn't think I was going to graduate." When they played "Pomp and Circumstance," he jokes, he was still taking tests for his makeup courses. This may be. It is verifiable, though, that Levinson was voted best-looking boy in the class of '60, boy with the best personality, and, although he never played varsity sports, second-best male athlete.

After graduation, he enrolled at Baltimore Junior College. "I didn't want to go into my father's business," he says. "Carpets and appliances didn't appeal to me at all." Neither did higher education. He dropped out after five months and, for a while, sold used cars. This was far from satisfying work, so he decided to do the right thing—that is, become a well-paid tax lawyer. Legal studies were also a disaster, and he re-enrolled at Baltimore Junior College, where broadcast journalism actually engaged him sufficiently to lure him on to American University in Washington. There he alternately studied broadcasting and practiced it as a floor director at a local television station. Eventually, he reached the point where he was doomed to be promoted. "I didn't want to be an administrator telling other people what to do," he says. "I like doing it all myself."

There was no reason to go to Los Angeles, and he hadn't fulfilled the language requirement at American University, but in 1967 Levinson headed west. There a new friend was on his way to an acting class. He suggested that Levinson come in. Levinson declined. In high school he had occasionally worked with the theater club; his big moment came when somebody yelled "Lights!" and he hit a switch. In college he had met many would-be actors, all of whom, he felt, seemed to come from England. The artistic side of show business, he concluded, had as little appeal as his father's store.

Somehow Levinson allowed himself to be dragged into the Oxford Theater. Inside he found regular people, some of them good-looking actresses. "Not too bad," he told himself. And signed up. There he met Craig T. Nelson, a young actor with a gift for improvisation. They worked up a comedy routine, they wrote some of the skits down, and, to their delight, they sold them. Barry Levinson was now a writer. In the next few years he wrote for Tim Conway, Marty Feldman, and Carol Burnett, collected his Emmys, and began to wonder about movies.

A successful screenplay, Bob Towne has said, consists of half a dozen big moments connected by other moments. That is a masterly summary of conventional screenplay form in Hollywood, where a screenplay's reception depends, in large part, on its ability to be summarized in a few sentences. This emphasis on big moments tends to reward clever technicians who can put straightforward characters into movies with clear-cut conflicts and lots of technology, special effects, and action sequences. As a result, Hollywood screenplays are generally plot-driven, not character studies. Typically, the conflict is laid out in the first few minutes, after which the plot proceeds at a pace that can practically be graphed—this is a world that lives and dies by Aristotle's *Poetics.* There are first-act climaxes, second-act complications, third-act wrap-ups; there is "dramatic arc," there is "subtext." And all of it is fully discussed and outlined before a word is written. The creativity thus tends to take place in the earliest stages of the screenplay, and the writing itself is less an act of discovery than of execution and manipulation.

Levinson was fortunate to enter this world with Mel Brooks as his protector; Brooks built his movies on gags and skits, and writing them didn't involve any abstract appreciation of screenplay form. "I am the last writer to have started in silent films," Levinson notes. Considering how verbally rich his Baltimore movies are, that first credit—as one of the writers of the Mel Brooks comedy, *Silent Movie*—is doubly ironic. The fact is, Levinson's work with Brooks was a virtual replay of the Hilltop Diner sessions. "You couldn't do better than work with Mel Brooks," Levinson says. "It was like hanging out and having coffee with the kid you thought was the funniest guy in the world."

Levinson very happily went on to co-write another Brooks film, *High Anxiety.* In the late seventies he married actress Valerie Curtin and began collaborating with her on scripts. Even then Levinson was eager to mine his personal experience—a minor car accident he'd been involved in inspired *. . . And Justice for All.* In 1980 Levinson and Curtin adapted *Inside Moves,* a heartfelt but unsentimental novel by Todd Walton about a crippled veteran of the Vietnam war. The following year they wrote a satire about the military and the toy industry that they called *Toys.* Twentieth Century Fox was going to finance it, and Barry Levinson would make his directorial debut. Then a new regime came in at Fox, and the project languished.

In 1981 Curtin got an acting job and left Los Angeles for a month. Levinson decided it was time to write something with a single byline. He had, he recalled, regaled Mel Brooks with the Hilltop Diner stories, and Brooks, who said they reminded him of Fellini's *I Vitelloni,* had encouraged him to use them in a screenplay. So Levinson put on a Pete Townsend tape called "Empty Glass" and let it play over and over while he wrote on a yellow pad. Three weeks later *Diner* was not just done—it was finished.

"When I write, I write the script," Levinson explains. "I can't write an outline. If I had to do an outline, I could never write the screenplay. What would be the point? I'm there. This way, the characters challenge one another and then I have to come back. The writing is like pure adrenaline.

Every day, I want to go. I get into the scene. Then I stop. Sometimes I don't do anything; I just listen to music and putter. I can't leap ahead—I'm waiting for the next thing. And I just go on like that until I'm done."

Two perceptions powered *Diner.* One was social: the difficulty young men have with women. The other was stylistic: the challenge of making movies lifelike. As it turned out, Levinson's dissatisfaction with traditional movies enabled him to devise a screenwriting style that neatly dramatized the social dilemmas of men who fear women. "I want to make the movie seem as if it's happening in front of you," he says. "I have a difficult time with other people's movies because my ear doesn't believe them a lot. And I can't watch sitcoms at all—it's like they invented another language, there's nothing that pushes through. The thing is, in life, conversations aren't very accurate or focused. We are fairly inarticulate—I know I am. We get screwed up, we go sideways. You don't end your sentence before I talk; there's overlap. A certain amount of improvisation occurs. In a mystery film, the script and language must be specific. The closer you get to life, the more you find digressions."

Diner is, in a sense, nothing but a digression—men stalling to avoid leaving their comfortable clique and confronting women. These young men are in their early twenties, but they're already nostalgic. As they dip their french fries into gravy, they talk wistfully of schoolboy pranks and the first time they felt a girl's breasts. Indeed, they are connoisseurs of youth—Shrevie is obsessed with his records, Fenwick takes pride in such juvenile stunts as rolling his car, Boogie gets a girl to touch his penis by inserting it surreptitiously in a popcorn box in a darkened movie theater. Adulthood is, for them, nothing but menace; something terrible may happen to Boogie if he doesn't pay off his bet, Eddie is terrified of getting married.

Through it all lurks their largest fear—that women are more than sexual vessels. There's something going on that they don't know about, and they know it, and because they can't deal with it, they huddle closer. As Eddie puts it, more in hope than belief, "You don't need a girl if you want to talk."

Levinson took this character study with its endlessly talky scenes and offbeat characters to Mark Johnson, a young producer who was then head of production for Jerry Weintraub. Johnson was marking time in that role; after graduating from the University of Virginia, he had spent two years in the Ph.D. program at the University of Iowa Film School. He immediately recognized that Levinson had created something unusual in *Diner*—he had stripped the story down to its essence, making its occasional set-pieces equivalent to the action sequences of more conventional films.

Johnson brought the script to Weintraub's attention. Weintraub seemed not to realize that although the movie was set in 1959, this wasn't an East Coast *American Graffiti.* The production staff of MGM, which was then headed by David Begelman, also missed the point that the diner crowd was made up of college students and a few college graduates. Everybody on the business side wanted to believe that, with big-budget films like *Victor, Victoria, Cannery Row,* and *Pennies from Heaven* in production, they had lucked into an inexpensive teen comedy, and that Barry Levinson, with his great credits and long silver hair and directorial okay from Fox, was, at thirty-nine, still young enough to direct it. And so, misunderstanding the director, his intentions, and his script, they gave Levinson $5.5 million and sent him to Baltimore to make his movie.

The backers of *Diner* soon discovered they had made a huge mistake. Not about Levinson's ability to make the movie—he and Johnson delivered the picture on time and $500,000 under budget. The problem was the movie itself. "You have a lot to learn about editing," an executive said after a screening of the rough cut. And he began to criticize the scene about the roast beef sandwich.

It's the first scene in the diner, and, after a debate about the relative merits of Johnny Mathis and Frank Sinatra and a little banter about sex, Modell asks Eddie if the sandwich is roast beef, which, as he well knows, it is. They go back and forth, with Eddie challenging Modell to say that he wants some of the sandwich. "I know what he means," Eddie complains, "but he beats about the bush. He beats about the bush. If he said the words, I'd give him a piece." Modell won't say the words, and it takes another full page of dialogue before the sandwich issue is—unexpectedly—resolved.

"That sandwich scene!" the MGM executive said. "Cut it out, get on with the story."

"That *is* the story," Levinson said. He did not explain that the scene was about friendship, and that, among friends, you never talk about friendship—he simply honored "the inarticulate language" and declined to cut the scene.

MGM's response was to test-market *Diner* in Phoenix and St. Louis, not cities known for their love of tradition-breaking movies. When business was awful, the studio then sat on the film, finally releasing it in Baltimore and Washington. A rabid New York publicist insisted on a screening for East Coast critics. Very reluctantly, the studio agreed. And, to MGM's surprise, several critics loved *Diner* so much they threatened to review it even if it never played in their local theaters.

At this point, in the spring of 1982, *Diner* finally and belatedly made its debut. And the reviews were, almost without exception, raves. "*Diner* isn't lavish or long, but it's the sort of small, honest, entertaining movie that should never go out of style," Janet Maslin wrote in the *New York Times*. "A wonderful movie," proclaimed Pauline Kael in *The New Yorker*. "Levinson doesn't violate his characters by summing them up—he understands that we never fully understand anybody." With proper marketing *Diner* went on to gross about $25 million and, just three years after . . . *And Justice for All*, get Levinson his second Academy Award nomination for Best Original Screenplay.

Barry Levinson was so sure that *Diner* would be his only film about Baltimore that he threw everything into its production, auditioning six hundred actors for the five lead roles and trucking in a diner from New Jersey when nothing in his hometown looked exactly right. "But as I was setting up the diner," Levinson says, "I told the assistant director, 'Over here are the older guys. A lot of tin men sit here.' And suddenly I thought, gee, I could make a movie about that."

This opportunity didn't come immediately. Levinson and Curtin next wrote *Best Friends*, a comedy about collaborators who happen to be married, and updated a 1948 Preston Sturges film called *Unfaithfully Yours*. At this point Robert Redford finally acquired the rights to a workable screenplay for *The Natural*, a Bernard Malamud novel he'd often discussed with the baseball-mad Levinson, and Levinson went off to direct his first big-budget movie. Levinson followed *The Natural* with *Young Sherlock Holmes*, again from another writer's script.

All this time, Baltimore wasn't far from his attention. After his divorce from Valerie Curtin, he married Diana Rhodes, a production designer for TV commercials who lived in Baltimore with her two children. Together they would start a second family, choose a Los Angeles home where Levinson could build an editing facility, and, in the ultimate expression of his love for his hometown, buy a home near Baltimore so the director could, when the mood struck, return to his favorite haunts. Meanwhile, he had his old diner friend Chip Silverman research the scams used by tin men, aluminum siding salesmen, in the 1950s and early 1960s. In 1985, Levinson was finally able to closet himself with a secretary and dictate his second Baltimore movie, this time to the incessant repetition of Nat King Cole singing "Sweet Lorraine" and Sinatra doing "In the Wee Small Hours."

Bill "BB" Babowsky and Ernest Tilley are a generation older than the diner crew, but they are no further along in their personal development—

this is another movie, Levinson says, in which the absence of women is what the story is all about. In this script Tilley's wife Nora serves as a ball tossed by one man to his enemy as they seek revenge on one another for a minor auto accident. But she is not nearly as passive as the women in *Diner.* As the story evolves, she begins to exert an enormous influence over both men. "She doesn't have the language of feminism—it's too soon," Levinson notes, "but she learns how to stand up for herself."

Tin Men draws upon many of the same devices as *Diner.* There are scams galore, and bets, and conversations about movies and television shows, and an orgiastic dance scene. Again, the dialogue overlaps; again, men talk at length. Just as Boogie comes to understand in *Diner* that it's not right to sleep with Shrevie's wife just to win a bet, BB realizes that he did "a lousy thing" by seducing Tilley's wife.

But BB goes further. After acknowledging that deceit is, for him, "an occupational hazard," he struggles to break through his insincerity:

> I don't like the idea that I'm not in control of this, but if this stuff's got to happen, I guess I've got no choice. I wanna . . . Ya know. . . . *He gets angry.* I wanna be with ya! OK, I said that. . . . I said it, OK?! I wanna be with you because . . .
>
> *(a beat)*
>
> I miss you, and I'd like to live with you. . . . I'd like to marry you. . . . And that's that!

When he finishes, Nora looks at him. She waits a long moment. And then, in a line that echoes Levinson's 1958 phone call to his prom date, she says, "I was hoping for something a little more romantic, . . . but, okay." (In another private reference, Levinson uses his family's former home for the *Life* magazine scene.)

Tin Men is also about another kind of growth. Levinson has great affection for these low-level con men—"as opposed to the big con guys like the President, who are the *worst,*" he says—as they bump up against recalcitrant customers, the Internal Revenue Service, and a Home Improvement Commission that threatens to put them all out of business. "Two salesmen who are rivals find themselves in an escalating conflict" is how the movie is often synopsized in TV guides. That's the plot; it's not the conflict. What Levinson is exploring here is each man's struggle with the world, and the forced reevaluation of his life and his career. And what he finds, for all the residual sexism that afflicts BB and Tilley, is that each man is able to change. BB, his heart opened by genuine emotion for Nora, finds it easier; he helps the Commission make the case against him. Tilley, protesting that aluminum siding is his "chosen field," fights the revocation of his license. But in the end the former salesmen go off into the sunset together like two cowboys—only in their case, they're heading for the next opportunity.

Tin Men built on the audience for *Diner,* and won some new converts. Budgeted at $14 million, it came in $3 million under budget and grossed more than $30 million. Levinson was pleased. "The kick to these movies—difficult but satisfying—is the hope of keeping an audience with you through these little turns," he says. "They may not gross the four hundred million dollars that make people look under a rock for the next one. I'm not concerned. If I can do what I'm doing, I'm happy. I'm able to make the movies I want."

Levinson felt that he had six or seven more Baltimore stories he might like to film after *Tin Men.* Typically, he didn't follow this one with another. But that's not to say he abandoned his exploration of character, circumstance, and communication. *Good Morning, Vietnam* is remembered for Robin Williams's manic bits, but its appeal for Levinson lies, in part, in its Baltimore connections. As a broadcasting student he worked at the campus radio station. "It was a time when FM meant fine music," he recalls, "and I'd get in trouble because I'd segue from Mantovani to rock." And, of course, Levinson saw in *Good Morning, Vietnam* an opportunity to dramatize human foibles in a place where miscommunication reaches its zenith—a war zone. "The point is, this guy can't figure Vietnam out through the men or the women, so he leaves," Levinson says. *Rain Man* is even more overtly about the difficulty of communication. Three directors tried to crack the script; all dropped out. What they saw as barriers, Levinson considered the movie's great asset. To him it didn't need more story, all it lacked was deeper characterization and a more explicit sense that these characters were related by disability as much as by blood; that is, Charlie (Tom Cruise) was as socially autistic as Raymond (Dustin Hoffman) was clinically unable to communicate.

Good Morning, Vietnam and *Rain Man* build on an idea that Levinson had explored in his first two Baltimore movies—character *is* story. These glossier, bigger-budget movies also benefit from Levinson's experiences with the actors in those films. As a former stand-up comic, Levinson had come to directing with no bias against "talent." To a great degree, in fact, he believed that much of his work as a director of actors was finished when he cast the movie. How an actor sounded, what he looked like, whether he or she fit with the rest of the cast—Levinson's overriding concern was building a credible world. Having done that, he encouraged his actors to explore it.

Levinson shoots fast, spending little time on rehearsals—some of the best scenes in his films are from early takes, when the actors are, in their opinion, still warming up. These scenes blend the scripted dialogue with improvisation, but because Levinson's scripts read so much like overheard conversation the line between prepared and invented material is rarely clear. Levinson is disciplined about his actors' improvisations; he knows his movies can run long and keeps only those moments that advance our appreciation of the characters.

This ability to let actors go while still hewing to the demands of an impatient audience was key to the success of *Rain Man,* and Levinson was praised for keeping control of the allegedly "difficult" Dustin Hoffman even as he gave Hoffman his head. Because of his skill in getting great performances from Hoffman and Cruise, Levinson was courted by many studios. Eventually, he made an agreement with Tri-Star that would allow his new company—which he predictably named Baltimore Pictures—to make films without any studio interference. And so, while others discussed, dissected, and honored *Rain Man,* Levinson found himself obsessed with one line of dialogue: "If I knew things would no longer be, I would have tried to remember better."

"I must have driven Diana crazy," he recalls. "I knew I'd do another Baltimore movie, and there were two or three I could write easily, but I had no desire to write them. I wanted something more, and I kept coming back to that one line. I hadn't written it down, I just asked myself, over and over: What does this line mean? What is this trying to hold on after it's gone?"

Levinson concluded that the line was about his family and all the changes that had occurred since his grandfather came to America. He went back to Baltimore, interviewed his relatives, and looked through photo albums. What he found was illuminating. His grandfather, he discovered, had not always been a paper hanger; at one point he owned a black nightclub and drove a motorcycle. One relative had a husband who died; when her sister's baby was born, she asked her to name the baby in his honor. The sister didn't, they never spoke again, and in family albums the sister's head is cut out of all the pictures. Three generations did live in a single row house, and then, when his father's business prospered, the Levinsons did move to the suburbs and split up.

All this gave Levinson the material for a screenplay about how America changed a very tight-knit family over three generations. Still, the story didn't reveal itself. "I have to justify the movie, it has to make sense," he says, "and even though I had the idea of *Avalon,* I didn't have the key. I thought, maybe there's a death in the family and they come together. But I'd seen that, or might have. All of a sudden, I remembered that my grandfather didn't enter this country through Ellis Island. Once I got rid of that stock opening, the movie made sense, I was able to start. Now, none of this had anything to do with the movie—it was about getting past convention and being able to make discoveries along the way." One key discovery was that television wasn't merely an amusing appliance—it was a character. "Television has had an enormous impact," Levinson explains. "It permeates our lives, it changes how we function, it affects how we relate to one another. Really, it takes over everything. In coming to terms with the evolution and impact of television, I realized I had a new character I could move around."

Avalon, for King Arthur, was an earthly paradise. In his screenplay Levinson is careful not to say whether Avalon is a street or a neighborhood; it is, for him, an idea of a glorious past in a city that has a strong English background. And so, for the writing of this script, he chose Randy Newman's songs from "Land of Dreams" as his background music. Once again he was finished in about a month and unable to rewrite or change his script. On the set his actors were unable to come up with improvised dialogue that improved it. And in the editing room, it proved impossible to move scenes around.

All this makes *Avalon* that rarest of American films—a summing-up that streams out of a writer-director. In form it is just that big: a tragedy with laughs that makes us feel we know the creator as well as we know his characters. In part this is inevitable in a movie that is, quite literally, inspired by the childhood memories of a man who forgets nothing. "The not-so-magnificent Ambersons," Levinson calls it, with characteristically self-deprecating humor. And so, although he doesn't like to conduct literary analyses of his scripts, he does take pleasure in noting the unseen connections between *Avalon* and his other Baltimore films. After the family car is smashed, he points out, the Krichinskys buy a Hudson; much later, Shrevie buys this car and drives it in *Diner.* The appliance store that Shrevie works in may be Izzy's—Levinson isn't sure. But he's quite certain that Tilley, in *Tin Men,* eventually comes to live in the house the Krichinskys leave when they move to the suburbs. And, of course, when Michael looks out of the car's back window and sees a diner being set into position, he's looking into his future—and Levinson's.

Levinson may not like to explicate his scripts, but he does not deny that they work on many levels. So while *Avalon* is, first and foremost, a story of a Jewish family as it is affected by success, the suburbs, and television, it is also, like every Levinson film, a parable about miscommunication. That is especially poignant here because, for the first time, the characters are relatives, not friends. And, on the deepest and most disquieting level, it's a chronicle of what our country has become: a land of strangers cut off from community, imprisoned by economic realities, with family and religious values eroded—a nation struggling to reconnect.

Although this last is a deeply disquieting vision, the movie is not the work of a polemicist. As in his earlier movies, Levinson refuses to create stereotypes or make judgments. As a result, *Avalon* is an eminently watchable movie with all the comedy front-loaded and all the tears coming in a flood at the end. Levinson doesn't neutralize the harshness, he just refuses to make it more than it is—his only enemy is, as ever, melodrama.

Toward the end, for example, the mother is in the hospital. Her son's appliance store has burned to the ground, and he is starting over as a space salesman for television advertising—as Levinson puts it, he's moved on from selling television sets to selling what makes them go. "I've never heard of such a thing," the mother says, so he explains what he does. "I hate commercials," she says. But wait—there's one she likes. Maybe he has something to do with that. He doesn't. "That's a shame," she tells her son.

"What she's saying, in effect, is 'I don't like what you do,' " Levinson explains. "She doesn't give him any support, but it's just said. You don't see villainy, it's not bad guys and good guys, it's attitudes and behavior. Sometimes we're affected, sometimes not. We slight each other all the time without meaning to."

The enduring charm of Barry Levinson's movies is that, more often than not, the characters forgive these slights and try to cherish one another. To be sure, one relative in *Avalon* cannot. Against his explicit wishes, the Thanksgiving turkey is cut before he arrives, an intolerable insult that he uses to separate himself from his family. More telling, though, is the way Michael (a stand-in for Levinson himself) names his son Sam (which is also the name of one of Levinson's sons) in honor of his grandfather. The Jewish tradition holds that children are only to be named for the dead, and at the nursing home where he is passing his last days, the grandfather reminds Michael of this. Then he relents: "That's good. . . . That's good. . . . Carry on the family name. . . . That's good."

"It's the death of the religion," Levinson acknowledges. "Michael feels a stronger connection to the man than to his heritage." But that is not, in

Levinson's scheme, a heresy. The important thing, as the grandfather seems to understand, is that someone does remember, that the past exists in the present and has the hope of being carried forward into the future. And indeed, in the film's last scene, when the young Sam notes that his great-grandfather "sounds funny," Levinson has Michael begin to tell his son the family's history. There is no more eloquent conclusion possible—and no more literary way of binding *Avalon* to the world that Levinson explores in his other Baltimore movies.

It is difficult to overstate Levinson's achievement in *Avalon.* In dealing with family issues it addresses a subject deeper and more central than dating and career—it's the work of a mature writer-director. *Avalon* also sustains a difficult cinematic trick: Though it spans half a century, we always feel as if we are observing life just as it happens.

In that sense, it is only for the sake of convenience that this volume of Levinson's screenplays will be found in the cinema section of bookstores. His obsession with the world he has created, his skill in moving readers around in it from script to script, his ability to define characters through language rather than action—these are skills usually reserved for novelists. To read these screenplays, then, is to do more than re-create some of our favorite movies in our heads. It is to follow the development of a point of view about life that finds expression nowhere else in American moviemaking.

When I look for writers who might be antecedents of Levinson's, I think not only of Faulkner but of Proust. And I'm reminded of a story about Proust on an evening when he went to the Ritz for dinner. A Prussian general was also dining there, and, seeing the fuss everyone made over the foppish man at a nearby table, he asked his aide who he was. "Marcel Proust, sir—he's a novelist," the aide replied. "What's his book like?" the general inquired. "It's not *like* anything," the aide said.

You could say the same about each of these screenplays.

JESSE KORNBLUTH
New York
July 1990

DINER

Fade in.

1. The screen

is black. We hear muffled rock-and-roll music. Then we read:

BALTIMORE
1959

Fade out.

Fade in.

2. Interior. Dance-hall basement. Night.

FENWICK *walks along the dimly lighted basement. Heavy winter coats hang from hooks on the wall. In the background there is constant traffic of people entering and leaving the rest rooms. From above we hear the muffled sound of the rock-and-roll* BAND.

FENWICK *is in his early twenties and is dressed in the Joe College style of the late fifties—sports jacket, button-down shirt, chino pants, and Bass Weejuns. We sense that he is a little lost in himself, confused. He looks out one of the windows onto the parking lot. Then, without any outward anger, he punches his fist through a windowpane. Seconds later he breaks another window with his fist.*

FENWICK, *picking up the beat of the music from above, struts to the sound as he approaches another bank of windows. He calmly breaks another windowpane with his fist.*

A GUY *coming out of the bathroom in the background sees* FENWICK*'s actions and then heads up the steps.*

Cut to

3. Interior. Dance hall.

The crowd is gathered around the bandstand, listening to the local group, THE SHAKERS, *playing their popular hit "Hot Nuts." The song is played toward the end of the evening because of its risqué lyrics.*

BAND LEADER

Hot nuts, hot nuts, get from the peanut man.
Hot nuts, hot nuts, get 'em any way you can.

As the crowd swings the verse back to the BAND LEADER, *the* GUY *who spotted* FENWICK *breaking the windows approaches* BOOGIE. BOOGIE *is something of a dandy, flashier in dress than others in his crowd. Although he isn't particularly good looking, something about his attitude is very appealing to girls.* BOOGIE, *after listening to the* GUY, *heads downstairs.*

4. Interior. Dance-hall basement.

FENWICK *casually breaks another window with his fist. His hand is bleeding.* BOOGIE *approaches.*

BOOGIE

What's up, Fen?

FENWICK

Just breaking windows, Boog.

BOOGIE

What for?

FENWICK

It's a smile.

He breaks another window with his fist.

BOOGIE

C'mon, don't be a schmuck.

FENWICK

I know that glass is made from sand, but how come you can see through it?

He breaks another window. BOOGIE *grabs him.*

BOOGIE

Leave the windows alone. What's the matter with you?

FENWICK

It's a smile, that's all.

BOOGIE

I'm cracking up.

FENWICK *struggles to get free.*

BOOGIE (*continuing*)

I'm warning you, Fen, break another window and you're gonna get a fat lip.

He lets FENWICK *go.*

BOOGIE (*continuing*)

Where's your date?

FENWICK

Gave her away.

BOOGIE

What?

FENWICK

Gave her away. David Frazer said she was death. So I said if you like the way she looks, take her.

BOOGIE

What are you, the Salvation Army?

FENWICK

Charged him five bucks.

BOOGIE

C'mon. Upstairs.

FENWICK *just stares at him.*

BOOGIE (*continuing*)

C'mon.

They walk away from the camera.

BOOGIE (*continuing*)

You really are nuts, you know that?

FENWICK

Me? What about her? She didn't have to go. I'm nuts. Get that.

BOOGIE

That's what you get from dating eleventh-graders. Brains aren't developed.

FENWICK

But her tits were.

BOOGIE

Falsies.

FENWICK

They were?

BOOGIE

Firsthand info.

FENWICK

Shit, then what am I pissed about?

They disappear up the steps.

Cut to

5. Interior. Dance hall. Slightly later.

The BAND *is on a break. A Frank Sinatra record is playing. The camera pans to* EDDIE, *who is in a corner with one foot up on a chair. He smokes a cigarette and taps his foot lightly to the music.* EDDIE *takes Sinatra very seriously.*

SHREVIE *approaches* EDDIE.

SHREVIE

Where's Elyse?

EDDIE

Talking with your wife about the fucking wedding plans.

SHREVIE

Gettin' cold feet?

EDDIE

They've never been warm.

BOOGIE *is talking with* DIANE, *the young eleventh-grader whom* FENWICK *had the falling-out with. She is an attractive, petite girl with large breasts.*

BOOGIE

How can you take Frazer over the Fen?

DIANE

'Cause.

BOOGIE

Diane, did you know that Frazer bought you for five bucks? That's the kinda guy he is.

DIANE

He did?

BOOGIE

Do you want to leave with Frazer?

DIANE

Not really, but Fenwick scares me. Why don't you take me home?

BOOGIE

Diane, I'm in law school at night. I have to go home and study. I just stopped by here 'cause I appreciate fine music.

DIANE

I thought you worked in a beauty parlor.

BOOGIE

I do during the day.

He puts his hand up and strokes her cheek. In the background we can see FRAZER *standing with another guy. He glances over.*

BOOGIE (*continuing*)

Diane, go with Fen. For me, OK?

Cut to

6. Exterior. Country road. Night.

FENWICK'S *TR3 speeds by.* DIANE *is in the car.* FENWICK *is telling her something, and she laughs.*

7. Interior. Fenwick's car. Night.

FENWICK

You cold?

DIANE

No.

FENWICK

I didn't turn the heater on.

7A. Exterior. Country road. Night.

BOOGIE *and* MODELL *follow. Behind them* SHREVIE *and his wife,* BETH, *follow in a 1950 Hudson Hornet.*

FENWICK *floors his car and disappears around a bend. The other cars do not keep pace.*

8. Interior. Boogie's car.

MODELL

You know what word I'm not comfortable with? *Nuance.* It's not really a word like *gesture. Gesture* is a good word. At least you know where you stand with *gesture.* . . . But *nuance,* I don't know. . . . Maybe I'm wrong.

9. Interior. Shrevie's car.

BETH

Elyse feels that Eddie is getting very sensitive about the wedding.

SHREVIE

I know. We were talking about it.

10. Interior. Fenwick's car.

DIANE

Aren't you chilly?

FENWICK

No, no . . . I feel good. . . . I feel good.

(*a beat*)

Am I going too fast for you?

DIANE

No, no.

11. Interior. Shrevie's car.

BETH

Elyse's mother is very upset with Eddie. They picked out a yellow and white motif for the wedding. You know, like we did—tablecloth, napkins, maids of honor. Anyway, Eddie objected. He wanted blue and white because that's the Colts' colors. Refused to give in.

SHREVIE

Yeah, so?

BETH

Well, you know how stubborn Eddie is.

SHREVIE

Could be worse. It could be black and gold. Steelers' colors.

SHREVIE *notices* BOOGIE'*s taillights come on. He slows down. Something is wrong up ahead.*

12. Exterior. Roadside. Night.

FENWICK*'s car is turned over. The headlights shine brightly against a tree.*

It's difficult to see exactly what has happened in the darkness. BOOGIE *and* MODELL, SHREVIE *and* BETH *exit their respective cars and walk toward the accident.*

As they approach, we see FENWICK *lying halfway out of the car covered in blood.* DIANE *cannot be seen.*

SHREVIE (*to* BETH)

Stay here.

The three guys move apprehensively toward the car. FENWICK*'s face is covered in blood, so much so that it can hardly be recognized.*

MODELL *reacts to the sight of* FENWICK*'s face.*

MODELL

Oh Jesus.

BOOGIE *kneels next to* FENWICK. *After a beat* FENWICK *explodes with laughter.*

BOOGIE

You son of a bitch!

FENWICK *screams with laughter.*

BOOGIE (*continuing*)

You asshole!

Then BOOGIE *laughs. The rest of the* GUYS *join in. Not* BETH. *She is not amused.* FENWICK *crawls out of the Triumph.*

FENWICK

I really got you guys, didn't I? Didn't I? Been carrying a ketchup bottle around for weeks.

DIANE *steps out of the woods. She laughs nervously.*

DIANE

I hid in the woods. Didn't want any ketchup on me.

FENWICK

Weeks. Just lookin' for the right time.

MODELL

You got me. Christ, I thought you bought it.

FENWICK

Real hard holding back the laughs. *Real* hard.

BOOGIE

You outdid yourself.

BETH

That's very mature, Fenwick.

FENWICK

Fuck mature.

SHREVIE

Hey!

FENWICK

Sorry, Beth.

BOOGIE

Turned the car over yourself?

FENWICK

Yeah. Give me a hand.

BOOGIE

No way.

FENWICK

C'mon.

BOOGIE *starts back to his car. The others follow.*

FENWICK *pleads with them.* BOOGIE, *with his back to* FENWICK, *is amused, delighted that he's got* FENWICK *on a number.*

BOOGIE (*with the authority of a schoolteacher*)

Fenwick, you turned that car over. You must put it upright yourself. You need some discipline in your life.

FENWICK

C'mon, guys. It was easy pushing it over 'cause of the angle. It'll be a bitch getting it up.

BOOGIE *and* MODELL *get into* BOOGIE*'s car.* SHREVIE *and* BETH *get into the Hudson.*

MODELL

Have you tried? You haven't tried.

FENWICK (*desperate*)

I'm buying at the diner.

Without missing a beat, BOOGIE *and* MODELL *exit the car.*

BOOGIE

Schmuck, another five seconds and you'd've had us for free.

They laugh. SHREVIE *starts his car.*

13. Interior. Shrevie's car. Night.

BETH

You guys really are sick, you know that?

SHREVIE

That's 'cause you got no sense of humor.

He pulls away from the side of the road.

SHREVIE (*continuing; yelling out the window*)

See you guys later at the diner.

Cut to

14. Exterior. Diner. Night.

The diner is a typical late-forties metal and glass structure, almost deco in design. Cars are parked in front, including SHREVIE's *Hudson Hornet. The camera pans to a car parked over in a corner.*

TABACK *has his trunk open. It is filled with pants. A few guys, including* FRAZER, *are going through the goods as* TABACK *tries to wheel and deal.*

TABACK (*to* FRAZER)

Seven bucks. All wool. You can't beat it.

FRAZER (*holding them up*)

The crotch looks too short. Don't care for that.

TABACK

What are you afraid it's gonna get caught in the crack between your legs?

The other GUYS *"Whooo" in reaction to* TABACK's *put-down.*

FRAZER

You sure are hot shit since you've taken over your father's business here.

He throws the pants back and walks away.

Cut to

15. Interior. Diner. Night.

The diner is the *late-night hangout. It attracts a mixed-bag crowd.*

Around one side are the aluminum-siding salesmen—guys in their thirties and forties. There are some HIGH-SCHOOLERS, *only there on the weekends, and the* BOOGIE-SHREVIE *crowd—the guys in their early twenties. One thing is quite apparent: there are no girls present, except the* WAITRESSES. *That is the unspoken rule—*no dates.

EDDIE, SHREVIE, *and* MODELL *sit in a booth. They eat french fries and gravy.*

EDDIE

You can't compare Mathis to Sinatra. No way.SHREVIE
They're both great singers.

EDDIE

Yeah, but you can't compare them. Sinatra is the lord. He's big in movies, everything.

SHREVIE

If Mathis wasn't a blue, he'd be a big movie star.

MODELL

That's true. There's hardly any blues in movies. Just sidekicks.

EDDIE

C'mon, they could've put Mathis in *From Here to Eternity.* They had blues in the war.

SHREVIE

Mathis didn't come around until after that movie.

EDDIE

Are you telling me Mathis could've played Maggio? Is that what I'm hearing?

MODELL

Who do you make out to? Sinatra or Mathis?

EDDIE

For that, Mathis.

SHREVIE

I'm married. We don't make out.

They laugh.

FENWICK *enters and approaches* GEORGE, *the manager, at the cashier area.*

FENWICK

George, you got a Band-Aid?

FRAZER *wanders by.*

FRAZER

Sorry about the Diane thing. I didn't know you, uh, had a thing for her.

FENWICK

Yeah, yeah. . . . It's OK; it's OK.

GEORGE

What'd you do, cut your hand?

FENWICK

Yeah, yeah . . . I don't know *what* happened.

FRAZER

What about my five bucks?

FENWICK

Gimme a couple of days.

Then FENWICK *heads toward the* GUYS *and passes the* WAITRESS.

FENWICK

Enid, french fries and gravy, and a cherry Coke.

He sits down and joins the GUYS.

SHREVIE

How'd it go?

FENWICK

Pretty good. Said she never wanted to see me again.

MODELL

Charmed her, huh?

FENWICK

All I did was park the car on a nice, lonely road. I looked at her and said, "Fuck or fight."

SHREVIE

Hey, that's a good line. . . . I'm gonna use that myself sometime.

MODELL

You always know the right thing to say.

SHREVIE

How old is she?

EDDIE

She's jailbait.

SHREVIE

What is she, twelve?

MODELL

She'll be twelve.

They all laugh.

SHREVIE

She'll be twelve.

FENWICK

She's old enough to know better. No, . . . I'm kidding.

16. Interior. Diner.

Angle on the WAITRESS *coming out of the kitchen*

ENID (*yelling to* GEORGE)

George, will you come here and talk to him. . . . He's driving me wild.

GEORGE *goes toward the kitchen, opens the door, and yells in Greek.*

17. Interior. Diner.

Angle on the GUYS *in the booth*

MODELL (*to* EDDIE)

What's that, roast beef?

EDDIE

Don't ask me this anymore, Modell. Yes.

MODELL

Gonna finish that?

EDDIE

Yeah, I'm gonna finish it. I paid for it; I'm not going to give it to you.

MODELL

Because if you're not gonna finish it, I would eat it, . . . but if you're gonna eat it—

EDDIE

What do you want?! Say the words.

MODELL

No, . . . if you're gonna eat it, you eat; that's all right.

EDDIE

Say the words: "I want the roast-beef sandwich." Say the words, and I'll give you a piece.

SHREVIE

Will you cut this out. I mean, every time!

EDDIE

He doesn't talk.

SHREVIE

But you know what he means, right?

EDDIE

Yeah, I know what he means, . . . but he beats about the bush. . . . He beats about the bush. If he said the words, I'd give him a piece.

MODELL

If I wanted it, wouldn't I ask?

EDDIE

Then ask. You know you want it.

SHREVIE

Will you let it go!

MODELL

You're an annoying asshole.

EDDIE

I'm annoying? I'm trying to eat a meal by myself.

SHREVIE

If you want to give him the sandwich, give him the sandwich. If you don't want to give him the sandwich, don't.

EDDIE

I don't want to. . . . Look at his eyes.

MODELL

I asked one, simple question. . . . You know, the trouble with you, you don't chew your food. . . . That's why you get so irritable. You've got lumps. . . . you've got like roast beef that just stays there.

EDDIE

Modell! Now you're really, really getting me mad. Now my blood is boiling.

SHREVIE

I'll take the sandwich.

He leans over to EDDIE*'s plate and picks up the roast-beef sandwich.*

EDDIE

You see. . . . You do this every time.

MODELL

Why are you blaming me? He took your sandwich. I'm sitting here having a cup of coffee. . . .

SHREVIE (*to* EDDIE)

You want this? You want this?

EDDIE (*getting madder*)

No, no!

FENWICK

I do.

EDDIE

I can't believe this. You two play against me; that's what the problem is. You're on each other's sides.

18. Interior. Diner.

Angle on BOOGIE *talking to* GEORGE *at the till*

BOOGIE

Come on, George.

GEORGE

You owe me ten dollars already.

BOOGIE

Don't be like that.

GEORGE

I don't want to talk to you.

19. Interior. Diner—the aluminum-siding guys' booth

Angle on BAGEL *holding court with his* GUYS.

BAGEL (*calling over to* BOOGIE)

Boog, come here.

BOOGIE *approaches.*

BAGEL (*continuing*)

You lay down a bet with Barnett?

BOOGIE

Don't remember.

BAGEL

C'mon, nobody bets two thousand and forgets.

BOOGIE

OK, so? What's the point, Bagel?

BAGEL

Where you getting two thousand? You haven't got a pot to piss in.

BOOGIE

Game's a lock.

BAGEL

Nothing's a lock. You want me to call it off? As a favor to your father, may he rest in peace.

BOOGIE

Leave my father out of it.

BOOGIE *walks off.*

BAGEL

Kids today. Nobody's interested in making an honest buck.

CARSON

Heard he wants to be a lawyer.

BAGEL

That's what I'm saying. You call that an honest buck?

BOOGIE *approaches the* GUYS *and sits down.*

BOOGIE

Bagel heard about my basketball bet.

MODELL

I'm down for fifty.

BOOGIE

Woo, big spender. I'm telling you. They're shaving points on the game. This is no bullshit tip. Get in, guys.

MODELL

You heard they're shaving points?

EDDIE

How do you know?

SHREVIE

I heard about your bets before. . . . It cost me fifty bucks.

EDDIE

What's your resource?

SHREVIE

Don't get in.

BOOGIE

Come on, they're shaving points on this game. You want in or what?

MODELL

They're definitely shaving points? You feel secure? Who's the guy?

BOOGIE

Why do you have to ask so many questions.

MODELL

Because I don't know who the guy is. Do you trust him? . . . Make it fifteen. . . . Make it fifteen. No, make it twenty.

SHREVIE

Don't do it, Modell. I mean, I lost fifty bucks on the last game.

EDDIE (*to* BOOGIE)

Let me ask you a question.

MODELL

Oh no.

EDDIE

Will you be quiet.

(*to* BOOGIE)

Listen, who do you pick? Sinatra or Mathis?

SHREVIE

Would you just let this die?

EDDIE

It's important to me.

SHREVIE

It's annoying to me, OK. You've been asking that question to every Mo that walks in here. Will you just forget it.

EDDIE

Maybe I've got something to gain from the answer, OK.

SHREVIE

It doesn't matter.

EDDIE

Let the man speak.

BOOGIE

Presley.

SHREVIE

There you go . . . the definitive answer. . . . It's Presley?

MODELL

It's Presley?

EDDIE

You're sick. You've gone two steps below in my book now. . . .

SHREVIE

Did you learn something from that?

20. Interior. Diner. Later.

The GUYS *are still hanging out at the diner.*

BOOGIE

Did I tell you guys I'm taking out Carol Heathrow tomorrow night?

FENWICK

You're taking out Carol Heathrow?

BOOGIE (*sarcastically*)

No, *you're* taking her out.

EDDIE

She is death.

BOOGIE

Only go for the best.

SHREVIE

Cold.

MODELL

She's not a smart girl. Did you ever talk to her?

BOOGIE

What's the bet she goes for my pecker on the first date?

FENWICK

The only hand on your schlong is gonna be yours.

BOOGIE

Bet me twenty.

FENWICK

You got it.

EDDIE

I'm in.

MODELL

Me too.

SHREVIE

I'm in, but we need validation.

BOOGIE

All right. I'll arrange it.

SHREVIE

How? What you gonna do, get fingerprints? I tell you, I'm not gonna do the testing.

They all laugh.

21. Exterior. Diner. Night.

EDDIE *and* MODELL *button up their coats against the cold as they leave the diner.*

MODELL

You bring your car?

EDDIE

No, I walked! Yeah, I brought my car.

MODELL

You going straight home, or you—

EDDIE

No, I'm going by way of Atlantic City! What kind of question is that?

MODELL

I'll wait for the other guys.

EDDIE

You constantly do this. You constantly walk out behind me. . . . You stand there. . . .

MODELL

Maybe you've got plans or something.

EDDIE

No, I don't have plans. It's four in the morning. I have no plans. You want a ride?

MODELL

I'll go with you if you want. You want me to—

EDDIE

Say the words: "I want a ride."

MODELL

I don't have to go home.

EDDIE

I enjoy your company. You want a ride?

MODELL

I'll go with you, sure.

EDDIE

You got gas money? Just kidding. You're so serious lately, Modell.

Cut to

22. Interior. B & O railroad station. Night.

The GUYS *mill around the platform as* PASSENGERS *leave a train that has just arrived and walk toward the camera.*

BILLY HALPERT *steps off the train.* BILLY *is in his early twenties and wears the typical button-down shirt, crew-neck sweater, chino pants, and Bass Weejuns. He sees the* GUYS.

BILLY

You guys are too much. How'd you know I was comin' in this morning?

BOOGIE

We know . . . we know everything.

SHREVIE

You up for some diner?

BILLY (*smiling*)

What do you think?

They start to pass the kiosk area in the center of the terminal.

FENWICK

Hold on a second. I'm gettin' some coffee here.

SHREVIE

Coffee? You have to have coffee before we go to the diner to have coffee?

BILLY (*to* BOOGIE)

I can't believe Eddie's gettin' married. I can't believe it!

BOOGIE

He's crazy is what he is. With the Shrevie here it was just nuts, but Eddie? That's lunacy.

SHREVIE

Marriage is all right. I'm not complaining.

BOOGIE

Not complaining. Ummm, sounds good.

FENWICK

'Course it isn't a hundred percent sure yet.

(*to* MAN *behind the counter*)

You got some cream?

BILLY

What? He's getting married on New Year's Eve.

BOOGIE

Not until she takes the test.

BILLY

Boog, what are you talking about?

FENWICK

Eddie's going to give Elyse a football test. If she fails, the marriage is off.

(*to* SHREVIE)

You got a nickel? I don't wanna break a five.

BILLY

What are you guys puttin' me on? This a joke or somethin'?

BOOGIE

You know Eddie and the Colts. Very serious. The test has something like a hundred and forty questions. True and false, multiple choice, short answer.

They start to walk away from the kiosk.

FENWICK

Oral test. He doesn't want any cheating.

BILLY

What happens if she fails? He's going to call it off? Is that what I hear?

SHREVIE

He swears to it. The test was supposed to be two months ago. Elyse keeps delaying. Heavy pressure.

Cut to

23. Exterior. B & O railroad station. Night.

The GUYS *walk across the parking lot toward* SHREVIE*'s car. The parking lot is relatively quiet, save for a half-dozen cars and a few taxicabs.*

FENWICK

Her plan could be, though, to stall until the last minute. Then if she fails, it doesn't matter. It's a *fait accompli.* Knot's tied.

BOOGIE

Fait accompli my ass. He walks.

BILLY

I doubt it. I tell you, it was a real surprise. No call. Just a note. Why do you figure, all of a sudden?

BOOGIE

Bottom line? Elyse turns into Iceland and Eddie's not the type to look elsewhere. Eddie goes for the marriage, and Elyse is back to being the Bahamas again.

They get into the Hudson.

SHREVIE

You don't know that for sure, Boog.

BOOGIE

I'm a good judge of human nature.

The Hudson starts to pull away. It moves down the parking lot away from the camera. As it turns at the corner, it disappears from sight.

Cut to

24. Exterior. Street. Daybreak.

The Hudson heads down a brick street and drives away from the camera.

Cut to

25–29. Exterior. Montage. Daybreak.

Five city scenes in the quiet, early morning

Cut to

30. Exterior. Harbor. Daybreak.

The sun is breaking over the water, the factory smokestacks billowing with white smoke. The Hudson drives by.

31. Exterior. Diner. Day.

The Hudson is parked out front. The morning light is just beginning to break. Through the windows we can see the GUYS *sitting in a booth eating. They are obviously having a good time.* SHREVIE *takes a sip of coffee.* BILLY *says something, and* SHREVIE *puts his hand to his mouth. Coffee pours through his fingers and down his chin.*

Cut to

32. Interior. Diner. Day.

BILLY

And that was nothing compared to what happened in Miss Nathan's class.

SHREVIE

This is great. I was there.

BILLY

Had her for art class. Third floor. She catches me talking. Tells me to see her after class. I jumped up from my seat and started screaming, "I can't take it any more! You're always picking on me! I can't stand it!" Then I ran to the window, opened it, and jumped out. She freaks and faints dead away. She forgot the gym roof was six feet below.

SHREVIE

Her eyes closed. She swayed for a moment and then toppled right over her high heels. Out cold. I was hysterical.

BILLY

The topper was the principal. Donley comes in and sees Miss Nathan on the floor. He doesn't know what to make of it.

SHREVIE

Then Sherman, remember him? Normally a schmuck, but he stands up and says, "Shhhhhh, she's sleeping, Mr. Donley." Then he sees Billy in the window.

BILLY

I said, "I'm sorry I'm late, sir, but my bus broke down. Is Miss Nathan up yet?"

All the GUYS *laugh.*

BOOGIE

You're missing the action now, Billy. Half the guys are at U of B night school. A lot of fucking laughs.

FENWICK (*to* BILLY)

A masters in business. That's the lowest.

BILLY *shrugs his shoulders as if to say, "What can I tell you?"*

BILLY

Who's there?

BOOGIE

Eddie, of course. Burton.

BILLY

Burton?

BOOGIE

Dropped out of rabbinical school. Henry . . .

FENWICK

Cliff, the Mouse . . .

SHREVIE

Youssel.

BOOGIE

Thrown out.

SHREVIE

Yeah?

BOOGIE

Accidentally stole some money from one of the teachers.

BILLY

U of B's busy at night, huh?

BOOGIE

And then there's me.

BILLY

Yeah? You at law school?

BOOGIE

Thought I'd take a pop with the law. Although I'm still working the beauty salon.

Cut to

33. Exterior. Residential neighborhood. Day.

The Hudson slowly moves down the quiet, tree-lined street. All is quiet, the morning having yet to begin. The neighborhood is well cared for—a pleasant, middle-class area. The car pulls up in front of a three-story, white shingled house. BILLY *exits the car with his suitcase.*

BILLY

See you guys at the diner tonight.

He slams the door shut. The car pulls away. BILLY *walks up the steps, pulls out a key, and opens the door.*

Cut to

34. Interior. Halperts' house. Day.

BILLY *walks up the steps to the second floor. He sees that his* PARENTS' *door is open and peeks inside. The bed is made. No one is there. He turns toward his* SISTER'*s room. The camera pans. The bed is also made. He goes up the stairs to the third floor.*

35. Interior. Halperts' house.

Angle on a black door

A sign reads NO ADMITTANCE. BILLY *enters.*

Cut to

36. Interior. Billy's room.

BILLY *lies on the bed in his shorts, smoking a cigarette. The camera slowly pans the room. An upright piano is in a corner. Then we see magazine pictures of various baseball stars tacked on the wall. The camera pans to pennants of the Baltimore Orioles and the Baltimore Colts. The camera drifts over to* Playboy *centerfolds. Then we see a photograph of* BILLY *and a bunch of the* GUYS *leaning against a railing in Atlantic City during their high-school years.*

Cut to

37. Exterior. Halperts' house. Day.

BILLY *walks away from his house, crosses the street, and climbs the steps of another house. He rings the doorbell.*

Seconds later the door opens. MRS. SIMMONS, *a short, heavyset woman, stands there.*

MRS. SIMMONS (*pleased*)

Billy, you're in town already?

BILLY

Yeah, thought I'd spend the holidays here. Lot of parties, I hear.

He enters.

38. Interior. Simmons' house. Day.

BILLY *and* MRS. SIMMONS *walk down the hallway. In the background* CLEANING LADY *is vacuuming.*

MRS. SIMMONS

Did you know your parents are out of town?

BILLY

No.

MRS. SIMMONS

They're in Florida. Be back for Eddie's wedding, though.

BILLY

He still sleeping?

MRS. SIMMONS

What else? It's only two thirty. Wake him.

BILLY *starts up the steps.*

MRS. SIMMONS (*continuing*)

I'll be happy when he's out of the house.

Cut to

39. Interior. Eddie's room.

It is a total mess. Clothes, underwear, and shoes are strewn all over the room. BILLY *shakes* EDDIE. *His eyes open.*

EDDIE

Whaddya say, Bill?

BILLY

Still the early riser, huh?

EDDIE *reaches over to the night table and lights a Pall Mall.*

EDDIE

Nothin' changes.

BILLY

Except you getting married.

EDDIE

Yeah, ain't that a kick.

He gets out of bed, picks up a pair of pants from the floor, and steps into them.

EDDIE (*continuing*)

Thought you weren't coming in until New Year's Eve.

BILLY

Nothing's happening around campus, so . . .

EDDIE *puts on a shirt and a tie with an already-made knot. He pulls the tie up and then starts buttoning the rest of the shirt.*

EDDIE

You bring in that girl with you?

BILLY

Broke up.

EDDIE

Shame. In that picture you sent, looked like she had great knockers.

BILLY

Yeah.

(*a beat*)

Didn't figure on you and Elyse so soon.

EDDIE *searches the floor and picks out two socks that are similar but not the same.*

EDDIE

I figured New Year's Eve would be good. Get married. Party through the night. You know.

He puts the socks on. They have holes in the heels.

BILLY

I was pissed off, Ed. Figured you would call or something. Let me know you were planning it.

EDDIE

Yeah, I know. But you're my best man.

BILLY

What do you think? Of course I'm your best man.

Eddie walks into the bathroom. The camera follows. He splashes some water on his face and wipes it with a wash rag.

BILLY

Boogie and the guys picked me up at the train station.

EDDIE *takes a drag on his cigarette and puts it on the toilet seat. Then he squirts some toothpaste onto the toothbrush.*

EDDIE (*with a mouth full of toothpaste*)

Yeah? I left the diner at five. They didn't say anything to me.

BILLY

Surprise, I guess.

EDDIE

How'd they know?

BILLY

Barbara Kohler told Fenwick.

EDDIE

You keep in touch, huh?

BILLY

Yeah.

EDDIE

You're still nailing her, aren't you, you son of a bitch.

EDDIE *spits the toothpaste out and sticks his mouth under the faucet to rinse, making sure to keep his tie dry.*

BILLY

Never did.

EDDIE *wipes his mouth with his hand.*

EDDIE

Who you kidding?

He puts the cigarette back in his mouth and starts out of the room. BILLY *follows.*

EDDIE (*continuing*)

What else would you be doing with her all these years?

BILLY

Talking.

40. Interior. Simmons' house.

Another angle as they start down the stairs

EDDIE

Talking? Shit, if you want to talk, there's always the guys at the diner. You don't need a girl if you want to talk.

BILLY

Eddie, you'll never change.

EDDIE

Damn right.

Cut to

41. Interior. Simmons' kitchen.

MRS. SIMMONS *is on the telephone as* EDDIE *and* BILLY *enter.*

MRS. SIMMONS

I saw it. It was in the papers this morning, Marion. . . . Yes, this morning.

EDDIE (*to* BILLY)

You and I'll shoot some pool.

BILLY

Haven't shot pool in ages.

EDDIE

Well, it's about time; otherwise you'll lose your edge.

MRS. SIMMONS

You still have the morning paper, Marion?

EDDIE

Ma, what's for breakfast?

MRS. SIMMONS

The kitchen is closed.

EDDIE *sits down at the table.* BILLY *sits down on a chair over by the wall.*

EDDIE

I'm hungry here.

MRS. SIMMONS

Hold on, Marion.

(*to* EDDIE)

You want something to eat? Make it. I haven't got all day to wait on you.

EDDIE

Come on, Ma. Don't give me that shit. A fried bologna sandwich will be good.

MRS. SIMMONS (*turning around angrily*)

Get out of the house! Billy, take him out of here!

EDDIE

A fried bologna sandwich is not a lot to ask for, for Christsake!

MRS. SIMMONS

Just a second, Marion.

MRS. SIMMONS *puts down the receiver, picks up a butcher knife from the counter by the sink, and waves it at* EDDIE.

MRS. SIMMONS

Eddie, you're giving me a headache! Take a walk.

EDDIE *rises from his chair.*

EDDIE

You want to stab me? Come on! Come on!

He brings up his fist and assumes a boxing position. MRS. SIMMONS *moves toward* EDDIE *wielding the knife.* EDDIE *backs around the table.* BILLY *watches this scene without expression.*

MRS. SIMMONS

You miserable creature.

EDDIE

Take your best shot. Then I'm going to punch your lights out, Ma.

MRS. SIMMONS (*stalking him*)

Who do you think you are!

EDDIE

Come on! Come on! Go for the cut; then you're down and out.

The short, heavyset woman continues to stalk EDDIE *as they move around the table.* BILLY *is not disturbed or surprised. This is apparently an ongoing occurrence.*

MRS. SIMMONS

How did you turn into such a thing!

EDDIE

I've got fists of granite. You're going down.

MRS. SIMMONS (*turning away*)

I'm not going to ruin a good knife on you. It's not worth it.

EDDIE *turns to* BILLY *and smiles.*

BILLY (*quietly*)

So what's new?

MRS. SIMMONS (*opening the refrigerator*)

Eat a sandwich, then give me some peace. Billy, you want something?

BILLY

No, thanks.

MRS. SIMMONS

You sure? It's no trouble.

BILLY

No, really.

MRS. SIMMONS (*picking up the telephone receiver*)

Marion, lemme call you back. I'm gonna fix the kids some breakfast.

Cut to

42. Interior. Appliance store. Day.

*Tight shot—TV screen—*Little Women, *an old feature film, is on the set.*

CUSTOMER (*offscreen*)

Is this show in color, or is there something wrong with the set?

SHREVIE (*offscreen*)

This is a black and white set, but I don't think that show is in color, anyway.

43. Interior. Appliance store.

*Another angle—*SHREVIE *and the* CUSTOMER *are standing in an aisle filled with rows of televisions.*

CUSTOMER

I don't like color television. Don't like that color for nothin'. Saw "Bonanza" at my in-laws; it's not for me. The Ponderosa looked fake. Hardly recognized Little Joe.

SHREVIE

It might have needed some tuning.

CUSTOMER

It's not for me. You got an Emerson? Hear they're real good.

SHREVIE *and the* CUSTOMER *move down the aisle, passing one black and white set after another. One set is in color—"Tom and Jerry" is on the set.* FENWICK *enters the store. He looks slightly drunk.*

SHREVIE

Here's an Emerson. This is portable.

The CUSTOMER *stares at it.* SHREVIE *notices* FENWICK *up at the front of the store. He nods to him.*

CUSTOMER

You got that twenty-one-inch Emerson? The cabinet type?

SHREVIE

The console model.

(*yelling toward the back*)

Kenny! We get some of the Emerson consoles in?!

KENNY (*offscreen*)

Let me check out in the warehouse!

SHREVIE

Be right back. That'll take a minute or two for him to check.

The CUSTOMER *nods, and* SHREVIE *walks up to* FENWICK.

FENWICK

I talked to Boog. He's going to take Carol to the Strand tonight.

SHREVIE

So what do you want to do?

FENWICK

I figure I'll be there. Sit a few seats away.

SHREVIE

Think I'll be there, too. Don't want any judgment calls.

FENWICK

Boog's got about a hundred dollars riding on this thing now. Making bets left and right.

SHREVIE

Jesus, hundred bucks, already?

FENWICK

Lot of people bettin' for Carol.

SHREVIE *senses that* FENWICK *is a little off.*

SHREVIE

What the hell you been doing? You been drinking already?

FENWICK

Yeah? I guess so.

SHREVIE

What for? It's too early.

FENWICK

I don't know. . . . I don't know. Gettin' antsy or something. Can't figure out what. . . . I don't know.

He turns and starts to head out of the store.

FENWICK (*continuing*)

See you at the Strand.

SHREVIE

Fen, sure you're OK?

FENWICK *turns back and smiles at* SHREVIE.

FENWICK

Hey . . . yeah.

He turns back and exits.

44. Exterior. Street. Day.

EDDIE *parks his Studebaker, and he and* BILLY *exit the car. They walk along a street of row houses and then cross an old brick street, heading for the pool hall on the corner.*

EDDIE

Colt championship is tomorrow. Want me to get you a ticket for the game?

BILLY

Can you get one this late?

EDDIE

Yeah. You can't be in Baltimore and not see the Colts win the championship. It would be sacrilegious.

They enter the pool hall.

Cut to

45. Interior. Pool hall. Day.

BILLY and EDDIE come down the steps into the poolroom. The place is old and dirty looking. Candy wrappers and cigarettes litter the floor. KNOCKO, a gray-haired man in his sixties, sits behind the cash register reading The Wall Street Journal. *On the back wall are pictures of the seminude girls from the men's magazines of the period. Some are inscribed to KNOCKO. A TV set is on in the background. A commercial for Renault is seen.*

As the GUYS approach, KNOCKO looks up and smiles.

KNOCKO

Billy, Billy, Billy.

BILLY

How you doing, Knocko?

KNOCKO

Eat, sleep, you know. Never see you and the guys anymore.

BILLY

You know how it is. Time to move on, I guess.

KNOCKO

Eddie's the only one who still pops in. Still loves the game.

(*very seriously*)

You doing OK, Billy?

BILLY

Going for my masters.

KNOCKO

Wonderful. All your crowd turned out fine. Take seven. It's got a new felt.

EDDIE

Eight's better.

KNOCKO

Take eight. The pool maven here.

They walk toward the tables. The place is quiet. Afternoons are not the action time.

Cut to

46. Interior. Pool hall. Slightly later.

Tight shot—a pool ball

After a beat EDDIE's head comes into the frame behind the ball. He closes one eye as he lines up a shot.

EDDIE

I'm scared shitless, to tell you the truth.

BILLY (*offscreen*)

You know anybody who's not?

EDDIE

If I had a choice, I'd just date Elyse all my life. Just date her and the hell with the rest. I like dating.

47. Interior. Pool hall.

Another angle as EDDIE *backs off the shot and starts to move around the table.* BILLY *sips an orange soda.*

BILLY

What are you doing it for?

EDDIE *approaches* BILLY, *reaches for the bottle, and takes a sip.*

EDDIE

What am I doing it for? I've been dating Elyse for five years. What am I . . . I have no choice. It gets to a point where a girl says, "Hey, where am I going?"

He hands the bottle back and chalks his pool cue.

EDDIE (*continuing*)

So, there is nobody else that I really care about. So, you know. I'm not saying that I'm doing it just to make her happy. The hell with that.

He shoots and sinks a ball.

EDDIE (*continuing*)

She's the only one I care about. I don't go looking for girls to date or anything like that. And, it seems like the time and all . . . so. At least she's not a ball breaker. Christ, if she were a ball breaker, there'd be no way.

BILLY *feels a certain sadness for* EDDIE, *but he doesn't know what to say.*

EDDIE *sees* METHAN, *a blond-haired kid several years younger than he.*

EDDIE (*continuing*)

How you doing, Methan?

METHAN *approaches* EDDIE *and stands inches away from* EDDIE*'s face.*

METHAN

"JJ, it's one thing to wear your dog collar, . . . but when it turns into a noose, . . . I'd rather have my freedom."

BILLY *has no idea what is going on.*

METHAN (*continuing*)

"The man in jail is always for freedom. Except, if you'll excuse me, JJ, I'm not in jail. You're blind, Mr. McGoo! This is the crossroads for me. I won't get Kello! Not for a lifetime pass to the Polo Grounds! Not if you serve me Cleopatra on a plate! Sidney, I told you . . ."

Suddenly METHAN *walks away, still mumbling the movie.*

METHAN

"And that is why you put your hands on my sister? JJ, please. . . . Susie tried to throw herself off the terrace. . . . Susie, tell 'im the truth. . . . Tell 'im . . . JJ, please. . . . Look. . . . I can explain. . . . JJ, . . . stop! Stop! . . . Stop! You're defending your sister, ya big phony! Didn't you tell me to get Kello? Didn't you . . . Susie, just as I know he's lying about your attempted suicide, . . . you know he's lying about me. But we can't leave it like this, can we? I suggest you go to bed, dear."

EDDIE (*to* BILLY)

Methan's favorite movie. *Sweet Smell of Success.*

BILLY

He memorized the whole movie?

EDDIE *lines up another shot.*

EDDIE

The younger guys, I tell ya, are crazier than we were.

He shoots and misses. From another table a GUY *yells out.*

GUY

Eddie, you taking any of Boogie's action?

EDDIE

Yeah! No way he pulls this off.

48. Exterior. The Strand Theater. Night.

There is a lot of milling around in front of the theater. The marquee reads TROY DONAHUE AND SANDRA DEE IN SUMMER PLACE.

49. Interior. The Strand Theater lobby. Night.

SHREVIE *stands with* BETH, *an attractive girl.* EDDIE *and* FENWICK *enter and walk over to* SHREVIE.

SHREVIE (*almost apologizing for bringing* BETH)

Beth heard the movie was pretty good.

BETH

Eddie, where's Elyse?

EDDIE

She's home studying for the football test.

BETH

You're kidding.

FENWICK

Seen the Boog yet?

SHREVIE

Not yet.

EARL MAGET, *an enormously fat guy, enters with a* FRIEND. *The* FRIEND *stops at the candy counter.*

FRIEND

Earl, want some candy?

EARL (*starting into the theater*)

No, don't care for sweets.

BOOGIE *enters with* CAROL HEATHROW. *She is a beautiful, shapely blonde.* BOOGIE *looks over at the group, nods, and walks to the candy counter with* CAROL.

BETH

Is that Carol Heathrow?

SHREVIE

Where?

BETH

With Boogie.

SHREVIE (*staring for a long beat*)

I think so.

BETH

I'm surprised she's with him. From what I've heard about her, Boogie wouldn't seem her type.

EDDIE *is amazed at how beautiful* CAROL *looks.*

EDDIE

She is death. Death.

FENWICK *spots the* GRIPPER *walking toward the men's room. The* GRIPPER *stands about six feet four inches and is all muscle.*

FENWICK

Damn! The Gripper's here.

SHREVIE

Where?

FENWICK *nods toward the men's room.*

SHREVIE (*continuing*)

Christ, the Grip's still growing, I think.

FENWICK

Hope he doesn't see me. Every time he sees me, he puts the grip on me.

EDDIE

Saw him put a grip on a guy at the diner. Gripped him right through his corduroy jacket. Made him stand on tiptoes.

SHREVIE

Where's Billy?

EDDIE

Comin' with that Barbara Kohler chick, I think.

BOOGIE *gets a large box of popcorn and a Coke and starts into the theater with* CAROL. *Just before he enters, he gives a smile to the guys.*

FENWICK

Guess I might as well get a seat.

(*to* EDDIE)

Comin'?

EDDIE *nods, and they start inside. After a beat* SHREVIE *and* BETH *start in.*

SHREVIE

Let's sit in the back.

BETH

Why?

SHREVIE

I'm tired of sittin' down close with the guys and all.

Just as they go into the theater, BILLY *enters alone.*

50. Interior. The Strand Theater.

BOOGIE *and* CAROL *sit watching the screen. The box of popcorn resting in his lap.* BOOGIE *keeps sneaking looks at* CAROL; *then slowly moves his hand down to his fly, and he quietly unzips it.*

51. Interior. The Strand Theater.

Angle to include FENWICK *looking over from his vantage point three seats away.* BOOGIE *squirms around ever so slightly and then places the box of popcorn back on his lap. Evidently he has stuck his penis into the bottom of the popcorn box.* FENWICK *nudges* EDDIE *and then whispers something into his ear.* EDDIE *smiles.*

CAROL *dips her hand into the popcorn box on* BOOGIE*'s lap and takes out a handful of popcorn.*

SHREVIE, *seated in the back, is restless, wondering what is happening.* BETH *is mesmerized by Troy Donahue.*

BILLY *sits on an aisle, unaware of the quiet intrigue that is taking place.*

CAROL *again reaches into the box and takes out a few kernels.* BOOGIE *glances toward* FENWICK. FENWICK *shakes his head and mouths, "Bet's off. Not fair."* BOOGIE *nods "yes."*

Troy and Sandra walk the beach. The romantic score swells. The young audience is caught up in this screen love affair.

CAROL *reaches into the popcorn box once again. Suddenly she screams. She bolts up from her seat and races up the aisle. The* AUDIENCE *is alive with chatter, wondering what has happened.*

BOOGIE *turns to* FENWICK *and smiles. Then he heads up the aisle after* CAROL.

BETH (*as she watches* BOOGIE *racing up the aisle after* CAROL)

BETH

What's going on?

SHREVIE (*playing dumb*)

I don't know. I don't know.

52. Interior. The Strand Theater lobby.

BOOGIE *catches up to* CAROL *just as she is about to enter the ladies' room.*

BOOGIE

Hold on. Hold on a second.

CAROL

You are disgusting!

BOOGIE

I know it was terrible, really horrible and all, but it was an accident.

CAROL

An accident!

She starts into the ladies' room. BOOGIE *holds her arm.*

BOOGIE

Wait! Carol! Woo! Seriously, it was an accident. Swear to God.

CAROL

An accident. Your *thing* just got into a box of popcorn?

BOOGIE

Damn near that. Can I be straight with you?

CAROL *tries to settle down.*

CAROL

Boogie . . .

BOOGIE

There's a good reason, but it's a little embarrassing to me. So maybe you don't want to hear it. I'll understand.

CAROL (*a long beat*)

Go on. Let me hear this.

BOOGIE

I don't like to tell this to girls, but you really are a knockout, really. And, uh, just sitting next to you in there got me crazy. I got a hard-on. I don't like to admit it, but I did. You don't know me, but I always try to come off being cool. Don't like to look like I'm hustling, and there I am, sitting next to you with a boner. Am I embarrassing you?

CAROL (*intrigued*)

Go on.

The "Summer Place *Theme" can be heard softly through the theater doors.*

BOOGIE

Well, it was killing me. So to stop the pain—it was digging into my pants and all—I opened my fly. Loosen everything up. Give it a little air, you know. And it worked. Everything settled down and I got caught up in the picture. Forgot all about it. Then when I saw Sandra wearing the bathing suit in that cove scene, you know, it just popped right out and went right through the bottom of the popcorn box. The force of it opened the flap.

CAROL *stares at him, wondering whether he is telling the truth. The beautiful theme from* A Summer Place *grows louder for a few seconds as someone comes through the doors and heads for the candy counter.*

CAROL

It just pushed the flap open?

BOOGIE

It's Ripley's, I tell ya. And I couldn't move the box, or you would have seen it.

CAROL

That's true.

BOOGIE

I was just hoping it would shrink back out.

He puts his hand up to her cheek and lovingly touches it.

BOOGIE

Come on, let's go back inside.

As they go through the doors, we hear the soundtrack.

TROY (*voice-over*)

I want to kiss you here in front of God and everyone.

Cut to

53. Exterior. The Strand Theater. Night.

SHREVIE *and* BETH *exit the theater.*

SHREVIE

What was the guy's name? The actor?

BETH

Troy Donahue.

SHREVIE

What kind of a name is Troy?

BETH

He's gorgeous.

SHREVIE (*mumbling to himself*)

Troy.

FENWICK *and* EDDIE *approach.*

SHREVIE (*continuing*)

Ever hear of a guy named Troy?

FENWICK (*sarcastically*)

Yeah, Troy Swartzman from Towanda.

SHREVIE

Cute.

BETH *is looking at the poster on the side of the theater.*

BETH

Hey, Shrevie, did you know that this movie was written by the author of *The Man in the Gray Flannel Suit*?

SHREVIE

No.

BETH

You know, I'd really like to see this again.

SHREVIE

Well, you can take Elyse.

BOOGIE *and* CAROL *exit the theater.*

BOOGIE (*as he passes the* GROUP)

See you guys at the diner. Bring some tens.

BOOGIE *walks on cockily with his arm around* CAROL'*s waist.*

BETH

Ten whats?

SHREVIE

Have no idea.

EDDIE *looks at* CAROL *as she walks away.*

EDDIE

Death.

(*to* FENWICK)

I'd give up *your* life if I could have her.

BILLY *exits the theater and starts toward the* CROWD. *Out of the corner of his eye he spots someone exiting through another door. He watches the* GUY *for a beat and then quickly moves toward him. He taps the* GUY *on the shoulder. As the* GUY *turns,* BILLY *punches him in the face. The* GUY *goes down.*

A CROWD *quickly forms. Confusion takes over as everyone moves to see what has happened.* SHREVIE, FENWICK, *and* EDDIE *move in for a better look.*

The GUY *sits on the ground holding his bleeding nose. He looks up at* BILLY.

BILLY

We're even.

BILLY *turns and moves away.* EDDIE, FENWICK, *and* SHREVIE *move to catch up with him.* BETH *trails along.*

EDDIE

I'll be damned. Willard Broxton!

FENWICK

Long time comin', huh, Billy?

BILLY (*excited*)

I couldn't believe it! There he was! I didn't want to hit him, but I had to, you know.

SHREVIE (*patting* BILLY*'s back*)

Outstanding! See you guys later. Come on, Beth.

BETH

Are we going to eat?

SHREVIE

Nah, not in the mood.

SHREVIE *heads toward his Hudson.* BETH *follows.*

BETH

Who's Willard Broxton?

SHREVIE

It was the eleventh . . . no, tenth grade. Billy was playing ball against one of the high-school fraternities. I think they were ULP. Billy came sliding into second base to break up a double play. The second baseman jumps Billy, thinking he was out to hurt him. Billy punches the guy and the whole ULP team jumped him. Beat the shit out of him.

They approach the Hudson. SHREVIE *goes around to the driver's side and opens the door.*

BETH

He's been after them all these years? That was forever ago.

SHREVIE

He swore he'd get them. Broxton makes eight . . . or seven. No, eight. There's one guy left.

BETH *stands by the car as* SHREVIE *gets in.*

SHREVIE

What are you waiting for? It's open.

Cut to

54. Exterior. Back alley. Night.

BILLY, EDDIE, *and* FENWICK *walk away from the theater toward their cars.*

FENWICK

I'm so pissed I missed the punch. I was watching out for the Gripper.

BILLY

Seven years. Seven years to get him.

EDDIE

Who's the last? Donald Tucker?

BILLY

No, I got Tucker in a bathroom at Chestnut Ridge. Moon Shaw.

EDDIE

Moon Shaw.

(*a beat*)

Who's Moon Shaw?

BILLY *gets in his car.*

BILLY

If you ever see him, you'll remember.

EDDIE

Going to the diner?

BILLY

In a while. I'm going to see Barbara.

EDDIE

Thought you were supposed to have a date.

BILLY

She had to work. I'm going to stop by the TV station and see her for a bit.

He starts his car and pulls away.

FENWICK

Wasn't Moon Shaw the toast who used to date Elaine?

EDDIE

That was my cousin Denny. You calling him an asshole?

FENWICK (*knowing he said the wrong thing*)

Oh, . . . not Elaine. Her name was Ellen. I'm thinking a whole other guy.

FENWICK *tiptoes away from* EDDIE, *playing as if he doesn't want to get hit.*

Cut to

55. Interior. Television-station corridor. Night.

BILLY *and* BARBARA *walk down the hallway quickly.* BARBARA *is a tall, thin brunet with classic features. She was never a girl. Born a woman. She moves down the hallway with great purpose.* BILLY *keeps pace.*

BARBARA

There's not much time before the news.

BILLY

I tried to call.

BARBARA

Switchboard closes down at ten.

BILLY

I was just getting the feeling you were avoiding me, Barb.

BARBARA

That's not true, Willy.

They enter the control room.

56. Interior. Television-station control room.

The control room overlooks the studio floor. Technicians are setting up the cameras, microphones, and lights. A bank of monitors hangs down from a metal shelf. The TECHNICAL DIRECTOR *is talking over a headset, balancing video levels.* BARBARA *slips on a headset and shuffles through some papers.*

BARBARA (*into the headset*)

Telecine, you want to run down the film chains for me?

BILLY *takes in all the activity. He is overwhelmed. His eye catches the Old Gold dancing boxes on one of the monitors.*

BARBARA (*continuing; getting information*)

Governor's press conference is on three? There's a B-roll to that. Four? OK. Goodwill charity Christmas party? Three also? And the slides? One?

BARBARA *looks up at the clock. It reads 10:58. The* DIRECTOR *rushes into the booth with the news script. He quickly sits and puts on his headset.*

DIRECTOR

Stand by for cold tease.

BARBARA

Ten seconds.

BILLY *steps forward to get a better view of the activity on the floor. The* DIRECTOR *becomes aware of his presence.*

DIRECTOR

Who's the visitor?

BARBARA

Friend of mine. Five seconds.

DIRECTOR

And one. Mike. Cue!

NEWSCASTER

President Eisenhower returns from world peace tour. Steel dispute continues. These and other stories next.

DIRECTOR

Roll three. Three and track.

A commercial comes up on the air monitor.

BARBARA

Willy, after this I still have a lot of work to do. Why don't you call in the morning?

DIRECTOR

Where's the news opening?

BARBARA

On six.

BILLY

What's good?

BARBARA

Church services are at ten; eight thirty, nine.

DIRECTOR

Punch ID and announce.

A slide of the television-station's call letters comes up. The ANNOUNCER *in a glass booth off to the right speaks.*

ANNOUNCER

This is WMAR-TV 2 in Baltimore, wishing all our viewers a merry Christmas and a happy New Year.

Cut to

57. Exterior. Saint Agnes's Church. Night.

A nativity scene is set up on the grounds. Wonderfully elaborate, it is about half life-size. The figures are made of clay and painted in fine detail. The camera pans over to FENWICK, *who is parked nearby. He leans on his Triumph, holding a half-pint of whiskey. He takes a big swig and shivers slightly. The air is cold, and his breath comes out in white puffs.*

Cut to

58. Exterior. Diner. Night.

EDDIE *and* SHREVIE *lean against a car parked in front of the hangout. The diner's blue neon sign above reflects off the cars, bathing the* GUYS *in a cold, blue light.*

EDDIE

Two days till the test. If she passes, three more days to the thing . . . the marriage.

SHREVIE

Where you going? Puerto Rico?

EDDIE

Cuba.

SHREVIE

My parents' friends, the Copelands, go every year. Nice.

There is a long pause.

EDDIE

Shrevie, you happy with your marriage, or what?

SHREVIE

To be honest, I don't know.

EDDIE

You know. How can you *not* know? It's not like you're trying to figure out the difference between Pepsi Cola and Royal Crown, for Christsake.

SHREVIE

Beth is terrific and everything, but I don't know.

EDDIE *looks off, not happy with the answer.*

SHREVIE (*continuing*)

You know the big part of the problem? When we were dating, we spent most of our time talking about sex. *Why* couldn't I do it? *Where* could we do it? Were her parents going to be out *so* we could do it. Talking about being alone for a weekend. A whole night. You know. Everything was talking about gettin' sex or planning our wedding. Then when you're married, . . . it's crazy. You can have it whenever you want. You wake up. She's there. You come home from work. She's there. So, all the sex-planning talk is over. And the wedding-planning talk. We can sit up here and bullshit the night away, but I can't have a five-minute conversation with Beth. But, I'm not putting the blame on her. We've just got nothing to talk about.

EDDIE *lights a Pall Mall.*

EDDIE

Well, that's OK. We've got the diner.

SHREVIE

Yeah, we've always got the diner. Don't worry about it.

EDDIE

I'm not worried.

SHREVIE

Don't back out on me.

EDDIE

I'm not going to back out on you either, unless she fails the test. It's out of my hands.

Cut to

59. Exterior. Heathrows' house. Night.

The house is a pleasant, two-story wooden structure. A yellow porch light is on. BOOGIE *and* CAROL *walk up the steps to the front door.* CAROL *opens the door with the key. She turns back toward* BOOGIE.

BOOGIE (*softly*)

I love you.

He gently kisses her forehead, then looks her in the eyes. CAROL *throws her arms around his neck and kisses him passionately.*

CAROL

Do you want to come inside?

BOOGIE

Are your parents around?

CAROL

They're probably in the basement watching TV.

BOOGIE

I'd love to, but I really should hit the law books. OK?

CAROL *nods. He strokes her cheek.*

BOOGIE (*continuing*)

I wish I could stay.

CAROL

Talk to you. Soon?

BOOGIE *nods and walks away.* CAROL *watches him with great affection; then she turns and enters the house.*

Cut to

60. Exterior. Diner. Night.

FENWICK *pulls over to the curb across the street from the diner. He exits the car.* EDDIE, SHREVIE, MODELL, *and a* GROUP *of others are all hanging out. A voice calls out—a soft, but very authoritative voice.*

VOICE

Whaddya say, Tim?

FENWICK *turns.* THE GRIPPER *is standing by his car.*

FENWICK

Whaddya say, Gripper?

GRIPPER

Not much, Tim.

He moves toward him ever so slowly.

FENWICK

Oh no, you're not going to put the grip on me.

GRIPPER

Where do you get that idea, Tim?

FENWICK *backs up; then he suddenly rips the antenna off his car and waves it like a sword.*

FENWICK

No! Stay away! I'm not going to get gripped! You're not going to get me to walk on my tiptoes in pain. Oh, no.

GRIPPER (*even more softly*)

Tim, I'm not going to grip you.

FENWICK (*waving the antenna*)

Yes, you are.

The GUYS *across the street are loving what is happening.*

GRIPPER

To be honest, I was. But not now. I like a guy who stands up to the Gripper. I like that, Tim.

FENWICK

You're not going to grip me?

GRIPPER

No, I just want to shake your hand.

FENWICK

You're settin' me up for a grip.

GRIPPER

Untrue, Tim.

FENWICK

Sure?

GRIPPER

I want to shake the hand of the man who stood up to the Gripper.

FENWICK

No grip?

GRIPPER

That's right, Tim.

FENWICK *drops the antenna. He moves toward* THE GRIPPER *slowly.* THE GRIPPER *extends his hand;* FENWICK *extends his hand. They shake. No grip.* FENWICK *is relieved.*

GRIPPER (*continuing*)

Let's go see the guys. The man who stood up to the Gripper.

FENWICK, *feeling very proud, walks with* THE GRIPPER *across the street toward the* GUYS. *Suddenly, halfway across the street,* THE GRIPPER *puts one of the greatest grips in his career on* FENWICK. *He squeezes* FENWICK'*s forearm right through his winter coat.* FENWICK *feels the pain. The famous grip is on.*

GRIPPER (*continuing*)

Up on your toes, Tim.

FENWICK

Oh no, Grip.

GRIPPER *puts on a little more pressure, and* FENWICK *is up on his toes. The* GUYS *cheer* GRIPPER.

GRIPPER

Tim, never doubt the Gripper. When I say I want to shake your hand, believe what I say. Never doubt, Tim.

FENWICK

Never doubt. Right.

THE GRIPPER *turns* FENWICK *around and leads him away from the* GUYS, *back to the other side of the street.* FENWICK *is up on his toes. The* GUYS *are eating it up. Then* THE GRIPPER *and* FENWICK *head back to the* GUYS. *The camera pans to* BOOGIE*'s car as it pulls into the parking lot on the left side of the building. He starts to pass* BAGEL, *who is about to drive out.* BAGEL *beeps his horn and rolls down the window.* BOOGIE *rolls his down.*

BAGEL

Did you hear? They won by fourteen.

BOOGIE

Fourteen? Shit. They weren't supposed to roll up that big a score.

BAGEL

Listen to me next time.

He pulls out. BOOGIE *pulls forward and parks. He slams his fist into the steering wheel. Again and again. Then he leans back in his car seat. He takes a deep breath and gets out of the car.*

61. Exterior. Diner.

Angle on car outside diner with GUYS *hanging around it*
TABACK *has the trunk of his car open and is trying to sell clothes. He grabs one of the* YOUNG GUYS.

TABACK

Hey you! Big time. Come here. Your mother let you loose like this? Look at them pants. I got charcoal pants here.

The KID *draws back.*

TABACK (*continuing*)

You want to get inside the diner? Come here. Look at these charcoal-gray pants. Special sale twelve fifty.

KID

Twelve fifty?

TABACK

All right. For you, eleven ninety-eight. Look, don't tell anybody where you got these, OK? How much money you got.

KID

Four bucks.

TABACK (*delving into his trunk*)

Come here, I got a good shirt for you.

62. Interior. Diner. Later.

EARL MAGET *sits in a booth alone, his enormous body taking up about one whole side. He finishes off one section of a club sandwich and very politely wipes his mouth with a napkin. Before him five deluxe sandwiches are waiting for his hungry mouth. He turns the financial page and picks up another sandwich.*

EDDIE, BILLY, *and* MODELL *are turned around in their booth watching* MAGET. BOOGIE, FENWICK, *and* SHREVIE *are discussing the pecker-in-the-popcorn bet.*

EDDIE (*watching* EARL)

Where's he now?

MODELL (*looking over the menu*)

He's on the Pimlico.

(*surveying the table*)

That's the George's Deluxe. The Garrison, The Avalon, and The Junction.

EDDIE (*amazed*)

The whole left side of the menu. What a triumph if he pulls it off.

MODELL *starts counting the sandwiches on the left side of the menu. We catch snatches of* BOOGIE, FENWICK, *and* SHREVIE *arguing.*

FENWICK

The bet was touch your pecker. Not pecker hidden in popcorn.

SHREVIE

It was pecker touching without intention.

BOOGIE

Listen to this.

MODELL *looks up from the menu.*

MODELL

Fifteen . . . or sixteen more. If you include the Maryland fried-chicken dinner.

EDDIE

I think he's just talking deluxe sandwiches.

MODELL (*yelling over*)

Earl! That include the fried-chicken dinner?

EARL

Yes.

EDDIE (*truly amazed*)

Twenty-two deluxe sandwiches *and* the fried-chicken dinner.

BILLY

And no bets.

EDDIE

Nope. Just a personal goal. Another private triumph. This'll top the eighty White Tower hamburgers.

MODELL

Unbelievable . . . like a building with feet.

BILLY

He ate eighty White Tower hamburgers?

EDDIE

Oh yeah, you didn't know? Thanksgiving night. Eighty-six he ate. Saw him later and said, 'Earl, your goal was eighty. Why eighty-six?' He looked at me and said, 'I got hungry.'

BILLY *laughs.*

MODELL

Truth.

They slide back down in the booth.

SHREVIE (*to* BOOGIE)

But it was a trick. I don't buy it.

EDDIE (*joining in the conversation*)

Me either. I want it on the up and up. Default.

BOOGIE

Let it all ride. Tell you what.

BOOGIE *stirs his french fry in the gravy for a long beat. The guys eagerly await his proposal.*

BOOGIE (*continuing*)

I bet I ball Carol Heathrow on the next date.

FENWICK

Now you're nuts.

BOOGIE

Fifty bucks a guy.

EDDIE

Fifty?

SHREVIE

It's like stealing money from you, Boog.

BOOGIE

In?

The guys all take the bet except BILLY.

BOOGIE (*continuing*)

And I'll take all the action I can get.

FENWICK

We need validation.

BOOGIE

I'll arrange it. You want to be there to validate?

FENWICK

Sure.

There's a slight sense of anxiety in BOOGIE'*s attitude.* BILLY *picks up on it.*

Cut to

63. Exterior. Diner. Night.

The first rays of morning light reflect off the diner's front windows. EARL MAGET *exits. The* GUYS *follow behind, applauding as he goes.*

MAGET *calmly crosses the parking lot, gets into his little, yellow Nash Metropolitan, and drives off.*

SHREVIE

You all want to meet here and go to the game in my car?

BOOGIE

Yeah, that's good.

SHREVIE (*getting into his car*)

Meet here at twelve.

EDDIE

Make it quarter to. Don't want to miss any of the pregame shit.

SHREVIE

Why don't you go now? Then you'll be sure not to miss anything.

He starts his car.

EDDIE

We're talking the championship game. Quarter to.

SHREVIE *nods. The* GUYS *all exchange see ya's, get into their cars, and drive off. The diner parking lot is now empty except for* FENWICK'*s Triumph.*

Cut to

64. Exterior. Countryside. Day.

The morning sun is up now. A very attractive GIRL *in full riding gear gallops along on a chestnut stallion. She rides expertly, seemingly unaffected by the cold morning air.*

The camera pulls back until we see BOOGIE'*s cherry and white DeSoto keeping pace on the road close by.*

65. Interior. Boogie's car. Day.

BOOGIE

I've got to meet this girl. She is *death!*

FENWICK

Very nice.

BOOGIE

I'm in love.

66. Exterior. Countryside. Day.

BOOGIE'*s car continues to trail alongside the* GIRL *on the horse.* BOOGIE *rolls down the window.*

BOOGIE (*yelling out*)

Miss! Miss! Woo! Miss!

The GIRL *pulls up on the reins and stops.* BOOGIE *quickly steps out of the car and approaches.*

GIRL

Yes.

BOOGIE *is amazed. She's more beautiful up close—long, black hair and deep, blue eyes—elegant.*

BOOGIE

I was admiring your horse.

GIRL (*very reserved*)

Were you?

BOOGIE

Do you ride western style as well?

FENWICK *gets out of the car and leans against the door.*

GIRL

I do, but I prefer English. There's a finer sense of control.

BOOGIE

What's your name?

GIRL

Jane Chisolm.

GIRL (*continuing, as* BOOGIE *stares*)

As in the Chisholm Trail.

She gallops away. BOOGIE *watches her go for a beat and then turns to* FENWICK.

BOOGIE

What fuckin' Chisholm Trail?

He walks back to the car and gets inside. FENWICK *does the same.*

67. Interior. Boogie's car. Day.

FENWICK

You get the feeling there's something going on that we don't know about?

BOOGIE

You get the feeling she gave me a false name?

(*starting up the car*)

Want to drive some more?

FENWICK

Naw, let's call it a night.

68. Exterior. Countryside. Day.

BOOGIE's DeSoto drives off, white picket fences framing the car as it heads down the road. We hear the sound of church bells.

Cut to

69. Exterior. Saint Agnes's Church. Day.

The bells in the tower ring. BILLY sits in his car waiting for BARBARA. Members of the congregation walk down the path, passing the nativity scene off to the left.

BILLY watches for BARBARA. The crowd thins. He exits his car and walks toward the church looking around, thinking he may have missed her somehow. He peeks inside the church, unsure whether to enter. A CHURCH MEMBER exits.

BILLY

Is there anyone inside?

CHURCH MEMBER

I didn't notice.

BILLY

Is it all right to go in?

CHURCH MEMBER

Of course.

BILLY enters.

Cut to

70. Interior. Saint Agnes's Church. Day.

BILLY stands at the back and looks around the large, stone structure. He sees BARBARA still sitting, all alone. He goes down the aisle quietly and joins her in the pew.

BILLY

Anything wrong, Barb?

BARBARA

No.

(*a long pause*)

Yes. I think I'm pregnant.

BILLY (*a long pause*)

Me?

BARBARA

Yes. Our one day in New York last month. Six years of a platonic relationship, then one night of sex, . . . and this happens.

They sit silently.

BILLY

Maybe it's for the best.

BARBARA

No, . . . I don't think so. Do you want to marry me?

BILLY

Yes.

BARBARA

Is that why you came back a few days early? To ask?

BILLY

I thought after New York, you know. Seven weeks is a long time when you miss someone.

BARBARA

New York was a mistake.

BILLY

Maybe it wasn't as romantic as we'd like it to be, but I think it will happen. It's not perfect, yet, but, . . . I love you, Barb.

BARBARA

You're confusing a friendship with a woman and love. It's not the same.

They sit saying nothing.

Cut to

71. Exterior. Memorial Stadium. Day.

Aerial view moving toward the main tower of the stadium. We hear the CROWD *yell,* "C!!! O!!!" *We move closer to the tower. The* CROWD *roars,* "L!!! T!!!" *We keep moving closer.* "S!!!" *We pass over the tower and enter the stadium. A deafening crowd roar is heard:* "COLTS!!!"

Cut to

72. Interior. Memorial Stadium. Day.

A COLT DEFENSIVE LINEMAN *smashes into the* GIANT'S QUARTERBACK, *knocking him to the ground with a thud. The* COLTS *are fired up. The championship is within their grasp.*

73. Interior. Memorial Stadium.

The scoreboard reads:
GIANTS *16* COLTS *31.*

74. Interior. Memorial Stadium.

Angle on EDDIE, BILLY, SHREVIE, BOOGIE *and* FENWICK. *They are on their feet. Victory is minutes away.*

EDDIE (*yelling*)

Gino! Gino!

(*to* BILLY)

He's incredible. They should build a statue, a monument to him. Something, you know.

SHREVIE *takes the binoculars from* BOOGIE *and looks through them.*

SHREVIE

Which one?

BOOGIE

Second from the right.

75. Interior. Memorial Stadium.

SHREVIE'*s point of view, through the binoculars. We see a* CHEERLEADER. *Then the camera pans to* ANOTHER CHEERLEADER.

BOOGIE (*offscreen*)

See her?

SHREVIE (*offscreen*)

Yeah. How can you tell she's not wearing panties?

76. Interior. Memorial Stadium.

Back to the GUYS. SHREVIE *puts down the binoculars.*

BOOGIE

You have to wait for her to jump.

SHREVIE

And when she jumped, you saw?

BOOGIE

I see everything.

SHREVIE *puts the glasses to his eyes again.*

SHREVIE

Come on! Jump!

BOOGIE *smiles at* FENWICK. FENWICK *holds back a laugh.*

FENWICK

I think there's a jump coming up.

The COLTS *take possession of the ball and start to run the clock down.*

EDDIE

More points! Johnny, the bomb!

BILLY

Ed, we've got it wrapped up.

EDDIE

I don't want just a win. I want humiliation. Goddamn New York teams think they're hot shit.

(*yelling out*)

Humiliation! Johnny, humiliation!

The CHEERLEADERS *give a big cheer.*

FENWICK

Quick, Shrevie. She's going to jump.

SHREVIE *quickly starts to bring the binoculars to his eyes, but* BOOGIE *has his arm through the strap.*

BOOGIE

Oops. Wait a second.

SHREVIE *tries to untangle* BOOGIE'S *arm.*

FENWICK

Too late.

SHREVIE *stares at* BOOGIE *a beat and then realizes he's been hustled.*

SHREVIE

Very good. Very good.

The scoreboard clock ticks. The CROWD *counts down the seconds. "FIVE . . . FOUR . . . THREE . . . TWO . . . ONE." Pandemonium. The* GUYS *go crazy, grabbing and hugging one another.*

Some of the CROWD *starts to swarm onto the field. The* GUYS *follow.*

The late afternoon sun has dropped below the stands. The lights are on. A gray-golden haze envelops the field.

FANS *are trying to tear down the goalpost.* BILLY, EDDIE, SHREVIE, BOOGIE, *and* FENWICK *hang from the goalpost singing the Baltimore Colt fight song. There may be happier days ahead for the* GUYS, *but this one will be hard to beat. The goalpost finally comes apart, and the* GUYS *fall to the ground in a heap laughing happily.*

Cut to

77. Interior. Fenwick's apartment. Night.

FENWICK *sits watching "GE College Bowl," the quiz show that pits one college team against another. It's a game of intellectual skill.*

The camera pans the apartment. It is imaginatively decorated in pink and turquoise. Five pink flamingos, four feet high, are placed around the room.

TV QUIZ MASTER

That's the opening whistle, and our game begins. Where you're still playing for a thirty-point bonus question, here's another toss-up in English. Are you ready? A spaceship is stranded on the planet Mercury outside of the libration areas; it's night and pitch black outside. For ten points, how long must the explorers wait until sunrise?

FENWICK

The sun doesn't rise on Mercury.

A buzzer sounds.

TV QUIZ MASTER

Bryn Mawr, Stebbins.

STEBBINS

They won't get a sunrise, because Mercury has one side perpetually turned toward the sun and the other side away from the sun.

FENWICK *licks his finger and draws a 1 in the air.*

FENWICK

Hey, Fenwick. Hey, hey.

TV QUIZ MASTER

That's right. They would have to wait forever. That's the answer.

(*beat*)

I have a twenty-point bonus coming up. Here's a toss-up. For ten points, what would a man probably have if he had a visual zygomatic contusion arch.

FENWICK

Black eye.

A buzzer sounds.

TV QUIZ MASTER

Cornell.

CORNELL TEAM LEADER

Sharp bump on his head.

FENWICK

Black eye! Black eye, you bozo.

TV QUIZ MASTER

No.

STEBBINS

He would have a bump here.

She indicates above her eyebrow.

FENWICK

You look like you've got a bump on your head! A black eye!

TV QUIZ MASTER

We were looking for a black eye, but I'll accept a bruised z-bone.

Cut to

78. Interior. Fenwick's bedroom.

The room is black. More pink flamingos are present. BOOGIE *is talking on the phone. Through the wall we hear the "GE College Bowl" and* FENWICK'*s answers.*

BOOGIE

Yeah, Ma, I know I owe two thousand dollars. Guess what? I heard it before you. What am I going to do? I'm choice. Got to find a way to pay it off. Me? I've got fifty-six dollars to my name. Yes, I know I'm in trouble. Then they'll kill me. What can I tell you?

Cut back to

79. Interior. Fenwick's living room.

TV QUIZ MASTER

Here's your toss-up for twenty points. What homegrown philosopher said, "The mass of men lead lives . . . "?

FENWICK

Thoreau.

A buzzer sounds.

TV QUIZ MASTER

Cornell, Pearlman.

PEARLMAN

Thoreau.

QUIZ MASTER

Right, Cornell.

FENWICK *looks smug.*

Cut back to

80. Interior. Fenwick's bedroom.

BOOGIE *sits looking worried. We hear the TV in the background.*

Cut back to

81. Interior. Fenwick's living room.

The quiz show continues.

TV QUIZ MASTER

That's right for ten points. Now you all know the insignia inscribed on the U.S. Post Office: "Neither snow nor rain nor heat nor gloom of night . . ."

FENWICK

Herodotus.

TV QUIZ MASTER

What classical author wrote it?

A buzzer sounds.

FENWICK

Hey, Cornell, . . . take a walk, bozo.

BOOGIE *comes into the living room.*

BOOGIE

Talked to Shrevie. He's going to lend me two hundred.

FENWICK

Going over now?

BOOGIE

Yeah.

FENWICK

I'm going to drop in on my brother. Might be able to get some bucks from the toast.

BOOGIE

Howard? Really?

FENWICK *shrugs his shoulders.*

BOOGIE (*continuing, with real sincerity*)

I appreciate that, Fen. I know how you guys feel about one another.

FENWICK *waves him off. He doesn't like any form of praise.* BOOGIE *starts for the door.*

BOOGIE (*continuing*)

With the Heathrow bet and all, I should be close. See ya.

He exits.

Cut to

82. Interior. Shrevie and Beth's house. Night.

A 45-rpm record drops down the spindle. The arm comes forward and gently rests on the record. A rock-and-roll song starts to play.

SHREVIE *is looking through his extremely large record rack. Something is bothering him. He pulls out one record, then another.*

SHREVIE

Beth! Beth!

BETH *is in another room.*

BETH (*offscreen*)

What?

SHREVIE

Come here!

BETH (*offscreen*)

I'm working on a crossword puzzle.

SHREVIE

Come here!

BETH *sticks her head in.*

BETH

What?

SHREVIE

Have you been playing my records?

BETH

Yeah. So?

SHREVIE

Didn't I tell you the procedure?

They have had this discussion before.

BETH

Yes. You told me all about it, Shrevie. They have to be in alphabetical order.

SHREVIE (*like a teacher to a student*)

And what else?

BETH

They have to be filed according to year as well. Alphabetically and according to year. OK?

SHREVIE

And what else?

BETH *thinks.*

SHREVIE (*continuing*)

And what else?

BETH (*confused, then angry*)

I don't know!

SHREVIE

Let me give you a hint. I found James Brown filed under the *J*'s instead of the *B*'s; but to top it off, you put him in the rock-and-roll section! Instead of the R-and-B section! How could you do that?!

BETH

It's too complicated! Every time I pull out a record, there's a whole procedure to go through. I just want to hear music; that's all!

SHREVIE

Is it too much to keep records in a category? R and B with R and B. Rock and roll with rock and roll. You wouldn't put Charlie Parker with rock and roll, would you?

BETH *says nothing.*

SHREVIE (*continuing*)

Would you?!!

BETH

I don't know! Who's Charlie Parker?

SHREVIE (*exasperated*)

Jazz!! Jazz!! Jazz!!!!

BETH

What are you getting so crazy about? It's only music. It's not that big a deal.

SHREVIE

It is! Don't you understand that?! It's important to me!

They stare at one another. SHREVIE *is trying to control his temper.* BETH*'s eyes become watery.*

BETH (*holding back tears*)

Why do you yell at me? I never see you yell at your friends.

SHREVIE

Pick a record. Any record.

BETH

What?

SHREVIE

Pick a record!

BETH *moves to the record rack and pulls out a record. She holds onto it, not sure what* SHREVIE *wants.*

SHREVIE (*continuing*)

What's the hit side?

BETH

"Good Golly Miss Molly."

SHREVIE

Ask me what's on the flip side?

BETH

Why?

SHREVIE

Ask me what's on the flip side.

BETH

What's on the flip side?

SHREVIE

"Hey, Hey, Hey, Hey"—1958—Specialty Records. You never ask me what's on the flip side!

BETH

Because I don't give a shit! Who cares about the flip side?!

SHREVIE

I do!

He gently thumbs through a handful of records.

SHREVIE (*continuing*)

Every one of these means something. The label. The producer. The year they were made. Who was copying whose style or expanding on it. I hear these, and they bring back certain times in my life.

He stares at her coldly.

SHREVIE (*continuing*)

Don't ever touch these again. Ever.

He starts out of the room. He turns back to BETH.

SHREVIE (*continuing*)

I first met you at Modell's sister's high-school graduation party. 1955. "Ain't That a Shame" was playing as I walked in the door.

He exits and slams the door shut.

Cut to

83. Exterior. Residential street. Night.

BOOGIE *drives down the quiet street and pulls over in front of* SHREVIE*'s modest duplex. He quietly gets out of his DeSoto and walks up to the front door. He rings the doorbell and waits.* BETH *opens the door. She holds some Kleenex in her hand.*

BETH

Oh, hi, Boogie.

He notices that she looks upset but says nothing.

BOOGIE

Shrevie here?

BETH

No.

BOOGIE

Is he coming back soon? I talked with him a little while ago. Said he'd be in.

BETH

I don't know.

She starts to cry. BOOGIE *puts his arms around her and holds her close.*

BOOGIE

What's wrong, babe?

BETH

He ever yell at you?

BOOGIE

What?

BETH (*choking back her tears*)

I don't know what to do. We've got a real problem.

BOOGIE (*stroking her hair*)

Go on, cry. Just cry, babe.

They stand in the doorway, BETH *crying uncontrollably and* BOOGIE *holding her, comforting her.*

Cut to

84. Interior Shrevie's car. Night.

SHREVIE *drives along in his car, singing with the radio.*

85. Exterior. Fenwick's brother's house. Night.

FENWICK *and his older brother,* HOWARD, *stand in the driveway arguing. It is dark, the main source of light coming from a wrought-iron lamppost on the property. The house is large and very modern in design. Through the picture window we see small* CHILDREN *at play in the living room.*

FENWICK

He's in trouble. Don't you know about friendship, Howard?

HOWARD

Five hundred dollars?

FENWICK

Four hundred, three hundred. Whatever you can afford.

HOWARD

Maybe this is a lesson for you. If you worked, you would have some money to lend him.

FENWICK

Yeah, I know. I'm irresponsible. Dropped out of college. Won't work in the family business. I'm a disgrace. That's a good reason for keeping me out of your house, God knows.

HOWARD

You're a bad example.

FENWICK

Far be it from me to disagree. Give me some money, Howard.

HOWARD

You ever read a book?

FENWICK

Huh?

HOWARD

Read. Do you ever read?

FENWICK

Never.

HOWARD

You should read Dale Carnegie's *How to Win Friends and Influence People.*

FENWICK

I have it on my night table. It's right under *How to Wax Your Car.* Give me some money, Howard.

HOWARD

Where did you get this attitude?

FENWICK

I borrowed it. Have to have it back by midnight. Howard.

FENWICK *starts to pace the driveway. His anger is building.*

HOWARD

I should talk to Daddy about stopping your trust fund. It's killing your initiative.

FENWICK

Big trust fund. One hundred dollars a month until I'm twenty-three. Granddad was a real Rockefeller.

Suddenly FENWICK *lunges at his* BROTHER, *grabbing his overcoat by the lapels and pushing him up against the lamppost.*

FENWICK (*continuing*)

Howard, it's important. I wouldn't come otherwise. I don't like to see you, so you know it's very important.

HOWARD

Get off.

FENWICK

I despise you, and yet I'm here.

HOWARD

Get off.

FENWICK *lets go of him and starts toward his car.*

FENWICK

Funny. As a little kid I always wanted a brother. I told that to Mom once. She said, "You *have* a brother." I said, "Oh, that's who the asshole in the other bed is."

FENWICK *gets into his Triumph and pulls away.* HOWARD *shakes his head in disgust.*

Cut to

86. Exterior. A movie theater. Night.

EDDIE *and* BILLY *walk toward the theater. The marquee reads* SEVENTH SEAL.

EDDIE

So what are you going to do?

BILLY

It's up to her.

EDDIE

Her? You've got a big decision to make. We could make it a double wedding.

They reach the box office, hand over a dollar apiece, and receive two tickets in return.

Cut to

87. Interior. The theater lobby. Night.

EDDIE *notices that there is no candy counter, no popcorn, and the only beverage served is coffee.*

EDDIE

What the hell's going on here? Nothing to eat.

BILLY

It's an art theater.

EDDIE (*throwing* BILLY *a look*)

Fuck art. They oughta get some popcorn in here.

They head into the theater.

Cut to

88. Interior. The theater.

The film is in progress. It's a "heavy" Bergman film, and the scene they're watching is very abstract.

EDDIE

What am I watching? It just started, and I don't know what's happening.

BILLY

It's symbolic.

EDDIE

Yeah?

He gives BILLY *the jerk-off motion. They continue to watch the movie.*

EDDIE

Who's that guy?

BILLY

That's Death walking on the beach.

EDDIE

I've been to Atlantic City a hundred times, and I've never seen Death walk on the beach.

89. Exterior. Saint Agnes's Church. Night.

The nativity scene—the camera pans the faces of the three wise men and then comes to rest on FENWICK*'s face. After a beat his half-pint comes into view, and he takes a swig. He shakes his head in disgust.*

As we move back, we see that the baby Jesus is gone. FENWICK *is very bothered by this.*

FENWICK

Kids. Kids did this. A sacrilege for Christsake.

He sits down on the hay next to one of the sheep. He takes another swig on the bottle.

Cut to

90. Interior. Shrevie's car. Night.

SHREVIE *drives along, still coming down from his fight with* BETH. *As he moves along, we see Saint Agnes's on the right up ahead. The nativity display cannot be seen clearly. We move closer and closer.*

SHREVIE *notices something unusual. Out of curiosity he pays closer attention.*

We see the nativity scene more clearly now. Everything is the same except FENWICK *has replaced the baby Jesus. He lies there next to the figure of Mary in his Jockey shorts. Because of the scale of the display,* FENWICK *looks like an enormous baby.*

SHREVIE *slams on his brakes and pulls over to the curb. He quickly gets out of the Hudson and walks up the slope toward the manger.*

Cut to

91. Interior. Movie theater.

EDDIE *is bored to death. He sits in the chair, his eyes drooping, fighting to stay awake.* BILLY *is completely involved. Suddenly a light flashes on them. They turn toward the source. An* USHER *stands holding a flashlight.* SHREVIE *is with him.*

SHREVIE (*to the* USHER)

That's the guys.

(*to* BILLY *and* EDDIE)

Come on! Emergency!

BILLY

What is it?

SHREVIE

Come on!!

The GUYS *get up quickly.*

EDDIE

What's wrong?

SHREVIE

Fenwick's in the manger.

BILLY (*as they head down the aisle*)

What?

SHREVIE

He's in the manger, and he won't leave.

EDDIE

The manger?

SHREVIE

I've never seen him like this.

They exit through the swinging door to the lobby.

Cut to

92. Exterior. Saint Agnes's Church. Night.

FENWICK *lies happily in the manger, sprawled out in the hay. Although he is almost naked, he seems immune to the cold night air. His bottle certainly helps as a warmer, however. He hums, "Oh, Little Town of Bethlehem."*

The GUYS *come across the church grounds.* FENWICK *sees them and smiles.*

FENWICK

Come, three more wise men. You've heard of the miracle.

EDDIE

Let's go, Fen.

FENWICK

You must have traveled far. Rest your weary feet.

BILLY

The police will be here. Somebody's going to spot you.

FENWICK

This is a big smile, don't you think?

SHREVIE

Yeah, come on.

The GUYS *prod him on.* FENWICK *will have none of it.* BILLY *reaches down to help* FENWICK *up.*

FENWICK (*pushing him away*)

No!

EDDIE and SHREVIE try to help out. FENWICK struggles with them. He grabs hold of a wise man. BILLY tries to pull him off it. The wise man topples over. The GUYS continue to struggle with him. BILLY is knocked backward, and part of the structure falls down.

Cut to

93. Interior. Police car. Night.

Two MEN drive along, patrolling the street. Off to the right they see what is happening in the nativity display. It looks as if a riot has broken out in the manger. A sheep suddenly sails through the air. The siren wails.

94. Exterior. Saint Agnes's Church. Night.

The GUYS are still struggling with FENWICK. Everything is a mess. They hear the siren, and the activity quickly comes to a halt.

As the POLICE approach, the GUYS stand very still. The three GUYS are standing side by side. FENWICK is in the hay. It looks oddly like a new version of the nativity.

EDDIE *(out of the side of his mouth)*

What do we do?

BILLY

Choice.

Cut to

95. Interior. Lockup. Night.

FENWICK is in a cell alone. EDDIE and SHREVIE are in the cell next to him. BILLY is directly across from them, locked up with another GUY. The lights are low. FENWICK and SHREVIE are asleep. BILLY and EDDIE stand by the bars talking to one another.

EDDIE

I added a couple killer questions to the test. Tomorrow night's the showdown.

BILLY

She studying hard?

EDDIE

Better be. Otherwise she's off to Cuba alone.

BILLY

Wish I knew what to do about Barbara.

The CELLMATE *starts putting his fingers in* BILLY*'s hair.* BILLY *pushes him away. He tries to ignore him.*

EDDIE

Get married. Take her back to school. Get a part-time job. By the time the kid arrives, you'll have your masters, and all's well.

BILLY

And what about her job?

EDDIE

Her job? I give you an answer, and you confuse it by bringing her into the problem.

BILLY *pushes the* GUY *away again.*

BILLY (*to the cellmate*)

Take a walk.

(*to* EDDIE)

Ed, she's in this thing. There's two of us. She loves her work, and . . . and she doesn't want to marry me. That's the bottom line.

EDDIE

You're dealing with an irrational girl. *That's* your problem.

BILLY *pushes the* GUY *away from him again.*

BILLY

Listen, find somewhere else to stand, buddy.

CELLMATE

What's wrong, cutie? Am I bothering you?

EDDIE

You heard him, back off.

The GUY *grabs at* BILLY. BILLY *pushes him off.*

CELLMATE

You going to do something about it?

He grabs at BILLY *again.*

CELLMATE

Huh?

EDDIE (*yelling*)

Back off him, schmuck!

CELLMATE (*to* BILLY)

You going to do something about it? Huh? Huh? Huh?

BILLY *pushes the* GUY *back against the wall and then goes into a boxing stance.*

BILLY (*very calmly*)

You want to fight? That what you want? Come on. Come on, you son of a bitch. I'll hit you so hard I'll kill your whole family.

BILLY *stands waiting.*

The GUY *doesn't know what to make of this threat. He could be dealing with a real tough kid. He looks at* BILLY, *unsure whether to test him.*

BILLY *stands ready.* EDDIE *watches. After a few seconds the* GUY *sits down on the cot.* BILLY *sneaks* EDDIE *a look and smiles.*

96. Interior. Police station. Night.

BILLY, EDDIE, SHREVIE, *and their* FATHERS *walk down the corridor.*

MR. SIMMONS

We called Timmy's father, but he said he wouldn't post bail until the morning. He wants to teach him a lesson.

The camera pans to BILLY *and his* FATHER.

MR. HALPERT

We get back from Florida, open the door, and the police call.

BILLY

That's what I call good timing. How's Mom?

MR. HALPERT

She's fine. I thought you were going to come down for a few days after the school break.

BILLY

Things came up.

They round a corner. The camera holds on the empty corridor.

Cut to

97. Interior. Diner. Night.

SHREVIE *and* MODELL *sit in a booth.*

MODELL

He was punching out wise men?

SHREVIE

Yeah, he was punching out the wise men. He was so incredibly drunk. I can't believe his father leaves him in jail overnight.

MODELL

He was punching out the wise men? He knocked over the whole manger?

SHREVIE

His family situation isn't the best—in between his father and his—

They're interrupted by METHAN, *who leans into their booth.*

METHAN

"And why furnish your enemies with ammunition? You're a family man, Harvey, and some day, God willing, you may want to be president, and there you are out in the open. For any hep person knows that this guy is toting this guy around with you. . . . Are we kids or what?"

SHREVIE

Will you get out of here, Methan.

METHAN

"Thanks, JJ, for what I consider sound advice."

SHREVIE

Take a walk. Would you get out of here!

METHAN *starts to walk away from the booth.*

MODELL

Is he crazy, or am I mistaken?

METHAN *walks off.*

SHREVIE

Movie freak.

98. Interior. Diner.

Angle on EDDIE *and* BOOGIE *sitting at the counter.*

EDDIE

Do you think I'm doing the right thing, getting married?

BOOGIE

Eddie, I can't tell you that.

EDDIE

I keep thinking I'm missing out on things, you know.

BOOGIE

That's what marriage is all about.

EDDIE

I never did a lot before, you know.

BOOGIE

What?

EDDIE

I never did a lot of screwing around. . . . Some of course . . . a little.

BOOGIE

A little?

EDDIE

A little.

BOOGIE

You son of a bitch! You're a virgin aren't ya?

EDDIE

Technically.

BOOGIE

Eddie, you've got a lot to learn.

EDDIE

And am I going to learn from Elyse? Elyse doesn't know anything. We'll be in trouble.

Cut to

99. Interior. Beauty salon. Day.

BOOGIE *is finishing putting rollers in a middle-aged* WOMAN*'s hair.*

WOMAN

One of these days I may try another hairstyle, not yet.

BOOGIE

Whenever you're ready.

BOOGIE *notices* BETH *enter the store. She looks around and then approaches* BOOGIE.

BETH

Hi, Boog.

BOOGIE (*with a hairpin in his mouth*)

Beth.

BETH

Is Mr. Sol here?

BOOGIE

He'll be back. He went down the street for some doughnuts and coffee. What's up?

He puts the last curler in place.

BETH

Well, you know, we're all getting our hair done for the wedding.

BOOGIE *leads the* WOMAN *toward the hair driers.* BETH *follows.*

BETH (*continuing*)

The bridesmaids, the whole group. And I'm in charge of making sure that Mr. Sol can handle us. Without any problems. Maybe have extra operators or something.

BOOGIE *sits the* WOMAN *down under the drier and turns the machine on. He hands her a magazine.*

BOOGIE (*to the* WOMAN)

Here's *The Saturday Evening Post.*

(*to* BETH)

I don't know what he's planned.

BETH

You're not working that day, are you?

A stocky GUY *enters the salon.* BOOGIE *notices.*

BOOGIE

No. So I guess he's got something arranged.

The GUY *motions for* BOOGIE *to come over.*

BOOGIE (*continuing*)

He'll be back. Wait around.

BOOGIE *walks to the front of the store, where the* GUY *waits.*

BOOGIE (*continuing*)

How you doing, Tank?

TANK *nods for* BOOGIE *to follow. They exit the beauty salon.*

Cut to

100. Exterior. Beauty salon. Day.

TANK *and* BOOGIE *come out of the shop and walk around the side of the building toward a small alley.*

TANK

You had a payment to make.

BOOGIE

Yeah, I'll have it tonight.

TANK

Suppose to have it last night. No one in the office got a call.

BOOGIE

It was a mistake. Forgot. Tonight. I've got some bets that I've called in. I'll have it.

TANK *looks* BOOGIE *straight in the eye.*

TANK

Don't bullshit me, Boogie.

BOOGIE

Straight. I'll have it.

TANK *starts to turn away. He quickly turns back and punches* BOOGIE *with a hard fist to the stomach.* BOOGIE *doubles up. His breathing comes hard and fast.*

TANK

Who do you think you're fucking with? You think this is kid's stuff?

He pushes the now helpless BOOGIE *against the wall.*

TANK (*continuing*)

You think this is fun and games? Little game that kids play, huh?

He slaps BOOGIE *around the head.*

TANK (*continuing*)

'Cause, I'm not amused. Tonight, Boogie. No if, and's, or but's.

TANK *walks away.* BOOGIE *slowly straightens up, takes in a few breaths, and feels his stomach.*

Cut to

101. Interior. Beauty salon. Minutes later.

BOOGIE *enters the shop.*

BEAUTICIAN

Boogie, there's a call for you.

BOOGIE *has got himself together. He walks to the phone and answers it.*

BOOGIE

Hello? . . . Carol? . . . Just thinking about you. . . . What? . . . The flu? Are you sure? . . . One hundred two, yeah, that doesn't sound good. . . . OK, babe. Take care. I'll call and check up on you. . . . Feel better. . . . Bye.

BOOGIE *hangs up the phone and leans back against the wall. He's in deep trouble. He looks across the room at* BETH, *who sits in a chair reading a magazine. He watches her. Thoughts race across his mind. He walks over to her and sits down.*

BOOGIE (*continuing*)

Feeling better today?

BETH

I'm not crying. That's about the only improvement. Thanks for last night. I needed someone to just be there.

BOOGIE

Felt like old times, you know. Standing in the doorway.

(*a small laugh*)

Like I was dating you again.

BETH

Boog, when we were dating, did you care for me?

BOOGIE

Sure I did.

BETH

Not because you could do things to me, but because you cared?

BOOGIE

Of course, Beth. There were plenty of girls for that, you know, if a guy wanted a pop. But I got to tell you, you were real good.

BETH

I was?

BOOGIE

Believe me.

BETH

How would I rate?

BOOGIE

Right up there. We had some good nights. Still think about those times, and that's long ago.

BETH *looks away. Her eyes start to tear. She is on the edge of breaking down.*

BETH

I don't have any sense what I'm like anymore. Don't know what I am. If what I wear is nice . . . If I look pretty . . . Just lost all sense of me.

BOOGIE

I don't know what Shrevie doesn't tell ya, but you have nothing to worry about. You're a definite looker. A sexy lady.

(*a beat*)

We should get together sometime.

They sit in the chairs, looking off in opposite directions.

BOOGIE (*continuing*)

Shrevie going over to Eddie's for Elyse's football test?

BETH

Yeah? Are you going?

BOOGIE

No.

BETH

Can we get together tonight, Boog?

BOOGIE *has accomplished what he wants, but he's not happy about it.*

BOOGIE

Yes.

Cut to

102. Interior. Television-station corridor. Night.

BILLY *and* BARBARA *walk down the corridor.* BILLY *is angry.*

BILLY

It's mine as well. I have something to say in this as well. Don't I?

BARBARA (*speaking quietly*)

I'm not talking about doing anything drastic, an abortion or anything like that.

BILLY

Well, I get the feeling I'm not even included.

BARBARA

Keep your voice down.

BILLY

I'm half-responsible for this mess!

BARBARA

Please. Don't be so loud.

She sees a door and opens it.

BARBARA (*continuing*)

In here.

BILLY *enters. She closes the door behind them.*

Cut to

103. Interior. Television news-announcer's booth.

Through the glass partition we see the control room and the studio floor below. There is some activity going on in preparation for the midday newscast.

BILLY

Have you been to the doctor yet?

BARBARA

No.

BILLY

Why not?

BARBARA

I'm afraid to. Confirm your worst fears, as they say.

Cut to

104. Interior. Television-station control room.

A TECHNICIAN *is checking out equipment prior to air time. In the background, through the glass partition, we see* BARBARA *and* BILLY *talking in the announcer's booth.*

On the monitors above we see the daily soap operas. The audio of one of them is on. The AUDIO MAN *asks for voice checks on the floor microphones.*

Cut back to

105. Interior. Television news-announcer's booth.

BILLY

What do we do? Don't you think we should explore the situation?

BARBARA *sits on the desk. A small light is directly behind her. It is not on.*

BARBARA

I can't believe this happened. I'm hardly the adventurous type. Somehow it just doesn't seem fair.

Cut back to

106. Interior. Television-station control room.

The AUDIO MAN *completes his check. Directly behind him we see* BILLY *and* BARBARA *in the glass booth.* BILLY *picks up a paper and puts his feet up on the audio console. Accidently he kicks on a switch.*

Cut back to

107. Interior. Television news-announcer's room.

The light behind BARBARA *turns red.*

BARBARA

And that makes it very difficult.

Cut back to

108. Interior. Television-station control room.

The soap opera continues. We hear the audio of the show. A COUPLE *is having lunch in a restaurant.*

We also hear BILLY *and* BARBARA*'s voices coming through, but very low key.*

SOAP OPERA MAN

I think it's important, and sometimes I feel that we've neglected to discuss it.

SOAP OPERA WOMAN

Are you saying that it's my fault?

SOAP OPERA MAN

No, no . . . of course not. It's no one's fault. But I only mentioned this because if you let time pass, the problems compound themselves. And that would be unfortunate for both of us.

SOAP OPERA WOMAN

Would it be better if we just let time pass?

SOAP OPERA MAN

He's very, very ill.

SOAP OPERA WOMAN

You were there?

BARBARA'S VOICE

I have a great affection for you, Willy. You're my closest friend.

SOAP OPERA WOMAN

If he dies, what will we do?

The camera holds on the soap opera monitors, the AUDIO MAN, *who is reading the paper, and* BILLY *and* BARBARA *in the background.*

BARBARA'S VOICE

I won't marry you, not out of convenience.

SOAP OPERA MAN

I think we should wait.

BARBARA'S VOICE

Not because it's the thing to do. God, I sound disgustingly brave.

SOAP OPERA WOMAN

It's not going to be easy when I talk to Terry.

SOAP OPERA MAN

Is it necessary that you talk to him?

SOAP OPERA WOMAN

What do *you* suggest?

SOAP OPERA MAN

I'm not sure, but I don't . . . I don't know.

SOAP OPERA WOMAN

Margaret did. She made the break. There were no hard feelings.

SOAP OPERA MAN

Well, good for Margaret, but that doesn't really pertain to us, does it?

SOAP OPERA WOMAN

I'm just trying to find an answer.

SOAP OPERA MAN

Something else to drink?

SOAP OPERA WOMAN

No . . .

Cut to

109. Interior. Simmons' basement. Night.

We are looking up a flight of steps. A door opens. MR. SIMMONS *stands there.*

MR. SIMMONS (*yelling down*)

How's she doing?

SHREVIE (*offscreen*)

Elyse has about a seventy-two so far, but she's hitting a bad streak.

EDDIE'*s* FATHER *comes down the steps. We see* SHREVIE, FENWICK, MODELL, *and* BILLY *gathered. The basement has a bar with neon lights around it, so as to set it off as a showpiece in the room. The walls are knotty pine.* EDDIE *and* ELYSE *are not in the room. They are in the laundry room. The door is partially open.*

EDDIE (*offscreen*)

Before the Cleveland Browns joined the NFL they were in another league. What was it called?

ELYSE (*offscreen*)

Another league?

EDDIE (*offscreen*)

Yes.

A long pause—the GUYS *eagerly await the answer.*

ELYSE (*offscreen*)

I don't know.

SHREVIE *shakes his head and makes a mark on a piece of paper.*

BILLY

What's it now?

SHREVIE

I don't know anymore. Maybe about a sixty-seven.

BILLY

Passing is sixty-five?

SHREVIE

Yep.

EDDIE (*offscreen*)

Buddy Young played for a team that no longer exists. What was the name of that team?

All the GUYS *look at one another. A very tough question.*

MR. SIMMONS

Anybody know that?

None of the GUYS *has the faintest idea.*

ELYSE (*offscreen*)

The New York Yankees football team.

EDDIE (*offscreen*)

Right.

MODELL

The New York Yankees football team?

MR. SIMMONS

They were also in the American Conference. I contributed that question.

EDDIE (*offscreen*)

What was the longest run from scrimmage by a rookie in his first game?

SHREVIE

Alan Ameche.

EDDIE (*offscreen*)

We heard that in here. I'm disqualifying that question.

ELYSE (*offscreen*)

I knew that. Seventy-nine yard run. Opening day 1955.

EDDIE (*offscreen*)

Sorry, Elyse.

BILLY

You blew that, Shrevie.

SHREVIE

Sorry. I got excited. It's one of the few questions I knew.

BILLY

How many more?

SHREVIE

I don't know. I've lost count.

The door to the top of the stairs opens. MRS. SIMMONS *stands there.*

MRS. SIMMONS

Elyse's mother is on the phone. How's she doing?

MR. SIMMONS

The guys think it could go either way.

MRS. SIMMONS

Either way. OK.

She closes the door.

EDDIE (*offscreen*)

The Colts signed him. A Heisman trophy winner who decided to play in Canada. Now, however, he plays for the team. What's his name.

The camera pans the faces of the GUYS.

ELYSE (*offscreen*)

Heisman trophy winner. L. G. Dupre.

EDDIE (*offscreen*)

No. Billy Vessels.

ELYSE (*offscreen*)

I should have known that.

EDDIE (*offscreen*)

Should of's don't count.

FENWICK

Vessels. Out of Oklahoma.

MODELL

She could of racked up points on that one.

SHREVIE

I have no idea what the score is now

MODELL

Want to bet she goes down for the count?

EDDIE (*offscreen*)

Last question.

The GUYS *and* MR. SIMMONS *tighten up. Tension fills the room.*

EDDIE (*offscreen, continuing*)

The Colts had a team here, lost the franchise, then got one from Dallas. What were the colors of the original Colt team?

FENWICK

Woo. A ball buster.

MODELL (*mumbling to himself*)

The original colors?

MR. SIMMONS

Also my question.

ELYSE (*offscreen*)

Original colors? Green and gray.

EDDIE (*offscreen*)

Right.

BILLY (*jumping up and applauding*)

A real scrapper! Tough question and she pulls it out of a hat.

The other GUYS *don't share his excitement.*

BILLY (*continuing*)

Come on, guys. Green and gray. Any of you guys know that? Come on. Give her credit.

We hear EDDIE'*s voice. The* GUYS *quickly shush* BILLY.

SHREVIE

Total's coming up.

EDDIE (*offscreen*)

True and false—seventy-two. Multiple choice—fifty-eight.

MODELL

Killer choices. Confusing.

EDDIE (*offscreen*)

Short answer—sixty-four.

EDDIE *totals. The* GUYS *wait.*

BILLY

What do you think?

MODELL

Pick 'em.

MR. SIMMONS *walks to the bar and pours a drink.*

EDDIE (*offscreen*)

The total is . . . sixty-three.

ELYSE (*offscreen*)

Oh no!

FENWICK

A cliff-hanger.

BILLY

Two points.

SHREVIE

What do you think he'll do?

MR. SIMMONS

He'll give it to her. Good sportsmanship is worth two points.

The door to the laundry room opens. EDDIE *steps into the room. He looks at the* GUYS *and his* FATHER.

EDDIE

The marriage is off.

Cut to

110. Interior. Boogie's car. Night.

He sits in the car and waits. BETH *comes out of the house and down the walk. She gets into the car and slams the door shut. She is excited. She leans over and kisses* BOOGIE *on the cheek.*

BETH

Where are we going?

BOOGIE

Fenwick's apartment.

He hands her a long, blond wig.

BOOGIE (*continuing*)

Here, put this on.

BETH

What's that for?

BOOGIE

Case someone sees us. They might think you're Carol Heathrow or somebody like that.

She slips the wig on and straightens it out.

BETH

How's it look?

BOOGIE

Fine. Just fine.

They drive away.

Cut to

111. Exterior. Simmons' house. Night.

FENWICK *and* SHREVIE *walk out the front door. From inside we hear yelling and screaming between* EDDIE *and his* PARENTS.

SHREVIE

You going up to the diner?

FENWICK

No, got to validate the Heathrow bet.

SHREVIE

Christ, yeah, of course.

They approach their cars.

SHREVIE (*continuing*)

Fen, you mind if I come along?

FENWICK *thinks about it.*

SHREVIE (*continuing*)

I won't make a sound.

FENWICK

It's a small closet. Gotta be still.

SHREVIE

Great.

They get into FENWICK*'s car and drive off.*

Cut to

112. Exterior. Street. Night.

BOOGIE *drives his DeSoto along.* BETH, *wearing the blond wig, sits by his side.*

Cut to

113. Exterior. Street. Night.

FENWICK*'s Triumph turns a corner and heads down another street.*

Cut to

114. Interior. Fenwick's car. Night.

FENWICK

"My Prayer"?

SHREVIE

Flip side—"Heaven on Earth"—recorded by The Platters for Mercury Records. Color of label—maroon.

FENWICK

"I'm Stickin' with You"?

SHREVIE

"I'm Stickin' with You"? Flip side is "Ever Lovin' Fingers" recorded by Jimmy Bowen for Roulette Records. Color of label is orange.

FENWICK

"Donna"?

SHREVIE

Flip side . . .

FENWICK

I thought that was the flip side.

SHREVIE

It's "La Bamba."

FENWICK *sings "La Bamba."*

115. Interior. Boogie's car. Night.

BOOGIE *is uncomfortable, knowing what he is about to do is wrong.* BETH *is silent.*

Cut to

116. Interior. Fenwick's apartment. Night.

FENWICK *and* SHREVIE *enter the dark apartment.* FENWICK *doesn't turn on the lights. They move toward the bedroom.*

Cut to

117. Interior. Fenwick's bedroom.

The room is dark. A shaft of light coming through a window offers the only illumination. FENWICK *opens the closet door.* SHREVIE *steps inside.*

FENWICK

You crouch. I'll stand.

SHREVIE *kneels down.* FENWICK *enters and closes the door. It remains about four inches open.*

Cut to

118. Interior. Fenwick's closet.

The GUYS' *point of view—part of the room and the bed*

FENWICK (*offscreen*)

Yeah, this'll be fine.

SHREVIE (*offscreen*)

Fine with me. Good view.

Cut to

119. Exterior. Fenwick's apartment. Night.

BOOGIE *and* BETH *are walking toward the apartment building.*

BOOGIE

You've got to be real quiet inside. No talking.

BETH

I think you're a little paranoid.

BOOGIE

The walls are very, very thin. Promise?

BETH

Sure.

They approach the door. BOOGIE *unlocks it. He starts to open the door, then closes it. He's changed his mind.*

BOOGIE

Let's go.

He takes her by the arm and leads her away. BETH *is confused.*

BOOGIE (*continuing*)

It's a mistake, Beth. Bet or no bet.

BETH

What?

They approach the car. BOOGIE *opens the door.* BETH *gets inside.*

BETH (*continuing*)

What are you talking about?

BOOGIE *closes the door and goes around to his side. He gets in, starts the engine, and pulls away.*

Cut to

120. Interior. Fenwick's bedroom.

Angle on the slightly opened closet door

FENWICK (*offscreen*)

They should be here now.

SHREVIE (*offscreen*)

Let's wait.

Cut to

121. Interior. Boogie's car.

BOOGIE *is very upset with himself.* BETH *is calm. She holds the blond wig in her lap.*

BETH

I was suppose to be Carol Heathrow?

BOOGIE

That's right. Sick thing to do. I'm real sorry.

They drive in silence. BETH *plays with the strands of hair on the wig.*

BETH

Thank you.

BOOGIE

For what?

BETH

At least you had enough respect for me to call it off. That says a lot.

BOOGIE (*a beat*)

Shrevie and you should work out your thing.

BETH

I wish I knew what to do.

BOOGIE

I'm not real good at talking to girls when there's problems and all. With me, if I have a hassle with a girl, I just split. But you guys should try something. It would be worth it.

BETH

Boog, when I came into the beauty parlor this morning, were you lying?

BOOGIE

You'll always rate right up there.

Cut to

122. Exterior. Shrevie and Beth's house. Night.

BOOGIE*'s car is pulled over.* BETH*'s door is open, and she stands on the curb talking to* BOOGIE *inside the car.*

BETH

What are you going to do about the money?

BOOGIE *shrugs his shoulders and smiles at her.*

BOOGIE

I don't know.

BETH *closes the door.* BOOGIE *drives away.* BETH *watches as he disappears down the street.*

Cut to

123. Interior. Fenwick's bedroom.

Angle on slightly opened closet door. FENWICK *and* SHREVIE *are still in the closet.*

FENWICK

Come on, Boogie.

SHREVIE

I bet he's getting her in the hallway.

124. Interior. Strip joint. Night.

BILLY *and* EDDIE *are in one of the clubs on Baltimore's famous Block. In the background a bored* STRIPPER *goes through the motions. The* DRUMMER *thumps out a monotonous beat and a* SAXOPHONIST *drones away. A few* SAILORS *and some other* CUSTOMERS *sit at tables around the stage. All the tables have wooden mallets. When the* STRIPPER *does something they especially like, the* CUSTOMERS *pound the table with the mallet.*

BILLY *and* EDDIE *both have beers and chasers in front of them.* BILLY *sips the chaser, and his body actually shakes from it for a few seconds.*

BILLY

There is no reason to actually like this; you know that.

EDDIE

An acquired taste.

BILLY

No matter how long I drink whiskey, I still don't like it.

He takes another sip and once again shakes. Then he sips the beer.

BILLY (*continuing*)

Now beer's another story.

EDDIE *watches the* STRIPPER *throwing a few bumps and grinds.*

EDDIE

You know something?

BILLY

What?

EDDIE

I don't like strippers. I mean, so they show a little here and there. So what? But give me a couple of mamoosas in a pink sweater . . . look out!

BILLY

Remember the first time we became aware of breasts on girls?

EDDIE

Arlene Stowe.

BILLY

Showed up for the new school year, and there they were.

EDDIE

Seventh grade. We gave little Joel Barry a nickel apiece to find out if they were real. Told him to be subtle. He walked over, reached up, and grabbed. Turned to us and yelled, "They're real!"

BILLY

The whole thing with girls is painful. And it keeps getting more painful . . . instead of easier.

BILLY *downs his beer and orders two more.*

EDDIE

Remember copping a feel? Boogie was the first. Said it was great. So when I took out Ruth Ray I figured I had to do it.

BILLY

Ruth Ray, eighth grade.

EDDIE

Right. Sat on the couch in her club cellar for hours trying to figure out a way to get my arm around her. Finally I learned the move. I yawned and put my arm around her shoulder.

He demonstrates on BILLY.

EDDIE (*continuing*)

Then came the big task of getting my hand down to her breast. By the time I worked up the nerve to move down, I realized my arm was asleep. Figured out there wasn't enough time to take it back, get the feeling again, and start over. Had to be in by eleven. Time was running out. So I move toward the breast with my arm asleep. My first copping a feel was like this.

He bangs his limp arm against BILLY*'s chest. He bumps it again.*

EDDIE (*continuing*)

Next time I saw the guys they said, "Did you cop a feel?" I said "Yeah." "How was it?" "Great."

BILLY

Now wait a second. You mean you never copped a feel for Ruth Ray?

EDDIE

You believed me.

They laugh.

Cut to

125. Exterior. Diner. Night.

BOOGIE *pulls into the diner parking lot.* FENWICK *and* SHREVIE *are there already, sitting in the Triumph.*

FENWICK

Hey, Boogie's here.

(*yelling over to* BOOGIE)

Hey, Boog, . . . where were you tonight, Mr. Boog?

SHREVIE

You chicken out?

BOOGIE

Yeah, I chickened out.

FENWICK

Boog, you should get outta here. Tank's inside.

BOOGIE *gets out of the car and slams the door shut. He looks toward the diner and thinks for a moment.*

SHREVIE

Why don't you wait until he splits?

BOOGIE

He'll just keep looking for me.

He starts toward the diner.

BOOGIE (*continuing*)

Hand's dealt. Might as well play the cards.

The GUYS *hang behind.* BOOGIE *continues on. Inside the diner we see* TANK *moving along the aisle toward the door. He comes outside.*

TANK

Boog.

BOOGIE

Tank.

TANK

Lucky man.

BOOGIE

That so.

TANK

Yeah. The Bagel just paid off your debt.

BOOGIE *looks at him, trying to size up the situation, wondering if he's running a number for some reason.*

BOOGIE

We're even? Straight?

TANK

That's the story.

TANK *starts past* BOOGIE.

BOOGIE

Tank!

TANK *turns.* BOOGIE *slams his fist into his stomach.* TANK *drops to one knee in pain. In the background we hear* SHREVIE *and* FENWICK *whooping and hollering.*

SHREVIE (*offscreen*)

He put him down! He put him down! Go Boogie.

FENWICK (*offscreen*)

Definitely the smile of the week.

BOOGIE (*to* TANK)

I still owed you that.

He enters the diner with SHREVIE *and* FENWICK *still yelling their approval.*

Cut to

126. Interior. Diner. Night.

BOOGIE *approaches* BAGEL, *who sits at a booth alone. He joins him.*

BOOGIE

Thanks, Bagel.

BAGEL

Your mother called. She was frantic. So out of respect for your father . . .

He sips his coffee. Then he picks up a toasted bagel and butters it.

BAGEL (*continuing*)

Your mother feels you're just wasting your time in law school. . . . It's not for you.

BOOGIE

Probably right.

BAGEL

Come to work for me. There's a lot of money to be made in the home-improvement business. You'd be very good at it.

BOOGIE *thinks about it.* BAGEL *chews on his bagel.*

BOOGIE

Well, I was only really using law as a come-on for the girls. They like that. But, what the hell.

(*smiling*)

I can always lie.

The WAITRESS *passes.*

BOOGIE (*continuing*)

Enid, some french fries and gravy.

BAGEL

Call the two thousand an advance.

BOOGIE

I'll work for you . . . for a while. Then I'll have to move on to bigger things.

BAGEL

Always a dreamer, eh Boog?

BOOGIE

If you don't have good dreams, Bagel, you've got nightmares.

He flashes him a smile.

Cut to

127. Interior. Strip joint. Night.

BILLY *and* EDDIE *are still drinking at the bar. They are not drunk, just very happy.*

EDDIE

I'll tell you one thing that happens when you get married. You have to give up your old friends.

BILLY *listens to the music, slapping his thighs, trying to get the band to pick up the beat.*

EDDIE (*continuing*)

The wife wants you to get new friends. 'Cause me and you have secrets she'll never know. And new friends can never be as good, 'cause we've got a history.

BILLY

It won't change, only if we let it.

BILLY *keeps slapping his thighs, but the* DRUMMER *and the* SAXOPHONIST *continue on, unaware of* BILLY'*s private urgings.*

BILLY (*continuing*)

This is getting me crazy.

BILLY *goes toward the small stage.*

BILLY (*offscreen continuing*)

Come on, guys! Pick up the beat!

They don't respond. EDDIE *sits at the bar amused.* BILLY *claps his hands to a strong rhythm, but of course the* GUYS *pay no attention.*

BILLY *goes up on the stage and pulls a cover off a small piano in the corner. He sits down, runs his fingers down the keyboard, then starts to play. It has a nice, pleasant sound to it. The* DRUMMER *and the* SAXOPHONIST *stop, not knowing what to do. The* STRIPPER *also stops.*

The club BOUNCER *at the front door turns toward the stage, notices something is wrong, and makes his way forward.*

BILLY*'s piano playing becomes more intense. He drives the keys hard—full-tilt rock and roll. The sound becomes infectious. The* SAILORS *and other* CUSTOMERS *pick up the beat. One after another they start to pound the table with the wooden mallets.*

EDDIE *moves toward the stage banging empty beer bottles together.*

The SAXOPHONIST *joins* BILLY. *Then the* DRUMMER. *The* STRIPPER *stands by the side of the stage watching. The music builds.*

BILLY*'s fingers pound the piano.* EDDIE *jumps up on the stage and starts dancing around. He grabs the* STRIPPER, *and they jitterbug.*

The SAILORS *and other* CUSTOMERS *are on their feet, banging the mallets on the tables for all they are worth—a room full of drummers. The tempo heightens.*

BILLY *kicks back the stool* à la *Jerry Lee Lewis. The* CROWD *cheers. The* BOUNCER *cheers along.*

The SAXOPHONIST *struts the stage playing his heart out. The* DRUMMER *drives the bass drum with his foot. His hands sweep back and forth across the skins.*

EDDIE*'s feet are flying—enthusiasm over grace. The* STRIPPER *is a whirlwind of motion and sexuality. The tempo is fierce.*

BILLY *gives a look to the* DRUMMER *and the* SAXOPHONIST. *The music builds and builds, and then altogether they shut down. The place explodes in cheers and applause.*

Cut to

128. Exterior. The Block. Night.

BILLY *and* EDDIE *walk with their arms around the* STRIPPER. *They are enjoying one another.*

EDDIE

Let's see.

STRIPPER

First joke you remember.

EDDIE

Ah, let's see. Fifth grade. *Junior Scholastic Magazine.* "Hickory dickory dock. The mouse ran up the clock. The clock struck one . . . and the other two escaped with minor injuries."

BILLY *and the* STRIPPER *boo.* EDDIE *laughs.*

STRIPPER

That's terrible.

EDDIE

Fifth-grade humor.

STRIPPER

Since then your humor has moved up to the sixth grade, is that it?

EDDIE *laughs. He enjoys the put-down.*

EDDIE

You're all right.

STRIPPER

You guys have made my night. You should come down and hang out more often.

EDDIE

Don't think I can. Getting married.

BILLY *looks at him.* EDDIE *smiles.*

EDDIE (*continuing, to* BILLY)

Figured she would have gotten the Alan Ameche question that Shrevie screwed up.

BILLY

Benefit of the doubt.

EDDIE

Exactly.

STRIPPER

I love weddings. Just never found the time to settle . . . or wanted to.

(*to* BILLY)

And you?

BILLY

No marriage.

STRIPPER

Got a girl?

BILLY

Not really. Just in love.

STRIPPER

Does the girl know?

BILLY

Yeah, I told her about it.

STRIPPER

Told her? Did you show her?

BILLY *thinks about that as they enter an all-night coffee shop.*

Cut to

129. Exterior. Coffee shop. Dawn.

BILLY, EDDIE, *and the* STRIPPER *sit in a booth by the window, eating, drinking, and laughing.*

The camera slowly pulls back. The first rays of morning light are breaking behind the building. The camera keeps pulling back.

Cut to

130. Exterior. Countryside. Day.

JANE CHISOLM *rides her horse across the gently rolling hills.*

The horse and she are as one—grace and beauty. She rides out of the frame. Seconds later BOOGIE *rides a horse into the frame. He pulls up on the horse and comes to a stop. He watches* JANE *ride, then pulls up the collar on his wool overcoat and rides off.*

BOOGIE *rides after* JANE. *Although he is not a good rider, he pushes to pick up ground. Finally he pulls alongside.*

JANE *slows her horse, and* BOOGIE *does the same with his.*

BOOGIE

Nice morning.

JANE

Yes, it is.

BOOGIE

Mornings I've always felt are a good time to ride.

JANE *doesn't respond.*

BOOGIE (*continuing*)

You live around here?

JANE

Not around here. Here.

BOOGIE *looks around what seems like endless countryside. He's overwhelmed.*

JANE (*continuing*)

Which means you are trespassing.

BOOGIE *looks her in the eye and flashes his smile.*

BOOGIE

I was waiting for an invite.

JANE *studies him.*

JANE

Let's ride.

She kicks her horse and gallops off.

BOOGIE *follows. They ride away from the camera.*

JANE (*continuing*)

What's your name?

BOOGIE

Boogie. As in Bobby Sheftel.

They ride over a crest and disappear from sight.

Cut to

131. Interior. Banquet-hall Wedding Room. Night.

The Wedding Room has been elaborately decorated. Potted blue and white flowers in stands line the aisle to the blue and white flowered altar. The room is a festival of blue and white.

The GUESTS *sit in folding chairs eagerly waiting for the wedding procession to begin.*

The music begins. It is not the traditional wedding march but rather the Baltimore Colts fight song. Even though the organist has softened it, there is still a rah-rah quality to it. The FLOWER GIRL *comes down the aisle throwing white flowers onto the blue aisle.*

MODELL'S GIRLFRIEND

What is that music?

MODELL

Colt marching song. Sounds good, huh? Very tasteful.

The USHERS *come forward—*BOOGIE *and* FENWICK, *followed by* SHREVIE, *who walks alone. They are all smartly dressed in black tuxedos.*

The BRIDESMAIDS *come forward—*BETH *and another* GIRL, *followed by two more* GIRLS, *followed by two more* GIRLS.

BILLY *and* EDDIE *start down the aisle. Behind them are* MR. *and* MRS. SIMMONS. *They walk on either side of* EDDIE'*s* GRANDMOTHER.

The Colts fight song continues.

EDDIE *sees someone sitting one seat in from the aisle. He whispers to* BILLY.

BILLY

Moon Shaw? Where?

EDDIE *indicates with a nod.* BILLY *looks over.*

BILLY (*continuing*)

You're right?

As they start to pass, BILLY *leans into the row and grabs* MOON SHAW *by the shirt. He pulls back his fist.* MOON *is shocked.*

BILLY (*continuing*)

Hi, Moon.

He smiles, lets him go, and rejoins EDDIE, *having missed only a few steps. No one is quite sure what has happened. Quickly the attention is back on the wedding procession.*

132. Interior. Banquet-hall Wedding Room.

Long shot—the hall—as ELYSE *and her* MOTHER *and* FATHER *come down the aisle.*

Cut to

133. Interior. Banquet-hall Wedding Room.

*Tight shot—*EDDIE'*s face*

RABBI (*offscreen*)

Do you, Edward, take this woman, Elyse, to be your lawful wedded wife? For better or worse, in sickness and in health, until death do you part?

EDDIE

I do.

RABBI (*offscreen*)

Do you, Elyse . . .

134. Interior. Banquet-hall Wedding Room.

*Tight shot—*FENWICK'*s face*

RABBI (*offscreen*)

take this man, Edward, to be . . .

135. Interior. Banquet-hall Wedding Room.

*Tight shot—*BOOGIE*'s face*

RABBI (*offscreen*)

your lawful wedded husband. For better or worse, . . .

136. Interior. Banquet-hall Wedding Room.

*Tight shot—*BILLY*'s face*

RABBI (*offscreen*)

in sickness and in health, till death do you part?

137. Interior. Banquet-hall Wedding Room.

*Tight shot—*EDDIE*'s face*

ELYSE (*offscreen*)

I do.

EDDIE *smiles.*

RABBI (*offscreen*)

I now pronounce you man and wife.

Cut to

138. Interior. Banquet hall.

The hall is also decorated in blue and white—the tablecloths, napkins, ribbons, flowers, the bandstand, the band.

The six-piece BAND *plays a nice, perky, dance tune. Some* WOMEN *dance with* WOMEN. MOTHERS *dance with* SONS, FATHERS *with* DAUGHTERS, *and some* HUSBANDS *with* WIVES.

The camera pans to a banner on the back wall. It reads EDDIE AND ELYSE—FOR THE 60S AND FOREVER.

SHREVIE *dances with* BETH, *and they seem to be enjoying themselves.* BETH *is counting the steps to the dance for* SHREVIE.

BETH

One, two, three. . . . One, two, three. . . .

SHREVIE

You look very pretty. Blue becomes you.

(*a beat*)

I've made us some reservations for the summer in the Poconos.

BETH

How long?

SHREVIE

I think we might go for ten days.

BETH

Ten days is good.

The camera pans to FENWICK *and the eleventh-grader,* DIANE.

FENWICK

I'm thinking of going to Europe.

DIANE

Why not travel the United States?

FENWICK

It's been done. Europe. Europe looks like a smile.

The camera pans to EDDIE *dancing with his* MOTHER.

EDDIE

It's not like I'm going to another country.

MRS. SIMMONS

Please come back soon. . . . I'll make you sandwiches.

139. Interior. Banquet hall.

Angle on SINGER *on stage. He is singing "Blue Moon."*

The camera pans to BOOGIE *and* JANE CHISOLM *sitting at a table.*

BOOGIE

Can I get you something?

JANE

Bobby, I think I will have a few more of . . .

(*holding up an hors d'oeuvre*)

whatever these are.

Cut to

140. Interior. Banquet hall. Slightly later.

A slow song is playing. BILLY *and* BARBARA *dance.*

BARBARA

I made arrangements with my boss. He said not to worry. The job was mine.

BILLY

That was nice of him.

BARBARA

So I'll work and care for the child. It can be done. I'll just have to put up with those who want to think badly of me.

BILLY

That's not going to be easy.

BARBARA

I know.

They move across the floor. BILLY *holds her close.*

BARBARA (*continuing*)

The baby is ours, Willy. We can both celebrate that. You can love him just as much, spend time with him or her.

BOOGIE *and* JANE *pass them.* BOOGIE *kisses* JANE *lightly on the cheek.*

BILLY

You know what I realized just yesterday? I've been intimidated by you. I always liked you because you were strong, independent, and all. But I've been intimidated by that as well. I've always held back with you. When we kissed, I held back. The same when we made love in New York. I keep thinking I have to be special, like normal passion wasn't proper . . . as if it were just too ordinary and we were beyond that.

BARBARA *pulls away from him slightly so she can see his face. There's a sad look in his eyes.*

BARBARA

If that's the case, I wouldn't think that's a hard thing to correct.

She kisses him; they hold each other tightly.

BARBARA (*continuing*)

We've got plenty of time to find out about one another. Plenty of time.

He kisses her. They stand still on the dance floor as others dance around them.

Cut to

141. Interior. Banquet hall later.

MODELL *gets up onto the stage and takes the microphone.*

MODELL

I don't want to bother you; I just wanted to say a few words. The guys wanted me to. . . . I didn't prepare anything. The guys told me to come up and say a few words. I was thinking that now Eddie's getting married, he won't really be hanging out with the guys anymore; I just wanted to say we were never really crazy about you. I'll be quite honest. I didn't want to tell you sooner because you're a sensitive person. I just wanted to thank everybody who's responsible for you being here, Elyse. I don't know if everybody knows what Elyse had to go through to get married. . . . She was just two points away from spending the rest of her life by herself. Now she knows more about football than most girls in America. It's important; it really is. We all know that most marriages rely on a firm grasp of football trivia. Eddie gets crazy sometimes with sports; I don't know whether you know.

During this dialogue the camera pans the faces of BILLY, EDDIE, SHREVIE, FENWICK, *and* BOOGIE *as they sit at a table together. As the dialogue continues,* ELYSE *stands with her back to the camera, holding the bouquet up toward the eagerly waiting crowd of* GIRLFRIENDS. *She tosses the bouquet.*

MODELL (*offscreen, continuing*)

It's one thing to dress the room blue and white with banners, and the cake in the shape of a football. . . . But personally I thought it was out of line when Eddie asked the rabbi to wear black and white stripes and a whistle.

Everyone laughs as we see the bouquet bouncing off several extended arms before it settles on the table where the GUYS *are sitting. They look down at the bouquet, then up at the camera. There is a faint smile on their faces. Freeze frame.*

The still turns to black and white.

Fade out.

TIN MEN

1. The screen

is black. In white letters we read:

BALTIMORE
1963

Fade in

2. Exterior. Cadillac dealership. Day.

BILL BABOWSKY, "BB," *a wiry, dapper-looking man in his mid-thirties, is circling a baby blue Cadillac. A* SALESMAN *follows on his heels.*

SALESMAN

She's a winner.

BB (*looking at the* SALESMAN)

Who?

SALESMAN

What?

BB

Who's the winner?

SALESMAN

The car.

BB

I thought maybe you saw some chick walking by. I lost my concentration. Why do they call cars "she"? They never say "he" . . . always "she."

The SALESMAN *shrugs his shoulders.* BB *walks around the Cadillac.*

SALESMAN

I guess it's just a custom. Well, what do you think?

BB

Don't press me.

Cut to

3. Exterior. Tilley's neighborhood. Day.

We see a line of row houses. We hear yelling.

4. Interior. Tilley's house. Day.

NORA, *a rather plain but attractive woman in her early thirties, is yelling up the stairs.*

NORA

You're a sick man! Sick! Do ya hear me?! Do ya hear me?!

Peeking around the banister from the second floor is ERNEST TILLEY, *also in his thirties, handsome in a boyish way.*

TILLEY

Who's sick?

NORA

Who do ya think I'm screaming at? How many of you are there up there? There's only you, and you're a sick human being.

TILLEY *comes down a few steps.*

TILLEY (*quietly*)

Where's my white-on-white shirt? The nice one, you know.

NORA

It's like yelling through a wall to you. I'm carrying on about what a disgusting human being you are, and all you want to know is where your white-on-white shirt is.

TILLEY

Yes, the one with the permanent stays.

Cut to

5. Exterior. Cadillac dealership. Day.

BB *is now sitting in a cubicle in the office with the* SALESMAN, *going over the contract on the car.*

BB

Now don't try to hustle me here. . . . You know what I mean.

I hate being hustled. Give me an honest price, not one of your "special" deals. . . . Give me an honest price. Do I make myself clear?

SALESMAN

Of course, Mr. Babowsky. . . . Now, how much are you willing to pay?

BB

There ya go. . . . There ya go. . . . You're doing it. . . . You're doing one of those hustle numbers.

SALESMAN

I'm just trying to get an idea how much you're willing to pay.

BB

Four dollars . . . I want to pay four dollars a month.

SALESMAN

That's not an honest answer.

BB

What do ya want to hear? Tell me how much you want me to pay, and I'll tell you how much I'll pay, but don't do a hustle on me. . . . I don't like that. How much do I want to pay? I'd like to pay nothing!

Cut to

6. Exterior. Tilley's house. Day.

TILLEY *is leaving the house with his tie undone, hanging around the neck of his white-on-white shirt. He carries his sports jacket, and* NORA *is standing at the door yelling at him.*

NORA

You're being unreasonable. You don't even want to listen.

TILLEY

I don't know what I did. . . . I got no idea. If it's my fault, I'm sorry. . . . I'm sorry. I can do no better than that. A full unconditional apology.

(*continuing*)

By the way, why don't you send a search party out for the white-on-white shirt. It's the best one I've got.

TILLEY *walks down the steps of the house and goes to his car—a Cadillac. He gets inside, starts the engine, and pulls away.* NORA *remains on the porch watching the car, one lonely figure in a neighborhood of hundreds of houses that all look alike.*

Cut to

7. Exterior. Cadillac dealership. Day.

BB *and the* SALESMAN *are coming out of the office.*

SALESMAN

If you even have the smallest problem, call me personally, and I'll just shoot you straight into the Service Department.

BB

And I get a loaner if the car's got to stay?

SALESMAN

As we discussed, you get a car if the car has to be kept overnight.

BB

I get a loaner?

The SALESMAN *nods.*

Cut to

8. Exterior. Tilley's car. Day.

Moving along a brick street lined with row houses

Cut to

9. Interior. Tilley's car. Day.

He drives along, mumbling to himself.

TILLEY

She's gonna drive me to my grave. . . . I'm headed to my grave. . . . The woman's driving me insane. . . . It's not supposed to happen this way.

He starts moving his head—stretching his neck from right to left.

TILLEY

It's not even eleven o'clock and my neck is stiffening up.

He juts his jaw out.

TILLEY

My neck's tight. . . . It's tight.

Cut to

10. Exterior. Cadillac dealership. Day.

BB *gets into the shiny, baby-blue Cadillac, puts it in reverse, and starts to back out of the lot.*

11. Interior. Tilley's car. Day.

TILLEY *is doing neck exercises, rolling his head from left to right as he drives. He sees a red light ahead and starts to slow down, continuing to roll his head.*

12. Exterior. BB's car.

BB *sees that the light is red and starts to back into the street.*

13. Interior. Tilley's car.

TILLEY *rolls his head back as he slows to fifteen miles an hour.*

14. Exterior. BB's car.

BB *backs into the street thinking that* TILLEY*'s car is going to stop.*

15. Interior. Tilley's car.

TILLEY *is still rolling his head.*

Cut to

16. Exterior. Street. Day.

TILLEY*'s Cadillac and* BB*'s Cadillac crash into one another. The entire right rear of* BB*'s shiny, baby-blue Cadillac is smashed. Both* MEN *are shocked and momentarily confused. After a beat both* TILLEY *and* BB *bolt from their cars.* TILLEY *looks at his buckled hood.* BB *races up to* TILLEY*'s face.*

BB

Are you a lunatic? Can't you see I'm trying to back out of this lot? There's a red light; you shoulda stopped.

TILLEY

Me? What are you, crazy? You just want to back into the middle of the street like that. A man's just driving along, and you back into the middle of the street. What kind of driving is that? What kind of driving?

BB

There's a red light; I'm making a space for myself. . . . That's what I'm doing, in order to get into the street. . . . That's something ya do!

TILLEY

You came out of nowhere. . . . You bolted out of no place. . . . Bolted out of nowhere.

BB

Bolted! At six miles an hour I'm bolting into the street! You schmuck! You schmuck!

He moves toward TILLEY.

TILLEY

Back away from me, do ya hear me? Back away from me.

BB

Back away? You want me to back away? I'll back away.

He turns to walk away from TILLEY, *walks, and then turns back and kicks in the headlight of* TILLEY'*s car.*

TILLEY

You're a fucking lunatic!

He goes for BB, *jumps him, and they both fall onto the trunk of* BB'*s car.* PEOPLE *have started to gather and immediately jump in and pull* BB *and* TILLEY *apart.*

BB

You're a madman! Smashes into me, attacks me. . . . The man is crazy!

PEOPLE *continue to pull them apart.*

MAN #1

Come on now, calm down; calm down.

He holds BB'*s arms. Another* MAN *grabs for* TILLEY *and tries to pull him off* BB.

MAN #2

Take it easy. . . . Take it easy. . . .

TILLEY (*to* PEOPLE *watching*)

Get this guy! Will ya get this guy? Backs in front of me, and then kicks my headlight in. . . . and *I'm* crazy. You lunatic!

TILLEY *makes another jump for* BB. *Again* PEOPLE *try to pull them apart.*

BB

You're going to prison. Death! Death! They're going to give you death!

BB *looks at his brand-new Cadillac with the smashed-in side.*

BB

Car only has one sixteenth of a mile, and I've been hit.

He turns back and looks at TILLEY.

BB

I'm gonna get even with you, you son of a bitch. . . . I'm gonna get even with you. This is no ordinary traffic accident.

TILLEY

You want to drive a Cadillac, learn how to drive. You want to get even with somebody? You picked the wrong person to get even with. Nobody backs into traffic, smashes my car, and says they want to get even. *I'm* gonna get even!

BB

We'll see about that.

BB *turns to the* SALESMAN *and grabs his collar.*

BB (*continuing*)

Now, a loaner . . . a loaner . . . no talk.

Cut to

17. Exterior. Industrial park. Day.

We are in a run-down part of town. We see BB *pulling up to a run-down building in his banged-up, brand-new Cadillac. There are three or four nice Cadillacs parked outside the building.*

Cut to

18. Interior. Gibraltar Aluminum Siding Company. Day.

The office is filled with secondhand furniture and mismatched desks in a conglomeration of styles. In one corner of the room are two or three GIRLS *working the telephones—*

canvassing—talking to people on the phone to see whether they're interested in a demonstration of the benefits of aluminum siding. They all speak in a congenial tone of voice.

GIRL #1

Good morning, I represent the Gibraltar Aluminum Siding Company. We will have a representative in your neighborhood today. Would you be interested in seeing the benefits of our aluminum product?

(*a beat*)

Yes. . . . Well, we do aluminum siding, which improves the appearance of your house and improves the insulation. . . .

The camera moves to another GIRL.

GIRL #2

Which improves the appearance of your house and improves the insulation. . . .

The camera moves to GIRL #3.

GIRL #3

Gibraltar Aluminum Siding Company. We will have a representative. . . .

The camera moves to another corner of the room, where we see four "tin" SALESMEN *sitting around one of the desks playing cards.* MOE *is beginning to tell a joke. He is a man in his fifties.*

MOE

So the guy goes to the doctor for a physical. . . . They do all those tests, all that stuff, blah, blah, blah. . . .

BB *enters the scene and goes to get himself a cup of coffee.*

MOE

Doctor says, "When we get all the information back, we'll give you a call." Leaves the doctor. One day the telephone rings. . . . The guy goes and picks it up.

CHEESE

The guy?

MOE (*immediately aggravated*)

The *guy!*

CHEESE

Not the doctor?

MOE

That's right, the *guy* picks it up. He gets a phone call. . . . It's the doctor on the line.

CHEESE

Don't get so irritable.

MOE

Doctor says, "I've got some bad news and some worse news."

BB *joins the tin men to listen to* MOE'*s joke.*

MOE

Guy says, "Well, let me hear the bad news first." "The bad news is you've got twenty-four hours to live." The guy says, "What's the worse news?" Doctor says, "I forgot to call you yesterday."

They all laugh. LOONEY, *a thin guy who twitches and blinks a lot, stands up.*

LOONEY

So the guy dies, right?

CHEESE

I never heard bad news and worse news. . . . Smart joke.

CARLY

It's dumb but good.

BB, *who is not laughing, stands behind* CHEESE, *who throws fifty cents into the card game.*

CHEESE

Up it fifty cents.

LOONEY

I call. . . . I call. I'm in on this one. . . . I call.

MOE

We get it; you're calling.

CARLY

I'm not sure.

BB

Stay with him.

CARLY

I don't know.

CHEESE

Carly, get out of the hand. . . . I'm holding serious cards. *Very* serious cards.

BB

He's bluffing.

CHEESE

If I'm lying, I'm dying.

CARLY

I'm out.

BB

Ballsy move.

MOE *throws his hand in, too.*

MOE (*to* BB)

Did you get the new Cadillac?

BB

Yeah. It's already been hit.

MOE

What?

BB

Didn't have it five minutes, backing out of the place, and a guy comes out of nowhere and bangs into my car.

LOONEY

So what ya got?

CHEESE *throws his hand down.*

CHEESE

Pair of sixes.

LOONEY

Jacks. Win.

CARLY

Shit! Pair of sixes.

MOE

How much damage?

BB

I bet it's six hundred bucks.

LOONEY

Six hundred bucks? I'd get rid of the car. That much damage it won't be any good. You may have dented the frame.

BB

I didn't dent the frame.

LOONEY

When you hit the frame, the car doesn't ride right.

BB

He didn't hit the frame! I'll tell you this; I'm gonna get the son of a bitch. If he would have apologized or something, but this guy gets out, tries to push me around.

CHEESE

You're kidding me?

BB

Yeah, . . . the guy's totally off the wall.

He takes a sip of his coffee.

BB (*continuing*)

I'm gonna get him . . . just for the fun of it.

Cut to

19. Interior. Diner. Day.

Seated at a booth are three aluminum-siding salesmen, SAM PICKLES, GIL, *and* MOUSE, *having their late-morning breakfast.* TILLEY *joins them at their table. He indicates to* SAM *to give him more room.*

TILLEY

Come on, give me a couple of more inches.

SAM

You want me to take my plate. . . . I'll eat in the parking lot.

TILLEY

Come on, Sam, I'm having a terrible morning. You're not going to believe this; some guy just crashed into me . . . right in the middle of the street. Rips off my side mirror; then he attacks me. One of the loonies.

SAM (*biting into his toast*)

Did ya live?

MOUSE

Did you get his name?

TILLEY

Yeah, I got his name. The police came. . . . God, I can't believe it. . . . The guy's an idiot.

He pulls a piece of paper from his pocket.

TILLEY (*continuing*)

Yeah, here it is. . . . Some Polish name . . . Babowsky . . . Bill Babowsky . . . fucking son of a bitch.

GIL

I know the guy. . . . They call him BB.

TILLEY

You know the son of a bitch?

GIL

Yeah, he works with Bagel.

TILLEY

He sells aluminum siding? I don't believe it. . . . Of all the people that could run into me, it has to be a fucking tin man. How come I don't know him?

GIL

You musta seen him. He hangs out with Cheese, Carly Benelli, . . . Gibraltar Siding. . . . You know, that group.

TILLEY

I don't know the guy.

GIL

Don't you remember, he was up at The Corral one night when we were there. . . . He's a good dancer. You must have seen him.

TILLEY

I don't know the guy.

SAM

Gil, he doesn't know the guy.

GIL

I thought he knew him, Sam. . . . I can't believe he doesn't know him.

SAM

He seems to be indicating that he doesn't know him.

TILLEY

I don't know the guy!

GIL

He's a good dancer.

TILLEY

What do you want me to do, date him? What do I give a shit if he's a good dancer?

GIL

I thought you saw him. I was amazed, he does a merengue . . . I tell you, if I was a girl, I'd be impressed.

SAM

You're *not* a girl, and you're impressed!

FLORENCE, *a waitress, comes over and puts down some coffee in front of* TILLEY.

TILLEY

Is it fresh?

FLORENCE

Yes, it's fresh!

TILLEY

Just asking, Florence.

FLORENCE (*walking away*)

You're always just asking.

GIL (*still talking about* BB)

I'm telling you, you just can't believe how well this guy does the merengue.

MOUSE

I can't wait to see it.

TILLEY

I'll tell you one thing, when I get a hold of this guy, I'll break both his legs, and then he won't dance the merengue too good.

(*continuing*)

Look at the nose on my car. . . . Take a look at that.

The GUYS *look out the window of the diner.*

GIL

Holy mackerel. . . . Look at that.

SAM

It was a beautiful car before.

MOUSE

Let me ask you something. You watch Ed Sullivan, right? Which act do you like better, the guy who spins the plates, or do you like the guy with the hand puppet—

TILLEY

Señor Wences.

MOUSE

Señor Wences, yes.

TILLEY

I love this guy.

SAM

He's good.

MOUSE

He's the best.

SAM

That's good comedy. . . . Better than the guy with the plates.

TILLEY

Plus he's got no overhead. Man's got a hand, a chalk, and a box, and that's it. . . . Every once in a while he puts on a wig.

He does an impression.

TILLEY (*continuing*)

Of course he's better than the guy who spins the plates. I love the guy. . . . I love the guy.

He drinks his coffee.

SAM

I'm gonna tell you something. . . . "Bonanza" is not an accurate depiction of the West. . . . That's all I'm saying. Did you ever see that show?

TILLEY (*looking around*)

Is someone talking about "Bonanza" in here?

MOUSE

Today's a "Bonanza" day. . . . It's Monday.

GIL

Big B-day.

TILLEY

Oh, it's Monday. How are Ben and the boys doing?

They all laugh.

SAM

You can laugh about it, but it's unbelievable. You've seen the show. . . . You've got a fifty-year-old father with three forty-seven-year-old sons. You know why they get along good, because they're all the same age. "Hey, Pa, I'll ride the horse, and you go to town." Come on, what kind of show is that?

TILLEY

I'm not an authority on it like you are, but I occasionally watch "Bonanza," and I think . . . it's like, can you believe here's a man who's got three kids from three different wives. They all died at childbirth.

SAM

He must have been a hell of a guy.

TILLEY

He's the kiss of death.

They all laugh.

SAM

It's called . . . one hump and out.

Cut to

20. Exterior. Lower-middle-class neighborhood. Day.

BB*'s Cadillac moves through the neighborhood, and we see homes that look to be about thirty to forty years old.* MOE *is in the passenger seat with* BB.

MOE (*offscreen*)

We've got a little time to kill; you want to get some coffee?

BB (*offscreen*)

No, let's do *Life* magazine.

MOE (*offscreen*)

Yeah, it'll be fun.

BB (*offscreen*)

Yeah, cheer me up.

21. Exterior. Wood-frame house. Day.

The house is slightly run-down. We're looking through the lens of a 35-millimeter camera.

BB (*offscreen*)

You know, I think we've got to come over about two feet.

The screen shakes as BB *moves the camera.*

Cut to

22. Interior. Wood-frame house. Day.

A HOUSEWIFE *is looking through the curtains suspiciously. The camera moves toward the window, and we see* MOE *and* BB *moving the 35-millimeter camera around on a tripod. We can faintly hear their talk.*

BB

I think this is a better position. . . . The light is hitting it, which is accentuating the effect we're going for. It's very good . . . very good.

MOE (*in a creative pose*)

This shows the flaws in the structure. . . .

Cut to

23. Exterior. Wood-frame house.

BB *and* MOE *stand at the camera and tripod.*

BB (*under his breath, to* MOE)

She's at the window.

MOE

Yeah.

BB (*in a loud voice*)

This is going to be terrific in *Life* magazine.

(*even louder*)

Terrific in Life *magazine!*

(*under his breath*)

Come on outside, honey.

MOE (*in loud voice*)

This should be our single biggest issue of *Life* magazine.

We see the HOUSEWIFE *coming out her front door.*

BB (*quietly*)

Bingo!

The HOUSEWIFE *approaches* BB *and* MOE *suspiciously.*

HOUSEWIFE

Excuse me. What are you doing?

MOE

Oh, I hope we're not disturbing you, ma'am. We're with *Life* magazine. . . . We'll be out of here in just a minute.

BB *continues to look through the camera.*

BB (*to* MOE)

Move the tripod another foot . . . another foot.

MOE *moves the tripod.*

HOUSEWIFE

What do you mean, *Life* magazine?

BB (*looking up from the camera*)

Two minutes, ma'am, and we'll be out of here. We just need the picture for *Life* magazine, and we'll be out of here.

HOUSEWIFE

Life magazine is here on my front lawn?

BB

It's very simple. Ya know, we're doing this layout about the benefits of aluminum siding—a before-and-after kind of presentation.

HOUSEWIFE

A "before" picture?

MOE

So they see your house and another one done with aluminum siding, . . . the other house looking so much more beautiful.

HOUSEWIFE

In *Life* magazine?

MOE

It's a special issue on home improvements and ways to beautify your home.

BB

A wonderful issue. . . . It's one of the finest pictorial things we've done here at *Life.* . . . The ways you can improve your house.

(*adjusting the camera*)

We're gonna be out of here in no time, ma'am.

MOE

It's gonna look very good, BB.

HOUSEWIFE

Our house is going to be the "before"? Are you crazy? We have *Life* magazine on our coffee table. Can't our house be the "after"?

BB

No, no, . . . we've got a house that looked like yours and it's been done in aluminum. . . . It's very nice.

MOE

Yeah, . . . really shows the contrast of what a house can look like.

HOUSEWIFE

What does it cost?

BB

What? The aluminum siding? Oh, . . . I don't know the figures offhand. Do you have any idea, Moe?

MOE

I think it's fairly reasonable.

HOUSEWIFE

Could my house be the "after" in *Life* magazine and you get another house for the "before"?

BB

You mean have your house as the "after" and find another house that looks like your house for the "before"?

HOUSEWIFE

Is it possible?

BB

What do ya think, Moe? Would that be ethical?

MOE

Well, we didn't sign any agreement with the "after" house. We'd have to move very quickly, ma'am. . . . You know what I mean?

BB

You'd have to work out an arrangement with an aluminum-siding company, and they'd have to do the job very quickly for us to make our deadline. . . . We've got a deadline; that's the problem.

HOUSEWIFE

How quickly?

MOE

BB, what do you think? Can we slide the deadline, or what? Six or seven days?

BB

Pressing it. Do you think we could manage it, Moe?

MOE

It's pushing it, BB.

(*to the* HOUSEWIFE)

What time would your husband be home, *'cause* he'd have to go over the figures with the salesman. . . . That's if there's a salesman available this evening.

HOUSEWIFE

He'll be home at seven.

BB

We might be able to work it.

HOUSEWIFE

That would be wonderful.

Cut to

24. Interior. Wood-frame house. Night.

BB *and* MOE *are sitting on a sofa sipping coffee, looking as if they were members of the family. The* HOUSEWIFE *and her* HUSBAND *are sitting across the dining-room table from* CARLY. CARLY *is going through papers, adding up figures.*

CARLY

OK, we've got a total of thirty-seven hundred dollars.

HUSBAND

Thirty-seven hundred dollars?

HOUSEWIFE

Honey, we're gonna be in *Life* magazine.

CARLY *takes a folder from his briefcase and opens it to display a photograph of a run-down wood-frame house.*

CARLY

Before . . .

He then lays a transparent frame over the photo of the house, which transforms the run-down house into a beautiful house done in aluminum siding.

CARLY

After.

25. Interior. Wood-frame house.

Angle on MOE *and* BB *on sofa*

BB (*to* MOE)

Moe, did you call the office and make sure we can hold up the issue until this job is completed? This house really could be a showcase.

HUSBAND

Thirty-seven hundred dollars!

CARLY

I tell you what. . . . I've got an idea. Do you mind my guys working on a Saturday? 'Cause if my crew can work on Saturday next, that'll free my guys up on Monday. Yeah, that'll really help me out on another job. Anyway, if we can do that, I think I'll be able to knock off three hundred and fifty dollars from the job. You see, I've got an overlapping situation on Monday. . . . I don't want to go into it. What do ya think? We got a deal?

HUSBAND

Yep.

Cut to

26. Interior House #1. Montage.

Angle on LOONEY

LOONEY

What are the benefits of aluminum siding? One: you never have to paint.

Cut to

27. Interior. House #2. Montage.

Angle on CHEESE

CHEESE

It'll never chip, peel, blister, crack, flake, or rust in any way. . . .

Cut to

28. Interior. House #3. Montage.

Angle on MOUSE

MOUSE

It affords much greater insulation, which, in turn, cuts down on your heating bills.

Cut to

29. Interior. House #4. Montage.

Angle on GIL

GIL

Only maintenance you ever have is to wash it down twice a year with a garden hose. In fact, I'm gonna throw in a garden hose with the sale.

Cut to

30. Interior. Tilley's car. Night.

SAM *is listening to the radio in the car.* TILLEY *opens the back door and throws his sample case inside. He gets in the driver's seat and slams the car door angrily.*

TILLEY

I thought I had 'em. . . . I was this close.

He demonstrates with his fingers.

SAM

The amount of time you spent there, I thought you were ready to send for me to close it up.

TILLEY

Damn! I thought I had 'em.

TILLEY *starts the car and pulls out.*

Cut to

31. Interior. Pimlico Hotel. Night.

This is a piano bar with an intimate restaurant at one end. The PIANIST *is playing "The Girl from Ipanema."*

PIANIST (*singing*)

Tall and tan and young and lovely,
The girl from Ipanema goes walking,
And when she passes, each one she passes
goes, "Ah!"

The last word of the verse, ah, is greatly emphasized and lengthened considerably. The PEOPLE *sitting around the piano all join the* PIANIST *and say "ah" in unison. The camera moves over to a table where* MOUSE, SAM, TILLEY, GIL, *and a few other* TIN MEN *sit.*

WING, *the head of Mason Dixon Aluminum Siding, a tall, strong, imposing figure, holds court. The table is filled with papers, folders, etc., as if* WING'*s office desk had been transported to the bar. He's reviewing a paper from a job that* MOUSE *has done.*

WING

Forty-six hundred dollars. This looks like a sound deal. They own their own house. . . . We won't have any problem getting the financing for them. Real good, Mouse.

He picks up his checkbook ledger and writes out a check.

WING (*writing*)

So that's one thousand one hundred and thirty-eight dollars.

He finishes writing the check and hands it to MOUSE.

MOUSE

Thanks, boss. Pleasure doing business with ya.

MOUSE *takes the check and pockets it.* WING *turns to* TILLEY *and* SAM.

WING

Now, what's your guys' story?

TILLEY

Nothing again. . . . Came up short. Let me get a little advance . . . three hundred, just to carry me for a bit.

WING

Tilley, I'm already carrying you for, what is it, twenty-three hundred? Something like that?

TILLEY

No problem. . . . Just in a little slump here.

WING

Don't try to go walking on me.

TILLEY

What do you mean, walking? You think I'm gonna work somewhere else. . . . You've been very good to me . . . very honorable.

SAM

He's always said that about you, Wing. Always said that about you . . . he has.

WING

I'll give you hundred and fifty.

TILLEY

Wing, I need a bit more than that. . . . I got expenses.

WING

What's wrong with your wife? She doesn't work?

TILLEY

Yeah, but how much is she gonna make working at the Social Security office?

WING *writes out a check and gives it to* TILLEY.

TILLEY

Come on, Wing, can't you do better than this? . . . A man in my position in terms of this firm. . . . I dunno . . .

WING

All right, I'll give you two hundred.

WING *changes amount of the check and hands it back to* TILLEY.

MOUSE (*yelling to the cocktail waitress*)

Honey, can you get me some Marlboros and a 7 and 7?

SAM

And some scotch, straight up.

TILLEY *pockets the check*

WING

Now listen, guys, we got a problem here.

SAM (*to* MOUSE)

Did she hear me say scotch straight up?

WING

My sources tell me this Home Improvement Commission is for real. . . . It's no jackpot. These guys are going to be a real pain in the ass, so any of the scams that you guys are pulling, they get wind of it, they take your license, and it's good-bye to this business.

MOUSE

They take away your license? They take away your livelihood? What kind of people are these?

SAM

They have no respect for the working man.

TILLEY

Which scams are they talking about? They got a list?

WING

Any irregularities. You know, selling a house on the pretense that it's a model house and every job sold in the area they get a kickback. . . . The *Life* magazine hustle. . . . You guys know all the bullshit numbers we can run.

SAM

Jesus! What a pain in the ass. Do you think this commission's gonna stick around, or is it gone with the wind?

TILLEY

They take your license?

WING

And I don't mean your car license, Tilley.

TILLEY

Don't mention cars.

Cut to

32. Exterior. Street. Night.

BB*'s Cadillac moves along the street.*

Cut to

33. Interior. BB's car. Night.

BB *and* MOE *are in the car driving along.*

MOE

I wouldn't mind seeing Africa sometime.

BB

Not me. I don't want to go where they've got snakes.

MOE

They've got snakes?

BB

I've heard they've got snakes that'll outrun a horse through the grass. They got a snake that bites you . . . you got eleven seconds to live. No, thank you. I don't want to spend my good money to visit with that kind of jeopardy. I'd like to go to a place where—Hold it!

He hits the brakes suddenly.

MOE

What's wrong?

BB *backs his car halfway up the street. He stops in the driveway of the Pimlico Hotel parking lot.*

BB

The guy who ran into me. . . . That's his car.

He puts the car into park and opens the car door.

BB

I'll be back, Moe. I'm gonna even the score.

He gets out of the car, quickly walks over to TILLEY'*s Cadillac, and with a swift kick kicks the headlight that isn't already broken.*

Cut to

34. Interior. Pimlico Hotel lobby. Night.

TILLEY, SAM, MOUSE, *and* GIL *are about to leave. They're putting on their coats just inside the closed door.* TILLEY *is halfway into his coat.*

TILLEY (*to* MOUSE)

Give me eight points I take the Knicks over the Lakers for twenty.

MOUSE

It's too big a spread.

We hear the sound of breaking glass. TILLEY *responds. He looks out the glass doors and sees* BB *kicking in the headlight of his car.* BB *runs back toward his own car.*

TILLEY

It's that fucking lunatic again.

35. Exterior. Pimlico Hotel. Night.

TILLEY *races out the door of the hotel toward* BB'*s car, which pulls away and speeds down the street. Several of the* TIN MEN *run after* TILLEY. *He stands in the street watching the car disappear.*

TILLEY (*still looking after the car*)

Can you believe this guy? Is he sane or what?

MOUSE

Isn't that something?

SAM

What's he got, a gnat up his ass? What the hell's wrong with the guy?

GIL

Don't you recognize him from The Corral?

TILLEY

I don't know the guy!

GIL

I'll never forget his merengue.

TILLEY

I'll tell you something. If Mr. Merengue wants to play, . . . we'll play.

Cut to

36. Exterior. Tilley's Street. Night.

Profile shot of the porches of one row house on top of another

37. Interior. Tilley's porch. Night.

TILLEY *lets himself into his house. He goes into the kitchen, where* NORA *is sitting, drinking a cup of coffee and working on a crossword puzzle. He takes off his coat and throws it on a chair.* NORA *doesn't look up from her puzzle.*

NORA

Look at you, quarter to three and home already. What happened? You and the fellas run out of things to talk about?

TILLEY

Please! I'm out there working myself to the bone, trying to make a living.

He goes to the refrigerator and gets himself some orange juice.

NORA

What's a five-letter word for a Portuguese overseas province?

TILLEY

Try Macao.

NORA

M-A-C-A-O . . . that fits.

TILLEY

What're you doing up so late?

NORA

We're off tomorrow.

TILLEY (*a beat*)

I think this place may be a little too large for us.

NORA

What are you talking about, . . . this matchbox?

TILLEY

It's got a lot of overhead to it. What do you do . . . spend your time in the bedroom and the kitchen; that's all. So why do you need a living room and a dining room?

He walks over to the back door and looks out.

TILLEY

Why do ya need a backyard?

NORA

You're not selling anything?

TILLEY

I'm in a slump.

NORA

It happens.

TILLEY

Last year I'm number-three top seller. . . . Year before, right up there. I can't get my momentum going this year.

NORA

Well, you will. You always do.

TILLEY (*a beat*)

I'm not sure I like the idea of all this overhead breathing down my neck. When you have a place like this, that's a lot of overhead.

NORA

What are you talking about? The monthly payments on your Cadillac are more than this whole house. Why don't you get yourself something cheaper, like a Chevy?

TILLEY

It doesn't instill confidence in my clients. Cadillac means that you're dealing with someone of importance.

(*a beat*)

I thought I had a couple tonight. . . . They just slipped away . . . slipped away.

(*a beat*)

I'm gonna take a bath—my neck's been tight since this morning.

NORA

I'll turn out the lights.

NORA *gets up and puts the cups in the sink. She gives a big sigh.*

Cut to

38. Interior. Tilley's bathroom. Night.

TILLEY *is in the tub lathering himself.* NORA *enters and sits on the side of the tub.*

NORA

You know, Tilley, we hardly ever do things together.

TILLEY

Like what?

NORA

Do things together that are enjoyable.

TILLEY

What would we do together for it to be enjoyable?

NORA

If we went on a picnic, . . . it would be fun.

TILLEY

I don't understand a picnic. . . . We just go someplace. . . . We put a thing on the ground, and we eat.

NORA

Yes, . . . it's nice to do that.

TILLEY

Why? I don't get it. It's better sitting at home and watching TV.

NORA

I think there's something nice about a picnic. . . . It's fun.

TILLEY

What's fun about it? Ants get into the food. . . . There's bees. I don't get it. We have to drive; it takes maybe an hour to get there, then you sit in grass and eat. Why is that fun?

NORA

I just thought it might be nice to do something together; that's all . . . thought it might be fun.

TILLEY

It doesn't sound like fun to me. . . . You take the stuff you've got here in the house; you take it someplace to eat it. It's just as much fun eating in front of the TV, and we do that together, don't we? No ants and no bees . . . much more comfortable.

NORA

It's not the same thing.

TILLEY

Will you wash my hair the way you do?

NORA *picks up the soap and starts lathering* TILLEY*'s hair.*

TILLEY

A little harder.

NORA *obliges.*

TILLEY (*continuing*)

Don't get me wrong, I'm willing to do anything with you. I'm just a little stymied by a picnic. If you want to go, send me a postcard.

NORA *drops the soap in the tub and walks out of the bathroom.*

TILLEY

What did I say?

Cut to

39. Exterior. Industrial Park. Day.

We see TILLEY*'s Cadillac cruising the streets, obviously looking for someone.*

GIL (*voice-over*)

You make a left here.

The car turns.

GIL (*continuing*)

There it is . . . over there.

Cut to

40. Interior. Tilley's car. Day.

TILLEY *pulls up outside the Gibraltar Aluminum Siding Company.* GIL *is in the passenger seat. We see* BB*'s car parked outside the building.*

TILLEY

OK, Mr. Merengue, . . . here I come.

He reaches into the back of the car, takes out a crowbar, gets out of the car, crosses to BB*'s Cadillac, and smashes in the windshield and all of the windows.*

TILLEY (*smashing wildly*)

There . . . you'll get a lot of air. . . . Car won't be too stuffy.

GIL (*calling from* TILLEY*'s car*)

Come on, Tilley, . . . let's get out of here.

TILLEY *runs back to his car and drives away.*

Cut to

41. Interior. Gibraltar Aluminum Siding Company. Day.

Tight shot of a map of a fifteen-block area of Baltimore. Colored pins indicate various homes that have been provided with aluminum siding. Another pin goes into place.

BAGEL (*offscreen*)

That was a good sale, Double B. Just got a call on a loan. . . . We're in business.

42. Interior. Gibraltar Aluminum Siding Company.

Another angle. We see BAGEL. *He's a little guy with a black fedora and baggy pants held up with suspenders.* BB *stands with him.*

BAGEL

This whole section has been very fertile for us.

(*to* BB)

Oh, I saw your car on the way in. It looks almost shiny brand-new.

BB

Yeah, yeah, . . . six hundred and forty-two dollars.

BAGEL

Six hundred and forty-two dollars?!

42. Interior. Gibraltar Aluminum Siding Company.

Another angle. MOE, CHEESE, *and* CARLY *are talking to* STANLEY, *a heavyset, balding man in his early thirties.*

MOE

Sure you wanna get into the tin game?

STANLEY

Money's good I understand.

CHEESE

Lot of crazy people you're gonna run into when you're knocking on those doors. Hermits that don't see the outside world. . . .

CARLY

People that are just lonely and want to have conversations. . . .

LOONEY

Kids crawling all over ya, . . . people with strange diseases.

STANLEY

Interesting.

MOE (*quizzing* STANLEY)

What's the best way to qualify a mark?

STANLEY

What?

MOE

How do you know if you can get the upper hand? How do you know if you're dealing with a guy who's in an inferior position to you, or superior position? How do you know?

MOE *puts* STANLEY *on the defensive.*

STANLEY

You just have to talk and feel your way.

MOE

Quick way . . . get a book of matches out of your pocket to light your cigarette. . . . You drop the matches on the floor.

STANLEY (*looking puzzled*)

Yeah.

MOE

Guy bends down to pick up the matches for you, you got a mark; . . . you got this guy in your pocket. If he looks to you to pick it up, you've got a long, hard, tough sell on your hands.

BB *walks over to the* GUYS, *having just poured himself some coffee.*

BB

You want to get in good with these people; . . . you want to win their confidence? Good thing to try . . . get a five-dollar bill; take it out when the guy's not looking; drop it on the ground. Bagel, give me a five-dollar bill.

BAGEL *hands him the bill.*

BB (*continuing*)

Guy looks back; pick it up; hand it to him and say, "Mr. Blah Blah, you musta dropped this five-dollar bill on the ground." Two things happen. . . . He says, "It's not mine." You say, "Musta been, 'cause it's certainly not mine." Or the guy takes it. Right away this guy is thinking you must be one hell of a honest guy; . . . you're in. You start chipping away; . . . you start getting inside those people.

STANLEY *is taken with their information.* BB *puts his cup down and grabs his coat.*

BB

Come on, Moe, let's split.

BAGEL (*running after* BB)

Hey, give me the five dollars. Hey, putz!

CHEESE (*to* STANLEY)

Yeah, we'd better go, too. Come on, Stanley.

(*to* CARLY, *who is hanging behind*)

Me and Stanley. It's like a first date.

Cut to

44. Exterior. Gibraltar Aluminum Siding Company. Day.

BB *and* MOE *approach* BB's *Cadillac. They see that all the windows have been smashed in.* MOE *looks to* BB. CHEESE *walks up from behind.*

CHEESE

What? You got a special bargain when you bought this car? They come cheaper without windows?

BB *reaches into the car and picks up a handful of broken glass. He tosses it up and down in his hands.*

BB

This guy's looking to play tit for tat. That's not my game. I'm gonna play hardball.

BB *throws the glass down on the ground.*

STANLEY (*quietly, to* CHEESE)

What's going on?

CHEESE *just nods for them to go, and they start to walk over to* CHEESE*'s Cadillac.*

BB

I'm gonna find out everything about this son of a bitch, and then I'm gonna find the one thing that cuts him to the quick.

MOE

Let's go inside . . . make some calls.

BB *nods, and they start back inside.*

BB

I wonder if he's married?

Cut to

45. Interior. Pool hall. Day.

Tight shot of a pool ball ricocheting off an eight ball. The eight ball drops into the pocket. TILLEY *throws down his pool stick. We see that his partner is* MOUSE. GIL *sits in a chair against a wall.*

TILLEY

Damn it! Damn it! I can't believe it. . . . I can't believe I did that.

MOUSE

Well, then, believe it. There's no sense not to believe it, because you did it. . . . So believe it. That's twenty more. . . . You owe me sixty.

TILLEY

You think I can't add?

He goes to rack to reset. MOUSE *goes over and puts a nickel in the jukebox. A record slips into position, and "La Bamba" begins.* MOUSE *sings in unison with the record, and is totally caught up in the song.*

Cut to

46. Interior. Room off the main pool hall.

SAM *is going through some papers on a desk and comes across an IRS letter addressed to* TILLEY. *He notices that it hasn't been opened. He looks at the postmark—January 3, 1963. It's five weeks old.*

SAM

Jesus Christ!

We can hear "La Bamba" through the door, with MOUSE *screeching along with it.* SAM *takes the letter and goes through the door to the pool hall.*

47. Interior. Pool hall.

He approaches TILLEY, *who's just finished racking the balls.*

SAM

Tilley.

He nods for TILLEY *to come to him. They start to walk together through the darkened areas of the pool hall.*

SAM

Found this on your desk while I was going over some papers.

He hands the letter to TILLEY.

TILLEY

From the IRS. I never even remember seeing it. I must have left it with my other bills. I wonder what it is?

SAM

Maybe it's a refund check.

TILLEY *opens the envelope and looks at the document.*

TILLEY

Hum . . . says here that they haven't received my 1962 taxes. They seem to be saying that they didn't get my check for four thousand dollars.

SAM

What? It must be a clerical error.

TILLEY

I can't believe they spend all that time and energy to write to me, . . . to single me out.

SAM

What are you talking about? You didn't pay your taxes?

TILLEY

I probably forgot. . . . People forget their taxes all the time. . . . Just slipped my mind. . . . I got so many things on my mind. I figured they could wait a few years. . . . It's not like they need my money to build a bomber. You think they're waiting for my money before they dig a new road? Are they all sitting there saying, "Well, it's time we went to see that guy on Pimlico Road. . . . Can't run this government without his four thousand dollars."

(*a beat*)

I figured they'd give me a little leeway. I'm going to pay them. . . . I know I've got a debt. . . . I just need a little leeway.

SAM

You can't mess around with the government. Why don't you go to H & R Block; they'll take care of your taxes for you.

TILLEY

You think I'm gonna let some stranger know all my business?

SAM

All I can say is you better get a lawyer or somebody to look into this, 'cause the IRS, they don't fuck around.

TILLEY

Just what I need in my life right now. . . . I'm in a slump, and I've got the IRS on me. Like when something goes wrong, it's like . . .

He throws his arms into the air in exasperation.

Cut to

48. Interior. Small neighborhood supermarket. Day.

NORA *enters. Ten seconds later* BB *enters. He pulls a shopping cart from the stall and follows* NORA.

49. Interior. Small neighborhood supermarket.

Angle on MOE *as he walks to the front of the supermarket and looks through the window*

50. Interior. Small neighborhood supermarket.

Angle on frozen-food section. NORA *is stopped with her cart and is deciding on vegetables.* BB *has a pile of frozen dinners in his arms.*

BB (*to* NORA)

Are these any good do ya know? These TV dinners?

NORA

I don't think they're too good for you, not a lot of 'em anyway.

She continues to choose her frozen foods. BB *continues talking to her.*

BB

My wife died.

NORA (*looking up*)

Oh, I'm sorry to hear that.

BB

I'm over it now, but it was a very trying time . . . very trying. . . . I've only just started eating again.

NORA

You know what would be a lot more healthy and satisfying is to get yourself a chicken. . . . Just pop it in the oven for a couple of hours with a little bit of seasoning on it. Makes a good meal, and you can make sandwiches with the leftovers.

BB

But then you have to sit and watch it cook. Something seems sad about a man sitting alone in a house and watching a chicken cook.

NORA

You should get yourself a timer.

BB

A timer . . . That's a good idea; I didn't think of that.

Cut to

51. Exterior. Small neighborhood supermarket. Day.

MOE *is looking through the window of the supermarket. From his point of view we see* BB *and* NORA. BB *says something, and* NORA *laughs. Then* NORA *says something, and* BB *laughs, holding her arm.*

MOE

He's an amazing sort. . . . He's got the gift.

Cut to

52. Interior. Modest house. Day.

TILLEY *is talking to a* MAN *and his* WIFE. *The* MAN *wears a seersucker suit and a bow tie—he is a mousie little man, and his* WIFE *is the female equivalent.*

WIFE

The Lord has certainly blessed us this evening.

TILLEY

Well, what can I say. . . . I'm just a modest salesman. . . . I do what I can to help.

MAN

Thanks again.

He opens the door for TILLEY, *and* TILLEY *walks out.*

Cut to

53. Exterior. Modest house. Day.

As the door closes behind him, TILLEY *goes to where* SAM's *car is parked and gets in on the passenger side.*

SAM

So, what's the scoop?

TILLEY

We got 'em!

He's very excited.

SAM

You're kidding?

TILLEY

Take a look at this, Sam.

TILLEY *shows him the written contract. Written across the front of the contract in big, bold, black letters are the words* THIS JOB IS FREE. SAM *looks at* TILLEY.

SAM

Are you fucking crazy? You just gave them forty-two hundred dollars in aluminum siding free?!

TILLEY (*smiling*)

This is the best scam I've ever thought of in my whole life.

He kisses his hands with wild smacking sounds. He's ecstatic.

TILLEY (*continuing*)

It's in my blood. . . . I'm brilliant. . . . I'm fucking brilliant. . . . This is such a brilliant scam. . . . I'm beside myself.

SAM

What are you talking about?

TILLEY

Here it is. . . . You go back in the house and this is what you say. . . .

Cut to

54. Interior. Modest house.

SAM

Mr. Tilley is crazy. . . . He had a nervous breakdown.

MAN

What's that?

SAM

He's been under a lot of pressure recently. . . . He snapped. . . . it's the saddest thing I've ever seen. Let's be honest about it, nobody gives away forty-two hundred dollars' worth of aluminum siding free.

MAN

I thought it was very generous, but sometimes the Lord moves in mysterious ways.

SAM

Let me tell you something, when I go and see his boss and show him this contract, he's out of this business. . . . He'll lose his home; . . . his wife and kids will be thrown out onto the street. He'll probably spend some time in an institution, so God knows what will happen to his wife and kids. Anyway, it's not your problem.

MAN

Why do they have to be thrown out onto the street?

SAM

You don't expect his boss to pick up the forty-two-hundred job, do ya?

MAN

Hmm.

SAM

Yeah, it's a sad state of affairs.

(*a beat*)

Let me ask you something, sir.

MAN

Yes?

SAM

You don't think there's some way you could work with me to try and resolve this, do you?

MAN

How so?

SAM

You got a cup of coffee?

WIFE

Won't be a minute.

SAM

Let's just sit down and kick this around.

The WIFE *goes into the kitchen.*

SAM (*calling to the* WIFE)

No hurry, ma'am.

The MAN *turns to sit down, and as he does,* SAM *throws a five-dollar bill on the ground.*

SAM

What you doing throwing your money around?

He bends to pick up the five-dollar note.

MAN

What's that?

SAM

I found a five-dollar bill, here by the side of the chair.

Cut to

55. Interior. The Corral Club. Night.

The place is crowded, jumping with activity. A local BAND *is playing on a tiny stage.* BB*'s on the floor dancing with a* GIRL*. He's doing some good moves, and it's obvious that he's a real crowd pleaser. Sitting at the bar are* LOONEY, STANLEY, *and* CARLY.

CARLY

The buzzard had a great gimmick. You know, when it came time to measure a job, he'd cut the yardstick and reglue it together. . . . He took out seven inches so his square footage would always be higher. That way he'd always make a few extra bucks on the job.

STANLEY *laughs and looks at* CARLY.

STANLEY

You're kidding?

CARLY

Yeah. He'd always put his hand over the break when he was measuring. Nobody looks at a yardstick to see how long it is.

STANLEY

I'd love to meet him.

CARLY

Maybe you will one day . . . if you play your cards right.

The song ends.

56. Interior. The Corral Club.

Angle on BB. *He pats his* DANCING PARTNER *on her rear. She walks back to her table, and* BB *walks over to where* MOE *is sitting.* BB *picks up his beer can and holds it up to* MOE *as if he's going to make a toast.*

BB

Here's to Nora.

MOE *smiles and picks up his can. They tap their cans, and both take a swig of their beer.*

57. Interior. The Corral Club.

Angle on CARLY, LOONEY, *and* STANLEY *sitting at the bar*

CARLY

Guy's got a million scams.

LOONEY

Oh, God.

LOONEY *disappears behind the bar.*

CARLY

That's not your wife. You can come up now.

Cut to

58. Interior. Sam's car. Night.

SAM *is driving, and* TILLEY *is rubbing his hands together with excitement.*

TILLEY

Fantastic, Sam! A twenty-seven-hundred sale! "This job is free!" What a beaut! I'm out of the slump! Tilley's riding high again. . . . Tilley's back! We ought to go and celebrate. Let's go to The Corral and have a drink. . . . We can turn the paperwork in a little later. Let's go and celebrate.

SAM

I didn't think you could pull it off, but you did.

TILLEY (*laughing and hitting the dashboard*)

I'm riding high. . . . Twenty-seven hundred dollars. . . . "This job is free." . . . The man went insane . . . lost control of himself. . . . His wife and children are out on the street!

(*laughing*)

Sometimes I'm brilliant. . . . I'm fucking brilliant. . . . I can't believe it.

Cut to

59. Interior. The Corral Club. Night.

Angle on the dance floor. BB *is dancing. He's not dancing with a girl; he's just moving around on the floor going through the famous* BB *moves. A couple of* GIRLS *smile at him; he glances back at a few other* GIRLS. *He does a nice, smooth dance step and smiles.*

60. Interior. The Corral Club.

Angle on the door. TILLEY *and* SAM *come through the door and walk over to the bar.*

TILLEY (*to* SAM)

Scotch straight up?

SAM

Yeah.

TILLEY (*to* BARMAN)

Scotch straight up and a rum and Coke for me.

He looks around the room at the WOMEN.

TILLEY

Looks like there's good action here tonight.

SAM

Must be half-price night for divorced women. The place is hopping.

61. Interior. The Corral Club.

Angle on BB, *who is now seated next to* MOE *at a table*

BB

Look how much more complicated things are now. There used to be a time you met a girl, you courted, and then you got married and lived happily ever after. Now, see that one over there. . . .

He points to a GIRL *at a table.*

BB (*continuing*)

That's Helen Arkon. . . . Maiden name used to be Tudor. Get this, she dated Charlie Rider when I was in high school, seemed like they were together forever. They broke up; she started to go with Lenny Mardigian; they got married; she's Helen Mardigian. That goes on two years, three years, something like that. They divorce, dates Billy Small for a couple of years, lives with John Bookly for a year, marries Tommy Selnini. . . . That marriage goes in the toilet, but fast. Now she's dating Charlie Rider, who was divorced by Evelyn Chartoff, who used to be Evelyn Gage before that.

A beat. He looks at MOE *and laughs.*

BB (*continuing*)

So much for relationships.

62. Interior. The Corral Club.

Angle on SAM *and* TILLEY *at the bar*

SAM

I'm beginning to believe in God.

TILLEY

You were never one of those atheists, were you?

SAM

No, I'm not saying that, but I'm beginning to give God more thought.

TILLEY

So, what did you do? Have some kind of religious experience?

SAM

I tell ya . . . I took my wife for lunch yesterday. . . . We went and had some smorgasbord, and it kind of happened.

TILLEY

You found God at the smorgasbord?

SAM

Yeah. I go there. . . . I see celery; I see the lettuce, tomatoes, cauliflower, . . . and I think, All these things come out of the ground. . . . they just grow out of the ground. They had corn—out of the ground; . . . radish—out of the ground. You say to yourself, How can all these things come out of the ground? You know what I'm talking about? All these things are out of the ground.

TILLEY (*not understanding*)

Yeah.

SAM

I mean, how can that be? Out of the dirt all those things came. And I'm not even getting into the fruits. . . . I'm just dealing with vegetables right now. With all those things coming out of the earth, there must be a God.

TILLEY (*looking at* SAM)

I'm not getting the same religious effect that came over you. I don't know why, but I don't feel like running to a church to pray right this second.

SAM

You gotta admit, it's amazing.

TILLEY

Yeah, yeah . . .

He turns away and looks across the room.

TILLEY (*continuing*)

I don't believe it. See the guy over there?

He looks in the direction of BB.

TILLEY (*continuing*)

That's the son of a bitch who crashed into my car. *Little Lord Fauntleroy.*

SAM *looks over to* BB.

63. Interior. The Corral Club.

Angle on BB *and* MOE. BB*'s looking through the* CROWD *and sees* TILLEY.

BB

I don't believe it! Mr. Banana Head is here.

MOE

Who's Mr. Banana Head?

BB

That crazy guy that banged into my car and smashed my windows in. I don't fucking believe it! I'm gonna get him.

64. Interior. The Corral Club.

Angle on TILLEY

TILLEY

I'm gonna get him!

Both BB *and* TILLEY *weave their way through the* CROWD *to get to one another. In the confusion of all the people, they both go right past one another and then look around for each other. They see that they're in the opposite direction and end up going toward one another again.* MOE *and* SAM *wander over to their* GUYS.

BB

You got a lot of nerve banging into my car, and you've got a lot of fucking nerve smashing my windows in.

TILLEY

What're you talking about? Why would I want to break your windows?

BB

You didn't smash my windows in?

TILLEY

I'm a hard-working guy. . . . I don't go around breaking windows. I've got better things to do.

BB

You didn't break my windows?! You didn't break my windows?!

He pushes TILLEY.

TILLEY

Push me one more time, and I'm gonna have to redefine your face.

BB *pushes him.* TILLEY *starts to go for* BB, *and they scuffle.* MOE *and* SAM *try to pull the* GUYS *apart.*

65. Interior. The Corral Club.

Angle on LOONEY *and* CARLY. *They move through the* CROWD *to* BB *and* MOE. *The* BAND *keeps playing.* MOE *and* SAM, *with the help of* LOONEY *and* CARLY, *pull* TILLEY *and* BB *apart.*

BB

Come on, let's go outside. . . . Let's settle this in the parking lot.

TILLEY

Oh, no! You're not gonna get near my car. . . . You're not gonna kick in my headlights again. . . .

(*a beat*)

What am I talking about? I didn't even drive tonight. You wanna duke it? Let's go.

They both head out the door. The other TIN MEN *follow, and* OTHERS *who have been paying attention to this altercation also follow.*

Cut to

66. Exterior. The Corral Club parking lot. Night.

TILLEY *and* BB *come out of the club and start to look for a place in the lot where there's some room to fight. The* CROWD *eagerly follows right on their heels.* BB *and* TILLEY *take off their sports jackets.* BB *sees the* PEOPLE *gathering around.*

BB

What is this? What is this crowd here? We're charging admission?

TILLEY

Back away. . . . Give me some elbow room.

BB *and* TILLEY *take up fighting stances and circle one another looking to take a shot. A police car pulls into the lot. The sound of the tires on the gravel catches* MOE*'s attention, and he sees it's the* POLICE.

MOE (*quietly to* BB *and* TILLEY)

Police!

TILLEY *and* BB *immediately drop their guard and lean against a car. One* COP *gets out of the police car and heads into the club; the other* COP *stays behind in the car. No one knows quite what to do since the* POLICEMAN *is so nearby.*

TILLEY (*casually, to* BB)

You're a lucky man . . . the police showed.

BB

We'll see who's the lucky one.

He picks up his coat and leaves with MOE.

TILLEY

Pansy-ass.

Puts on his coat.

TILLEY (*to* SAM)

Chinese?

SAM

Well I could go for some wonton soup.

They walk away.

Cut to

67. Interior. Social Security office. Day.

Tight shot of a large cake with lighted candles on it. The cake reads FAREWELL ADA.

SECRETARIES (*offscreen*)

Surprise!!!

The lights go on, and we see a group of GIRLS *gathered around the cake, which sits on one of the desks. At the center of the group is* ADA, *in her late twenties and very pregnant.*

ADA

I never expected this. What a lovely cake.

GIRL #1

Blow out the candles then.

ADA *blows out the candles, missing a couple and getting help from one of the other* GIRLS.

GIRL #2

Nine candles for nine months!

Everyone laughs.

GIRL #3

We'll miss you, Ada. . . . You'd better bring that baby in to visit us.

GIRL #1

Register him for his Social Security number.

A couple of GIRLS *hand around glasses of Coca-Cola.* NORA *stands in the midst of the* GIRLS, *pleased for* ADA. *She yells out.*

NORA

I love ya, Ada, and if you're smart, you won't come back.

The cake is passed out, and PEOPLE *are talking. It has become somewhat of a party atmosphere.* NORA *turns to her friend* NELLIE.

NORA

I've just decided. . . . I'm going out with him.

NELLIE

You're kidding?

NORA

I have to. I just want to know what it's like to be with someone else.

She sips her Coke.

NORA (*continuing*)

Because if what I've got with Tilley is as good as it gets, I just . . .

She shrugs her shoulders.

NORA (*continuing*)

I gotta know.

NELLIE

Well, how are you going to manage it? You and Tilley aren't exactly Jackie and JFK.

NORA

Tilley doesn't get home until at least two in the morning.

NELLIE

I hope you know what you're doing. . . . You speak to some guy at the frozen-food section for five minutes, you could jeopardize your whole marriage.

NORA

Everything I've done in my life has been safe and practical, and where's that gotten me?

(*lifting her paper cup*)

Well, here's to who knows what.

They touch their cups.

Cut to

68. Interior. BB's living room. Night.

This is a two-story apartment in a renovated building. It has high ceilings and exposed brick. It is sparsely furnished, but what there is is decent-looking. We see NORA *and* BB *dancing closely in the shadows of the darkened room. A Frank Sinatra record is playing on the record player in the background—"In the Wee Small Hours of the Morning." A bottle of wine is on the coffee table. The remains of Chinese food in containers are alongside.*

NORA

I'm still nervous.

BB

Well, I guess that's to be expected. You want me to take you home?

NORA

No, not right now.

They dance quietly for a moment.

BB

Every time I listen to Sinatra, I always remember when I used to work in Atlantic City back in the late forties . . . you know, a busboy job. . . . Sinatra used to play at The 500 Club, and we used to take our dates and say, "Hey, you wanna go and hear Sinatra?" Then we'd just lean on the door of the club in the alley and listen to the music. I think the girls were looking for something a bit more uptown.

NORA *laughs.*

NORA

I'd go with you and lean against the door.

They dance for a bit and look at one another. He leans toward her, holds her tight, and kisses her. Then the record sticks on the words "that's the time" . . . "that's the time" . . . "that's the time" . . . BB *slips off one of his loafers while still embracing* NORA *and kicks it so that it hits the side of the record table. The record slips a little and continues to play correctly.*

NORA (*looking at* BB)

You've got a pretty good aim.

DD

I sure do.

Cut to

69. Interior. BB's bedroom. Night.

NORA *is sleeping.* BB *slips on a robe, looks at her, and then goes down the stairs to the living room. He takes a piece of paper out of his jacket pocket on the back of a chair and dials a number on the telephone.*

Cut to

70. Interior. Pimlico Hotel. Night.

A telephone rings at the bar; the BARMAN *picks it up.*

BARMAN (*into the phone*)

Yeah, he's here. . . . Just a minute.

The BARMAN *calls over to* TILLEY, *who we see sitting at a table with some of the other* TIN MEN.

BARMAN

Hey, Tilley, somebody wants ya on the phone.

TILLEY *gets up from the table and goes over to the phone.*

TILLEY

Yeah, this is Tilley . . .

Cut to

71. Interior. BB's living room.

BB (*on the phone*)

Hey, asshole, . . . here's the ultimate fuck you. . . . I just poked your wife!

Cut to

72. Interior. Pimlico Hotel.

TILLEY (*on the phone*)

What are you talking about?

Cut to

73. Interior. BB's living room.

BB (*on the phone*)

She's in my bed right now with a big smile on her face.

Cut to

74. Interior. Pimlico Hotel.

TILLEY (*on the phone*)

Well, that's just fine by me. . . . She's a pain in the ass. . . . an albatross around my neck. You're welcome to her. . . . Keep her . . . and may you both rot in hell!

TILLEY *slams down the phone.*

Cut to

75. Interior. BB's living room.

BB *puts down the phone. He looks puzzled.*

BB

Is this a setup? That son of a bitch . . . I bet he set me up. . . . I thought I got him, and he got me. That son of a bitch!

Cut to

76. Exterior. Tilley's street. Night.

TILLEY *pulls up in front of his house. He runs up the front steps.*

77. Interior. Tilley's house. Night.

TILLEY *opens the door, flips on the lights, and looks around.*

TILLEY

Time to hit the road, Nora!

He races upstairs and starts rifling through the closet and drawers, pulling out NORA'S *clothes—her dresses, skirts, blouses, and coats. He opens the window wide and throws them out. He screams as he tosses underwear and the rest of her clothes.*

TILLEY

I'm a free man! I'm a free man!

He grabs NORA'S *shoes and throws them out onto the street. Then he goes into the bathroom and piles all of her toiletries in his arms and tosses them into a trash can. He takes a suitcase from a shelf in the bedroom, opens it, and throws it in the trash can. He clears out her underwear drawers and empties them into the suitcase, closes the suitcase, and then throws that out the window. He's out of breath, exhausted and sweating. He goes downstairs to the kitchen to get himself a drink. He sees a pair of* NORA'S *slippers under the kitchen table, picks them up, opens the back door, and tosses them outside. He locks the door. He stands there as if a motor were running inside of him. He walks out of the kitchen.*

78. Exterior. Tilley's house. Night.

He leaves the house, gets into his car, and drives away.

Cut to

79. Interior. Tilley's car. Night.

TILLEY *is driving. The same Sinatra record, "In the Wee Small Hours of the Morning," is playing on the car radio.* TILLEY *does his now-familiar neck exercises to relieve tension. He's hard to read—a mixture of happiness and sadness.*

Cut to

80. Exterior. Diner. Night.

Through the window of the diner we see TILLEY *sitting alone at a table drinking a cup of coffee. "In the Wee Small Hours of the Morning" plays over this.*

Cut to

81. Exterior. Tilley's street. Night.

NORA is getting out of her car in front of her house. She starts to walk toward the house and stops as she sees her clothing, shoes, etc., scattered all over the lawn. She tries to take in the scene—coats are lying on hedges, underwear on the flower beds. She's shocked.

NORA (*quietly*)

Oh, my God!

She stands there, and tears run down her face.

82. Exterior. Tilley's street.

Long, wide shot of NORA's back to the camera, with all her possessions strewn over the front garden of her house

Cut to

83. Interior. BB's apartment. Night.

The elevator door in BB's apartment opens, and NORA stands there, suitcase in hand. BB stands by the elevator.

NORA

He must have gone crazy. . . . I don't know what happened to him. . . . He must have found out I was with you. . . . I don't know. . . . I don't know what to do.

She starts to cry. She goes to hug BB.

NORA (*continuing*)

Can I stay with you for a day or two?

BB puts his arms around NORA.

BB

Sure.

Cut to

84. Interior. Room off the main pool hall. Day.

Long shot of a nearly empty pool hall. One GUY plays alone in the far corner of the room. TILLEY comes down the stairs of the pool hall and starts to walk toward the back rooms. The camera follows him. He opens the door and goes through.

85. Interior. Mason Dixon Aluminum Siding Company. Day.

The camera continues to follow TILLEY *into the offices of Mason Dixon Aluminum Siding Company. We pass by three* GIRLS *on telephones—they are soliciting jobs for the salesmen. The camera goes from one* GIRL *to the other.*

GIRL #1

Hello, this is Mason Dixon Aluminum Siding Company. We're taking a survey . . .

GIRL #2

Would you be interested in our field representative giving you a home demonstration?

GIRL #3

Home demonstration. We will have some factory representatives in your area today as it happens.

A voice calls out.

VOICE (*offscreen*)

Tilley! Let me see you.

TILLEY *walks over to the coffee machine.*

TILLEY

Wing, give me a minute to get a cup of coffee here.

TILLEY *passes* SAM *on the way to the coffee machine.* SAM *is looking through the sports page of the newspaper, along with* MOUSE *and* GIL.

SAM

What about Super Highway in the seventh. . . . It's paying seven to one. Ran well in its last race.

GIL (*looking at the newspaper*)

Super Highway . . .

TILLEY

Four in the fourth . . . twenty bucks.

SAM

Who's that?

TILLEY

I don't know. . . . It just came to me—number four in the fourth.

SAM (*looking at* TILLEY)

Number four in the fourth—Rider's Revenge—sixty to one, never been in the money. Nice pick, Tilley. Why don't you just throw the twenty dollars in the trash can right now.

TILLEY

Rider's Revenge . . . I like that name. I've gotta go and see Wing.

(*a little pissed off*)

Look, we can be scientific from now to doomsday, but we gotta be gutsy and go for the big one.

TILLEY *goes through the door into* WING'*s office.*

86. Interior. Wing's office.

The office is as messy and thrown together as everything else in the Mason Dixon offices. As TILLEY *closes the door, his coffee, which is filled to the top of his cup, spills over and burns his hand.*

TILLEY

Ah! Ah!

He jumps back, puts the cup down on a desk, and wipes his hand on the back of his jacket.

TILLEY

What's up, Wing?

WING *is sitting at his desk, which is cluttered with papers.*

WING

You lost a sale, Tilley. The Hudsons' loan didn't go through.

TILLEY

What do ya mean? They wouldn't clear the loan?

WING

This Mr. Hudson's some guy. He's got three outstanding shoplifting charges, failure to pay child support from a previous marriage. . . . Guy's overdue on his mortgage, overdue on his car loan, and he was fired from his last job for misappropriation of funds.

TILLEY

What's wrong with this world? There are sick people out there! Thievin' son of a bitch like that takes up my time, . . . cuts into the amount of hours I have available to deal with other people interested in my wares! There's no fucking sympathy for the working man in this country.

WING

They don't make our job easy, Tilley.

(*a beat*)

Did you see the paper?

TILLEY

What section?

WING

Take a look at this.

He hands the newspaper to TILLEY. TILLEY *reads.*

TILLEY

Ocean Front Recreation . . .

WING

No, no, . . . Home Improvement Commission . . .

TILLEY (*reading*)

"Home Improvement Commission . . . Hearings begin today. . . ." Is this McCarthyism? What are they gonna see? If there are any Communists?

WING

Just cool down the scams, OK, Tilley?

TILLEY *shrugs his shoulders.*

Cut to

87. Interior. Converted tobacco warehouse. Day.

An area has been set up for hearings to take place. This seems to be a temporary headquarters, until something substantial can be worked out. There are boxes and crates all over. There's a long table with a number of commissioners behind it and a defense table a little ways across the room. Microphones are being used, and the sound booms, echoing off the walls. A small gallery of PEOPLE *watches the proceedings.*

88. Interior. Converted tobacco warehouse.

Angle on JOHN MASTERS, *who is presiding over the hearings. Even though he wears a tie and a vest, he is sloppily dressed. To his left and right are two other* HOME IMPROVEMENT COMMISSIONERS.

MASTERS

Now, when you made your initial sales pitch, did you indicate that you would be giving free storm windows with the job?

89. Interior. Converted tobacco warehouse.

Angle on MURRAY BANKS, *a typical aluminum-siding salesman, in his early forties. He leans into the microphone.*

MURRAY

Free storm windows?

MASTERS

Yes. That you would provide a free set of storm windows with the sale of aluminum siding.

MURRAY

No, sir. I wouldn't be able to make any money if I was giving away storm windows. My cost of a storm window is somewhere like—

MASTERS (*cutting him off*)

The point being that you had no intention of giving away the storm windows.

90. Interior. Converted tobacco warehouse.

Angle on BB *and* MOE *standing by the door at the back of the warehouse*

MURRAY (*offscreen*)

The storm windows, as I can recall, was not an issue.

MASTERS (*offscreen*)

So, you weren't dangling a free set of storm windows as a come-on to selling them the aluminum-siding job? Because it says here, and I'm reading from a statement from Mr. Tabaleri . . .

MOE (*to* BB)

What do ya make of all this?

BB

It's the future, Moe. . . . It's the future.

MASTERS (*offscreen*)

"It was my understanding that the storm windows were included in the price of the sale."

Cut to

91. Exterior. Converted tobacco warehouse. Day.

MOE *and* BB *are walking away from the warehouse toward* BB*'s car, away from the camera.*

MOE

Where do you think they're getting this information from?

BB

I dunno. . . . Looks like any tin man gets in that hot seat, then he's had it.

MOE

Then they can take your license forever. . . . It don't seem fair.

They walk by a Volkswagen beetle that's parked in front of BB*'s Cadillac.* BB *stops and looks at it.*

BB

Boy, I tell ya, I bet you could sell a ton of these things.

MOE

That? Too silly-looking.

BB *looks at the car for a few more seconds and then goes to get into his car.*

BB

Ever see a dealership?

MOE

No.

BB

Interesting.

They get into the car and drive off.

Cut to

92. Exterior. Racetrack. Day.

Angle on the starting gate as it bolts open and the horses charge out

Cut to

93. Interior. The Turf Club at the racetrack. Day.

Angle on SAM *and* TILLEY *sitting at a table.* SAM *is studying the racing form, and* TILLEY *is concentrating hard.*

TILLEY (*putting his hand to his forehead*)

Six . . . six . . . six . . . six.

(*a beat*)

I'm thinking one. Who's one?

SAM

Mr. Motor.

TILLEY

Then that's it; I'm going with one.

SAM

Tilley, this is insane. You're picking horses because you think you're clairvoyant or something.

TILLEY

Sam, I'm not doing too well by checking the stats, so why not? I put my hand to my forehead, I see a one—Mr. Motor in the second . . . twenty bucks.

They both look toward the track. The horses race to the finish line. Number nine streaks across the finish line.

SAM

Hallihan's Daughter.

TILLEY (*laughing*)

I got it. . . . I got it. . . .

He picks up the racing form.

TILLEY

Three to one. . . . Hundred and sixty smackers.

(*laughing*)

Hand to the forehead! Hand to the forehead!

SAM

You're not exactly talking about a long shot. Mr. Motor, for instance, is coming off at fifty to one.

TILLEY *taps his forehead with his eyes closed.*

TILLEY

Third race I see a six. . . . I see a three. I don't think the verdict's in on that one yet.

TILLEY *stands up and is going through his money and tickets.*

TILLEY

Wing paid a hundred on number five; he loses. I got hundred and forty. . . . Next race I'll lay down the bet.

(*a beat*)

What you taking in this race?

SAM

Thrifty's Delight—number four—twenty bucks.

TILLEY

You take Thrifty's Delight—twenty bucks; I got twenty on Mr. Motor, Wing's got a hundred on Night Fire. What's the odds on Night Fire?

SAM

Twenty to one.

TILLEY

I don't see Night Fire winning. Fuck it, I'm not gonna even place the bet. . . . I just made a hundred bucks.

SAM

What are you, crazy? What happens if he wins?

TILLEY

He's not gonna win. . . . I feel it.

TILLEY *heads toward the betting booths.* WING *enters near the booths.*

TILLEY (*yelling to him*)

Hey, Wing, we're sitting just off the left of the entrance. I'm gonna lay down your bet right now. See you in a minute. You lost the first race, in case you don't know.

Cut to

94. Exterior. Corner drugstore. Day.

BB *and* MOE *come out of the drugstore eating Snowball Ices.*

BB

I tell you something; she's getting on my nerves.

MOE

Who, Nora?

BB

Yeah, yeah, . . . who else is it gonna be? . . . "Who, Nora"! . . . Who else is there?

They walk over to a bench in front of a painted brick wall and sit down.

BB

The whole idea of being with a girl on consecutive nights is new to me. It's one thing when they're with you for a night, but when they live with ya, it's stretching the point. They got a lot of things they bring with them. . . . You go to the bathroom, you see "things" you never saw before.

MOE

So, what's the to-do?

BB

Well, they move your stuff around, and it's not where it used to be. . . . I'm not used to that.

MOE

You mean all this time you've never lived with a girl?

BB

What?! Did we just meet? How long we been partners? No, I've never lived with a girl!

MOE

Boy, oh boy! Did you wake up on the wrong side of the bed today?

BB

Yes, I did. I came in last night, she was sleeping on my side of the bed. In my life I never got out of bed on the left side . . . in my life, never from the left.

(*a beat*)

I got close once up in the Catskills. I met this girl, Dorian. For a week we were together, but it wasn't the same because she always went to her room to change and do all that stuff. She didn't have things in my room.

BB *gives a big sigh.*

BB (*continuing*)

All this 'cause I'm trying to get even with some guy.

(*a beat*)

You know what? I think I got to see her and put an end to this.

Cut to

95. Interior. Social Security office. Day.

We see hundreds of SECRETARIES *typing away and* CLERKS *sitting at desks.* BB *walks into the office, peeking his head around the corner, feeling a little uncomfortable. He starts to walk around, trying to find* NORA *among all the* SECRETARIES *and* CLERKS.

96. Interior. Social Security office.

Angle on NELLIE, NORA*'s friend. She looks up from her typewriter and sees* BB. *In his thick overcoat, huddled up, he seems a little lost, and it's obvious that he's looking for someone. She calls across to* NORA *at the next desk.*

NELLIE

Is that him?

Nora looks up and sees BB *wandering around.* ,

NORA

Yes.

She smiles.

NORA (*yelling*)

Bill!

BB *turns toward* NORA. *She waves to him happily, with a twinkle in her eye.* BB *feels conspicuous*—PEOPLE *are looking at him. He gives a little wave.*

BB (*softly*)

Yeah.

Cut to

97. Interior. Social Security office.

BB *and* NORA *are standing by the partitioned coffee area.* NORA *gives* BB *a small kiss.*

NORA

I'm glad you stopped by. This is a real surprise.

BB

Listen, I got a problem.

NORA

Oh. How can I help?

BB

Um . . . er . . .

He realizes that NORA *hasn't got the point.*

BB (*continuing*)

Well, the problem is . . . like . . . is like . . . eh, you know. . . . You're the problem.

NORA *is obviously really taken with* BB.

NORA (*quietly*)

Really. How so?

BB

There's things that are bothering me.

NORA

Like what?

BB

You know, . . . things.

NORA

Things?

BB

You know, like things that come up . . . stuff . . . like . . . you know, annoyances.

NORA

Annoyances?

BB

Hard to explain . . . very hard.

NORA

Well, try.

BB

As an example, . . . I came home last night, I get undressed, and I realize you're sleeping on my side of the bed. I've always slept on that side. . . . It's something I've always done.

NORA

Then why didn't you just nudge me a bit and tell me to go and sleep on the other side?

BB

I didn't want to wake you up. . . . I thought you might think it was kind of stupid or something.

NORA

Well, that's easily changed.

BB

But there are other things, . . . bigger things. But I realize just talking about it, they all sound petty and silly.

NORA

Listen, if you think all of this is going too fast, maybe I should move out. Is that what you want, Bill?

BB *looks around, very uncomfortable, and he shrugs.*

NORA

I really care for you, but if you think it's best.

(*a beat*)

I don't want to make you unhappy.

BB (*a long beat*)

I don't think we've got to take drastic action.

NORA *smiles.*

BB (*continuing*)

Thought I'd come by and get things off my chest, . . . talk it out.

(*a beat*)

Listen, I'm going over to Pimlico . . . catch the seventh race. . . . Wanna come?

NORA

I can't get away from work.

BB

I know.

He starts to walk away, then turns back and gives her a quick kiss. He turns and walks away. NORA *watches him as he walks by the rows and rows of* SECRETARIES *and* CLERKS.

Cut to

98. Interior. The Turf Club. Day.

Close-up of TILLEY *watching a race*

TILLEY (*very excited and animated*)

We're taking a thirty-to-one shot . . . number eight. . . . Come on, number eight. . . . Streamers, . . . come on, you sucker!

Cut to

99. Exterior. Racetrack Day.

We see horse number eight in the lead, coming around the home stretch.

Cut to

100. Exterior. Racetrack grandstand.

MOE *and* BB *are watching the race.*

Cut to

101. Interior. The Turf Club.

Angle on TILLEY, SAM, *and* WING. TILLEY *is still yelling for his horse.* SAM *and* WING *watch quietly.*

TILLEY

Thirty-to-one . . . a hundred bucks on you, number eight. There's a guy up here who put a hundred on ya. Come on, . . . come on, . . . come on, baby. . . . Come on, baby!

Cut to

102. Exterior. Racetrack.

At the finish line another horse—number fourteen—races past the winning post.

Cut to

103. Interior. The Turf Club.

Angle on SAM, TILLEY, *and* WING

TILLEY

Nooooooo!

WING *smiles.*

WING (*quietly*)

I've got myself a winner.

TILLEY *turns to look at* WING. SAM *turns toward* TILLEY, *looking concerned. We see the totals flash on the board indicating that the winning horse pays $16.30.*

Cut to

104. Exterior. Racetrack grandstand.

Angle on MOE *and* BB

BB (*smiling*)

Way to go, . . . Southern Belle.

MOE *tears up his ticket.*

BB

Should have bet with me, Moe.

Cut to

105. Interior. The Turf Club.

Angle on WING, SAM, *and* TILLEY. WING *smiles.*

WING

Very nice!

TILLEY

That was your horse, Wing?

WING

Yeah, . . . Southern Belle. You oughta know, you bet her for me.

TILLEY

Of course.

WING *goes to look at the racing form.*

WING (*to* TILLEY)

I'm gonna go with the favorite in this one—Fordnee Lane. I tell you what, I won sixteen plus on the other race; from those winnings you can bet me eight hundred.

TILLEY

Eight hundred?

WING

Yeah. . . . I wanna bet eight hundred on Fordnee Lane.

TILLEY (*feeling uncomfortable*)

Fordnee Lane—eight hundred.

SAM *is looking at* TILLEY *knowing that he's really in a jam.*

TILLEY

Eight hundred.

WING (*calling to a* WAITER)

Waiter, can you get me a cup of coffee?

TILLEY *looks over to* SAM *with panic on his face.* WING *turns back to* TILLEY *and* SAM.

WING

You guys want anything else?

TILLEY *nods "no."*

TILLEY

Er . . . hum . . . er . . . hey, Wing, . . . I tell you, I got a problem.

WING

What is it?

TILLEY

It's the eight hundred on Fordnee Lane. I haven't got it.

WING

No, you got it wrong. You take it from the sixteen plus I won . . . the eight hundred.

TILLEY

I haven't got the winnings.

WING (*angry*)

What do ya mean, you don't have my winnings?

TILLEY

Wing, it was the craziest thing. . . . I didn't want to mention it earlier because it was so nuts. . . . it was the craziest thing.

WING

What?

TILLEY

I don't know how to even tell you this without being embarrassed for myself. It was an accident. . . . It's like one of those things out of the blue. . . . It's crazy. . . . You can't explain it. . . . It happens.

WING (*to* SAM)

Sam, what is he talking about?

SAM (*quietly*)

He had an accident of some sort.

TILLEY

It happens. . . . I don't know how . . . I don't know how to explain. It's too crazy, I swear to God, Wing.

WING

Wait a minute. . . . You're telling me that I didn't win the last race?

TILLEY

You won, Wing, . . . you won; it's just that you're not getting any money. . . . It was a fluke. I swear, I don't know how it could have happened. A ten year old couldn't have made the mistake I made. . . . I don't know, I swear.

WING (*to* SAM)

What the fuck is he talking about?

TILLEY

If there was some way I could make it up, believe me, I would, because you know where I stand.

There's a beat while WING *just looks at* TILLEY.

TILLEY (*continuing*)

You know where I stand, Wing. If there was any way, believe me, I'd make it up. I'd give you thirty percent of what you didn't get because it was a fluke. . . . I'm willing to make some kind of retribution.

WING

You just pocketed the goddamn money. . . . You just took my money and slipped it into your goddamn pocket, didn't you?

TILLEY

No. I'd split fifty-fifty with you; that's how badly I feel under the circumstances.

WING

You get this straight, you son of a bitch, you owe me sixteen plus. . . . I want sixteen plus.

TILLEY

Am I trying to shirk my responsibility? That's not the way I see it. . . . It was a fluke, a crazy thing that happened, but I stand behind my honor on this. . . . Put it on my tab.

WING (*to* SAM)

What the hell is wrong with him? What the hell is wrong with him? He's stealing money from me. . . . What the hell is wrong with him? Can you tell me?

SAM

I don't know the whole story.

WING

You work with him, Sam, . . . for Christsake.

WING *is totally frustrated.*

TILLEY

What do you mean, wrong? It was a fluke. . . . It was an accident. I don't know what the hell went wrong. It was a one-in-a-million thing that happened to me when I went to place that bet. I'm trying to do what I can.

WING (*shaking his head*)

Tilley, what the hell happened to you?

Cut to

106. Exterior. Racetrack. Late afternoon.

TILLEY *and* SAM *are leaving the racetrack and walking to* TILLEY*'s Cadillac.*

SAM

Why didn't you at least give him the six hundred that you pocketed from the six races he lost?

TILLEY

Fuck him! It's on my tab. At least I've got six hundred in my pocket right now. It's like another loan. Sam, you got to think about today. Today, I got six hundred bucks in my pocket. You know what I'm saying?

SAM

Yeah.

TILLEY

It's like some guy trying to sell me life insurance. You think I'm gonna take some money out of my pocket to give to some jerk so that somebody can take it when I'm dead? No, Sam, you gotta live for today. I'm gonna live as good as I can every day. You know what I'm saying?

As SAM *and* TILLEY *walk toward* TILLEY*'s Cadillac,* BB *and* MOE *are walking to* BB*'s Cadillac, which is parked close to* TILLEY*'s. They see each other.*

TILLEY (*yelling to* BB)

Hey, Mr. Merengue went to the track!

BB

Did you bother to bet, or did you just hand your money to the tellers?

TILLEY (*laughing*)

The sarcasm's killing me.

(*a beat*)

I thought you were looking to get even.

BB

Who's your accountant, mister, 'cause I think you're down in the debit side.

TILLEY

Who's stuck with my wife. You or me?

He laughs.

BB

You want me to believe that you were setting me up with your wife as some kind of decoy?

TILLEY

Decoy is the word!

There's a long beat as the two GUYS *eye one another. Then, almost in a soft apologetic manner,* BB *speaks.*

BB

OK then, you win.

BB *gets into his car.*

TILLEY

I win?

(*to* SAM)

That guy would never let me win. He must be setting me up. The son of a bitch is setting me up, Sam.

SAM

For crying out loud, why don't you just leave it at that: . . . you win.

TILLEY

I couldn't have won.

(*a beat*)

I smell a rat.

BB*'s car pulls away.* TILLEY *and* SAM *watch him go.*

Cut to

107. Interior. BB's car. Day.

BB*'s driving, and* MOE *is in the passenger seat.*

MOE

BB, I think you're getting a little humility in your blood.

BB

If getting Nora is part of losing, Thank God I didn't win.

Cut to

108. Exterior street. Night.

BB*'s Cadillac is parked in front of a house.*

MOE (*offscreen*)

What do you think if we made this one of our factory showcase houses?

MAN (*offscreen*)

What's that?

BB (*offscreen*)

It's a good location. . . . Get a lot of traffic on this street.

Cut to

109. Interior. House. Night.

BB *and* MOE *are selling to* MR. *and* MRS. SHUBNER, *a young couple. The television is on in the background.*

MR. SHUBNER

What does that mean, Mr. Gable?

MOE

You know what I do, Alan? I pick certain houses that are strategically located; we put up the aluminum siding; and for every referral, for every person who sees this quality job that we do, . . . sees how beautiful it is, . . . I give you two hundred dollars.

MR. SHUBNER

Two hundred dollars?

MOE

That's right. God knows how many homes we could sell by people passing this house. It's perfectly placed for that.

(*taking out his wallet*)

Alan, this is how confident I feel that this house will drum up business for me.

He peels off four hundred dollars and hands the money to SHUBNER.

MOE

Four hundred dollars. . . . I'm giving you commission on two house referrals before I put a panel on the side of your house. . . . That's how confident I feel.

MR. SHUBNER

You think that many people are going to—

MOE (*interrupting*)

I'm certain of it. I'm not giving away four hundred dollars for my health. . . . I'm a businessman, and I'm a good businessman. This is good business for me. I'm giving it away 'cause I believe in this house, believe that it will refer me to other jobs, which means money in my pocket, which means money in your pocket.

MR. SHUBNER

You got a deal, Mr. Gable.

BB *smiles. Suddenly* MOE *winces in pain.*

MR. SHUBNER

Something wrong, sir?

MOE *collapses, falling to the floor.*

Cut to

110. Interior. Hospital corridor. Night.

MOE *is being wheeled on a gurney by a couple of* ATTENDANTS. BB *walks alongside.*

BB

I finally got hold of May. . . . She was over your sister's.

MOE (*breathing heavily*)

Oh, I forgot.

BB

She'll be down here shortly.

MOE

BB, I don't have any insurance. If I die, May's got nothing, . . . nothing, . . . nothing for Leonard. The only money I've got is in my pocket. That's all I got.

BB

Just take it easy, Moe. . . . Rest.

MOE

Did they sign? Did they sign?

BB

Don't worry about it now.

MOE

Goddamn it, BB! Did you sign them?

BB

Don't worry. . . . Don't worry. I'll take care of it tomorrow.

MOE

Goddamn, my chest hurts.

(*a beat*)

I always taught you, BB, never walk out of a place without a signed contract. Somebody's word ain't spit.

BB

They'll sign, Moe. Don't worry, they'll sign.

They round the bend of the corridor.

Cut to

111. Interior. Another hospital corridor.

BB *is on a public phone to* NORA. *We never see* NORA; *we just hear her voice.*

BB

This is kind of new to me, but I thought I better call and tell you I'm gonna be late . . . maybe two or three. I never had anyone there to call before, but I thought I should call, you know.

NORA (*voice-over*)

Why? Do you think you have some obligation?

BB

I dunno. . . . I thought I'd better call; that's all.

NORA (*voice-over*)

Well, I'm glad you did.

BB

I don't know what's gonna happen to Moe.

NORA (*voice-over*)

Well, I hope he's OK.

(*a beat*)

I'll see you when you get in.

She gives BB *a kiss over the phone.*

BB (*looking at the receiver*)

Yeah.

He hangs up the phone and walks to a room opposite. He opens the door and stands in the doorway looking at MOE, *who is lying beneath an oxygen tent.*

Cut to

112. Interior. Diner. Day.

TILLEY, SAM, MOUSE, *and* GIL *are sitting in a booth, having just finished breakfast.*

SAM

Let me see what the damage is.

He reaches for the bill, humming as he reads.

SAM (*continuing*)

Babum . . . babum . . . babum . . . babum . . .

He hands the bill to MOUSE.

SAM (*continuing*)

Mouse, figure it out, will ya?

GIL

Why don't we just split it four ways?

TILLEY

No way! I didn't eat anything, so why should I pay for Mouse? . . . He eats like an animal.

SAM

Well, sometimes you'll eat more than he does, and it'll even out.

TILLEY

No way! He's a pig! He always eats more than anyone else. Why should I pay for his food?

MOUSE

What're you talking about? Today I happened to have eggs and flapjacks, some cantaloupe, some juice, and then another juice.

TILLEY

Like an animal! Like an animal!

MOUSE

But yesterday, what did I have?

TILLEY

What did he have?

(*turning to* SAM)
Sam, what did he have?

SAM
Let me get out my notebook. How the fuck do I know what he had?

TILLEY
Well I don't remember what he had. Gil, what did he have?

GIL
Yesterday? Pancakes?

MOUSE
No.

Through the diner window we see NORA*'s car pull up and park outside the diner.*

TILLEY (*to* MOUSE)
Then what did you have?

MOUSE
Guess.

TILLEY
What is this, a quiz show? We don't know what you had. What did you have?

MOUSE
I had very little.

TILLEY
Very little!! You eat like an animal! It couldn't have been very little.

MOUSE
I didn't have that much. . . . Doesn't anybody remember?

SAM
We don't remember, I don't know why.

GIL
I could have sworn he had pancakes.

TILLEY
He said he didn't have pancakes.

MOUSE
I'll give you a clue. . . . Maple syrup was used.

TILLEY
I don't give a shit.

SAM

French toast.

There's a knock at the window of the diner.

TILLEY

French toast? He had more than French toast.

MOUSE

Yes, but not a lot more.

We hear more rapping on the window.

TILLEY

I don't give a damn. . . . It's split four ways.

GIL (*to* TILLEY)

Your wife's knocking on the window here.

TILLEY *looks to the window, acknowledges* NORA, *and points to the far end of the diner. She nods and starts walking across the front of the diner to the door.* TILLEY *gets up and walks toward her.*

TILLEY (*to the* GUYS)

OK, we'll divvy it up . . . four ways!

113. Interior. Diner.

NORA *and* TILLEY *are sitting alone at a table drinking coffee.*

TILLEY

Was not long ago you never would have seen a woman in here.

NORA

You don't have to tell me. How many nights did you drop me off and come up here till all hours of the morning?

TILLEY

I know. I was just trying to be congenial. . . . You know, start a conversation off, on a nice kind of light level, you know. So, what's the scoop, Nora?

NORA

Well you know, I think we really should get divorced.

TILLEY

Makes sense. You want some more coffee?

NORA

Yeah, I'll have some.

TILLEY (*shouting to the* WAITRESS)

Florence, some coffee here.

FLORENCE (*offscreen*)

I'm busy, give me a minute.

TILLEY (*to* NORA)

It's for the best.

(*a beat*)

You know, we were kind of fooling ourselves, weren't we?

NORA

Yes, it went wrong somewhere along the line. . . . I don't know where, though. You used to make me laugh, Tilley. . . . You used to really make me laugh.

TILLEY

Yes, something went wrong. . . . I don't know.

FLORENCE *walks over and pours coffee for* TILLEY *and* NORA; *then she walks away.*

TILLEY

So you like this guy?

NORA

Yeah, I like him.

TILLEY

All in all, I guess it'll all work out for the best.

NORA

I'm glad you feel that way.

TILLEY

Yeah, can you figure it out? A guy bangs into my car, thinks I did him in, tries to get even with me by stealing my wife, you two people fall in love. . . . Can you figure that out?

NORA

What?

TILLEY

You telling me you didn't know this was the guy?

NORA

This was *that* guy?

TILLEY

Yeah, I told you I ran into another tin man.

NORA

He didn't tell me he was a tin man. . . . He told me he sold baby pictures.

TILLEY

It's your life. All I know is this guy has a bent weather vane.

NORA

Oh, God! Not another tin man.

TILLEY

He didn't tell you he was the guy who crashed my car? I can't believe this.

NORA *is getting very agitated.*

TILLEY (*continuing*)

Nora, you OK? You want me to get you a Bromo Seltzer or something?

NORA *becomes more and more agitated.*

TILLEY (*continuing*)

I'm telling you, this guy is nuts. He attacked me in the middle of the street.

NORA (*getting up*)

I've got to go.

Cut to

114. Exterior. Industrial Park. Day.

Angle on BB *as he comes out of the Gibraltar Aluminum Siding building and walks toward his car. We see* NORA *driving her Chevy in front of* BB*'s car. She drives her car forward and then reverses it hard into* BB*'s Cadillac. He runs over to the driver's side of* NORA*'s Chevy.*

BB

What are you, crazy?!

NORA *drives the car forward and then backward again, almost running* BB *down. She rolls down the window, automatically, so that she can yell.*

NORA

You're a goddamn tin man!

Then she backs up the car. BB *tries to go around the front of the car.*

BB

Wait a minute! Wait a minute!

NORA *starts to move the car toward him. He moves away, and her car smashes into the side of his car.*

NORA (*yelling out of window*)

You wanted to win me just to get even with my husband. . . . Screw you!

She rolls up the window, floors the car, and drives away.

115. Exterior. Industrial Park.

Angle on CHEESE *as he walks out of the building. He sees* BB*'s car all smashed up.*

CHEESE (*to* BB)

I think you ought to get rid of this car. . . . It's bad luck.

NORA*'s car screeches around the corner.*

CHEESE

Is that the guy again?

BB

No, it's his wife.

CHEESE

There's some kind of sickness that runs in that family.

Cut to

116. Interior. Pool hall. Day.

Tight shot of MOUSE. *He's singing "La Bamba" and teaching it to a* POOL-HALL WORKER.

MOUSE

"La, la, la, la, la, Bamba . . ."

The POOL-HALL WORKER *sings the same words.*

117. Interior. Pool hall.

Angle on TILLEY *and* GIL *sitting at the bar. We hear "La Bamba" in the background with* MOUSE *and the* POOL-HALL WORKER *singing to the music.*

TILLEY

Is he gonna teach everyone that song?

GIL

He's terrific. I have a lesson at three thirty.

TILLEY

And you'll both be out the window at four!

118. Interior. Pool hall.

Angle on SAM. *He comes out of the back room into the pool hall and walks over to where* TILLEY *and* GIL *are sitting. He hands* TILLEY *a letter.*

SAM

Take a look at this crap.

TILLEY

IRS? They're not gonna leave me alone!

SAM

Home Improvement Commission.

With those words there's a genuine moment of concern from all of the TIN MEN*—even* MOUSE *stops singing.* TILLEY *picks up the envelope and pulls out the letter.*

TILLEY

We've got to appear?

SAM

I think that's the gist of what they're saying.

GIL *looks at the letter over* TILLEY*'s shoulder.* MOUSE *comes over.*

MOUSE

Holy Christ!

TILLEY

Can't we just ignore it? How do they know we got the letter.

SAM

It's certified.

TILLEY

What do you think, Sam?

SAM

I dunno. . . . I don't know what they've got.

TILLEY

Why is this happening?! Am I paranoid or something? I mean, why is this happening?!

Cut to

119. Interior. The Corral Club. Night.

BB *is sitting at the bar getting drunk.* STANLEY *sits next to him. A girl,* RUTHIE, *approaches.*

RUTHIE

Come on, Beeb, let's dance.

BB

Not tonight, Ruthie, my dancing shoes are on holiday.

RUTHIE

You sure?

BB

I'm more than sure.

RUTHIE *moves off.* BB *takes a shot of whiskey, downs it, and then drinks some beer.*

STANLEY

Who was the best you ever saw?

BB

Best I ever saw? Best tin man I ever saw?

He holds up his shot glass toward the BARTENDER, *and the* BARTENDER *fills it.*

BB

Harry Fennerman . . . Dandy Flynn . . . those guys had good lines, but they burned themselves out too fast. Best? Moe's the best. . . . The best there ever was. If he's in the door, he's got a sale. The best closer ever.

STANLEY

What's some of the hustles he used to pull?

BB *downs another shot glass of whiskey.*

BB

Goddamn Nora. . . . Goddamn Nora! I'm trying to adjust. . . . I'm putting up with things I never put up with in my life. I mean, give me a break. . . . Give me a break, woman.

STANLEY *wants to get back to the topic of best tin man.*

STANLEY (*making light*)

So, what are a couple of things you and Moe have done?

BB (*still on the subject of* NORA)

It was getting to be real pleasant. . . . Figure that.

(*a long beat*)

More than pleasant. To hell with her!

STANLEY

How come Moe's so good? Why do you think, huh?

BB

Great man, Moe. Great man.

BB *again holds out his glass to the* BARTENDER, *who refills it.* BB *downs the shot and drinks more beer.*

BB

I don't know why they're so irrational, . . . chicks. I dunno. I think it's because air gets inside 'em.

(*a beat*)

She probably went back home, to her husband.

He looks at his watch.

BB (*continuing*)

Eleven thirty . . . he wouldn't be home yet.

He takes a ten-dollar bill from his wallet.

BB (*continuing*)

This ought to cover it, Stanley.

He puts the money down on the bar and walks out of the club.

Cut to

120. Exterior. Street. Night.

SAM'*s Cadillac is moving along a row of houses.*

Cut to

121. Interior. Sam's car. Night.

SAM *is driving his Cadillac;* TILLEY *is in the passenger seat, very drunk.*

TILLEY

They got no right. You know what I'm saying, Sam? They've got no right.

TILLEY *takes a drink from a pint of whiskey he has open.*

SAM

They've got nothing concrete against us, because if it's just hearsay stuff, it's neither here nor there.

TILLEY (*looking around*)

Where's my car? What happened to my car?

SAM

It's better I drop you off.

TILLEY

Yeah, it's better.

Cut to

122. Interior. Tilley's bathroom. Night.

TILLEY *is in the bathroom washing his face in the sink, trying to sober up. He lifts his head out of the stream of water and bangs it on the faucet. He grabs his head in pain and then slides down the tiled wall to the floor.*

Cut to

123. Exterior. Tilley's street. Night.

BB*'s Cadillac pulls up in front of* TILLEY*'s house. We see* BB *looking up and down the street with his head out of the car window. He's very drunk.*

BB

He ain't here.

He gets out of the car and looks around the street some more. He stumbles up to a couple of parked cars, looking for NORA*'s car. He falls into some trash cans in front of the house.*

Cut to

124. Interior. Tilley's bathroom. Night.

TILLEY *is lying on the floor. His eyes open at the sound of the trash cans falling. He struggles to his feet and walks through the bedroom. We hear the sound of more trash cans rattling.* TILLEY *goes to the bedroom window and looks out. He sees* BB *struggling to his feet, surrounded by trash cans and garbage.*

TILLEY

I knew I could smell a rat! The son of a bitch is coming for me. . . . The son of a bitch never wants to leave me alone!

TILLEY *walks over to the night table, opens the drawer, and pulls out a revolver.*

Cut to

125. Exterior. Tilley's street. Night.

BB is making his way up the front steps of TILLEY's house.

Cut to

126. Interior. Tilley's house. Night.

TILLEY makes his way down the stairs and creeps to the front door.

TILLEY (*quietly*)

You want to rob my goddamn house? I'm gonna make it easy for you.

He unlocks the door and leaves it ajar.

TILLEY (*continuing*)

Come and rob Tilley. . . . Come on, . . . take everything he's got.

Cut to

127. Exterior. Front door of Tilley's house. Night.

BB knocks on the door. The door swings open. He waits a moment, unsure of what to do.

Cut to

128. Interior. Other side of Tilley's front door.

TILLEY stands behind the door with the gun, waiting. BB steps inside.

BB

Hel—

Before he can finish saying hello, TILLEY hits him hard in the head with the butt of the gun. BB falls to the ground unconscious.

Cut to

129. Interior. Tilley's house.

The screen is black. Then a light goes on, and we see the inside of a refrigerator. The camera pulls back to reveal TILLEY at the refrigerator in the kitchen of his home. He is putting eggs and rotten tomatoes from the refrigerator into a bowl. He looks at a piece of celery. It's too wilted and has no strength for his purpose so he throws it down. He picks up other vegetables but settles for the eggs and tomatoes. He closes the refrigerator door and makes his way to the living room. We see BB *lying on the floor, unconscious.* TILLEY *sits down across from him with the bowl in his lap. . . . He watches* BB. BB *starts to come to.*

TILLEY

You're a sick man! You smash my car, you steal my wife, and now you come to rob me! You're one demented human being.

BB *tries to focus on* TILLEY.

TILLEY

I'm going to call the police and send you to jail, . . . but I'm going to humiliate you first.

TILLEY *throws an egg at* BB *and hits him in the head.* BB *is groggy and confused and still drunk.*

BB

What're you doing?

TILLEY

What do ya want to break into my house for? This ain't the fucking Rockefeller mansion! There ain't thirty-eight television sets here. They ain't saying "Nelson, I think we've had a break-in; . . . count the sets to see how many we've got left." There ain't tons of jewelry hanging out of drawers. . . . It ain't like I don't know which watch to put on I got so many. I'm a working man, trying to make an honest living. What fucking morality you got, asshole?!!

TILLEY *throws another egg at* BB *and hits him in the head again. Egg yolk drips down* BB*'s face. He tries to get off the floor but can't.*

BB

You're the craziest human being on the face of this earth!

TILLEY *gets ready with another egg.*

TILLEY

What else do you want from me? Huh? What else?! I've got enough problems with the IRS busting my balls and the Home Improvement Commission bullshit to contend with. I don't need aggravation from you.

BB *is still trying to get up. He wipes his face.*

BB

Nobody does this to me and lives! Nobody!

TILLEY *throws an egg.*

TILLEY

How do ya like your eggs? Over easy?

He picks up a tomato.

TILLEY (*continuing*)

Side of tomatoes?

He throws the tomato.

BB

You're going to rue the day you ran into my car. This ain't the end. . . . This is just the beginning.

TILLEY *throws another egg.*

Cut to

130. Interior. Police station. Night.

A POLICE OFFICER *is interrogating* TILLEY *behind the main desk of the police station. There's a lot of activity during this interaction;* PEOPLE *are coming and going.*

TILLEY

A guy breaks into my house and I'm being charged with assault? It makes no sense. . . .

POLICE OFFICER (*with pencil and paper*)

Let's get it down right. The guy broke into your house; you hit him in the head with a gun, went to the refrigerator, took out eggs and tomatoes, and threw them at him.

TILLEY

I was defending myself. . . . He was stealing from me.

POLICE OFFICER

It doesn't sound like defense to me.

TILLEY

I wanted to humiliate the guy. Here I am out busting my ass all day making a decent living; I come home, and some schmuck is trying to steal from me.

POLICE OFFICER

So you hit him with a gun and pelted him with eggs and tomatoes?

TILLEY

If I had some soup I would have thrown soup at him. . . . Is there any law you can't throw eggs?

POLICE OFFICER

Mr. Babowsky claims he didn't break into your house.

TILLEY

What did I do? Invite him in so that I could throw eggs at him?

POLICE OFFICER

Maybe Mr. Babowsky intended to break into your house, but these circumstances of the guy being pelted with eggs and tomatoes is something we need to look into.

TILLEY *shrugs his shoulders.*

TILLEY

He's lucky that he didn't rob me last week, 'cause then my wife was living at home and we had all kinds of things in the fridge. . . . I could have thrown barley soup, pumpkin pie, candied yams. . . . Yeah, he got off light.

Cut to

131. Exterior. Police station. Day.

BB *and* BAGEL *come out of the police station.* BB *is covered with eggs and looks a mess. They cross the road toward* BAGEL*'s car.*

BB

I can't believe it; the man throws eggs at me and now I'm gonna have breakfast with him.

BAGEL

I thought if the two of you could sit down, you might be able to come to some kind of settlement. You guys have got to put an end to this.

BAGEL *opens the door of his convertible, and* BB *opens the door on the passenger side.*

BAGEL

Now sit on the paper. I put paper down there for you. I don't want you getting eggs all over my seat.

BB *sits in the car.*

BAGEL

And keep your feet off my rug.

BB

What do you want me to do with them?

BAGEL

Just suspend them up in the air, OK. I cleaned the rug.

BB *groans.*

Cut to

132. Interior. Tilley's car. Day.

TILLEY *is sitting in the driver's seat, and* SAM *is next to him.*

TILLEY

What am I supposed to say to him? The man has been a pain in the ass since the day he rammed into my car.

SAM

Just air your differences, and we'll put an end to this.

Cut to

133. Exterior. Police station. Day.

Long shot of the police station and the two Cadillacs as they start to pull out of the parking lot

Cut to

134. Interior. Coffee shop. Day.

TILLEY, SAM, BB, *and* BAGEL *are sitting at a table together looking at menus.* BB *looks up from his menu.*

BB

I tell you what. . . . I'll drop the charges against you, and we can wipe the slate clean.

TILLEY

I appreciate it.

SAM

See how quickly you can clear it up?

BAGEL

That's it. . . . That's the end of it. Let's eat!

TILLEY

But I don't understand how the slate gets wiped clean when he breaks into my house and I'm the one charged.

BB

I told you, I wasn't breaking into your house. I was looking for your wife.

BAGEL

Hey! Put it to bed!

TILLEY

All right, . . . all right. . . . I'm too tired. . . . The slate's clean. . . . The slate's clean.

The WAITRESS *approaches.*

WAITRESS

What will you have?

TILLEY

Couple of eggs over, some hash browns, some toast—toasted dark, . . . butter on the side—large grapefruit juice, and some coffee.

The WAITRESS *writes down his order.*

TILLEY (*continuing*)

On second thought, instead of the eggs over, if I ordered soft-boiled eggs do you take them out of the shell or leave them in the shells?

We can see that BB *is getting a little irritable.*

WAITRESS

We leave them in the shell.

TILLEY

I don't like them that way, because they get hot in the hand and it's hard to scoop the stuff out. . . . It's not good, . . . and you get little bits of shell in there, and it doesn't taste good.

BB

Why don't you just order some scrambled eggs and be done with it, . . . all right?

TILLEY

If I'm going to order, at least I ought to be content with my food.

BB

I'm getting a little hungry. . . . I've got a headache as it is. Just order some eggs so some other people can have something to eat before the lunch trade comes in.

TILLEY *looks to* SAM.

The cast and crew shooting a scene from *Diner* outside the Fells Point Diner in Baltimore.

The *Diner* guys (left to right): Shrevie (Daniel Stern), Boogie (Mickey Rourke), Eddie (Steve Guttenberg), Fenwick (Kevin Bacon), and Billy (Timothy Daly) at Eddie's wedding.

Beth (Ellen Barkin) and Shrevie discuss his record collection.

Fenwick fakes a car accident.

Boogie with Carol (Colette Blonigan) at the movies.

BB (Richard Dreyfuss) with his "tin men" (from left to right): Looney (Matt Craven), Carly (Richard Portnow), Stanley (Allen Blumenfeld), Moe (John Mahoney), and Cheese (Seymour Cassel).

BB contemplating buying a new Cadillac from a salesman (Walt MacPherson).

BB wants to know why Tilley (Danny DeVito) crashed into his new Cadillac.

Tilley smashes BB's car windows to get even.

Tilley praying at the salad bar.

BB trying to make up with Nora (Barbara Hershey).

Avalon's Sam (Armin Mueller-Stahl) tells Michael (Elijah Wood) and his cousins the story of when he came to America.

From left to right: Dottie (Eve Gordon), Izzy (Kevin Pollack), Ann (Elizabeth Perkins), and Jules (Aidan Quinn) enjoying the band at a nightclub.

From left to right: Mindy (Mindy Isenstein), Teddy (Grant Gelt), Robert (Robert Zalkind), and Michael build a model airplane.

The Krichinsky family looking at the television set that's just arrived for Jules.

Jules and Izzy filming a television commercial to promote the opening of K&K Discount Warehouse.

From left to right: Eva (Joan Plowright), Alice (Mina Bern), Sam, and Hymie (Leo Fuchs) relaxing at Frock's Farm.

TILLEY

Why do I need a guy telling me what I should or shouldn't eat?

BB

This is not a four-star restaurant. . . . We're not having a gourmet meal, . . . we're ordering breakfast, for Christsake!

TILLEY

It so happens I haven't been to this restaurant before. I don't know how they do their eggs. . . . If they're over easy and they're gooey, I'm not happy with it, . . . and I'm not happy if the soft-boiled eggs are left in the shell—

BB (*to the* WAITRESS, *cutting* TILLEY *off*)

Can I have some French toast and a cup of coffee?

(*to* BAGEL)

Bagel, what do you want?

TILLEY

Hey! I'm ordering here. At least you can have the courtesy to let a man order his breakfast.

BB (*to the* WAITRESS, *ignoring* TILLEY)

French toast and a cup of coffee.

TILLEY (*to* SAM)

Sam, this guy gets on my nerves . . . from day one! I knew it then, and I know it now.

TILLEY *stands up and starts to leave.*

BB

I'm back to pressing charges against you!

TILLEY *turns and is face-to-face with* BB.

TILLEY

You want to play that way? This game ain't over, mister. . . . It ain't over. . . .

BB *stands up. The* WAITRESS *steps back and looks concerned.*

BB

All right, you want to finish it now? You want to finish it right now? I'm ready. . . . I'm ready *now!*

TILLEY

You're ready?! You're ready, that's what you're saying?! You're ready now?! I have to be intimidated. . . . I have to be brought here to be intimidated. . . .

BB

I can't stand it any longer. You're driving me out of my mind.

BB *lunges for* TILLEY *across the table.* SAM *and* BAGEL *try to intervene. The* WAITRESS *doesn't know what to do.*

BAGEL

Come on, guys, . . . take it easy. . . . Take it easy.

TILLEY

Get the people with the straitjackets. . . . This man is out of control.

TILLEY *and* BB *pull at one another.*

BB

We're gonna finish it. . . . We're gonna finish it.

BAGEL *and* SAM *pull them apart.*

SAM (*to* TILLEY)

Come on, let's get out of here.

SAM *ushers* TILLEY *to the door.*

TILLEY

I'm not finished with him, Sam.

(*to* BB)

You heard me. . . . I'm not finished with you, mister.

He storms out of the coffee shop with SAM. BAGEL *sits back, looking relieved.* BB *composes himself. The* WAITRESS *nervously stands by.*

BB (*to the* WAITRESS)

So, I'm having French toast and coffee.

(*to* BAGEL)

Bagel?

Cut to

135. Exterior. Hospital. Day.

Establishing shot

136. Interior. Hospital room. Day.

MOE *is in bed, still hooked up to tubes. His breathing is deliberate, and he seems weak. The camera slowly pans to* BB, *who is sitting by* MOE*'s side.*

BB

Moe, when you decided to marry May, how did you know?

MOE

Know what?

BB

How did ya know?

MOE

You mean to make up my mind to marry her?

BB

Yeah. How did ya know?

MOE *shrugs his shoulders as if he doesn't know.*

BB (*suddenly angry*)

This Nora is a pain in the ass, Moe, . . . a pain in the ass. It's worse now than when she used to be around.

MOE *smiles.*

BB

You wanna hear something? The other night at The Corral Club, I turned down a dance.

MOE

You turned down a dance?

BB

What's the odds on that? You think you can come up with odds on that one?

MOE

Hundred to one BB don't dance. . . . A hundred to one against.

(*a beat*)

I'm getting out of the business, BB. . . . I've got nothing for all this.

BB

Lot of good times, Moe.

MOE

A lot of good times, but I can't live off the good times.

(*a beat*)

You know, my brother-in-law has offered me a job at Hess Shoes. I think maybe I should do it. You get there in the morning, you come home at night, . . . you get health benefits. . . . I get to be assistant manager.

BB

That's it, Moe? You're gonna spend the day measuring people's feet? "You're an E fit." . . . "You're a D wide." . . . "You got a high arch." . . . "I'll show you something in an alligator, . . . something with a wing tip." How can you talk about that all day long?

(*a beat*)

Moe, you're the best tin man there ever was. Nobody's a better closer.

MOE

It's over, BB. . . . It's over.

BB *looks at* MOE *for a long beat. He's obviously greatly affected by this.*

BB

So, May's happy about this Hess Shoe thing, heh?

MOE

To say the least.

Cut to

137. Interior. Sam's car. Day.

SAM *is driving, and* TILLEY *is in the passenger seat.*

SAM

You know, when I saw "Bonanza" the other day, something occurred to me. There's those four guys living on the Ponderosa, and you never hear them say anything about wanting to get laid. You never hear Hoss turn to Little Joe and say, "I had such a hard-on when I woke up this morning." You know, . . . they never talk about broads, . . . nothing. Ya never hear Little Joe say, "Hey, Hoss, I went into Virginia City and saw a girl with the greatest ass I ever saw in my life." Ya just see 'em walking around the Ponderosa saying, "Yes, Pa," and, "Where's Little Joe?" Nothing about broads. I don't think I'm being too picky. . . . At least once if they talked about getting horny. I don't care if you're living on the Ponderosa or right here in Baltimore, guys talk about getting laid.

(*a beat*)

I'm beginning to think that show doesn't have too much realism. What do you think, Tilley?

TILLEY

Sam, I can't concentrate on "Bonanza" shit. . . . I've got too much on my brain. What with that asshole and the Home Improvement Commission, I don't want to have to worry about whether Little Joe got laid last night.

(*a beat*)

Let's go and eat something.

SAM

Yeah, we'll go and have some lunch at the smorgasbord.

Cut to

138. Interior. Thor's Smorgasbord Restaurant. Day.

TILLEY *and* SAM *are in line at the buffet.* SAM *fills up his tray and moves off to the cashier.* TILLEY *hangs behind staring at all the food. He looks up to the ceiling.*

TILLEY (*very quietly*)

God, if you're responsible for all the stuff down here, maybe you got a moment's attention for me.

(*a beat*)

Between the IRS, this Home Improvement Commission, and Mr. Merengue, I got it up to here with this bullshit. To be frank with you, I'm in the toilet here. If you can see your way . . .

A WOMAN *with a tray starts to approach* TILLEY. TILLEY *turns to her.*

TILLEY (*continuing*)

Listen, I'm praying here. . . . Go around.

WOMAN

I wanted to get some of the salad.

TILLEY

It's out of order. . . . Go around.

He signals for her to walk around him. The WOMAN *looks at him and moves down the line.*

TILLEY (*looking up to ceiling*)

Do what you can, all right? I appreciate it. Amen.

TILLEY *helps himself to some salad.*

Cut to

140. Interior. Gibraltar Aluminum Siding Company. Day.

The usual office activity. BB *is at a desk. He picks up the phone and dials.*

BB

Nora Tilley, please.

We hear a WOMAN*'s voice on the other end of the phone.*

WOMAN (*voice-over*)

What department is she with?

BB

She's with Social Security.

WOMAN (*voice-over*)

Which department in Social Security?

BB

I dunno. . . . She's there somewhere. . . . Yeah, on the third floor. . . . she's got a desk towards the back.

WOMAN (*voice-over*)

Just a moment . . . checking.

141. Interior. Gibraltar Aluminum Siding Company.

Another angle. In the background STANLEY *has gone over to a filing cabinet and is starting to look through the files.* CHEESE *wanders over to him.*

CHEESE

Stanley, can I help you look for something?

STANLEY

No, I'm just making myself busy.

CHEESE

Well, I wouldn't do that. Bagel don't like nobody looking at the files.

143. Interior. Gibraltar Aluminum Siding Company.

Back to BB *on the phone. He's still holding for* NORA. *We hear a ring on the other end of the phone.*

NORA (*voice-over*)

Mrs. Tilley.

BB

Nora, this is BB.

The phone goes dead. BB *reluctantly puts the receiver down.*

Cut to

142. Interior. Converted tobacco warehouse. Day.

The Home Improvement Commission is in session. TILLEY *and* SAM *sit at the defense table.* MASTERS *presides over the commission table, where four or five other* COMMISSIONERS *sit.*

MASTERS (*into the microphone to* TILLEY *and* SAM)

Didn't you approach Mr. Boloshevski August 18, 1961, while he was cutting his front lawn and tell him that his house had been selected, as one of only sixteen homes in the state of Maryland, for a free aluminum-siding job?

TILLEY

What's the name again?

MASTERS

Boloshevski.

TILLEY

Doesn't ring a bell.

(*to* SAM)

Sam, does it ring a bell to you?

SAM (*leaning into the microphone*)

It doesn't ring a bell to me either, sir.

MASTERS

Didn't you suggest that for a nominal labor charge, he would receive over five thousand dollars' worth of aluminum siding?

TILLEY

That's an awful lot for nothing. Doesn't sound like good business to me.

MASTERS

Mr. Boloshevski was ultimately charged twenty-four hundred dollars for labor, which, according to our figures, is about the average cost of an aluminum-siding job.

SAM (*leaning into the microphone*)

I don't get the point of this.

MASTERS

Twenty-four hundred dollars that you charged for labor is the same as if Mr. Boloshevski had purchased the aluminum siding and had the labor done.

TILLEY

Maybe I'm missing the point here, but if he paid twenty-four hundred, which is the cost of the job, I can't see anything wrong with that.

MASTERS

What we're getting at here, . . . what we're trying to stress, is that the job was sold under false terms. The man didn't win any award. . . . He was not getting aluminum siding at a special price. A clear case of deception was involved here.

TILLEY (*to* SAM)

What's he talking about? The man got the job for twenty-four hundred dollars, and that's what it costs in aluminum siding.

(*leaning into the microphone*)

Um . . . I don't know. . . . We have no recollection of this particular job, but I don't know if this is deception. Look, if you work in a clothing store, some guy tries on a suit, it looks like shit, but you tell him it looks wonderful. The guy's standing there looking like a sack of shit, the salesman says what a great suit, and the man buys it. That's deception as far as I can see, but I don't understand the deceptiveness that you say we're responsible for, . . . if I make myself clear.

SAM (*leaning into the microphone*)

I'd go along with that as well.

MASTERS

What we're trying to establish are the principles that have been laid down as part of the Home Improvement code of ethics . . . that you cannot mislead someone intentionally, and I think that's the principle that applies to this.

TILLEY

Did somebody put a gun to this guy's head and make him spend twenty-four hundred dollars? I don't get the point here. All I can say is this guy got a fair price for a fair job.

MASTERS (*leaning into the microphone*)

Excuse us for one moment.

He confers with the other COMMISSIONERS. *They nod in approval; then* MASTERS *leans back into the microphone.*

MASTERS

Thank you very much, gentlemen. Should there be a reason in the future to call you back, we would like to reserve that right.

TILLEY (*leaning into the microphone*)

Glad we could be of some service.

TILLEY *and* SAM *get up from the table and walk out of the building.*

Cut to

143. Exterior. Converted tobacco warehouse. Day.

TILLEY *and* SAM *are walking toward* TILLEY'*s car.*

TILLEY (*rubbing his hands gleefully*)

We beat 'em, Sam. . . . We beat 'em! What a piece of cake! No problem! They ain't got nothing on us. . . . Clean as a whistle. . . . We're clean as a whistle!

SAM

I need a drink. I hate inquisitions.

Cut to

144. Exterior. Social Security office. Night.

Heavy rain is falling. NORA, *holding an umbrella, walks quickly across the parking lot. Suddenly* BB *slips under the umbrella with her.*

NORA (*reacting sharply*)

I don't want to see you anymore.

She pulls away from BB *and continues walking.* BB *walks behind her, getting soaked in the rain.*

BB

I gotta talk to you.

NORA

I don't want to listen.

BB

Give me a chance to explain. You owe me that much.

NORA *continues to walk toward her car in the downpour.*

NORA

I don't owe you anything.

BB *lets her walk away. After a beat he yells out.*

BB

It was a lousy thing to do, OK? It was a lousy thing to use you to get back at your husband, . . . but the fact is that I never would have met you otherwise.

NORA *stops and turns to look at* BB.

BB (*more quietly*)

It was lousy. . . . It was a disgusting, terrible thing, . . . but a lot of good came out of it.

NORA

What kind of a person would come up with such a devious thing?

BB

I'm not always a nice guy; I admit that. I got a lot of training in deceit. . . . It's an occupational hazard.

They stand looking at one another in the rain.

NORA

I'd like to know what it is about me that I have to fall for tin men. What kind of character flaw do I have?

BB

I didn't want to have to come here. I wish that I didn't have to ever see you again. I've gone this far in my life without having to have this kind of thing happen to me. I was going through life, sailing along, pretty good, . . . doing OK, and I tried to get even with some crazy guy, . . . and I'm here.

NORA

The wet becomes you. Gets rid of some of the slickness.

BB

I don't like the idea that I'm not in control of this, but if this stuff's got to happen, I guess I've got no choice. I wanna . . . Ya know. . . .

He gets angry.

BB (*continuing*)

I wanna be with ya! OK, I said that. . . . I said it, OK?! I wanna be with you because . . .

(*a beat*)

I miss you, and I'd like to live with you. . . . I'd like to marry you. . . . And that's that!

NORA *eyes him carefully. The rain falls on her umbrella, and the rain beats on* BB'*s head.*

NORA (*after a long moment*)

I was hoping for something a little more romantic, . . . but, OK.

A slight smile comes to BB'*s face.*

Cut to

145. Interior. Crab house. Night.

TILLEY *and* SAM *are eating steamed crabs. The crab house is filled with* PEOPLE *eating crabs and drinking pitchers of beer. An Oriole game is on the television in the background.*

SAM

Ya know, Tilley, we been working together for over a year.

TILLEY

Yeah, must be about that.

SAM

I've been thinking that sometimes a different combination makes for better luck. Ya know what I mean? I mean, maybe the two of us ain't the right combination.

TILLEY

I'm just getting used to ya, Sam.

SAM

Let's face it, we're not exactly setting the world on fire.

TILLEY

It's a slump. . . . It's a slump, Sam.

SAM

Maybe it's a slump, but like baseball, sometime they have to change the lineup to get the team going again.

TILLEY

You're not serious about this, are you, Sam?

SAM

Yeah.

TILLEY

You're serious? You wanna get another partner? You don't think I'm gonna pull out of this?

SAM

I know you're gonna. . . . I know you're gonna.

TILLEY

So?

SAM

Look, we beat the commission today. . . . You know, we got a little bit of a victory. We split right now, and maybe we can add to that. . . . You know what I'm saying?

TILLEY

I know. . . . I know. Change in the lineup. OK, maybe it'll help. . . . Maybe it'll help.

TILLEY *drinks his whiskey.*

TILLEY (*continuing*)

You got any ideas for a new partner?

SAM

Well, I had a conversation with Solly Suvicks, so . . . maybe I'll go with him.

(*a beat*)

Mouse is gonna need a new partner because Dennis is going into used cars.

TILLEY

Mouse! Mouse! He gets on my nerves. . . . He eats too much.

A beat. He holds up his whiskey glass.

TILLEY (*continuing*)

Here's to some pretty good times, huh?

SAM *smiles.*

Cut to

146. Interior. The Corral Club. Night.

CHEESE, *looking tanned, sits with* STANLEY *at the bar.* BB *and* NORA *are dancing in the background.*

CHEESE

I don't get it. . . . The broad smashes into his car, and he takes her dancing. Some kind of dating ritual that I'm not familiar with.

STANLEY

BB's a pretty good tin man, huh?

CHEESE

Pretty good? Whew! Man's what legends are made of. Started selling pots and pans door-to-door at sixteen. Nothing he can't sell.

147. Interior. The Corral Club.

Angle on BB *and* NORA. *The song ends, and* BB *walks* NORA *back to the table they were sitting at.*

BB

You're gonna come back and stay the night?

NORA

I dunno. . . . All my things are back at Nellie's—the other side of town.

(*a beat*)

I know what I could do; I'll go back to the house. . . . There's still a few things I left behind. . . . At least I can get a change of clothes.

They both sit down. BB *looks at* NORA.

BB

I'm glad this is working out.

NORA

You really happy?

BB

Yeah.

NORA

You don't really show a great deal of exuberance.

BB

Honey, for me . . . I'm a parade.

Cut to

148. Exterior. Tilley's street and house. Night.

Tight shot of hand rattling a special padlock. Pull back to reveal TILLEY *at his front door trying to get in. The camera pans to* NORA*'s car pulling up in front of the house.* NORA *turns off the car lights and gets out of the car. She starts up the front walk and stops.*

NORA

What happened?

TILLEY

The IRS . . . they need the furniture. They got some living room somewhere in this country that needs to be furnished.

NORA

They're taking the furniture?

TILLEY

The furniture, the whole house. They locked it up. . . . They confiscated it.

NORA (*yelling up to* TILLEY *on the porch*)

What do you expect? You expect to get some preferential treatment . . . you're some special case? You've got to pay your taxes just like everybody else.

TILLEY *shrugs and sits down on the steps.* NORA *sits down next to him.*

NORA (*as she sits*)

There's a responsibility that somehow you can't seem to get a handle on.

TILLEY

I was doing pretty good there for a while. . . . doing pretty good. Had my house, had a wife, a Cadillac. . . . I still got my Cadillac.

NORA

Where are you gonna sleep?

TILLEY

I'll stay at Sam's for a couple of days until I get set up.

(*a beat*)

What're you doing here, anyway?

NORA

There's just a couple of things you didn't throw out of the house . . . a couple of things I didn't find on the lawn. I assume they're still in the drawer.

TILLEY

I don't know. . . . I did a pretty good house-cleaning number on you.

NORA

Listen, about the divorce. Do you want to file, or should I file?

TILLEY

I got to be frank with you, this guy is nuts.

NORA

He told me all about it. . . . All about how you threw eggs at him.

TILLEY

He told you it was about eggs? The guy tried to break into my house. He tried to steal things from me.

NORA

He was trying to find me. We had an argument.

TILLEY

I think you'd be making a big mistake if you married him.

NORA

It's not for you to make decisions for me.

TILLEY

I think maybe I should, because I think you're being misled. . . . I think you're confused. I think—

NORA (*interrupting*)

I know what I'm doing—

TILLEY (*interrupting*)

Nora, listen to me. I know about guys—

NORA (*cutting him off*)

I appreciate your concern, but it's not for you—

TILLEY (*interrupting*)

But this guy is as bad a choice as you could make. Bad choice.

NORA

You're a good one to give advice. . . . You're sitting on the steps, locked out of your house because you can't pay your taxes, and you're going to give me advice on life?

TILLEY

I'm not giving you a divorce, and that's it. I'm looking out for your welfare. No divorce.

NORA *looks at him, starts to say something, then stands up and walks down the steps of the house toward her car.*

TILLEY (*yelling to her*)

It's for your own benefit, and you'll thank me for it.

NORA *turns toward* TILLEY.

NORA (*suddenly*)

My benefit! You don't give a damn about me! You don't give a damn who I marry. The reason you don't want me to marry him is because he's the one taking your wife, and you've got your own problems with him. You don't care about me. . . . It's the same bullshit you're doing. That's what it always is with you, Tilley. It's always you! The IRS took *your* house, . . . *your* furniture! You don't say anything about *my* things in the house. I've got things in the house I worked damn hard for and things that belonged to my family. . . . The headboard that was given to me by Aunt Josephine, it's got to be at least a hundred years old, . . . and the hand-embroidered footstool . . .

TILLEY

What footstool?

NORA

The hand-embroidered footstool over by the T.V.

TILLEY

I don't remember seeing that.

NORA

It's been there forever. . . . It was my granny's.

TILLEY

It's been there forever? I've never seen it.

NORA

You've never seen it?! You've never seen it?! You put your feet on it to watch TV. . . . The hand-embroidered footstool.

TILLEY

I don't know what you're talking about. I never put my feet up to watch TV.

NORA

That's the way you are, Tilley; it doesn't mean anything to you. You don't care if they take it all away. It's all you, Tilley! That's the way it's always been.

She stands there for a moment, then turns back to her car, gets in, slams the door, and drives off. TILLEY *stands on the front steps with a puzzled look on his face.*

TILLEY

Hand-embroidered footstool?

He walks over to his car, gets in, and starts the engine, shaking his head in disbelief.

Cut to

149. Exterior. Gibraltar Aluminum Siding Company. Night.

BB *drives up to the building in his Cadillac. The passenger door opens, and* STANLEY *gets out.*

STANLEY

Thanks for the lift back, BB. See ya around.

BB (*offscreen*)

OK, Stanley.

STANLEY *closes the car door, and* BB *drives off.* STANLEY *watches* BB*'s car turn the bend, and then he goes toward the office door.*

Cut to

150. Interior. Gibraltar Aluminum Siding Company. Night.

STANLEY *is standing at the filing cabinet going through files. He takes some files and puts them to one side. Then, satisfied that he's got everything he needs, he picks up the files and turns to leave.* BB *is standing at the door watching him.*

BB

You know something, Stanley, I can always smell a guy who's not made of tin.

He walks over to STANLEY.

BB (*continuing*)

It's against the law to steal files. I could call and have you arrested and sent to jail, right now.

STANLEY

I'll put everything back; nobody's the wiser.

BB

You work for the commission, is that it?

STANLEY *nods yes.*

BB (*continuing*)

Doesn't the commission have enough information? They got to send out guys like you to spy?

STANLEY

Well, we just started out, and if we had some really good, hard facts of some infractions, it would give us a lot of credibility in the community.

BB *walks closer to* STANLEY, *looks at him for a second, grabs him by his tie, and pushes him backward.* STANLEY *crashes into the filing cabinet.*

BB

You know what your big problem is, Stanley? You're lazy. If you want to find out stuff, then you dig. . . . You get on the phone; . . . you canvas. . . . "We're from the Home Improvement Commission." . . . Go find your leads. . . . That's what we do all the time. You're just lazy, Stanley. If we're doing something wrong, you should collect all your evidence. Instead, you snoop around, . . . steal files. What is this? Undercover time? You think you're breaking up some big drug ring? Is this the Mafia you've infiltrated? All you've got here is a bunch of guys selling tin for Christsake!

(*a beat*)

You want some files?

He walks over to the filing cabinet, flips through some files, and pulls out three. STANLEY *has got up from the floor.* BB *throws the files down on the desk.*

BB

Here. . . . Here's some jobs I did. Leave Moe out of this. . . . He quit the business.

STANLEY *gathers up the files from the desk.*

BB

Go on, get out of here.

STANLEY *starts for the door and turns back.*

STANLEY

Why are you doing this?

BB

If it's not gonna be you, it's gonna be somebody else, . . . and if it's not tonight, it's gonna be another time.

STANLEY *leaves the office.* BB *picks up the files that* STANLEY *had taken out of the filing cabinet and starts to put them back. Then he slams the filing drawers closed very hard.*

Cut to

151. Interior. BB's bedroom. Night.

BB *and* NORA *are in bed together.*

NORA

Maybe if I talked to him another day, he'll change his mind. I mean, he's like that. . . . One day he's this way, and another day he's that way.

BB

You don't need to talk to him.

NORA

I mean, he's probably, you know, upset about the IRS taking the house and all our stuff.

BB (*a beat*)

Ever see a Volkswagen?

NORA

What?

BB

You know, those little Volkswagens. It's a car, . . . a little car.

NORA

What does that have to do with anything?

BB

I dunno. . . . They're interesting.

Cut to

152. Interior. Mason Dixon Aluminum Siding Company. Day.

WING *is standing up at the blackboard chalking out schedules and sales.* TILLEY *stands back and looks at the board, seeing his name up with* MOUSE*'s.*

TILLEY (*to* WING)

Tilley and Mouse. It looks weird, doesn't it? Looks very weird.

WING

Let's hope you have some better luck with Mouse.

Cut to

153. Interior. Pool hall. Day.

The pool hall is poorly lighted, except for the slight shaft of light falling over several tables.

GIL *is playing with another* TIN MAN. MOUSE, SAM, *and three or four other* TIN MEN *are also playing pool.*

154. Interior. Stairs to the pool hall.

Angle on BB *coming down the stairs into the pool hall*

155. Interior. Pool hall.

Angle on GIL. *He stops playing pool.*

GIL (*under his breath*)

Mr. Merengue.

He goes over to the office door, opens it, and yells to TILLEY.

GIL

Hey, Tilley, . . . Mr. Merengue's out here.

TILLEY *comes out of the office and stands looking at* BB.

BB

Can I talk to you in private, or do I have to talk to you over fourteen pool tables?

TILLEY *moves down the hall toward* BB.

BB (*continuing*)

We've got enough that's going down between the two of us, but the fact of the matter is that I love your wife, and I want to marry her.

TILLEY

I don't care who she marries, but I don't want her marrying you!

BB

Why don't we just talk about this in a nice, rational manner.

TILLEY

Rational? You're going to be rational?

BB

We've got our problems, but let's try and isolate this particular situation.

TILLEY

Isolate . . . isolate. . . . I like this kind of talk. What the hell nonsense is that?

BB

What are you gonna gain from this thing here?

TILLEY

Now let me see here. . . . I've got to isolate that for a moment and think it over.

BB

Nobody's going to benefit from making me mad.

TILLEY

You ought to hear yourself. You know that? You ought to listen to the way you talk. You come in here, you want to take my wife, . . . you want to isolate this situation, . . . you want to be rational. I've got no tolerance for you, mister. You know what I'm saying?

BB

What you're saying is you don't want to discuss this, am I right?

TILLEY (*after a beat*)

You like pool?

The other TIN MEN *move closer to* TILLEY *and* BB, *crowding in.*

BB

I enjoy the game.

TILLEY

Why don't we play a little game of eight ball? If I lose, I consent to the divorce. . . . If you lose, you give Nora up. . . . Walk away from her.

BB *stares at* TILLEY; TILLEY *eyes* BB.

BB (*quietly*)

Rack 'em.

Cut to

156. Exterior. Gibraltar Aluminum Siding Company. Day.

We see a MAN *get out of a car parked outside the building and walk toward the Gibraltar Aluminum Siding Company.*

157. Interior. Gibraltar Aluminum Siding Company. Day.

CARLY, CHEESE, *and* LOONEY *are sitting around a desk drinking coffee.*

CHEESE

You know who's no longer married to who?

CARLY

Well, we ought to know. There's like a million fucking people living in Baltimore. How many guesses do we get?

NOTE: The following action and dialogue run concurrently.

CHEESE

It's not that hard if you think about it.

LOONEY

Ruby and Joe.

CHEESE

No, but they're friends of them.

LOONEY

Friends of them . . .

CARLY

Ed and Ethel?

CHEESE

Ed and Ethel aren't that friendly with Ruby and Joe.

CARLY

What are you talking about? I went to a party not two weeks ago at Ed and Ethel's, and they invited Ruby and Joe over.

CHEESE

It doesn't mean they're friendly because they're invited to a party. They're friendly, but not that friendly. Couple I'm thinking about were very, very tight with Ruby and Joe.

LOONEY

Do we have any money bet on this, because otherwise we could be thinking and

The MAN *comes into the office from outside. He's carrying an envelope. He approaches* NICK, *who is closest to the door.*

MAN

I have a certified letter here for William Babowsky.

NICK (*pointing to* BB)

The guy over there.

The MAN *approaches* BB, *who is standing back from the group a little.*

MAN

William Babowsky?

BB

Yeah.

MAN

I have a certified letter for you.

BB *takes the letter. The* MAN *hands* BB *a piece of paper.*

MAN (*continuing*)

Would you please sign.

BB *picks up a pen and signs the paper.*

not gaining anything from this discussion.

CARLY

Frank and Vivien?

LOONEY

Frank and Vivien broke up?

CARLY

I don't know. . . . I'm just making names up for Christsake.

CHEESE

They did break up, but that's not who I was thinking about.

LOONEY

I'd like to call on Vivien. . . . She's one hot broad.

CARLY

Then why don't you call her?

LOONEY

I stood her up in high school. . . . She's hated me for nearly fifteen years.

CHEESE

You stood up Vivien Carsoll? Are you an idiot! What an idiot.

LOONEY

I stood her up for Denise, who happened to have been my wife. So, yes, I was an idiot. If I knew then what I know now . . .

CARLY

What was your ex-wife's maiden name?

LOONEY

Essex.

CARLY

Denise Essex. Did she have a sister named Wilma?

MAN (*continuing*)

Thank you.

He turns and leaves the office. BB *looks at the envelope, opens it, and pulls out a summons. He reads it:* YOU ARE SUMMONED TO APPEAR BEFORE THE HOME IMPROVEMENT COMMISSION AT 9:30 A.M. ON WEDNESDAY, APRIL 6, 1963. BB *smiles and walks over to* BAGEL, *who is standing outside his office looking through some files.* BB *hands him the summons.* BAGEL *looks at it.*

BAGEL

Jesus Christ! I think you should take some legal counsel, Double B.

BB

Not necessary.

BAGEL

Better to err on the safe side.

BB

I'd rather handle it myself.

BAGEL

Want me to find out what they've got against you? I know a clerk down there. For a price I could get the inside scoop. These guys are just fishing right now.

BB *just shakes his head no.* BAGEL *looks at him.*

BAGEL

You OK, Double B?

BB

Yeah. . . . Yeah.

BAGEL

Because ever since Moe went down, you seem a little off your feed to me.

LOONEY

Yeah.

CARLY

You're kidding me.

CHEESE

What does this have to do with the couple who broke up?

CARLY

We'll get to that once we've discussed Wilma. . . . They'll still be broken up. . . . We'll get to that in a minute.

LOONEY

How do you know Wilma?

Cut to

BB

Thanks for the concern, Bagel, but I'll be all right.

BB *puts the summons into his breast pocket and leaves the office.*

158. Exterior. Pimlico Hotel. Night.

TILLEY *drives into the parking lot of the Pimlico. He heads for a dark corner where about eight other cars are parked. As he's about to park his car, he sees* WING *talking to* MASTERS *in the car next to his.* TILLEY*'s a bit confused; he stays in his car watching them. After a couple of beats,* WING *gets out of the car and heads for the Pimlico.* MASTERS *drives off.* TILLEY *gets out of his car and catches up to* WING.

TILLEY

Hey, Wing, isn't that the putz from the commission?

He points to the car leaving the parking lot.

WING

Masters? Yeah.

TILLEY

What the hell's he doing hanging around here?

WING

He wants information.

TILLEY

I nailed his ass the other day, Wing. Can't lay a finger on me. I was amazing; you should have been there. I was amazing. . . . I was respectful, courteous, but I was slipping and sliding. . . . They couldn't touch me.

WING

I got a real problem, Tilley. Come inside; I'll buy you a drink.

Cut to

159. Interior. Pimlico Hotel. Night.

TILLEY *and* WING *are sitting at a table in the bar. The* PIANIST *is playing, and* PEOPLE *are sitting around the piano joining in on the song.*

TILLEY

You're gonna sell me out to the commission? Wing, am I hearing this right?

WING

I'm up front with you about this. . . . I'm up front with ya, Tilley. I've got my balls in a vice. . . . What am I gonna do?

TILLEY

Is this about the money I owe you? Are you just pissed? You want to get even because of the horserace? I told ya it was an accident.

WING

Tilley, it's got nothing to do with the money.

TILLEY

You're selling me out? You're gonna let them bury me? Jesus Christ, Wing. . . . Jesus Christ! I'm not gonna be able to work in this business? Wing, this was my chosen field!

WING

Masters was gonna take this company apart. You're the low man on the totem pole, Tilley. There's a lot of guys earning a good living. . . . No sense for it all to go up in smoke. You understand, don't you, Tilley? It's just business.

TILLEY

Jesus Christ!

WING

Listen, Tilley, you owe me sixteen plus from the race, and you're in for over two grand on the books, so I tell you what. . . . I'll wipe the slate clean.

He takes his wallet from his pocket and peels off a few notes.

WING

Here's a thou until you get yourself set up. I can do no better than that.

TILLEY (*looking at the money*)

You'd sell me out for a lousy three thousand dollars? Three thousand dollars and I got to go down the toilet? Jesus Christ,

Wing, how long the two of us been busting our asses together?! We got some history to this relationship for Christsake. Masters puts a little squeeze on you, you just sell out. Three thousand dollars?!

WING

The bottom line is I'm running a business, Tilley.

He peels off another couple of hundred dollars from his wallet.

WING (*continuing*)

Here's another deuce. I carried you a long time, Tilley. I've done a damn sight more than a lot of other guys would have done for you, . . . and I don't see no gratitude from you.

He gets up to leave.

WING (*continuing*)

You can finish up whenever you like.

He throws a few dollars on the table.

WING (*continuing*)

I'm sorry, Tilley. That's the way of the world.

He pats TILLEY *on the back and walks away.*

Cut to

160. Exterior. Vacant parking lot. Night.

TILLEY'*s Cadillac drives into a lot that overlooks the harbor. We see the city lights surrounding the lot.*

Cut to

161. Interior. Tilley's car. Night.

The radio is playing. TILLEY *stops the car, turns off the lights, but leaves the radio playing. He leans into the back of the car and takes a pillow off the backseat. He props the cushion up against the passenger side and lies down, looking up to the roof of the car.*

Cut to

162. Exterior. Vacant parking lot. Night.

Long shot of the Cadillac in the deserted lot.

Fade to black

Fade up on

163. Interior. BB's kitchen. Day.

Eggs are being fried in a frying pan on a stove.

NORA (*offscreen yelling*)

Bill! Better hurry up; everything's ready.

164. Interior. BB's kitchen.

Another angle on the eggs as they are slipped onto a plate with some bacon and hash browns

165. Interior. BB's kitchen.

Another angle. BB *comes into the kitchen. He is tying his tie. Shot widens to include* NORA.

NORA

I can't believe that you're up so early. This is a rare occasion.

BB

Yeah. I just got some business downtown I gotta take care of.

He stands watching NORA *as she prepares the plates of food.*

NORA

Toast will be ready in a second. Coffee's on the table.

He continues to stand watching her. She's not aware that he's doing so. She waits for the toast to pop up out of the toaster.

BB

Listen, Nora. I . . . um . . . I . . . er . . . lied to you the other day.

NORA *is still waiting for the toast, looking inside the toaster to see if it's getting brown.*

NORA

How so?

BB

I went to see Tilley about the divorce.

She turns to look at him.

BB (*continuing*)

He was not too agreeable, and one thing led to another, and we decided to shoot some pool to settle the matter.

NORA

What?!

The toast pops up. She ignores it.

BB

We played pool. If I won, he'd give you up; if I lost, I'd give you up.

NORA

You played pool for me?

BB

Nora, I had no choice.

NORA

It's the most despicable thing I've ever heard in my life. I mean, it's disgusting. . . . Guys shooting pool to determine my future.

BB

Nora, I had no choice!

(*a beat*)

Hand me the toast.

NORA

Get the toast yourself.

BB *takes the toast out of the toaster.*

BB

I'm just trying to be honest. It's been on my mind, . . . on my conscience.

He picks up a plate.

BB (*continuing*)

This plate yours or mine?

NORA

Why don't you take both. . . . Maybe you can choke to death on one of them.

BB *takes one of the plates and goes toward the table.* NORA *watches him a beat, amazed that he doesn't seem to recognize the seriousness of the situation.*

NORA (*angry*)

How can you be so . . . How can you not understand how wrong that is? I can't understand that mentality! Shoot pool for me! It's insane.

BB *dips his toast into his eggs.*

BB

Tilley is not the most rational man in this world. I tried to talk to him. . . . He wouldn't listen. So, what are my options? You know what I'm saying? What are my options?

NORA

I can't believe you had to shoot pool! Don't you understand that . . . Don't you understand how crazy that is? You're sitting there . . . You're eating your eggs as if it's normal business in life here! Like feudal lords or something you used to read about in history books.

BB

All right, I'm sorry.

NORA (*a beat*)

What happened?

BB

I lost.

He dips more toast into his eggs and eats.

NORA

You lost?

BB

I blew the eight ball.

NORA

You lost?

BB

Yeah.

NORA

What does that mean?

BB

It means I'm supposed to give you up, and I'm never supposed to see you again.

NORA

Will you stop eating the eggs for a minute! How can you tell me things like this and casually eat your eggs?! What does this mean, Bill?

BB

Well, I'm supposed to give you up as part of honoring that agreement, but I'm not that honorable a guy.

He smiles and takes a quick sip of his coffee.

BB (*continuing*)

I gotta go.

NORA

Why are you running off so fast here?

BB

I told you; I got some business downtown.

He gives her a kiss, starts to go, turns back, and gives her another kiss, more passionate this time.

BB

I'll see you later.

He goes down the hall to the front door.

166. Exterior. BB's apartment. Day.

NORA *walks behind* BB *to the front door and watches him go out the door and down the front steps. He gets into his car and drives off.* NORA *stands at the door watching the car drive away.*

Cut to

167. Exterior. Downtown street. Day.

TILLEY *pulls his Cadillac into a parking space just a little up the street from the tobacco warehouse that houses the Home Improvement Commission. He gets out of his car, locks the door, and starts down the street.* BB*'s car passes* TILLEY. *The camera follows* BB*'s car as he pulls into a parking space close to the commission building.*

Cut to

168. Interior. Converted tobacco warehouse. Day.

A corridor off the main hearing room. The hearing is not yet in session. TILLEY *sits on a bench against a wall. He glances up, his eyes drop, and then he looks across the camera. The camera pans to the opposite side of the corridor, where* BB *sits on another bench against a wall.* BB *glances off at* TILLEY *and then drops his eyes. The camera pans back to* TILLEY. *A few beats go by. Both* MEN *are uncomfortable with one another's presence.*

TILLEY (*finally*)

You gotta testify, huh?

BB

You?

TILLEY

Yeah.

BB

You got a lawyer?

TILLEY

Nah. I already testified once. I beat 'em before; I'll beat 'em again.

(*a beat*)

You got a high-priced mouthpiece to speak for ya?

BB

I don't need one. I don't expect to win.

TILLEY

How so?

BB

I gave them some pretty incriminating evidence.

TILLEY

You gave them evidence?

BB

The only way I could think to get out of this business.

He smiles.

TILLEY (*pointing and laughing*)

Hey, that's good. . . . That's good, yeah.

There's activity in the hallway.

VOICE (*offscreen*)

The hearing for the Home Improvement Commission is now in session.

TILLEY *stands.*

TILLEY (*to* BB)

So . . . how's Nora?

BB

She's doin' all right.

A MAN *comes out of the hearing room.*

MAN

Ernest Tilley?

TILLEY

Yeah. . . . Here.

(*turns to* BB)

Take good care of her.

Cut to

169. Interior. Converted tobacco warehouse.

Long shot of the hearing room of the Home Improvement Commission. Five or six COMMISSIONERS *are behind a long table, led by* JOHN MASTERS. *There is a gallery of* OBSERVERS, *and* TILLEY *sits at the defense table across from the* COMMISSIONERS.

MASTERS (*into the microphone*)

Are you aware that that's a violation of Sections 258 and 261?

TILLEY

I'm not aware of the section numbers. Sometimes you get a little overzealous in the heat of the sales pitch, that's all.

BB *is watching the proceedings. The camera holds on him.*

MASTERS (*offscreen*)

Was it the heat of the sales pitch on February twenty-third of this year that made you write across a contract "This job is free"?

170. Interior. Converted tobacco warehouse.

Angle on TILLEY, *who is falling apart*

TILLEY

As I remember, no sale was made concerning those customers.

MASTERS

It fell out because a loan couldn't be arranged, but the people did agree in principle.

(*a beat*)

The point that we'd like to stress is that you misled these people. Told them the job was free. Then you sent in your closer with some cover story about how you had suffered a nervous breakdown, and a sale was ultimately made for twenty-three hundred and seventy-seven dollars. That is misleading and deceptive sales practice.

TILLEY

It was temporary insanity. I don't know. . . . It just came over me. . . . It might have been something I ate. I don't know. . . . It was crazy; I'm the first to admit it was a crazy thing to do. Believe me—

MASTERS (*cutting him off*)

We have other specific examples of deceptive sales practices on your behalf concerning a job carried out on December 11, 1962. You violated Sections 241 and 247. And concerning a job sold to Mr. and Mrs. DeFranco on October 9, 1962, violations of Sections 251 and 257 took place.

TILLEY

What are all these numbers here? I'm not familiar with all these section violations.

171. Interior. Converted tobacco warehouse.

Angle on BB, *who is watching the proceedings intently*

MASTERS (*offscreen*)

It is the feeling of this commission that these infractions are severe violations of the Home Improvement Laws and therefore constitute misuse of the license to sell aluminum siding as approved by this state.

172. Interior. Converted tobacco warehouse.

The camera is on MASTERS.

MASTERS

It is the decision of this commission to revoke your license to sell aluminum siding, . . .

173. Interior. Converted tobacco warehouse.

The camera is on TILLEY. *He's not very happy.*

MASTERS (*offscreen*)

which will prohibit you from practicing in the state of Maryland.

TILLEY

Are you sure? Maybe the guys want to think this over.

174. Interior. Converted tobacco warehouse.

The camera returns to MASTERS.

MASTERS

Thank you, Mr. Tilley. You may hand over your license to the clerk of the commission on your way out.

175. Interior. Converted tobacco warehouse.

TILLEY *gets up from the table and goes to the back of the room to exit the building. He stops at a desk just inside the door, where the* CLERK *is sitting.* TILLEY *pulls out his wallet, takes out a small document, and throws it down on the desk. He exits the building.*

Cut to

176. Interior. Converted tobacco warehouse.

Same as before, except now we see STANLEY *enter and sit among the* OBSERVERS

177. Interior. Converted tobacco warehouse.

Angle on MASTERS

MASTERS

Will Mr. William Babowsky please come forward.

BB *walks to the defense table and sits down.*

MASTERS

You have the right to have a lawyer present if you so wish.

BB

I do not wish.

Cut to

178. Exterior. Converted tobacco warehouse. Day.

TILLEY *walks down the street toward his car. Suddenly he realizes that there's an empty space and his car is gone. He's a little confused, thinking that perhaps he parked elsewhere. A young black* KID *walks up to him.*

KID

Did you have a car parked here? A Cadillac?

TILLEY

Yeah. What about it?

KID

A man told me to say they took it.

TILLEY

Who took it?

KID

Man said, "the tax man." Gave me a dollar to tell you so.

TILLEY *walks over and stands in the empty space where his car had been.*

TILLEY

Tax man! Fucking IRS. How low can you get? How low can you get?

He walks around in the space as if somehow his car might reappear.

TILLEY (*mumbling to himself*)

They're lowlife. How can people come and take a man's car? . . . His Cadillac?

Cut to

179. Interior. Converted tobacco warehouse. Day.

The hearing is continuing. BB *is at the defense table, and* STANLEY *is watching.*

MASTERS

I think with the number of violations on your record, Mr. Babowsky, this commission has no recourse but to revoke your state license.

180. Interior. Converted tobacco warehouse.

The camera is on STANLEY.

MASTERS (*offscreen*)

Would you please drop off your license with the clerk of the commission on your way out.

181. Interior. Converted tobacco warehouse.

The camera is on BB.

BB (*leaning into the microphone*)

Thank you.

BB *gets up and walks to the back of the room. He stops at the same desk* TILLEY *stopped at, but instead of going into his wallet as* TILLEY *did, he just reaches into his suit pocket, pulls out the document, and tosses it onto the table. Then he heads out the door.*

Cut to

182. Exterior. Converted tobacco warehouse. Day.

BB *walks down the street, making for his car. He sees* TILLEY *still standing in the vacant parking space.* TILLEY *sees* BB. BB *stops.*

BB

Sorry about your license.

TILLEY

Yeah. You in there?

BB

Yeah. They got my license as well.

TILLEY

Sorry to hear it.

BB

What are you doing standing there?

TILLEY

This is where my car used to be.

BB

Stolen?

TILLEY

IRS. Fucking bandits! Bandits! Thieving sons of bitches!

BB *looks at* TILLEY *for a beat.*

BB

You need a ride uptown?

TILLEY

I could use one.

BB

Come on.

They cross the street and go toward BB*'s Cadillac.* BB *gets in the driver's side,* TILLEY *gets in the passenger side, and the car pulls out.*

Cut to

183. Interior. BB's car. Day.

BB*'s driving, and* TILLEY*'s in the passenger seat.*

TILLEY

Some bullshit commission, huh?

(*a beat*)

Tell me, where's it written in the Constitution that says you can't hustle for money? Where's it written? It ain't like I went into an alley and hit a guy over the head with a brick and stole his money. . . . Not like I broke into somebody's house and stole his stuff. All I'm doing is selling. . . . Where's the crime in that?

BB

I don't know what the world's coming to.

TILLEY

You're telling me. I don't know what the world's coming to.

Cut to

184. Interior. BB's car. A little later.

BB*'s still driving, and* TILLEY*'s in the passenger seat.*

BB

You know what our big crime is? We're nickel-and-dime guys. We're small-time hustlers. They got us because we're hustling nickels and dimes.

TILLEY

Nickels and dimes. You got a good point there, BB. You're right on the money with that kind of thinking.

BB *stops the car at a stop sign. Something catches* BB*'s eye. Through the windshield we see a Volkswagen beetle going from right to left.*

185. Interior. BB's car.

Angle on BB *as he watches the car.*

BB

Gotta find a new business to get into.

TILLEY

New? Very hard to find something new to get into.

BB *puts his foot on the gas and starts to drive.*

BB

Maybe . . . maybe not.

TILLEY

Better put on my thinking cap. . . . Not easy to think of something new.

Cut to

186. Exterior. Street. Day.

Long telephoto shot of the city showing stacks of houses as the Cadillac drives away. A pair of McDonald's golden arches is being put in place by a crane on the horizon. It's almost as if it's a rainbow across the far side of town and the Cadillac will drive through it.

BB

Believe me, we'll find something. It's just a matter of time.

TILLEY

Yeah . . . matter of time.

BB (*a beat*)

You know, I hear the new Cadillac's gonna be out in a couple of months.

TILLEY

You're kidding?

BB

Yeah, . . . they're changing the body. I hear it's a beaut.

TILLEY

Maybe I should put in my order now.

BB

What're you talking about? You ain't got a pot to piss in.

TILLEY

Give me the pot; . . . I'll fill it.

Both GUYS *speak at the same time.*

TILLEY	BB
I've got an idea.	You know, I've got an idea.

BB

What were you going to say?

TILLEY

No, you go first . . .

BB

No, you go first. . . . My idea will keep; you're the guest.

TILLEY

No, you go first. I want to hear yours.

BB

It's irrelevant. . . . Go ahead.

As the car continues toward the golden arches, BB *and* TILLEY *banter back and forth.*

BB (*voice-over, continuing*)

OK, we'll flip a coin for it. . . .

Dialogue continues as the credits begin to crawl.

Fade to black.

AVALON

1. The screen

is black. We hear:

SAM (*voice-over*)

I came to America in 1914, . . . by way of Philadelphia. . . . That's where I got off the boat, and then I came to Baltimore. It was the most beautiful place you've ever seen in your life.

Fade in:

2. Exterior. Street. Night.

SAM KRICHINSKY, *a man in his early twenties, walks along a main street in Baltimore. It is glowing with lights. The lights arch from one side of the street to the other in a magnificent array of electricity.*

SAM (*voice-over*)

There were lights everywhere, . . . what lights they had. It was a celebration of lights. I thought they were for me: . . . Sam was in America! I didn't know what holiday it was, but there were lights, . . . and I walked under them.

We see SAM *walking beneath the lights.*

SAM (*voice-over, continuing*)

The sky exploded; people cheered; . . . there were fireworks. What a welcome it was.

The scene is in black and white, but the fireworks are in color.

As SAM *walks observing the splendor, he carries an envelope in his hand. He walks among the crowds of* PEOPLE, *who are waving flags, dancing in the streets, and generally having a wonderful time. There are* VENDORS *selling food and drinks and others with banners, flags, etc.* SAM *gets caught up in the excitement, and we see him talking to one* PERSON *then another, showing them the envelope and obviously asking for directions.* PEOPLE *shake their heads, not knowing the address, and then a* MAN *finally walks with* SAM *to the address on the envelope—a street close by. We see that this is not the right house, but someone in the house tells* SAM *to follow him, and we see them walking to another street while the celebrations continue. They meet up with a* MAN *with very large shoes.*

SAM (*voice-over*)

I didn't know where my brothers were. I had an address on an envelope, but when I went there, they'd moved. I found a man who knew the name Krichinsky. . . . He was a little man with big shoes. I'll never forget him. . . . He had such big shoes. They were brand new, . . . beautiful shoes. He told me this was how he made his living: . . . he would break in shoes for the wealthy. Stuff them with newspaper and walk in them.

We see SAM *and the* MAN *with the shoes walking and* SAM *looking down at the shoes and shaking his head.*

SAM (*voice-over*)

I said, What a country this is! What a country! Wealthy didn't even have to break in their own shoes.

(*a beat*)

So this man with the shoes took me down one street after another. . . . We walked and walked, and the skies would light up and explode in a celebration. Then we arrived at this building, and the man with the shoes yelled, "Krichinsky!" A window opened up, and my four brothers looked down and saw me. . . . "Sam!"

All action follows the dialogue as above. We see the four brothers, GABRIEL, HYMIE, WILLIAM, *and* NATHAN, *in a burst of light from the fireworks. We see* SAM *looking up to them as another burst of fireworks lights his face. One spark of light remains in the sky with a red glow, and suddenly we realize that it is the puff of a cigar in a dark room.*

3. Interior. Sam's house. Late afternoon.

We see SAM *in the shadow of the late afternoon puffing on his cigar.*

SAM

And that's when I came to America. It was the Fourth of July.

4. Interior. Sam's house.

Different angle. SAM *is sitting in a chair in the living room of his row house. The year is 1948, and* SAM *is in his mid-fifties. A number of* CHILDREN *(probably eight), between the ages of five and ten, are sitting on the floor at his feet listening to his story. There's a lot of activity in the room—dinner is being prepared; dishes are being laid on the table;* PEOPLE *are getting drinks; and so on.*

SAM (*continuing*)

Boy, did they used to celebrate, . . . big celebrations then. They closed the streets and would celebrate through the night.

MINDY, *a six year old, wants to know more about the man with the shoes.*

MINDY

What happened to the man who wore the big shoes?

SAM

The funny thing is that he did it for another two years. He brought his brother into the business. . . . Both of them would walk the streets breaking in shoes. Then he got an idea. Why not make shoes that fit right; so they became custom shoemakers. The Solomon Brothers. They made shoes, pants, . . . and then they were a department store. . . . But the Krichinsky Brothers . . . wallpaper hangers. The Five Krichinsky Brothers—Wallpaper Hangers.

Cut to

5. Exterior. Street. Day.

A van with KRICHINSKY WALLPAPER HANGERS *painted on its side is parked outside a row house.*

SAM (*voice-over*)

And we worked.

Cut to

6. Interior. House. Day.

We see the five brothers, GABRIEL, HYMIE, WILLIAM, NATHAN, *and* SAM, *putting up wallpaper in a row house.*

SAM (*voice-over*)

Except Gabriel didn't work. Gabriel used to point a lot. . . . "There's a crease. . . . It's not straight." He was the inspector.

Cut to

7. Interior. Sam's house. Late afternoon.

The CHILDREN *are listening intently.*

MINDY

How did you all get to be wallpaper hangers?

SAM

It was your grandfather, William; he came to America first, and he worked in a department store where they used to sell wallpaper and do wallpaper hanging for people. So, he became a wallpaper hanger, and as each brother came over, we all became wallpaper hangers.

MINDY

Is that what you wanted to do?

SAM

Who knew what to be? You make money wallpaper hanging, so you become wallpaper hangers, . . . but on the weekend we made music. What music it was.

Cut to

8. Interior. Elegant ballroom. Night.

The five KRICHINSKY BROTHERS, *varying in age from their early twenties to their early thirties, are on a platform stage playing various instruments—*SAM *is at the piano. The music they are playing is the music we have heard in the background throughout the film so far, only now it comes up to full volume. The* BROTHERS *are playing their hearts out and having a great time doing it.*

The camera pans the ornate ballroom and the elegantly dressed CROWD. *Many* PEOPLE *are dancing. There are* PEOPLE *standing at a bar and sitting in wicker chairs around tables surrounding the dance floor. It's a very happy atmosphere. It's obvious that* SAM *is an accomplished piano player, and as he plays we see him scanning the room.*

SAM (*voice-over*)

We liked American music, and we were very popular ourselves.

(*a beat*)

One night I looked across the floor, and I saw this young, lovely girl.

We see a young EVA, *in her early twenties, dancing with a young* MAN. *She catches* SAM'*s eye. He smiles at her, and she just stares at him. Then she smiles.*

9. Interior. Elegant ballroom.

Angle on SAM *playing the piano as he watches* EVA

SAM (*voice-over*)

I wasn't a handsome man; I didn't have a beautiful body. But when I touched a woman, they fell in love with me.

10. Interior. Elegant ballroom.

The camera begins to sweep in, revealing SAM *and* EVA *in wedding clothes. It is their wedding. They dance slowly together, and then they begin to spin faster and faster, until the two of them become almost a blur.*

11. Interior. Elegant ballroom.

Then we see a PHOTOGRAPHER *lining up a shot. He has a large camera of the period. He puts a black cloth over himself and the camera and lights the powder. There's an explosion of light; then we see the five younger* BROTHERS *and their* WIVES *seated in a pose, with their* CHILDREN *(five boys and three girls between the ages of three and nine) sitting on the floor in front of them—the whole of the* KRICHINSKY FAMILY *together.*

Cut to

12. Interior. Sam's living room. Late afternoon.

The family photograph taken above sits in a frame on a shelf next to SAM. *He looks over to it as he continues with his story for the* CHILDREN.

SAM

Oh, the family, how it grew. The wives, the children, . . . and like that, I was married. Hymie was married; Gabriel was married. A whole family we had. Krichinskys everywhere.

(*a beat*)

So, we had the family circle meetings.

Cut to

13. Interior. House. Day.

We see the five BROTHERS *and their* WIVES *and the* CHILDREN *from the photograph in a gathering similar to the present one in* SAM*'s house. A hat is being passed around, and the* ADULTS *are putting money into it.*

SAM (*voice-over*)

We put money in the hat to bring over the cousins, the aunts, the uncles.

(*a beat*)

Then out of the blue William gets the flu. It was a terrible epidemic—the flu of 1919. Thousands died.

Cut to

14. Interior. Hallway in house.

We see the whole FAMILY *gathered in the hallway. A bedroom door opens, and we see* WILLIAM *in bed. It is clear that he is seriously ill. He is sweating profusely and is delirious.*

SAM (*voice-over*)

William died. He was a young man. He left three children.

(*a beat*)

How quickly the time goes.

Cut to

15. Interior. Sam's house. Late afternoon.

EVA, *also in her mid-fifties, passes* SAM *in his chair as he's reminiscing and takes a bowl out of a cupboard close to him.*

EVA

Sam, how many times do we have to hear this story. We know the story. . . . We've heard it before.

SAM

If you don't tell the children, they don't know.

SAM *continues his story to the* CHILDREN *sitting on the floor.*

SAM

And Belle last year . . . Last year Belle died. It was very warm last year when Belle died.

(*to* EVA)

Wasn't it warm?

EVA

Sam, how many times do we have to hear the story? The children know the story.

SAM

I'm telling them about when I came to America.

EVA

We know about it. . . . We've all heard it before.

JULES, SAM's *son, a man in his late twenties, walks through from the kitchen.*

JULES (*to* SAM)

Dad, you want to cut the turkey, or do you want me to cut the turkey?

SAM

It's done? I wanted to tell them about when my father came to the country.

EVA

Plenty of time to talk about your father.

JULES

Dad, let's get on with it.

The camera pans to front door, and we see GABRIEL *and his wife,* NELLIE, *coming through the door.*

GABRIEL

Sorry we're late.

EVA

Another minute and we would have cut the turkey without you and started to eat.

GABRIEL

The turkey is cut without me present, we leave. . . . We leave the house!

SAM

We didn't cut the turkey.

GABRIEL

I heard the turkey was cut.

SAM

I was just talking about when Belle died.

NELLIE

Thank God we're late.

Cut to

16. Interior. Sam's dining room.

The family members are seated around the dining-room table: HYMIE *and his wife,* ALICE; NATHAN *and his wife,* ADA; GABRIEL *and* NELLIE; WILLIAM's *widow,* MOLLY; SAM *and*

EVA; *and all of their respective* CHILDREN *and* GRANDCHILDREN. SAM *is carving the turkey and serving it. Others are piling their plate with food. There's a lot of chatter and activity as everyone digs into his or her food and takes seconds. The atmosphere is noisy, and general confusion abounds.*

EVA

I don't understand this holiday. I'll never understand this holiday.

SAM

What's not to understand?

EVA

Thanksgiving! Thanksgiving! We're giving thanks to who?

JULES

You give thanks for what you have.

SAM

How many times do we have to go through this?

EVA

All I'm saying is we had to get the turkey and we had to kill it to give thanks. If it wasn't this holiday, we wouldn't have turkey. I don't eat turkey the rest of the year; why do I have to eat it now?

JULES

Mom, don't give thanks, OK?

SAM

Time to tell the kids when my father came to America.

ANN

Can't we wait until later?

SAM *pauses and looks at* ANN, JULES'*s wife.*

SAM

You've heard this story?

Several of the CHILDREN *say they want to hear it.*

SAM

See, the children, . . . they want to hear it.

NELLIE (*cutting her meat*)

Eva, this is very tender.

EVA

Of course it is.

MICHAEL

The turkey was in the basement alive. She killed it.

EVA

A beautiful bird.

SAM

We brought my father over in . . .

He thinks.

SAM (*continuing*)

Twenty-five.

GABRIEL

Twenty-five? It was later than twenty-five.

SAM

William died in 1919.

He counts on his fingers.

SAM (*continuing*)

Twenty-five. . . . Twenty-five.

GABRIEL

Twenty-five?

SAM

He came the same year that we brought Belle and Edith over.

GABRIEL

Belle and Edith came after.

SAM

After?

GABRIEL

After!

JULES

Gabriel, Dad, what's the difference? He came to America, right?

GABRIEL

It's a big difference between twenty-five and twenty-six. One is twenty-five, and the other is twenty-six.

JULES

All's I'm saying is who cares if it was twenty-five or twenty-six?

SAM

Jules, Jules, if you stop remembering, you forget.

(*a beat*)

It was twenty-six, and I remember the excitement when we went to meet him. Finally, the father was coming. We saved the money and sent it to him. The whole family went to the boat.

Cut to

17. Exterior. Street. Day.

We see the four BROTHERS *and their* WIVES *and some of the* CHILDREN *walking toward the docks.*

SAM (*voice-over*)

The whole family. . . . Jules, you were just a little child, a very little child. We went through the marketplace. . . . Ooh, it was cold.

We see this image of the FAMILY *bundled up against the cold and walking through a busy marketplace full with* VENDORS, CUSTOMERS, *and livestock.*

Cut to

18. Interior. Sam's dining room.

Back to the dinner table, as before

EVA

What are you talking about? It was cold? It was May. . . . It was late May.

SAM

May? I remember cold.

EVA

You're thinking of when Irene was getting married. It was bitter cold then. It was May seventeenth when your father came.

Cut to

19. Exterior. Street. Day.

The FAMILY *is walking together through the marketplace as before, only now it's summer, and they are all dressed in lighter clothes.*

SAM (*voice-over*)

Anyway, we went. The whole family: . . . the brothers, the wives, the children.

NELLIE (*voice-over*)

I didn't go. And the kids didn't go. We waited at the house.

Now we see fewer PEOPLE *in the crowd walking to the dock.*

Cut to

20. Interior. Sam's dining room.

The dinner table, as before

EVA

There was such excitement. . . . The father . . . The father was coming.

JULES

All I ever heard . . . All I ever heard was "wait until the father comes, . . . the head of the family."

(*a beat*)

I pictured this big, powerful man.

Cut to

21. Exterior. The docks. Day.

We see a ship docked in the harbor, and a little old MAN *in a black coat and hat comes down the gangplank.*

JULES (*voice-over*)

Because all I'd heard was "wait until the father comes. . . . The father's word . . . When he speaks . . ."

The FAMILY MEMBERS *go toward the old* MAN, *and the* BROTHERS *embrace him.*

JULES (*voice-over*)

So, I'm there, I see him. He's shorter than me, and I'm only six! He was this little, itsy-bitsy man. He was a little, little man.

Cut to

22. Interior. Sam's dining room.

The dinner table, as before

SAM

I never said he was big, . . . but he was the father.

Cut to

23. Exterior. The father's house. Day.

The FATHER *sits in a chair on the porch of a row house like a king holding court. There is a small metal pot by the side of the chair.*

SAM (*voice-over*)

From the day he came to America, he never had to work, . . . not a day in his life. Each of us would give him ten percent of our salary. He was the father.

We see the BROTHERS *and* COUSINS *putting money into the pot at the side of the* FATHER*'s chair.*

24. Exterior. The father's house.

Another angle. CHILDREN *are playing out in front.*

Cut to

25. Interior. Sam's dining room.

The dinner table, as before

GABRIEL

He never drank water. The entire time he was in America, . . . from the day he came, . . . he had whiskey or seltzer water. Never drank water, and boy could he drink.

(*to* SAM)

What was that stuff called he always used to drink?

SAM

Schlivovitz. He used to call it block 'n fall.

JULES

What?

SAM

Block 'n fall. You have one drink of that, you walk one block, and you fall.

SAM *and the* CHILDREN *laugh.*

GABRIEL

You have one drink, it burned the gums out.

SAM (*laughing*)

You have one drink, you walk one block, and you fall. Block

'n fall. . . . Block 'n fall. He was funny, . . . very funny.

IZZY

How often did he drink water?

GABRIEL

Never, ever touched it! How many times—I'm sitting across from you; you can't hear? Never. He never drank water!

IZZY

He didn't drink it. . . . I got it.

GABRIEL

All right.

IZZY

Occasionally, maybe, he had some water.

GABRIEL

He never drank water.

The FAMILY MEMBERS *all raise their glasses in a toast.*

Cut to

26. Interior. Sam's house.

The camera pans to the CHILDREN *sitting on the stairs, and now* ANN *has joined them. Her son,* MICHAEL *(a nine year old), sits next to her. Also present are* MARION, *a ten year old; her twelve-year-old brother,* TERRY; *their first cousins* TEDDY, *who is nine, and* MINDY; WILLY, *who is* HERBIE'*s son and* GABRIEL'*s grandson and is also nine;* LIBBY, WILLIE'*s seven-year-old sister; and* ROBERT.

MARION (*to* TEDDY)

We're first cousins, and that's because your father and my mother are brother and sister, right?

TEDDY

Right.

TERRY

Then what's a second cousin?

TEDDY

Second cousin? I don't know. What is a second cousin?

MICHAEL

That would be if your father and my father are first cousins, then your father's cousin is my cousin.

TEDDY

Who's my second cousin then?

MICHAEL

You're my second cousin; then if I had kids—

WILLIE

But what happens if the kid is the same age?

MICHAEL

What's the difference? You're not my cousin anyway.

WILLIE

Yes I am. We're all first cousins.

TEDDY

Are aunts kids before they become aunts?

ANN

Yeah, everybody's a kid before they become an aunt, a mom—

TEDDY

Really?

The CHILDREN *continue to discuss their family genealogy as the camera pans to the living room, where* SAM *and* GABRIEL *sit on the sofa. The weight of the Thanksgiving dinner is taking its toll and has drained the blood from their brains. They are trying to stay awake but nodding off. On the opposite side of the room,* JULES *is talking to his cousin* IZZY.

IZZY

I think the time is right to open a business.

JULES

I don't know; it's risky. I got a good route; . . . you've got a good route. Why gamble?

IZZY

Look, it's a perfect situation. We've got built-in customers; we open our own place. We hold onto the route; we just start to switch people over to us. We don't let the routes go. We sell the same goods, except the money's going into our pockets.

JULES

You don't think Gable's is going to sit still? We open our own place; they're going to put someone on our route.

IZZY

But we can hold onto a lot of the customers.

JULES

Yes, but we're not going to hold onto everybody. We're going to lose customers. . . . This is less dollars, and we've suddenly got to find new customers out of the store.

IZZY

I don't know. . . . The war's over; there's a lot of people with a lot of money. It's a good time to gamble.

JULES

Yeah, it's a gamble. . . . That's for sure.

IZZY

Yeah, everything's a gamble, but there's a good time to gamble and a bad time to gamble.

EVA *enters the living room from the dining room.*

EVA

Dessert!

At the sound of this word, both GABRIEL *and* SAM *open their eyes.*

GABRIEL

I hear dessert?

SAM

I heard dessert.

They get up and start to walk to the dining room.

SAM (*to* EVA)

The children aren't having dessert?

He doesn't see the CHILDREN *sitting on the stairs.*

EVA

They ate it already. . . . They ate it already.

MICHAEL

So my grandmother is grandmother to me, but she's not a grandmother to Teddy?

ANN

That's right.

MICHAEL

Then what is she?

ANN

She's Teddy's great-aunt.

TEDDY

There are aunts and great-aunts?

ANN

Yes.

MICHAEL

What's the difference between a regular aunt and a great-aunt?

LIBBY

They're older; that's the difference.

ANN

No, it's not just that they're older; otherwise all aunts would become great-aunts one day.

ROBERT

Why are aunts just called great-aunts? Why couldn't they be good aunts, or fantastic aunts or terrible aunts?

ANN

No, no, it doesn't have anything to do with what kind of a person they are. It's got to do with, great. You know, they're great, they're older.

ROBERT

And what about those red ants that crawl around on the floor and bite you?

ANN

No, that's A-N-T ant. A-U-N-T is aunt, the other aunt.

MINDY

This family stuff's giving me a headache!

ROBERT

What's a first cousin twice removed?

ANN

I have absolutely no idea.

Cut to

27. Exterior. Sam's house Day.

It is winter, and snow is on the ground. SAM *comes out of his house dressed in overalls. He's carrying rolls of wallpaper.* MICHAEL *is behind him carrying buckets and brushes and putting them in the back of* SAM*'s old jalopy, "The Coffee Grinder," a very noisy Hudson.*

MICHAEL

I'm going selling with my dad today.

SAM

You mean you're not going to school?

MICHAEL

It's the Christmas holidays. . . . No school for a while.

SAM *gets into the driver's seat of his car and starts the engine while* MICHAEL *waits on the sidewalk.*

SAM

Keep your nose clean.

SAM *drives off.*

Cut to

28. Interior. Jules's car. Day.

JULES *is driving, and* MICHAEL *is in the passenger seat.*

MICHAEL

How come you didn't become a wallpaper hanger like Sam?

JULES

Sam always thought that doing manual labor had no dignity. But selling, . . . selling was security. "No matter where you are, no matter what you're selling, you can always make a living."

MICHAEL

Can you sell anything? Anything?

JULES

Anything. I can sell anything. It's all a question of being able to talk to people. The product doesn't make any difference. It's all a question of being able to talk to people.

MICHAEL

Can you sell model trains?

JULES

As many as they can make.

MICHAEL

Can you sell toothbrushes?

JULES

To as many people as have teeth.

(*a beat*)

Quick, what car is that?

A car comes in the opposite direction.

MICHAEL

Crosley.

JULES

One parked on the right?

MICHAEL

Nash.

JULES'*s car heads on down the street.*

Cut to

29. Exterior. House #1. Montage.

We see JULES *on the steps showing a* HOUSEWIFE *pots and pans and irons.* MICHAEL *is tagging along.*

30. Exterior. House #2. Montage.

Here JULES *is selling vacuum cleaners.* MICHAEL *tags along.*

31. Exterior. House #3. Montage.

JULES *is displaying towels and facecloths.* MICHAEL *tags along.*

32. Exterior. Jules's car. Montage.

We see MICHAEL *growing weary and getting into the backseat of the car and going to sleep as the sun sets.*

33. Exterior. Street. Night.

As night falls, the city comes alive with Christmas decorations. Lights are strewn across streets, around house windows, on trees, etc. There's a blaze of light and color in this festive setting as JULES *trudges along in the snow back to his car, having made his last sale of the day. As he approaches his car, a middle-aged* MAN *comes up to him.*

MAN

Give me your money!

JULES

What?

MAN

Give me your money.

JULES

What, are you kidding me?

MAN

No, I'm not kidding you.

JULES

You're kidding! Right here on this street! With all these houses, you're robbing me?

MAN

Yeah, I'm robbing you.

The MAN struggles with JULES and pushes him against the car. JULES drops his case as the MAN bangs him against the car to get his money.

34. Exterior. Street.

Another angle, from inside the car, where the noise has awakened MICHAEL, and he sees the struggle. Suddenly the MAN runs off, and JULES falls down the side of the car, his hands on the window looking in at MICHAEL. He's calling to MICHAEL for help, and we see the blood from his hands trickling down the window of the car.

Cut to

35. Interior. Ambulance. Night.

JULES is on a stretcher, and MICHAEL is at his side. An ATTENDANT sits opposite. As the ambulance races to the hospital with its lights flashing, we hear a piano playing a tune similar to the one we heard previously.

36. Exterior. Street. Day.

We see a piano being pushed over a hill by SAM, NATHAN, and GABRIEL. It's a hot summer afternoon, and the street is teeming with CHILDREN and VENDORS. PEOPLE are shopping, and the atmosphere is busy and bustling. As the MEN struggle with the piano, PEOPLE comment on it and try to help carry it.

MAN #1

You bought a piano, Sam?

SAM

It's for Jules. . . . It's time. He's gonna play.

MAN #2

It's a beautiful piano. . . . He'll for sure make lovely notes with that thing.

MAN #3

What an instrument. . . . What an instrument! He's a lucky boy, your son.

Cut to

37. Exterior. Sam's house. Day.

SAM *and the* BROTHERS *arrive with the piano and lift it onto the porch. Several* NEIGHBORS *come out of their houses to watch and comment on the arrival of the piano.* SAM *calls into the house to* JULES.

SAM

Jules, come down here! You have a piano.

Cut to

JULES, *eight years old, is sitting at the piano, trying to play. He's making a terrible noise.*

SAM

See, he can't play. . . . He can't play, . . . but he'll learn. . . . He'll learn to play.

Cut to

38. Interior. Hospital corridor. Night.

JULES *is being wheeled down the corridor. He's delirious.*

JULES

I can't play. . . . I can't play.

JULES *is sweating profusely as he tosses and turns on the hospital stretcher, and the piano music gets louder.*

JULES

I can't play. . . . I never learned.

39. Interior. Sam's house.

Intercut with JULES *as a boy sitting at the piano trying his hardest to play a tune*

40. Interior. Hospital corridor.

Back to the gurney carrying JULES. *The* NURSES *and hospital* STAFF *accompanying* JULES *are puzzled as he continues to rant.*

JULES

I never learned to play the piano. I never learned . . .

Cut to

41. Interior. Hospital waiting room. Night.

The four elder brothers, SAM, NATHAN, HYMIE, *and* GABRIEL, *are sitting in chairs side by side against a white wall. They are wearing hats and heavy overcoats.*

SAM

That's the problem with collecting.

NATHAN

Yes, that's the problem.

HYMIE

When you got lots of money, somebody wants the money.

SAM

That's the problem.

GABRIEL

It's unheard of. Somebody stabs you to take money. . . . It's unheard of. I never heard about it. I want to know about it! Not like in the old days!

HYMIE

When they know you've got a lot of money on ya, somebody wants the money.

GABRIEL

We know, we know that, but who wants it? I don't know anything about it, and it's not like it used to be! You can't walk in the street!

SAM

Never. Never.

(*a long beat*)

It's the money that's the problem. Somebody tries to kill my boy just for money. It's not good.

HYMIE

It's the money; it's the money.

NATHAN

No good.

GABRIEL

That's the whole problem.

Cut to

42. Interior. Intensive Care Unit. Day.

MICHAEL *is standing looking through the glass doors of the Intensive Care Unit, where his father is lying in bed hooked up to various tubes and other hospital paraphernalia. Suddenly a hand is placed on* MICHAEL'*s shoulder.* MICHAEL *looks up and is shocked to see his* FATHER, *in a hospital gown, standing beside him.* MICHAEL *looks back to the hospital ward and sees his* FATHER *lying there as before.*

43. Interior. Hospital corridor.

The second image that MICHAEL *sees, that of his* FATHER *standing beside him, now quietly leads him away from the ward and down the corridor.* MICHAEL *listens incredulously as his* FATHER *begins to speak.*

JULES

When I was a little younger than you, I used to think the world was made up of big people and little people, and that's where everyone would always stay.

MICHAEL *looks up at his* FATHER, *still not understanding what is happening.*

JULES (*continuing*)

And then I always wondered why sinks were too high. . . . You had to climb up to wash your face. . . . Cupboards were too high. Nothing was made for us. Just a world of big people and little people. You never got any older, and nobody ever died.

44. Interior. Hospital corridor.

Another angle of MICHAEL *walking down the hallway alone. His* MOTHER *is calling to him.*

ANN (*offscreen*)

Michael!

MICHAEL *looks up at his* FATHER, *but his* FATHER *is no longer there. He looks toward his* MOTHER, *who is walking toward him.*

ANN

I've just talked with the doctor. Your father's going to be all right.

Cut to

45. Exterior. Sam's house. Late afternoon.

Snow is on the ground, and Christmas decorations are hanging in the street and around some of the houses. SAM, NATHAN, *and* IZZY *are carrying a large package into the house.*

46. Interior. Sam's house. Late afternoon.

As SAM, NATHAN, *and* IZZY *enter the house, we see that the house is full with the whole* FAMILY—*three generations of Krichinskys.* JULES *is sitting in an easy chair wearing a dressing gown. Everyone's excited and curious.*

MICHAEL

What is it? What is it?

ANN

What could it be?

EVA

It's so big!

SAM

It's a holiday gift.

TEDDY, IZZY'*s son, feels the package.*

TEDDY

What is it?

SAM

What is it?! What is it?! It's a surprise. . . . Wait and see.

The three MEN *set the package down on a table, and* SAM *starts to unwrap it with the help of the* CHILDREN, *who tear away at the paper to reveal a television set. All the* FAMILY MEMBERS *have now congregated in the living room and are gathered around the television.*

SAM (*to* JULES)

The family voted, and so we decided to get you a holiday get-well gift.

SAM, *with the help of* IZZY, *hooks up the television, plugs it into a wall socket, and turns on a knob on the set.*

EVA

So, what is this?

IZZY

Television.

The whole FAMILY *silently watches as a test pattern appears, accompanied by a steady hum. They continue to stare at the test pattern for a period of twenty seconds. Then* SAM *speaks.*

SAM

So, that's television, huh? You can only watch for so long.

(*a beat*)

To me, it doesn't have what radio has.

The FAMILY MEMBERS *begin to disperse. Some of them shake their head commenting on this new electronic invention. The* WOMEN *go toward the kitchen, some stay in the living room, and the* CHILDREN *are scattered around all the rooms and in the hallway and on the stairs. It's definitely a very full house, . . . noisy and smoky. . . . Everyone is talking and hustling and bustling.* TEDDY *and* MICHAEL *are on the floor in the living room under a table; there's a lamp on the table, and the* RELATIVES *are milling around, eating, talking, and drinking.*

EVA

So does anybody want some coffee?

IZZY

Nice picture, huh?

JULES

There's more than this.

NATHAN

Something more is coming?

JULES

Yeah, something more is gonna come.

TEDDY

I've got a great idea.

MICHAEL

Yeah?

TEDDY

A way never to get called on when you don't know the answer.

MICHAEL

Yeah?

TEDDY

Wanna know?

MICHAEL

Yeah.

TEDDY

When Mrs. Parkes asks a question, she looks around the room and everyone goes . . .

He shoots his arm up into the air.

TEDDY (*continuing*]

"Ooh, ooh, Mrs. Parkes, ooh, Mrs. Parkes, Mrs. Parkes," and she's looking to see who doesn't know the answer?

MICHAEL

Yeah?

TEDDY

Next time you don't know the answer, get your hand up. . . . "Ooh, ooh, Mrs. Parkes, Mrs. Parkes," just like you know it.

MICHAEL

This is very valuable.

TEDDY

Never did anyone say, "Ooh, ooh, Mrs. Parkes, Mrs. Parkes" and she calls on 'em and they say, "I have no idea."

MICHAEL

This is *very* valuable.

MICHAEL *laughs as* TEDDY *reaches his hand up to the table and grabs a handful of nuts from a dish.*

TEDDY (*very sure of himself*)

And here's the other part.

(*a beat*)

If you know the answer, make like you don't. Daydream; stare in space; make like you're looking in your desk for something.

He shares some nuts with MICHAEL.

TEDDY (*continuing*)

Then when she calls on you, you say, "What"? She thinks she's got you. "How much is seven times eight?" she says. You think.

He pauses.

TEDDY (*continuing*)

"Fifty-six! That's right." But she's disappointed you beat her. She won't call on you for a while. . . . You're home free.

47. Interior. Sam's living room.

Another angle of the living room. SAM, HYMIE, NATHAN, *and* GABRIEL *are sitting together talking.*

GABRIEL

Never happened. In the old country never heard of anyone stabbing someone to take their money.

NATHAN

You're right. But the government would kill ya and take your money, . . . your property, . . . whatever ya had.

SAM

Ya know what you have to do? You have to be like in the westerns, have a stagecoach and sit with a shotgun when you collect. That's what they had in the Wild West because of the outlaws.

HYMIE

Yeah, that's what ya need. There's always robbers.

SAM

What was that movie we saw with the stagecoach? It was a good movie.

HYMIE

Stagecoach.

SAM

The movie had a stagecoach.

HYMIE

Stagecoach.

SAM

A very active movie. . . . John Wayne. He was an outlaw but not an outlaw. What was that movie called with the stagecoach?

HYMIE

Stagecoach!

SAM

That's what I'm saying, with a stagecoach.

HYMIE

Stagecoach!!

SAM

Stagecoach is not the name of the movie. It had a stagecoach!

48. Interior. Sam's living room.

Another angle on JULES *and* IZZY *in another corner of the room.*

IZZY

There's a nice shop right off the Lexington Market, on Saratoga, the southeast corner.

JULES

All right, supposing we do this. What do we sell? The same things we're selling now?

IZZY

Yeah. We can sell 'em for less than running the routes.

JULES (*thinking*)

Pots and pans.

IZZY

Pots, pans, vacuum cleaners, brooms, toasters. . . . I'm telling you, the time is right to get out on our own.

ANN

We don't have the money in savings. Now is not the right time.

JULES

Ann, please.

Cut to

49. Interior. Bedroom in Sam's house. Night.

JULES *and* ANN *are getting ready for bed.*

ANN

The thing is, Jules, there's not a moment's privacy. Everyone's on top of everybody. We can never get away. We need our own place.

JULES

We'll get it. . . . We'll get it, . . . but this is the time to use our savings for our own business. We can get off the street. . . . See if we can make a go of it.

ANN

I know it's the best thing to do, . . . but I can't promise I'm going to remain sane.

She smiles.

Cut to

50. Exterior. Sam's house. Day.

Row houses line both sides of the street, a mirror image of one another. MICHAEL *comes out of* SAM*'s house.* EVA *comes to the door.*

EVA

Did you put on a little sweater?

MICHAEL *just nods and heads down the steps.*

EVA

Be sure to take small steps. There's a little wind.

The camera pans across the street as TEDDY *leaves his row house. His mother,* DOTTIE, *watches after him.*

The camera pans back to SAM*'s house as* ANN *joins* EVA *on the porch and steps out.*

ANN (*yelling*)

Michael! You forgot your lunch money.

MICHAEL

Toss it!

ANN *throws a quarter, and* MICHAEL *tries to make a major-league outfielder catch, comes under it, settles in place, and misses it. He picks it up, runs to catch up with* TEDDY, *and the two* BOYS *head down the street.*

DOTTIE (*yelling*)

Ann! Should we leave at ten thirty?

ANN

Yeah, that would be fine, because I've got to be back at one o'clock to go with Jules to the doctor.

EVA

You're not driving, are you?

ANN

No, I'm still taking lessons.

EVA

Oh, thank God.

Cut to

51. Interior. Classroom. Day.

A middle-aged female teacher, MRS. PARKES, *stands at the front of a class of* BOYS *and* GIRLS, *who have books laid out on their desks.*

MRS. PARKES

Can is whether you are capable of doing something.

She writes on the blackboard.

MRS. PARKES (*continuing*)

May is asking for permission.

MICHAEL *is moving around in his seat, and then shoots his hand into the air.*

MRS. PARKES

Yes, Michael?

MICHAEL

Can I go to the bathroom?

MRS. PARKES

Michael, do you want to repeat that question?

MICHAEL (*to* TEDDY, *at the next desk*)

Oh, no! I'm going to be made an example of. . . . Ugh!

MRS. PARKES

Michael?

MICHAEL

I said, "Can I go to the bathroom?"

MRS. PARKES

You can, but you may not.

MICHAEL

Well, can I, or can't I?

MRS. PARKES

I don't think you've been paying attention to this lesson, have you, Michael Kaye?

MICHAEL

Yes, I have.

MRS. PARKES

So, how would you rephrase that question?

MICHAEL

Can I *please* go to the bathroom?

MRS. PARKES

Michael Kaye, why don't you just spend some time in the hallway until you learn the difference between *can* and *may.*

MRS. PARKES *walks over to* MICHAEL, *takes him by the arm, and leads him to the classroom door. She opens it, and* MICHAEL *walks into the hallway.*

MRS. PARKES

When you've learned the difference, then you may come back in.

The TEACHER *returns to the classroom, and* MICHAEL *stands in the hallway looking through the window to the class as it continues. Various* CHILDREN *look at* MICHAEL, TEDDY *pulls a face, and then the* TEACHER *brings them to attention.*

ROBERT

I have to go to the bathroom, but I'm afraid to ask.

MRS. PARKES

Now does anyone know the difference between *may* and *can?*

Several CHILDREN *raise their hand.*

Cut to

52. Interior. School corridor. Day.

MICHAEL *is pacing the hallway. The classroom door opens, and the* TEACHER *puts her head out.*

MRS. PARKES

Well, young man, have you learned the difference between *may* and *can?*

MICHAEL

Not yet.

MRS. PARKES

Well, you stay out there until you've learned the difference.

MICHAEL

Yes, Mrs. Parkes.

She leaves, and MICHAEL *begins tap-dancing down the hall.*

Dissolve to

53. Interior. School corridor.

Again MICHAEL *is pacing the hallway. The* TEACHER *pokes her head out the classroom door.*

MRS. PARKES

Well, are you ready to rejoin the class, Michael?

MICHAEL

Yes, Mrs. Parkes.

He moves toward the classroom door.

MRS. PARKES (*holding the door*)

And what's the difference between *may* and *can?*

MICHAEL *stops and looks up at the ceiling for a minute, and then he looks at her. There is a long pause.*

MICHAEL

Give me a little more time.

The door to the classroom closes. MICHAEL *starts to pace again.*

54. Interior. School corridor.

Angle on the principal, MR. DUNN, *coming up some steps near where* MICHAEL *is pacing. He approaches* MICHAEL.

MR. DUNN

Young man, what are you doing in the hallway?

MICHAEL

I'm learning the difference between *may* and *can.*

MR. DUNN

And how long do you think it'll take you to learn this?

Cut to

55. Interior. Sam's house. Day.

The telephone is ringing. SAM *picks up the phone in his living room.*

MR. DUNN (*voice-over, on the phone*)

Is this Mr. Kaye?

SAM

This is his father, Mr. Krichinsky.

MR. DUNN (*voice-over*)

Is Mr. Kaye there?

56. Interior. Mr. Dunn's office. Day.

Intercut with Mr. Dunn on the telephone in his office and Michael sitting across from his desk

57. Interior. Sam's living room.

SAM (*on the phone*)

No, he's at the doctor's, but he's doing fine. Who is this?

58. Interior. Mr. Dunn's office.

MR. DUNN

This is Mr. Dunn, the principal of Michael's school. We seem to have a problem.

59. Interior. Sam's living room.

SAM

Is he sick?

60. Interior. Mr. Dunn's office.

MR. DUNN

We seem to have a problem between *may* and *can.*

Overlap from the phone conversation; cut to

61. Interior. Mr. Dunn's office.

SAM *is seated next to* MICHAEL, *and* MR. DUNN *is sitting behind his desk.*

SAM

Well, what's the problem?

MR. DUNN

That was the lesson they were learning, and Michael asked

if he could go to the bathroom. He said, "Can I go to the bathroom?" and the teacher said, "You can, but you may not."

SAM

So, what's the problem? He asked to go to the bathroom.

MR. DUNN

He asked, but he didn't ask correctly.

SAM

He raised his hand, didn't he?

MR. DUNN

Yes, he did, Mr. Krichinsky, but the point is it was a lesson, and they were learning about *may* and *can.*

SAM

OK, it's fine with me. So what's the problem?

MR. DUNN

He asked, "Can I go to the bathroom?" The teacher said, "You can, but you may not."

SAM

This is confusing to the child, because you're saying you can, and then you say you can but you can't.

MR. DUNN

I think that you don't understand the subtleties of the English language, Mr. Krichinsky.

Cut to

62. Exterior. Park. Day.

SAM *walks home with* MICHAEL *through the park.*

SAM

This English is very difficult. I never realized how difficult English is. . . . *May* or *can.* . . . You can, but you may not. We've come a long way. In the old days if you had to pee, you peed on a tree with no *may* or *can.* That's progress for you.

MICHAEL *laughs.*

Cut to

63. Interior. Sam's living room. Day.

Angle on the blank television screen.

We see a reflection of JULES *sitting in his pajamas and robe staring at his reflection on the screen.*

64. Interior. Sam's living room. Day.

JULES *is sitting in a chair in the living room, and the television set is on the other side of the room. There's a slight smile on his face. He gets out of the chair and walks into the kitchen, where* ANN *is preparing dinner.*

JULES

I got it.

ANN

What?

JULES

The store. Televisions . . .

Cut to

65. Interior. Empty store. Day.

JULES *and* IZZY *stand in the center of the empty store, and as* JULES *speaks, the camera swirls around them from one side of the store to the other.*

JULES

Televisions . . . televisions packed to the walls.

JULES *points to different walls as the camera continues to swirl around him, up and down the walls.*

JULES

Wall-to-wall televisions. . . . We'll pack them in. . . . We'll sell more of them. . . . We'll sell them cheaper. . . . Televisions . . . Televisions . . . from one end of the shop to the other. . . . Nothing but televisions. . . . Televisions!!

Cut to

66. Interior. Jules and Izzy's store. Day.

Angle on a television with a test pattern humming and then another and another, all showing a black and white test pattern with an Indian's face in the center of it. The camera pans from one television to another, all showing the test pattern and humming.

67. Interior. Jules and Izzy's store. Day.

Another angle. The store is filled with television sets, but there's not one customer in the shop. MICHAEL *and* TEDDY *are sitting on the floor watching one of the sets.* SAM *is also there.*

SAM (*to* JULES)

You better hope they start getting some more interesting programs.

MICHAEL

I think something's about to happen. Seems like the humming is getting less. . . . That's when something's about to happen.

TEDDY

Seems like it's humming the same hum to me.

68. Interior. Jules and Izzy's store.

Angle on a TV set. The network logo appears, and then we hear

TV ANNOUNCER (*voice-over*)

"It's Howdy Doody time!"

MICHAEL (*to* TEDDY)

See, I told you something was going to happen. It's "Howdy Doody."

69. Interior. Jules and Izzy's store.

Another angle on JULES, IZZY, *and* SAM

IZZY

Maybe we're just getting ahead of ourselves. . . . We better add toasters, brooms, pots and pans, linoleum. . . .

As the "Howdy Doody" jingle plays, the camera pulls back, out the door.

70. Exterior. Lexington Market. Day.

We see the front of the store with its sign, KIRK AND KAYE'S DEPARTMENT STORE, *and then the camera continues into the bustling market-place, where* VENDORS *are selling live chickens, all kinds of food, clothes, household wares, etc. There are* PEOPLE *huddled around fires burning in large metal canisters by the side of the stalls to keep warm. The music from "Howdy Doody" continues to play as we fade out on this scene.*

Cut to

71. Exterior. Sam's street. Day.

It is summertime in the Krichinsky neighborhood, and we see two moving vans—one in front of IZZY*'s house and the other on the opposite side of the road, in front of* SAM*'s house. Both* FAMILIES *are out in the street watching their possessions being loaded into the vans.*

MICHAEL (*to* ANN)

What does it mean?

ANN *is distracted, watching her furniture being loaded.*

ANN

What?

MICHAEL

What does it mean, the suburbs?

ANN

Just a nicer place to live.

MICHAEL

That's what it means, a nicer place?

ANN

It's nicer. It has lawns, big trees.

MICHAEL

And Uncle Izzy and Teddy and everyone, they're gonna be there too, in one house in the suburbs?

ANN (*to one of the* MOVING MEN)

Watch that. . . . Be very careful with that. It's a very old piece.

MICHAEL

Huh? In one house?

ANN

No, no, Michael. . . . It's going to be the same. . . . Us and your grandparents will be in our house, and they'll be in another house. We'll live near each other just as it is now. It's going to rain any minute. I've got furniture spread out all up and down the street. I'm in a panic. Please don't distract me right now, OK?

She hurries after the MOVING MAN *who is carrying an antique chair.* MICHAEL *walks over to the other side of the road, where the second moving van is being loaded. He goes to* TEDDY*'s mother,* DOTTIE.

MICHAEL

Is this a good thing that's happening?

DOTTIE

What?

MICHAEL

Is this a good thing, going to the suburbs? We're going to like it?

DOTTIE

Yes, you boys are going to love it there.

MICHAEL *goes over to* TEDDY *and* TEDDY'*s sister,* MINDY, *who are leaning against the porch steps.*

MICHAEL

We've been here forever.

TEDDY

We've got to go to a new school, too.

MINDY

Everybody we've ever known we're never gonna see again . . . ever, living way out in the suburbs.

MICHAEL

Ever been to the suburbs?

TEDDY

I'd never even heard of the suburbs until this thing happened.

MICHAEL

We still gonna be in Maryland when we're in the suburbs?

72. Exterior. Sam's street.

Angle on the street outside SAM'*s house.* EVA *is running out of the house after a* MOVING MAN *who is carrying a large vase.*

EVA

Wait a minute! Where you running with that? Wait a minute!

ANN

It's OK, Mom, they'll wrap it.

EVA

Nah, nah.

She catches up with the MOVING MAN *and tries to take the vase from him.*

EVA

We'll take this in the car. It'll be safer.

MOVING MAN

It'll be wrapped. It's gonna be fine.

EVA

Nah, nah, . . . We'll take it in the car. The truck hits a bump, anything can happen.

The MOVING MAN *hands the vase to* EVA.

Cut to

73. Interior. Sam's house. Day.

The house is almost empty. SAM *is standing in the empty living room with* JULES.

SAM

Remember, Michael learned how to walk right here. Held onto the sofa and he took his first steps. . . . He went right to you.

JULES

I remember. What was he, a year old?

SAM

Not a year, . . . nine months. Held the sofa and took steps. . . . Nine months.

SAM *walks into another room, and the camera follows him. He's obviously upset.* JULES *moves behind him at a distance.*

JULES

What's wrong, Pop?

SAM

I don't know; I don't know. I get nervous about making a change.

JULES

What are you talking about? You came all the way to America.

SAM

I came to America in 1914, but I was a young man.

JULES

You saw the house. . . . Forest Park area . . . It's beautiful. We'll have more room for the whole family.

SAM

We're getting further and further away from Avalon.

(*a beat*)

I think I'm getting too old for change.

Cut to

74. Exterior. House in the suburbs. Early evening.

Establishing shot of the KRICHINSKYS *and* KAYES' *new abode, a three-story shingle house, probably built around the turn of the century. It has a front lawn.*

Cut to

75. Interior. Krichinsky-Kaye house. Early evening.

SAM, EVA, JULES, ANN, *and* MICHAEL *are having dinner in the kitchen, and their dog,* NIMO, *hovers around the table. The house is still in a state of disarray and it's clear that they haven't got everything in its place since the move. The* DOG *settles between* SAM *and* EVA *and puts his head on the table.* SAM *feeds the* DOG *a piece of steak, and the* DOG *disappears under the table.*

EVA

Sam, don't feed the dog from the table.

SAM

He likes meat.

EVA

Don't give him big pieces; he has a small throat.

SAM *pushes his green beans to the side of his plate.*

EVA (*continuing*)

What's wrong with the green beans?

SAM

I don't like green beans.

EVA

Since when you don't like green beans?

SAM

I never eat green beans.

ANN

I can't believe that we're going to have an argument about this again.

(*to* EVA)

He never eats the green beans. As long as I've been around, he's never touched green beans.

EVA

Since when he never eats green beans?

(*to* SAM)

You used to love green beans.

SAM

Never!

SAM *gives the* DOG *another piece of meat. The* DOG *goes under the table again.*

SAM

Too stringy . . . Tickles me here.

He touches his throat.

Suddenly we hear the DOG *choking under the table.*

EVA

See! I told you. Don't give him big pieces. He has a small throat.

ANN

I can't believe we have the same kind of argument over the dog and green beans every meal. Green beans and the dog . . . It's like it's the first time it happened. You constantly argue over the same things.

SAM

It's not an argument. . . . It's dinner talk.

JULES *sees that* ANN *is a little upset.*

JULES

Dad, this goes on all the time, whether it's the green beans or feeding Nimo. Constantly the two of you have a problem at dinner.

SAM

Constantly?

JULES

What about drinks? How you argue about how you can mix drinks and Mom says you can't.

EVA

He can't! The mixes he makes is not a good drink.

ANN

Please, don't let's get into the drinks thing now!

SAM (*to* EVA)

What are you talking about? I take the juice from the pears in the can and mix it with a little Coca-Cola. . . . It's a good drink.

EVA

That's a terrible drink.

SAM

Also cherry juice with orange soda, that's a good drink.

EVA

Please, you're going to make me sick with this.

SAM *gives the* DOG *another piece of meat.*

EVA

I said, Sam, don't feed the dog from the table!

ANN (*disturbed*)

Oh, my God!

JULES (*to* ANN)

We're thinking of keeping the store open a couple of nights a week until nine.

ANN

Do you have to?

JULES

We'll alternate, but I think if we want to be competitive with the other shops staying open later, we're gonna have to do it.

SAM

Cherry juice with soda water is a good mixture

EVA

The things he'll mix.

ANN (*to* JULES)

What nights?

JULES

Friday and Saturday.

ANN

I guess if you have to be open—

We hear the DOG *choking under the table.*

EVA

He's gonna choke to death! One night we'll look under the table, and the dog'll be laying there dead.

JULES

Dad, I spoke to Izzy about the family circle meeting this Sunday. It's supposed to be here, but some of the brothers feel it's too far to go.

SAM

Too far? How far can it be? They shoot up Reisterstown, go down Rogers, over the Liberty Heights—

ANN

We know the way to go.

EVA

Why go Rogers? You take Greenspring, you don't have the light.

SAM

To take Greenspring you have to go across Garrison. Garrison's a bottleneck! It's a bottleneck with the construction.

EVA

It's not a bottleneck.

SAM

I say you take Rogers.

EVA

For Gabe to go to Rogers, he's gonna go up Park Circle. Why should he have to go to Rogers?

JULES

The question is not which way they're going to come. . . . They think it's too far.

Suddenly we hear a fire alarm, and in the flash of a moment everyone jumps up from the dinner table and rushes into the living room, where the television, sitting on a packing box, is on and the "Texaco Star Theatre" with Milton Berle has just begun. In the center of the bare floor of the living room, which does not yet have any furniture in place, is a rolled-up carpet. The FAMILY MEMBERS *sit in a line on the rolled-up carpet in front of the television set. As they watch the set,* MILTON BERLE *comes onto the screen, and the* FAMILY *is mesmerized. The small box has captured everyone's attention.*

MILTON BERLE *starts strutting around the stage making a face, and the whole* FAMILY *laughs.*

Cut to

76. Interior. Jules and Ann's bedroom. Night.

JULES *and* ANN *are getting ready for bed.*

JULES

What'd you want? You want me to tell them to move out? What'd you want?

ANN

I don't want you to tell them to move out. I was just expressing a feeling, that maybe, you know, we could get them their own place, chip in or something.

JULES

Get them their own place? Where the hell would the money come from? I don't have that kind of money yet. They don't have that kind of money.

ANN

I know, I just feel like there's always somebody watching over me. I feel like somebody's thinking they could do it better. That's what I feel. I put something down. I like the way it looks on the coffee table. I come back, and it's moved.

JULES

You want me to talk to her?

ANN

. . . but I'd like to be able to put something down, and if it's nice there, have it there when I return. That's all.

JULES

You want me to talk to her? I'll talk to her. I'll talk to her again and again, but you know it doesn't do any good.

ANN

I feel like I'm still living at my house, like I'm still with Mom and Dad. And I'd like to feel like this is my home. I'd like to feel like the mom in my own house.

JULES

I understand.

ANN

I go out; I'll buy what I consider to be an attractive outfit. I come home. "It's too tight here." "The fabric's not becoming to you." "It looks too heavy for summer."

JULES

She speaks her mind. She's got opinions.

ANN

I'd like to feel good about something I buy or put in my house or put on myself.

JULES

Don't let her make you feel bad.

ANN

How can I help it?

JULES

Put her in her place. You've gotta do that sometimes. I put her in her place sometimes. Him, too.

ANN

I know. I would just like to feel as though I live in my own house.

JULES

You live here. What do you want from me?

ANN

I . . . I'm just talking.

Cut to

77. Exterior. Krichinsky-Kaye house. Day.

EVA *comes out the front door and hurries down the steps and along the path to a small lane that is a few houses away. She's obviously excited about something and moves very quickly.*

Cut to

78. Exterior. Izzy's house. Day.

TEDDY, MICHAEL, *and* MINDY *are playing step ball on the steps of* IZZY'*s house, which is a duplicate of the Kaye-Krichinsky house—a three-story wooden structure.* EVA *hurries up to the house.*

EVA (*to* MICHAEL)

Where's your mother, Michael?

MICHAEL

She's in the kitchen with Aunt Dottie.

EVA *goes up the steps and into the house as* TEDDY *throws his tennis ball against the steps.*

79. Exterior. Izzy's house.

Angle underneath the porch. The camera closes in on a beehive beneath the wooden porch. As the ball hits the step, the vibration creates a disturbance in the beehive, and the BEES *begin to stir.*

Cut to

80. Interior. Izzy's house. Day.

EVA *makes her way through the hallway of the house to the kitchen, where* ANN *and* DOTTIE *are sitting at a table drinking lemonade.*

EVA (*out of breath*)

You're not going to believe this! I got a call . . . the American Red Cross. . . . My brother's alive in Europe.

ANN

What?

EVA

I can't believe it. . . . I have to sit down.

She coughs and sputters and pats her chest.

EVA (*continuing*)

I need something to drink. . . . I ran to get here.

DOTTIE *gets up and pulls a chair out from the table for* EVA *to sit on and moves toward the refrigerator.*

DOTTIE

I'll get you some lemonade.

EVA

Not too sweet.

(*fanning herself*)

My heart, . . . my heart is running.

ANN

Mom, . . . so what happened?

EVA

I don't know exactly. He was in a concentration camp. . . . He lived through the concentration camp. They found him. . . . I don't know; I don't know how he lived through it. . . . I don't know.

DOTTIE *brings* EVA *a glass of lemonade, and* EVA *takes a big gulp as both* ANN *and* DOTTIE *sit silently, shocked at this revelation.*

DOTTIE

To have been in a concentration camp. My God!

EVA

I never saw him. . . . I heard about him from letters.

She drinks more lemonade.

EVA (*continuing*)

When I came to this country, he wasn't born; and when he was old enough to come, he wouldn't leave my father. He was blind and dying, . . . and then the war started.

ANN

So where is your brother now?

EVA

I don't know . . . With refugees . . . But now they've found me, they'll make plans for him to come to America.

Cut to

81. Exterior. Izzy's porch. Day.

MINDY *is at the steps now throwing the ball. The camera closes in on the beehive underneath the porch as the* BEES *continue to stir, a little more actively this time.*

Cut to

82. Interior. Izzy's kitchen. Day.

EVA, ANN, *and* DOTTIE *sit around the kitchen table as before.*

EVA

After the concentration camp he's put in a camp with the displaced people. He says he has a sister in Baltimore, but he can't remember my married name, Krichinsky. He doesn't have his letters anymore; they were all destroyed. He knows the name's Russian, not Polish: . . . "It's a *y,* not an *i,*" . . . but he can't remember the name.

ANN

I can't imagine having a brother I've never seen.

EVA

Never seen. . . . thought was dead.

Cut to

83. Exterior. Izzy's porch.

MICHAEL *is at the steps for his so-called at bat. He's aiming for the point in the step.* TEDDY *and* MINDY *are on the walkway ready to catch the ball.* MICHAEL *throws it hard. The tennis ball hits the flat dividing part of the step and bounces to* TEDDY. TEDDY *picks it up, and there's a look of surprise on his face. Suddenly we see bees pouring out from the latticework that surrounds the underside of the porch.* MICHAEL *is in shock as the* BEES *make their way toward him.*

TEDDY (*yelling*)

Bees!

MINDY *and* TEDDY *start to run down the street.*

MICHAEL

Stand still! You're supposed to stand still!!

The BEES *are now swarming all around* MICHAEL, *and he begins to scream.*

Cut to

84. Interior. Izzy's kitchen.

EVA, ANN, *and* DOTTIE *hear* MICHAEL *screaming, and they run to the front door and out onto the porch.*

85. Exterior. Izzy's porch.

EVA, ANN, *and* DOTTIE *see* MICHAEL *holding his hands over his face and head, screaming as the* BEES *surround him, stinging him.*

86. Exterior. Izzy's porch.

Angle on the three WOMEN

EVA

Oh my God! Oh my God!

ANN *sees a broom on the porch. She runs for it and starts down the steps, swinging away at the* BEES *with the broom.*

Cut to

87. Interior. Doctor's office. Day.

Tight shot of a needle being injected into an arm

88. Interior. Doctor's office.

Another angle of MICHAEL, ANN, *and* DR. KALIN. MICHAEL'*s face and hands are covered with bee stings, and there's some kind of white cream spread all over him.*

DR. KALIN

He's not allergic to the bees, so there's no real problem. He's just going to be a little uncomfortable for a while.

MICHAEL

I hate the suburbs!

DR. KALIN (*to* ANN)

I'm surprised your mother-in-law didn't come along.

ANN

She refuses to get into the car with me. She's never been in a car when a woman drives.

DR. KALIN

It's tough for them. . . . They've got the old ways.

Cut to

89. Exterior. Back alley in between row houses. Day.

Clothes are strung across the backyards, and the KRICHINSKY CHILDREN *are playing.*

Cut to

90. Interior. Hymie's house. Day.

The KRICHINSKY ELDERS, *dressed in their Sunday visiting clothes, are congregated around a large table in the living room. The windows are wide open, and several of the* WOMEN *hold fans. This is the family circle meeting.* GABRIEL *is presiding over the meeting and is reading the minutes.*

GABRIEL

The election of a new family circle president takes place three weeks from this Sunday, so we have some serious decision making.

EVA (*to one of the other* WOMEN)

It's like a furnace in here. Like a furnace.

GABRIEL

That concludes old business.

IZZY

If we're moving to new business, let's make a motion that the next meeting be held at Frock's Farm, where it'll be cooler, and we won't be suffocating to death.

Several of the FAMILY MEMBERS *concur by saying "Hear, hear!"*

GABRIEL

This is a family circle meeting; this is not an outing!

IZZY

Why can't we combine the two when it's this hot? We have an outing and a family circle meeting at the same time.

GABRIEL

Because an outing is an outing, and a family circle is a family circle!

EVA

I'm dripping.

JULES

Why don't we just finish the meeting quickly, and that'll be it?

NATHAN

That'll be it! That'll be it! When Father was alive, we sat; we had a meeting. When the meeting was finished, then we left. If it was hot, if it was cold, if there was snow, if there was rain, . . . we sat and we had a meeting. If we don't want to meet because it's hot, then don't meet anymore. . . . Don't meet!

SAM

No one said not to meet.

EVA

It's a furnace.

GABRIEL *is trying to get on with the meeting.*

GABRIEL

We need to make a decision as to how much money we want to give to our charities this year.

HYMIE

It's too hot! It's too hot for a family circle meeting! It's too hot!

IZZY

This is a heat wave.

NATHAN

It was hotter at Avalon. We had a meeting one time, it was so hot you couldn't stand at Avalon. No one complained. Molly fainted, . . . the meeting still went on.

GABRIEL

Last year we gave . . . Let me look. . . .

He shuffles some papers.

GABRIEL (*continuing*)

We gave to six charities . . .

91. Interior. Hymie's house.

Angle on EVA *looking out the window. From her point of view we see what looks like the top of an elephant's head going down the street.*

EVA

An elephant just went by the window.

92. Interior. Hymie's house.

Angle on IZZY, *who can't see the window from where he sits*

IZZY

It's the heat, . . . the heat. You're hallucinating.

EVA

Well, then, the heat made me see another elephant, because another one's going by the window.

93. Interior. Hymie's house.

Angle on the CHILDREN *as they run into the house very excited and screaming, "The circus . . . The circus is outside!!"*

Suddenly there's total confusion as everyone runs to the windows and out onto the front porch.

Cut to

94. Exterior. Hymie's street. Day.

Sure enough, there are ELEPHANTS *and* HORSES, LIONS *and* TIGERS *in cages, wagons and* CIRCUS PERFORMERS*—all heading down the street, led by a* BRASS BAND. *It's an odd sight as the row houses frame the circus procession.*

95. Exterior. Hymie's street.

Angle on the front porch of the row house, where the majority of the FAMILY MEMBERS *are standing watching the parade.* JULES *stands next to* ANN.

JULES (*to* ANN)

They must be going through here to get to the tent sight. I think I read they're going to have the tents at Edmondson Avenue.

Cut to

96. Interior. Hymie's house. Day.

GABRIEL *is the only one in the room. He is sitting at the table as before.*

GABRIEL (*yelling*)

Are we going to have a meeting! It's a circus going down the street. . . . No one's ever seen a circus?!

Cut to

97. Exterior. Hymie's street. Day.

The circus is traveling down the street as before.

98. Exterior. Hymie's street.

Angle on the PEOPLE *gathered on the street and the excited faces of the* CHILDREN *watching as the circus continues on its way.*

JULES

Look at the midgets.

IZZY

No, I don't want to look at the midgets.

JULES

Why? Why don't you want to look at the midgets?

IZZY

They make me nervous. Well, they do.

JULES *laughs.*

IZZY (*continuing*)

Well, they do.

99. Exterior. Hymie's street.

Another angle on MICHAEL *as he watches the parade pass by. He runs along the street, peeking through gaps in the crowd of* SPECTATORS, *trying to follow the parade. The* BAND *plays on. There's some things in life you know you'll never forget.*

Cut to

100. Exterior. Krichinsky-Kaye house. Night.

SAM *is coming out of the house with* MICHAEL, TEDDY, *and* MINDY. *He's carrying a thermos and a small picnic basket.* MICHAEL *has a flashlight. They're all holding their own pillows and a sheet.* EVA *stands on the porch.*

EVA

And stay with Sam. . . . Don't go wandering off around the reservoir without him, understand?

MICHAEL and TEDDY (*together*)

We know. . . . We know.

EVA

I'll make breakfast.

They head down the steps of the house toward the car.

SAM

You'll love it. It's cool. The breeze comes off the reservoir. . . . With the breeze, you can sleep.

As they arrive at the car, they load the pillows, etc.

SAM (*continuing*)

We used to go every night to the reservoir.

TEDDY

Every night?

SAM

In the old days it used to be hotter in the summertime.

He walks around to the driver's side as the CHILDREN *pile into the car.*

SAM (*continuing*)

You'll love it. That breeze comes off the reservoir. You'll love it.

He gets into the car, and they drive off.

Cut to

101. Exterior. Druid Hill Reservoir. Night.

Cars are parked all over the place, and PEOPLE *are sleeping around the reservoir. It's a strange sight and looks like a nighttime picnic area, but this is the way to beat the heat of a hot summer night.*

102. Exterior. Druid Hill Reservoir.

High shot looking down on SAM *flanked by* TEDDY, MICHAEL, *and* MINDY *as they lie on the grass looking up at the stars.* SAM *smokes a cigar.*

SAM

Did I ever tell you that my father never drank water in America? The whole time he was alive . . . Never drank water in America.

MICHAEL

What did he drink? Coca-Cola?

SAM

No, whiskey, . . . and if he didn't drink whiskey, mineral water. But never drank from the faucet.

TEDDY

Why?

SAM

Well, he had the old ways. You see, we drank from a well, spring water, and he said water that comes through a pipe under the streets of the city can't be good water, . . . can't be good for you. He was a very stubborn man, and we could never convince him otherwise.

He pauses.

SAM (*continuing*)

Your grandmother is a stubborn woman.

TEDDY and MINDY (*together*)

We know.

The camera moves toward the sky, which is scattered with stars. As the stars twinkle and shine, SAM *continues with his stories.*

SAM (*voice-over*)

I came to America in 1914, and when I came to Baltimore, it was the most beautiful place you ever saw.

The lights of the stars suddenly explode into fireworks, and as the sparks trickle down from the fireworks, they turn into the lights lacing the streets and buildings we saw in the opening scene.

103. Exterior. Street. Night.

Once again we see SAM *walking below this magnificent array of lights.*

MICHAEL (*voice-over*)

We know that story, Sam. Tell us another one.

Cut to

104. Exterior. Druid Hill Reservoir.

Back to the CHILDREN *and* SAM *lying on the grass as before*

SAM

Did I tell you when I used to own a nightclub?

In the background we hear the tinkling of a piano playing light jazz.

MICHAEL

You used to own a nightclub?

SAM

Not a big nightclub.

105. Interior. Nightclub. Night.

We see hands playing a piano. The camera pulls back to reveal SAM *at the piano and four other* MUSICIANS, *all black, on a stage in the club. The camera pans the club, and we see that it's crowded and that all of the* CLIENTELE *is black.* MEN *and* WOMEN *are dancing and sitting around the floor at tables drinking. The camera moves to the front door of the club, and* JULES, ANN, IZZY, *and* DOTTIE *enter. They are all in their early twenties. They stand in the doorway and watch the activity in the smoke-filled room, looking over to* SAM *at the piano.*

Cut to

106. Interior. Nightclub.

JULES, ANN, IZZY, DOTTIE, *and* SAM *are sitting together in a corner of the club.*

SAM

You ran off and got married?!

JULES

Well, we didn't plan to get married. We were taking them to Elkton to get married.

IZZY

Yeah, Jules has the car, and we needed a ride . . .

SAM

So, because you needed a ride, my son is now married!

ANN

We got caught up in the moment.

JULES

It was so . . . Ya know. . . .

ANN

We were going to get married sooner or later.

IZZY

The justice of the peace made a deal. It's normally ten bucks a piece, but he made it two for fifteen dollars.

SAM

That's wonderful! Just what my son needed, a bargain wedding! He saved five dollars by getting married. I'm so pleased!

JULES

Come on, Dad, be happy for us.

SAM (*to* ANN)

Do ya love my boy?

ANN

Yes, I do, very much.

SAM

Good, good, 'cause that's one young man that's crazy about you.

(*to* JULES)

Kiss the bride at least. Let me see you kiss the bride.

JULES *kisses* ANN.

SAM (*continuing*)

Izzy, kiss your bride.

The two COUPLES *kiss while* SAM *looks on.*

SAM (*continuing*)

That's it.

JULES

Dad, it's all right she's going to sleep at the house tonight?

SAM

Where's that marriage certificate? Let me see that marriage certificate. I don't want any hanky-panky going on in my house.

JULES *puts his hand in his inside jacket pocket and pulls out the marriage certificate.* SAM *inspects it.*

SAM (*continuing*)

Wait a minute. . . . Wait a minute. . . . Who's this Jules Kaye here?

JULES

That's me, Dad. I changed my name.

IZZY

Me too, I changed my name to Kirk. . . . Better than Krichinsky . . . Much easier to say.

SAM

Easier to say?! Who said names are supposed to be easy to say? What are you, a candy bar? You got a name, Krichinsky. . . . It's a name. Kirk, Kaye . . . Two cousins, different names! How can this be a family when the father's called Sam Krichinsky, his son is called Jules Kaye, and his first cousin is called Izzy Kirk!!

SAM'*s anger is increasing.*

SAM (*continuing*)

This is a family, goddamn it!! Krichinsky is the name of this family! It's not Kaye. . . . It's not Kirk. . . . It's Krichinsky!!

There's a long pause, and no one knows what to say.

Cut to

107. Exterior. Druid Hill Reservoir.

SAM *and the* CHILDREN *are lying on the grass as before. The camera picks up a side angle of* SAM *puffing on his cigar.*

SAM

We argued. . . . We argued. And then, the way things are in life, you stop arguing.

Cut to

108. Interior. Nightclub.

JULES, ANN, IZZY, DOTTIE, *and* SAM *as before*

SAM

It's your life; you're gonna have to live it.

(*a beat*)

What about a celebration!

They all hug.

Cut to

109. Interior. Nightclub.

IZZY, DOTTIE, JULES, *and* ANN *are dancing in the club along with all of the black clientele. The music is loud and raucous. There's a wild celebration. The place is alive.* SAM *is dancing with a black woman, something between a jitterbug and a Russian folk dance.*

SAM (*voice-over*)

And we celebrated that night. I gave everyone free drinks. It wasn't your ordinary family celebration.

Cut to

110. Exterior. Nightclub. Daybreak.

JULES, ANN, IZZY, *and* DOTTIE *drive off in* JULES'S *car.* SAM *stands alone on the street as the rhythmic piano music plays softly.* SAM *moves to the music, tapping his feet and swaying. He struts down the street, smiling as he goes.*

Cut to

111. Exterior. Druid Hill Reservoir.

The CHILDREN *are sleeping. The piano music continues lightly.* SAM *is in profile.*

SAM

It was the best wedding I ever went to.

The camera pulls away from SAM *and the* CHILDREN *and widens to show* PEOPLE *sleeping all around the reservoir. Snores emanate from some of the* SLEEPERS.

SAM (*voice-over*)

It's nice. It's easy to sleep when you have a breeze.

Fade to black.

Fade up.

112. Exterior. Lexington Market. Day.

The market and streets are teeming with PEOPLE, *who are busy shopping.*

113. Exterior. Lexington Market.

Angle on sign that reads KIRK AND KAYE'S DEPARTMENT STORE, *as earlier, except the sign is larger and covers three buildings—the original store and two buildings on either side.*

114. Interior. Kirk and Kaye's Department Store. Day.

There is a flurry of activity inside the store, which is being expanded across the two other spaces. WORKMEN *are hammering and plastering, and boxes of supplies are piled high. It's a very busy scene.* JULES *and* IZZY *are supervising the* WORKERS.

JULES

I'm getting nervous. This is too much expansion. We bought out that store, the other store, the one upstairs. We got all this merchandise. We got money going out and not coming in. I'm a little nervous. More than a little nervous.

IZZY

You're not the only one.

(*to one of the* WORKERS)

Paul, are we going to be done by the end of the week?

PAUL

Should be. . . . Should be.

IZZY

What do you mean, "Should be, should be"? Can't be "should be." . . . It has to be.

Cut to

115. Exterior. Lexington Market. Day.

IZZY *and* JULES *are walking through the marketplace.*

JULES

I've been asking some of the people around here in the market-place. . . . I'm not sure anyone knows what discount is. I don't know whether it means anything to anybody.

IZZY

It's not like we invented the word.

JULES

Yeah, but it doesn't mean anything.

IZZY

So, what are you saying?

JULES

I think we've got to be more clear. I think we need a catchy slogan or something.

Cut to

116. Interior. Coffee shop. Day.

IZZY *and* JULES *are sitting at a table drinking coffee.*

IZZY

We sell for less.

JULES (*thinking*)

Sell for less . . .

IZZY

Every day's a sale.

JULES *shakes his head.*

IZZY (*continuing*)

Sale prices every day?

JULES

Even if we find the right thing to say, how are we gonna let people know?

(*a beat*)

We're getting in over our heads. We're expanding the store, . . . carrying more product. . . . We've borrowed a lot of money. . . . We're getting in over our heads.

IZZY

You're getting eleventh-hour jitters.

(*a beat*)

Guaranteed the lowest prices in town!

JULES

That's good.

Cut to

117. Exterior. Lexington Market. Day.

A flier is posted on the market wall. It reads KIRK AND KAYE'S DISCOUNT DEPARTMENT STORE—GUARANTEED LOWEST PRICES IN TOWN. NEW STORE OPENS 10 A.M. MONDAY, OCTOBER 3, 1949.

The camera pans the whole of the Lexington Market area and the streets adjacent to it, and we see that the fliers are everywhere—on buildings, lampposts, windshields, and steps of buildings. PEOPLE *walking along the street are reading them.*

Cut to

118. Exterior. Kirk and Kaye's Department Store. Day.

A sign is being hoisted above the store. It reads GUARANTEED LOWEST PRICES IN TOWN. SAM *and* HYMIE *are putting it in place on top of the building, and* GABRIEL *is supervising from below.*

GABRIEL

A little higher . . . Higher!

HYMIE (*to* SAM)

What if somebody buys and it's cheaper, cheaper than they guaranteed is the lowest price? What do they do then?

JULES *is standing outside the store looking at the sign.* IZZY *stands in the doorway.*

SAM (*yelling to* JULES)

Jules, what happens if somebody buys cheaper than what you sell?

JULES

I don't know.

(*to* IZZY)

Izzy, what are we gonna do if they get it cheaper some place else and we guarantee it's the lowest price in town?

IZZY

If they buy it cheaper somewhere else, then we'll match it at that price.

JULES

That's good.

(*yelling up to* SAM)

We'll match it.

HYMIE (*to* SAM *as they fix the sign*)

They'll match it? What does that mean?

SAM

That means whatever the guy buys somewhere else, he can get it here for the same price.

HYMIE

What the hell's he wanna do that for?

SAM *thinks.*

SAM

He bought it, and then they guarantee they'll give him the same price.

HYMIE

That makes no sense. He's got to take it back to the shop and then get it here for the same price.

SAM

Why wouldn't that make sense?

HYMIE

They guarantee it?

SAM

That's what they said. . . . They'd guarantee it. Maybe they'll make it lower.

HYMIE

How much lower. Because if it's a nickle lower, I'm not gonna take it all the way back to get it here for a nickle less.

GABRIEL (*calling up from the street*)

A little higher on the right . . . A little higher.

SAM

How much lower?

HYMIE

And the other thing is if another store can make it lower, then you've got to lower your price more. Then they go lower again, so you've got to make your prices still lower than the other place. That forces you out of business because you can't even buy it at that price.

SAM

Can we just put up the sign!

119. Exterior. Kirk and Kaye's Department Store.

Angle on the front of store. ANN *is standing beside* JULES *as he watches the sign being hoisted.*

ANN (*to* JULES)

I've got to go to the doctor's and then get the kids. I said I'd pick them up from the movies at four.

JULES

I can't believe how they do it, from ten o'clock in the morning until four in the afternoon . . . Just a minute, you're going to the doctor's?

ANN

Just for a checkup.

(*a beat*)

What time will you be home?

JULES

Probably around seven.

(*a beat*)

See if my mother wants to go back with you.

ANN *starts to walk into the store, and the camera follows.*

120. Interior. Kirk and Kaye's Department Store. Day.

EVA *is doing some little job inside the store.* ANN *approaches her.*

ANN

Mom, do you want to ride back with me?

EVA

With you?

ANN

Yes.

EVA

I think it's still too soon.

ANN

I've been driving now for six months.

EVA

Still too soon. You got to go all the way uptown. . . . You got a lot of turns to make. It's too soon.

ANN

Otherwise you're going to have to wait until seven o'clock. That's when Jules says they're going to head home.

EVA

I'll take the streetcar. It's on tracks. . . . You take a thirty-two and you're there.

ANN (*exasperated*)

Fine!

Cut to

121. Exterior. Kirk and Kaye's Department Store. Day.

ANN *goes outside again.* JULES *is still in front of the store.* GABRIEL *is supervising the hanging of the sign as before, and* SAM *and* HYMIE *are still on top of the building.*

JULES

She's not going with you?

ANN

I can't believe your mother. I haven't been driving long enough for her.

She throws up her hands and starts walking through the CROWD *in Lexington Market.*

Cut to

122. Exterior. Movie theater. Day.

A paper airplane is flying in the air. We see that it is made out of one of the fliers—part of the print is visible. The paper plane flies across the theater marquee. The marquee announces: SANDS OF IWO JIMA KING OF THE ROCKET MEN—CHAP. 6 RADAR PATROL VS. SPY KING—CHAP. 10.

Cut to

123. Interior. Movie theater Day.

Rocket Man goes shooting across the sky on the screen.

124. Interior. Movie theater.

Another angle on the theater. It is packed with CHILDREN, *including* MICHAEL *and* TEDDY. *It's general chaos. The* CHILDREN *have peashooters and are shooting at the screen. There are popcorn fights, and candy and drinks are overflowing.* CHILDREN *are in the aisles and clambering all over the seats.*

MICHAEL (*to* TEDDY)

I wonder how long it's gonna be before we can all get our own rocket suits?

TEDDY

Yeah, it'll be great. You'll be able to rocket to school. . . . You'll be able to rocket back home. It'll be great.

MICHAEL

Can't be that long, can it?

(*a beat*)

I'd love to see my grandmother rocketing to the store to get bread.

They both laugh.

125. Interior. Movie theater.

Angle on the screen. A trail of gunpowder is on fire and is making its way toward a warehouse. It reaches the warehouse and explodes. The screen reads END OF CHAPTER SIX.

Cut to

126. Exterior. Gas station. Day.

ANN *drives into the gas station. An* ATTENDANT *approaches. She gets out of the car.*

ANN (*to the* ATTENDANT)

Can you fill it up? I'll be right back. I'm going to get the kids from the movie theater.

ATTENDANT

OK.

She heads across the street just as MICHAEL *and* TEDDY *are coming out of the theater. The* BOYS *react to the light as if they were animals emerging from a long period of hibernation. They squint.* ANN *catches up to them.*

MICHAEL

Oh, I can't see!

ANN

Well, that's because you've been sitting in a dark movie theater all afternoon.

Then, from MICHAEL*'s point of view, we see a streetcar coming around the corner. It jumps the track, goes up the sidewalk, heads for the gas station, shears off two of the pumps, crashes into* ANN*'s car, and comes to a stop against a wall. The whole scene is overlighted, as if* MICHAEL*'s eyes are trying to adjust to the light, and the dust that the streetcar kicks up almost makes it dreamlike. There's no explosion, but suddenly there's confusion in the street—*PEOPLE *are running in every direction.*

MICHAEL

Wow! End of Chapter Six!

Cut to

127. Interior. Krichinsky-Kaye house. Night.

Upstairs ANN *and* JULES *are getting ready to go out for the evening.* JULES *is in the bathroom shaving, and* ANN *is dressing in the bedroom.* EVA *stands in the door of the bedroom talking to* ANN.

ANN (*to* EVA)

What are you saying? It's my fault?

EVA

I'm not saying it's your fault.

ANN (*continuing to dress*)

The way you say it sounds like it's my fault the streetcar smashed into my car.

EVA *straightens* ANN*'s dress for her.*

EVA

I'm not saying it's your fault. . . . You took the car, and it got hit, and I could have been sitting in it.

The camera follows ANN *as she walks out of the bedroom and toward the bathroom.* EVA *follows her.*

ANN (*exasperated*)

But don't you understand, you keep making it sound as if I'm responsible for it, . . . as if it's my fault.

EVA

I've been in this country forty years; I've never seen a streetcar jump the track and hit a car.

ANN *is in the bathroom, and while* JULES *combs his hair, she shares the bathroom mirror, touching up her own hair.* EVA *stands in the bathroom doorway.*

ANN

Am I crazy, or does it sound like she's making it my fault?

JULES (*finishing combing his hair*)

I think you're being too sensitive about this. She's not trying to blame you. You're not trying to blame her, are you, Ma?

He comes out of the bathroom, and ANN *follows. They start down the stairs.* EVA *follows them.*

EVA

Oh, no. I'm not blaming her. . . . What I'm saying is they should get rid of the streetcars.

The camera follows as they all continue down the stairs.

EVA (*continuing*)

They got buses; why do they need streetcars? The tracks are too slippery. I don't even like Sam to drive in the rain with the tracks. . . . It's dangerous.

They reach the bottom of the stairs, and ANN *goes to the coat closet in the hall.* JULES *continues along the hall and goes into the kitchen.* EVA *stops at the living room, where* SAM *is watching TV with* MICHAEL.

EVA (*to* SAM)

Did you ever know anyone whose car got hit by a streetcar that went off its tracks?

SAM

It's a first.

EVA (*in the hallway*)

When I think I could have been sitting in that car? Thank God I didn't get into that machine, that's all I'm saying.

ANN, *frustrated with* EVA, *is looking for her coat.*

ANN

I can't believe this!

JULES *comes out of the kitchen with a glass of milk, comes down the hall to* EVA *and* ANN, *and goes into the living room.*

JULES

Let's put this streetcar talk to rest, OK? We're lucky nothing serious happened, and that's the end of it, all right?!

MICHAEL

You should have seen it, Dad, it was just like the cliff-hangers.

JULES

All right, Michael.

He finishes his milk, turns back, and heads toward the kitchen.

SAM (*offscreen*)

Alan . . . er . . . Ferguson.

JULES *puts his glass in the sink.*

JULES (*yelling*)

What?

SAM

Alan Ferguson's car got hit by a streetcar.

JULES *comes out of the kitchen and heads back to the living room.* EVA *goes into the living room in front of him.* ANN *continues to look for her coat.*

EVA (*to* SAM)

It wasn't a streetcar, it was a train, . . . off of Saratoga, a freight train. It wasn't a streetcar

SAM

It wasn't a streetcar?

ANN *comes into the living room.*

EVA

It was a train.

ANN (*very flustered*)

Do you know where my new coat is?

EVA

Yeah, it's in the back closet. It was too crowded.

ANN, *very annoyed, goes to the back closet to get her coat.*

EVA

Never has there ever been a streetcar jumped its track. . . . A train has jumped its tracks, but never a streetcar.

JULES (*putting on his coat*)

Must have circulated over ten thousand fliers for the opening of the new store, Dad.

SAM

I never believed in fliers. I always think if people don't pay for something, they don't bother to read it. The newspaper you pay for; then you read an ad.

JULES (*buttoning up his coat*)

Let's hope you're wrong, because we can't afford to advertise in the newspaper.

SAM

Well, it's a good time to gamble. You're young. . . . You make mistakes, you can always start again. Look what Solomon did. He could have stayed in the business of just breaking in shoes, but he gambled, and today he's got—

JULES (*interrupting*)

Yeah, I know, . . . one of the biggest department stores in Baltimore.

ANN *comes back into the living room.*

ANN (*exasperated*)

I can't find the coat.

EVA

Oh God. I sent it to the cleaners.

ANN *goes back to the closet and finds another coat while* JULES *prepares to leave.* JULES *stops and turns back to* SAM.

JULES

Dad, where's the keys to the car?

SAM *puts his hand in his pocket and throws the keys to* JULES. EVA *is sitting down next to* SAM *watching TV.*

JULES

Michael, be good.

MICHAEL

I will.

JULES

You ready, hon?

ANN

I'm just putting on my coat!

They head out the front door.

SAM

Well, it's true with Solomon.

Cut to

128. Exterior. Krichinsky-Kaye house. Night.

JULES *and* ANN *come out of the house and head down the steps toward* SAM'*s Coffee Grinder.*

ANN (*exasperated*)

I'm just this far away from losing my mind!

She holds her fingers as if measuring.

Cut to

129. Exterior. Nightclub. Night.

Establishing shot

130. Interior. Nightclub. Night.

Angle on CAMERA GIRL *as she moves through the crowded club stopping to take photographs.* COUPLES *dance to a* BIG BAND. JULES, ANN, IZZY, *and* DOTTIE *are sitting at a table.*

IZZY (*offscreen*)

Miss, can you take our picture?

The CAMERA GIRL *comes over to their table.*

IZZY

OK. Come on, . . . come on, everybody smile. Don't laugh, smile. Stop making a face.

DOTTIE (*smiling*)

I am. I can feel it.

JULES

Yes, you are. I can see it from here.

The CAMERA GIRL *takes the photo and leaves.*

IZZY

Miss, Miss? We gotta do it again.

DOTTIE

What? What do you want?

IZZY

I don't think my eyes were open.

DOTTIE

Oh, they were fine. What's your problem?

IZZY

I'm getting nervous now.

ANN

You? You, getting nervous?

IZZY

Your husband makes me nervous. He started it. "Maybe they won't show up. . . . Maybe no customers will show. . . . Maybe we're expanding too much. . . . in over our heads . . ."

JULES (*laughing*)

Well, it was a genuine concern.

IZZY

Genuine concern. I like that. Genuine concern . . . Very nice phrase.

ANN

Well, he does tend to be a little on the conservative side.

JULES

Let's face it, if this expansion doesn't go over, we're out of the suburbs, and we're back into row houses.

DOTTIE

That's a genuine concern.

IZZY

I think we should toast to genuine concern. . . . It has been acknowledged.

They all raise their glasses and clink them together.

JULES

To the suburbs.

Cut to

131. Interior. Nightclub.

ANN *and* JULES *are dancing to a slow number.* IZZY *and* DOTTIE *are also dancing, as are other* COUPLES.

ANN

Honey, don't count. Just—

They laugh.

JULES

I'm doing good, aren't I?

ANN

You're doing wonderfully.

JULES

Thank you. Who would have thought that a bargain marriage would have lasted this long?

ANN

I didn't get a chance to tell you, but . . .

She hesitates.

JULES

But what?

ANN

I'm pregnant.

JULES

You're what?

ANN

I'm pregnant.

JULES

You're kidding.

ANN

No, I'm not kidding.

JULES

You're kidding?! Some great news like that, and you wait until now to tell me? This is incredible!

ANN

I would have told you earlier, but the streetcar discussion got in the way. Didn't seem like the proper time to try to get in the fact that I was pregnant.

JULES (*smiling*)

That's true.

ANN

Let's face it, the streetcar story was all consuming.

JULES *laughs.*

JULES

This is great news. Hey, Izzy, guess what!

IZZY

What?

JULES

We're pregnant. We're having another child.

IZZY

What!

DOTTIE

No!

JULES

We're having another child!

IZZY *and* DOTTIE *come over to congratulate* JULES *and* ANN.

JULES *dances* ANN *into a dip and kisses her. Then they twirl around the dance floor.*

Cut to

132. Interior. Nightclub. Later.

The four are sitting around a table. They're all in a great mood and having a good time. They're singing "It's a Big, Wide, Wonderful World We Live In."

DOTTIE (*to* IZZY *about his singing*)

Please, it's bad enough over there.

The theme music to the film begins to rise in volume as the singing continues, and then the singing gradually fades, so that we hear only the theme music, which carries over into the next scene.

Cut to

133. Exterior. Street. Day.

IZZY *is driving his car down a street leading to Lexington Market, and* JULES *is in the passenger seat. They're heading toward their store, and from their point of view, through the windshield of the car, we see a crowd of* PEOPLE *on the street outside the store.*

134. Exterior. Kirk and Kaye's Department Store.

Angle on a line of PEOPLE *that winds around the length of the block. We see that the line begins at the front door of the store and goes on forever.*

JULES (*voice-over*)

What is this?

IZZY (*voice-over*)

I don't know. There's a lot of people waiting for something.

135. Exterior. Kirk and Kaye's Department Store.

Another angle of JULES *and* IZZY *in the car as they realize that the* PEOPLE *are waiting for their store to open*

JULES

This is us! This is for us!

IZZY

This is good.

JULES

Look at this! Discount is here.

IZZY

This is good.

JULES

Don't go anywhere. We're coming right out.

Fade to black

Fade in

136. Exterior. Penn Station, Baltimore. Day.

It is an autumn day. We hear a train coming into the terminal.

Cut to

137. Exterior. Station platform. Day.

A train pulls into the station, and the platform is crowded with PEOPLE *ready to meet passengers or get on the train.* SAM *and* EVA, *dressed in their best clothes, are waiting on the platform. The train stops. A* CONDUCTOR *opens the doors of the train, and* PEOPLE *start getting off the train.*

EVA

I don't even know what he looks like. Where are the people who know where the people are?

As PEOPLE *pour off the train, we see a tall, thin* MAN *come down the steps. He wears an old, leather three-quarter-length coat buttoned up to the neck. He stands on the step for a moment and looks around. He has dark eyes, and there's something very gaunt about him. Although he's in his thirties, he seems much older.* EVA *looks toward him. He looks back at her.*

EVA (*yelling*)

Simka?!

He nods. She goes toward him excitedly, and the two of them hug. Two Polish immigrants, brother and sister, meet for the first time. They step back from one another, and he says something to her in Polish. Then he turns back to the train and waves to a WOMAN *and a six-year-old* GIRL. *They step down from the train. This is* SIMKA*'s wife,* GITTLE, *and their daughter,* ELKA. *None of them speaks English.* SAM *stands back on the platform and watches.*

Cut to

138. Interior. Krichinsky-Kaye house. Night.

It is the annual KRICHINSKY FAMILY *Thanksgiving get-together.* SIMKA *and* GITTLE *are in the living room being introduced to the family. Most of the dialogue is in Polish.*

139. Interior. Krichinsky-Kaye house.

Angle on the kitchen as ANN *comes out of that room carrying a dish of cranberry sauce.* DOTTIE *follows, carrying a plate of pickles.*

The camera follows them into the dining room.

ANN

To be honest with you, I'm not exactly sure what happened.

DOTTIE

I don't know if they met in a concentration camp. Couldn't be that, right? So it has to have been a refugee camp.

They place the dishes on the table.

ANN

I'm not sure she was in a camp. Her husband might have died in the war.

DOTTIE

No, I didn't get that.

ANN

It must be. The child couldn't have been born in a concentration camp. I'm pretty sure that he met her after the war.

DOTTIE

To think that a woman could survive a concentration camp with a child. Ugh! My God, . . . it gives me the chills.

ANN

I don't think that she was in a concentration camp. I got that they met in a refugee camp and that her husband had died.

DOTTIE

But the refugee camp is really recently and the kid is like . . . six. . . . No.

ANN

We'll have to ask later.

Cut to

140. Interior. Krichinsky-Kaye basement.

Angle on a German fighter plane, a Messerschmitt. *It's obviously from a kit and is made out of balsa wood, crudely done.* MICHAEL*'s head comes into the shot.*

MICHAEL

See, there's nothing else to do with it. . . . It's done.

141. Interior. Krichinsky-Kaye basement.

Another angle. We see that all of the CHILDREN *are in the basement.* MINDY, TEDDY, *and* ELKA *are sitting on the steps of the cellar, and a few other* CHILDREN *are either sitting or standing looking at the plane.*

TEDDY

That's the problem with model planes. There's nothing left to do but look at 'em.

MICHAEL *looks at the plane as it lies on the floor.*

MICHAEL

It doesn't fly.

MINDY

It'll never fly.

ROBERT

We can throw it off a building and watch it crash.

MICHAEL

How about a cliff-hanger?

TEDDY

Now that's an idea.

With that TEDDY *squirts some glue onto the end of the fuselage and then onto the cellar floor, and he starts making a long trail. The* CHILDREN *understand what he's doing, and they respond with "Oohs" and "Aahs" as the trail goes under an ironing board, under an old chair, and halfway across the cellar floor.*

TEDDY (*excited*)

This plane's in trouble.

MICHAEL *grabs some matches from the top of a fuse box. He lights the end of the glue trail, and the fire moves along the trail as it did in the movie serial, working its way toward the German* Messerschmitt. ELKA *watches with no expression at all on her face. The fire works its way around the ironing board.* TEDDY *lies down with his face on the floor as if to examine it more closely and make it much bigger and more lifelike.*

The camera closes in for a tight shot on TEDDY*'s face as the flame flickers past him and into the camera.*

TEDDY

This looks good. The plane's definitely in danger.

Several of the other CHILDREN *get down on the floor to view the trail of fire closer. All of their faces are close to the floor and as close to the fire as they can stand it. Tight shot of their individual faces as the fire passes by, then a tight shot of the fire moving along the trail. As the flame works its way to the plane, the* CHILDREN *start humming exciting climax-type music similar to that heard at the movies when the serial is playing. As the fire quickly spreads along the fuselage, the* CHILDREN*'s voices grow louder, and when the flame hits its target and the plane explodes, the* CHILDREN *scream in mock fright. It is very melodramatic.*

MICHAEL (*screaming*)

End of the chapter! Boom! Boom! Boom!!

The CHILDREN *all yell with him.*

Suddenly EVA *appears at the top of the stairs to the basement and starts to make her way down to announce dinner. She sees the plane on fire.*

EVA

Oh my God! Oh my God! What are you doing?!! Are you crazy? You'll burn the house down!

She runs down the steps and starts to stomp on the plane to put out the fire. A piece of the wing that's on fire sticks to her shoe.

MICHAEL (*yelling*)

The wing's on your foot! You've got the wing on your foot!

EVA *grabs a towel out of one of the laundry baskets, throws it over the plane, and stamps her foot furiously on the wing that's stuck to her foot. It falls off, and she stamps it out.*

EVA

Michael, are you crazy?! You're going to burn the house to the ground!!

MICHAEL

It was just a cliff-hanger.

Cut to

142. Interior. Krichinsky-Kaye house.

All the members of the KRICHINSKY, KAYE, *and* KIRK FAMILIES *are gathered for Thanksgiving dinner. Everyone is congregated in the dining room and is seated around the table. It is obvious that* ANN *is pregnant. The table is laden with food, and a very large turkey sits in the center.* SAM *and* EVA *are trying to explain the holiday to* SIMKA, GITTLE, *and* ELKA, *who are slightly puzzled by this celebration.*

SAM

We give thanks. . . . We give thanks . . .

He thinks.

SAM (*continuing*)

The Pilgrims started it, whoever they were, . . . and now we all have to give thanks. We kill a turkey, and everybody says thank-you. . . . It's a holiday.

EVA *slowly tries to expand on* SAM'*s explanation.*

EVA

We never have turkey the rest of the year, and now we have to eat it. . . . It's a funny holiday if you ask me. Makes no sense.

SIMKA (*laughing*)

Funny holiday!

ANN

I think he's getting the wrong impression of this holiday.

MICHAEL

Are we going to eat?

SAM

Gabriel should be here any minute.

EVA

The man will be late for his own funeral.

TEDDY

We'll just eat a little bit. . . . It won't be really eating.

JULES

Dad, why don't we eat?

Several of the CHILDREN *concur, saying, "We're hungry. . . . We want to eat something."*

SAM

We should wait for Gabriel.

JULES

Come on, Dad, every year we have to go through the same thing. . . . We can't cut the turkey.

SAM

All right, Jules, cut the turkey.

All the CHILDREN *yell, "Hooray."*

JULES (*starting to cut the turkey*)

Who wants white meat?

Some of the CHILDREN *wave their hands.*

EVA (*to nobody in particular*)

I hate the white meat. . . . It's too dry. . . . It sticks. . . . It lays on you.

ANN *heaps a spoonful of mashed potatoes on* MICHAEL'*s plate and then puts a few green beans next to the potatoes.*

MICHAEL (*disgusted*)

Ugh! I hate when food touches. . . . Ugh!

ANN

What's the difference? It's going to end up in the same place.

MICHAEL *moves the green beans away from the potatoes with his knife.*

MICHAEL

I hate that. . . . I hate when it touches. . . . Ugh!

143. Interior. Krichinsky-Kaye house.

Another angle on GABRIEL *and* NELLIE *as they come through the front door and go through the living room toward the dining room.* GABRIEL *sees* JULES *cutting the turkey.*

GABRIEL (*screaming*)

You started without me?!! You cut the turkey without me?!!

(*to* NELLIE)

Come on; we're going. . . . They start without us, we leave.

SAM

Every year you're late Gabriel. We were hungry. . . . The children wanted to eat. . . . We were ready. . . . We couldn't wait.

GABRIEL

Your own flesh and blood, and you couldn't wait?!! Ya cut the turkey?!!

He turns to his wife and starts to usher her out of the room.

GABRIEL (*continuing*)

That's it! That's the last time we come for Thanksgiving.

He heads out of the dining room with NELLIE.

EVA

Such a lunatic.

SAM *gets up from the table.*

SAM

Gabriel, come here, for God's sake!

IZZY

This is ridiculous! Every year we have to go through the same thing. . . . We wait for him before we cut the turkey.

Cut to

144. Exterior. Krichinsky-Kaye house. Night.

GABRIEL *and* NELLIE *are walking to their car as* SAM *runs down the steps of the house after them.*

SAM

Come on, Gabriel, for God's sake. . . . There's food on the table. . . . It's Thanksgiving. . . . Come on.

GABRIEL

I'm not eating! You couldn't wait. . . . You couldn't wait! Ya cut the turkey!

(*a beat*)

It took us hours to get here . . . you live miles from nowhere. . . . It's too far, for God's sake. Too far for relatives.

He puts the key in his car door.

GABRIEL (*continuing*)

Get new relatives. . . . Get relatives that live near you and who you'll wait for!

He opens the car door for NELLIE, *and she gets in. He starts to walk around the car to the driver's side.*

SAM

Gabriel, for God's sake!

GABRIEL

You know what it is? That's what happens when you get to be wealthy. . . . You have a wealthy son, you don't even wait for your brother to come before you cut the turkey. To hell with ya!

SAM

To hell with me?! Jules making a good living has nothing to do with when we cut the turkey. . . . Nothing!

GABRIEL

When we were on Avalon, nobody ate! You wait for everybody before you eat, much less cut the turkey without a brother! You move out here to the suburbs, you don't think it matters anymore?!!

SAM

The young ones are hungry. . . . They carry on. . . . They make a commotion. What do you want to do, stand on ceremony with the family?

GABRIEL

There's always young ones. . . . There's always young ones that are hungry, and they're carrying on and want to eat. They've got to wait until every relative is there before the turkey's cut.

(*getting into his car*)

I've said enough!

He gets into his car, and he and NELLIE *drive off.* SAM *just stands and watches him go.*

Cut to

145. Interior. Michael's bedroom. Later that night.

MICHAEL *is in bed, and* ELKA, *who is sharing his bedroom, has a bed next to his. They are both sleeping. Suddenly* ELKA *bolts up and screams. She wakes* MICHAEL.

MICHAEL (*to* ELKA)

What's wrong?

She looks at him for a long beat and then lies back down and goes back to sleep. He just stares at her, wondering what kind of nightmare she had.

Cut to

146. Exterior. Warehouse. Dockside. Day.

Establishing shot of an old, seven-story building. This is not exactly a refined-looking structure.

Cut to

147. Interior. Warehouse. Day.

IZZY *and* JULES *are at the far end of a large, open floor space in this big warehouse. The windows cast a hard morning light on the scene as the* MEN *examine the space.*

IZZY

You can put all kitchen appliances over through here. . . . Washing machines, refrigerators, stoves . . . You know, make a whole department out of it. One entire floor just for bedroom sets, sofas, sleepers . . .

148. Interior. Warehouse.

Angle on JULES *as he glances around looking a little nervous*

JULES

Whew! I don't know. What a gamble this is.

IZZY

That's it, a gamble. That's what it's all about.

JULES

It's been no time since we just expanded the other place. Where is the money coming from?

IZZY

Look, the bank is financing us. . . . This is the time. We've got no real competition. We open a place like this, we're so big nobody will be able to compete with us. We got a chance, we might as well run with it.

JULES

A discount department store?

IZZY

What's the worse thing that can happen? It goes under.

JULES

That's not bad enough?

IZZY

How much money do you have right now? You've got nothing, right? It's all borrowed.

JULES

I got nothing because every time I make a dollar, you want to expand.

IZZY

God forbid the place goes under, you can't have less than nothing. It's not allowed.

JULES *nods his head.*

IZZY

What are we? We're a discount warehouse. There's never been nothing like it. We have no frills, no fixtures. . . . we're stripped down. Nobody's ever done it before. We can tear up this city.

JULES *looks a little apprehensive.*

JULES

Let's do it!

IZZY *laughs.*

IZZY

Did you ever think you were going to owe so much money in your whole life?

They both laugh.

Cut to

149. Exterior. Krichinsky-Kaye house. Day.

SAM *drives up to the back of the house; parks The Coffee Grinder, and gets out. It's obvious he's returning from work because he has his overalls on, and his glasses and hair are splattered with wallpaper paste and paint. He goes in the back door of the house to the kitchen.*

Cut to

150. Interior. Krichinsky-Kaye kitchen. Day.

As SAM *enters the kitchen,* SIMKA, *who is sitting at the kitchen table, jumps up excitedly and begins to tell* SAM, *in Polish, that he's got a job at McCormack's Spice Company.*

SAM

A job at McCormack's Spice Company? Very good.

SAM *goes to a kitchen cabinet and takes out a bottle of his favorite whiskey and, from another shelf, a glass and pours himself a shot of whiskey.*

SAM

We'll have a family circle meeting. Get everybody to help you get your own place.

He takes a drink of the whiskey. His body shudders as the whiskey goes down, and he hits the side of the counter with his hand.

SAM

That's a good drink!

(*a beat*)

You'll have your own place. You'll be an American like us.

EVA *comes into the kitchen and sees* SAM *with his splattered eyeglasses.*

EVA

How can you see?! How can you see?! You drive a car! I don't know how you can see?

SAM (*laughing*)

I see!

EVA (*to* SIMKA)

He'll crash into a car and kill himself!

Cut to

151. Interior. Krichinsky-Kaye living room. Night.

We still hear EVA *carrying on in the background about* SAM*'s splattered glasses and how he can't see to drive.* MICHAEL *is teaching* ELKA *about the intricacies of television. He flicks the knob on the set.*

MICHAEL

Two, eleven, and thirteen—that's the only channels we've got.

He flicks back and forth between the three channels.

MICHAEL (*continuing*)

"Howdy Doody" on eleven, so that's the channel you want to be on in the afternoon. You want to try it?

ELKA *turns the dial as* MICHAEL *did and speaks as if learning for the first time.*

ELKA

Two, eleven, thirteen . . . "Howdy Doody."

MICHAEL

Monday through Friday "Captain Video" . . . That one's great. Did you ever see "Captain Video" where you come from?

ELKA (*trying to pronounce it*)

"Captain Video"?

MICHAEL

"Captain Video."

Cut to

152. Exterior. Street. Day.

SAM'*s Coffee Grinder is moving along a city street on a winter's day.*

Cut to

153. Interior. Sam's car. Day.

SAM *is at the wheel,* EVA *sits beside him, and* MICHAEL *and* ANN *are sitting in the back. They are all dressed in their Sunday best—heavy winter clothes.*

SAM (*to* ANN)

What time is Jules coming to the family circle?

ANN

He'll be there on time. He said he wanted to take some golf lessons . . . see how it goes.

EVA

Golf? He's gonna learn golf?

SAM

That's what I said when I heard. A working person doesn't play golf. It's for people with sweaters and a cap.

EVA

Where does he get such crazy ideas?

ANN

Why is that such an unusual thing?

EVA

It's not unusual. I just never heard of it.

ANN

You mean to say you've never heard of people playing golf?

EVA

Of course I've heard of people playing golf, . . . but not working people.

MICHAEL

What about Mr. Rhodes? He plays golf.

SAM

That's not the same thing. His father was already wealthy, way before I came to this country.

EVA

It isn't the same thing.

ANN

I can't believe you're gonna make an issue out of the fact that he's out there taking golf lessons.

SAM

There's no issue.

EVA

An issue? Who's making an issue? I find it strange that he's playing golf. It's not an issue.

(*a beat*)

Sam, don't run with the machine!

SAM

I'm not running! I'm going thirty-five miles an hour.

EVA

You're running. . . . You're running! The telegraph poles are going by too quick!

Cut to

154. Exterior. Gabriel's house. Day.

Long shot of the row houses stacked on top of one another. Tight shot of a baseball card floating up to the edge of a step. It has a picture of Joe DiMaggio on it.

155. Exterior. Gabriel's house.

Angle on TERRY, *one of the older children, as he aims a card at the step. He tosses his card. It spins in the air and floats up to the step. It's a Ted Williams. It's not as close to the step as the Joe DiMaggio.*

TERRY

Whoa!

He's not happy—he didn't win.

The camera pans over to TEDDY *and* MICHAEL *sitting on the steps of a row house.*

MICHAEL

They say that Stuart Baum was the best at eating in class.

TEDDY

Really?

MICHAEL

They say he could eat sunflower seeds in his class and not get caught.

TEDDY

It's impossible.

MICHAEL

Kept the sunflower seeds in his right cheek. Then he'd move them one at a time to the center of his mouth, open it with his tongue, separate it, eat the seed, and move the old shell to the left side of his cheek.

TEDDY

Like a chipmunk, huh?

MICHAEL

Then when he'd eat a mouthful, and he had these old shells in his cheek. Then he'd lean over to the ink well on the desk, and he'd let them fall out. He was famous.

TEDDY

Never heard of him.

MICHAEL

I think you've got to be eleven or twelve to do that.

Over this last piece of dialogue we hear yelling from inside HYMIE'*s row house, where the family circle meeting is taking place, but we can't quite make it out.*

The camera starts to move off MICHAEL *and* TEDDY *toward the front window of the house.* MICHAEL'*s voice trails off.*

MICHAEL

This is very hard, because the tongue has to move with such small movements, and you have to shell without making a noise, so you have to muffle it somehow.

The camera closes in on the front window, and we see that the FAMILY MEMBERS *are gathered around the dining-room table. The dining room and living room is packed with* FAMILY MEMBERS *and is smoke filled from cigars and cigarettes.*

Cut to

156. Interior. Gabriel's living and dining rooms. Day.

SAM *is president of the family circle and sits at the head of the dining-room table. A very heated argument is taking place, and there's a lot of tension in the room.*

GABRIEL

I don't think that we should have to chip in for Simka. That's all I'm saying.

SAM (*angry*)

This is part of our tradition! One brings another over. We supported them. . . . we took care of them.

(*to* GABRIEL)

You brought me.

GABRIEL

When's the last time that we gave percentages of our money? How long has that been? It's got to have been twenty-five years, hasn't it?

HYMIE

Belle came over . . . It was in the late twenties. No, it wouldn't be twenty-five years.

(*thinking*)

Let's see now, that was 1929 or 1930—

GABRIEL (*interrupting*)

It's close to twenty-five years!

GABRIEL'*s son,* HERBIE, *a man in his early forties, speaks up.*

HERBIE

What are we gonna do? You want to start supporting every Tom, Dick, and Harry?

SAM (*getting angrier*)

We're not talking about Tom, Dick, and Harry, we're talking about my wife's brother!! Herbie, you talk like an idiot!

GABRIEL (*also now very angry*)

Don't call my son an idiot! He's not an idiot!!

SAM

Tom, Dick, and Harry for God's sakes!

EVA (*interrupting*)

He never had any sense. He has never had common sense.

GABRIEL

Just because Jules is making money, you got a right to call Herbie an idiot?!!

NATHAN

Nobody's calling anybody an idiot.

GABRIEL (*to* NATHAN)

He called my son an idiot! His son makes money; then all of a sudden they've got this kind of an attitude.

JULES

What are you talking about? What kind of an attitude?

GABRIEL

You're living out there in the sticks. . . . You don't wait for anyone before you cut the turkey!

SAM

So, this is about the turkey! This is about the goddamn turkey again!

EVA

Oh my God! The turkey thing! The man has a mind like an elephant.

HERBIE

You don't think that wasn't unfair that he drove all that time, and you go ahead and eat the dinner before they got there?

NELLIE

We were starving.

SAM

Who ate? We didn't eat the dinner; we cut the turkey!

GABRIEL

It isn't how much you ate or didn't eat, it was the act. It was the disregard for an older brother. You might as well have stabbed me in the heart.

IZZY

What's this about? Is it the fact that they cut a turkey, . . . or is it about Simka? Let's get back to the issue and talk about some kind of support for him and his family.

GABRIEL

Huh! Another member of the wealthy contingent is speaking!!

JULES

Uncle Gabe, we're out there busting our asses to make a living. Why are you so contemptuous about that?

HYMIE

Sshh!! the language . . . The language . . . The children are outside.

NATHAN

We're not talking about a lot of money for Eva's brother.

GABRIEL

What do you mean, it's not a lot of money?

JULES

Enough of this! I'll give Simka the money, and that'll put an end to it.

IZZY

I'm with you.

GABRIEL

Good, now let's move on to next business.

SAM

Next business?!! . . . I resign! That's the next business!!

NATHAN

What do you mean, you resign?

IZZY

What are you talking about?

SAM (*getting up from the table*)

That's it! I'm finished! I'm finished with this family circle! Come on, Eva, we're going. . . . Get your coat. Jules, Ann . . .

JULES

Dad, let's try to settle this.

SAM *heads for the hall and the front door.*

SAM

I'm insulted! I'm not gonna stay where I'm not wanted!

Cut to

157. Exterior. Gabriel's house. Day.

The front door bursts open, and SAM *comes out, putting on his overcoat.* EVA *is right behind him trying to put her coat on. There's total confusion as* FAMILY MEMBERS *emerge from the house on top of one another and call to their* CHILDREN.

IZZY

Teddy . . . Mindy! Come on!

JULES

Michael! Come on, we're going. . . . Get in the car.

NATHAN *and* HYMIE *stand on the porch watching the* FAMILY *leave the house.*

NATHAN

Sam, come on, let's talk! Come back and let's talk for God's sakes!

SAM, EVA, JULES, ANN, *and* MICHAEL *start to get into* SAM*'s car.*

MICHAEL (*to* ANN)

Is it over already? Are we going for Chinese?

ANN (*sharply*)

Get in the car!

158. Exterior. Gabriel's house.

Angle on HYMIE *on the porch as he yells back into the house to* GABRIEL

HYMIE

Gabriel! Talk to him! Settle this!

159. Exterior. Gabriel's house.

Angle on SAM*'s car and the* FAMILY *getting into the car*

EVA (*to* JULES)

Where's your car?

JULES

The golf pro dropped Izzy and me off.

SAM *is muttering as he ushers everyone into the car.*

SAM

Never do I come back. . . . Never!

160. Exterior. Gabriel's house.

Angle on the front porch and GABRIEL, *who comes blustering out the front door, down the steps, and onto the street*

GABRIEL (*yelling at* SAM)

We brought you to this country. . . . We took you into the paper-hanging business. If I didn't give the say-so, you'd be in the old country. You wanted to quit the paper-hanging business. . . . You wanted to open your own club. . . . I said OK. When the nightclub was over and you wanted to come back to the business, I say OK!

161. Exterior. Gabriel's house.

Angle now includes SAM *and the others at the car.*

SAM

That's got nothing to do with nothing!

GABRIEL *starts to move around the car to where* SAM *is.*

SAM

Get away from the car!

GABRIEL

I came to a Thanksgiving dinner proud to have dinner at my brother's house, but you have no respect! No respect!

SAM *looks at him for a brief moment then gets into the car.* EVA, JULES, *and* ANN *follow. They drive off.*

The rest of the KRICHINSKY FAMILY MEMBERS *are scattered over the street, on the lawn. Some are just standing; others are making their way to their cars. There's a great deal of confusion.* GABRIEL *stands in the street and watches the car drive off.*

Cut to

162. Interior. Sam's car. Dusk.

SAM, EVA, JULES, ANN, *and* MICHAEL *ride along in silence. The piano-music score starts to play and continues throughout the following montage.* MICHAEL *stares out the back side window, and he notices in the last light of day that a diner is being unloaded from a truck in a large, vacant lot. He watches in silence. As the car passes, he looks through the back window at the diner.*

163. Exterior. Diner. Dusk.

MICHAEL*'s point of view of the semiprefab diner as it's being moved onto its pad in a gravel parking lot*

164. Interior. Sam's car. Dusk.

Another angle of MICHAEL *looking through the rear window as he continues to watch in fascination*

165. Exterior. Street. Dusk.

The car slowly moves away from the camera as it heads down the street, farther and farther from view, with MICHAEL*'s face still pressed against the back window.*

Cut to

166. Interior. Krichinsky-Kaye living room. Day.

Tight shot of hands playing the piano score

167. Interior. Krichinsky-Kaye house. Day.

The camera pulls back to reveal SAM *playing the piano and* MICHAEL *standing watching him.*

SAM (*as he plays*)

I remember when I brought the piano home for Jules. It was a beautiful sunny day.

(*a beat*)

You should learn how to play.

MICHAEL

Aaw, I dunno.

SAM

I tried to teach your father, but he never learned how to play the piano. Never. That's a shame.

SAM *continues to play as the camera slowly moves in for a close-up, and we see that he has a very pensive look on his face.*

Cut to

168. The screen

is white, and then suddenly we have a tight shot of a wallpaper brush coming through the frame, and we see going up onto a wall a sheet of wallpaper with a print of a bear sitting in a rocking chair. Then the brush smooths the wallpaper out.

169. Interior. Sam and Eva's bedroom. Day.

Another angle. SAM *is wallpapering the bedroom with nursery paper.* MICHAEL *is with him. The bedroom furniture is piled in the middle of the room.*

MICHAEL

If the baby's going in here, where are you going to go?

SAM

Well, Michael, there comes a time when you have to leave your kids. Your mom and dad need their own place.

MICHAEL

But where are you going to be?

SAM

We'll get a place with Simka, Gittle, and Elka.

MICHAEL

You mean you won't live here?

SAM *secures the panel of wallpaper on the wall.*

SAM

See this seam? You get a bubble in it, you use the brush like this and smooth it out.

MICHAEL

Can I try it?

SAM

It's not important for you to know how to wallpaper, because you should never do this in your life.

MICHAEL

I don't want you to ever leave.

SAM

One way or another we all have to leave.

170. Exterior. Kirk and Kaye's Department Store. Day.

Tight shot as the wallpapering brush goes across the frame, and then we see a cartoon of George Washington with an ax in the frame. The cartoon character is cutting through dollar signs with the ax, axing prices, and the dollar signs are scattering everywhere on this graphic.

The camera slowly pulls back to reveal that this is a large poster in the window of Kirk and Kaye's Department Store. Then the camera moves slowly in through the window.

171. Interior. Kirk and Kaye's Department Store. Day.

We see inside the store, which is festooned with large, colorful banners that read BIGGEST SALE IN THE WORLD—BEST VALUE FOR MONEY ANYWHERE, *etc. The store is crowded wall-to-wall with* PEOPLE, *and a* FIRE MARSHALL *is trying to keep some order at the entrance to the store. It's a zoo, and one would think that the merchandise was being given away.*

172. Exterior. Kirk and Kaye's Department Store. Day.

As the piano music continues, the camera pulls back to the sidewalk outside, which is crowded with PEOPLE *waiting to get into the store. The camera moves through the marketplace, where there is the usual activity, smoke curls in the air from the fires burning in steel canisters at the sides of stalls, and a great deal of hustle and bustle.*

Dissolve to

173. Exterior. Street. Day.

The camera pans a suburban street and its houses and arrives at the Krichinsky-Kaye house.

174. Exterior. Krichinsky-Kaye house. Day.

Angle on a very pregnant ANN *coming down the steps of the house helped by* JULES, SAM, *and* EVA. DOTTIE *stands on the porch with* MICHAEL, TEDDY, *and* MINDY. SAM *opens the car door, and* JULES *and* EVA *help* ANN *into the car. The car drives off.*

Cut to

175. Exterior. Hospital. Day.

ANN *leaves the hospital with her new* BABY, *accompanied by* SAM, EVA, *and* JULES.

Cut to

176. Exterior. Kaye house. Day.

SAM and EVA's furniture is being loaded onto a moving van. SAM and EVA are putting some things into their car. JULES, ANN, and MICHAEL stand on the porch. ANN holds a small baby, DAVID, in a blanket. SIMKA, GITTLE, and ELKA are putting a few things in the trunk of the car. Then they get into the car. MICHAEL has tears in his eyes. He runs down the steps and jumps up into SAM's arms. SAM holds him as the moving van pulls away from the house. SAM releases MICHAEL and turns and gets into the car with EVA. They wave to JULES, ANN, and MICHAEL, who just stand and watch as they drive off.

The piano music ends as we fade to black.

Fade up.

177. Interior. Warehouse. Day.

Tight shot of JULES

JULES (*into the camera*)

On July Fourth, the largest discount department store warehouse in the state of Maryland opens its doors.

(*a beat*)

Hi, I'm Jules Kaye.

Pull back to reveal

178. Interior. Warehouse.

JULES and IZZY are standing in front of a canvas drawing of the warehouse interior. They are dressed in their best suits. A film camera is ready to shoot a commercial, and various STUDIO TECHNICIANS mill around. The camera pans to IZZY.

IZZY

And I'm Izzy Kirk.

(*to JULES on camera*)

That's right, Jules, July Fourth, the day that you'll get independence from higher prices when K & K expands to serve you better. Sixty thousand square feet of discounted merchandise.

The camera pans back to JULES.

JULES

And with that lowest-guaranteed-price-in-town sticker price—

He suddenly stops and turns to IZZY.

JULES

That doesn't sound right, does it?

We hear a voice.

TECHNICIAN (*voice-over*)

OK! Cut it!

IZZY

It sounded good to me.

TECHNICIAN (*voice-over*)

No, you said *price* twice. . . . That's what threw you off.

(*a little exasperated*)

OK, gentlemen, let's reset to try to do that again.

JULES (*thinking to himself*)

With that guaranteed-lowest-price sticker . . .

(*to* IZZY)

Lowest-price-guaranteed sticker?

IZZY

I think it's "with our guaranteed-lowest-price sticker."

JULES

It's tough. Maybe this was not such a good idea. Maybe we should have got one of those announcer guys.

IZZY

Nah, too professional. We're salesmen. Who better to sell than salesmen? Anyway, we can't even afford these spots.

JULES (*laughing*)

You're gonna kill me with this! Every time I turn around, you remind me of how broke we are.

IZZY *also laughs.*

IZZY

Seriously, this whole TV thing is way beyond the budget that we set aside for advertising.

JULES

But nothing gets the message across like this thing.

IZZY

Yeah, yeah, yeah, . . . I know. You love television.

A makeup WOMAN *comes over to* JULES *and powders his face.*

JULES (*to* IZZY)

So what are you saying? What are we gonna do?

The makeup WOMAN *is touching up* IZZY*'s makeup.*

IZZY

Don't worry. I'll just shift some money around. Take a little from this area, . . . borrow from here; take it to there. Ya know, a little creative financing . . . bum bum bum.

JULES (*to himself*)

Guaranteed-lowest-prices-in-town sticker

(*to someone off-camera*)

Can I see that card again?

Another voice calls from off camera.

TECHNICIAN (*voice-over*)

Mr. Kaye, your mother's on the phone.

JULES *walks over to a telephone that is sitting on the floor in an unfinished part of the warehouse. He picks up the phone.*

JULES

What's up? . . . What do you mean, they're moving to New Jersey? . . . What's he doing moving to Vineland, New Jersey?

IZZY *joins* JULES *at the phone.*

IZZY

Jules, time is money.

JULES (*into the phone*)

Hold on, Mom, hold on for a minute.

(*to* IZZY)

Can you believe this? Simka's moving to Vineland, New Jersey. . . . He's gonna work on a farm.

IZZY

A farm?

JULES (*back on the phone*)

How did this happen? I don't understand.

IZZY (*as* JULES *listens*)

With cows?

JULES

One of the people he works with at the Spices? . . . All right, all right . . . I'll see you later on. You're OK, aren't you? . . . OK, . . . see you later.

JULES *hangs up the phone.*

IZZY

What the hell was that about?

JULES

One of the workers at McCormack's has a brother who's got a farm in Vineland, New Jersey. He made Simka a deal. He's gonna be the farm manager or whatever the hell they call it when you run a farm. He thinks it's too busy in a big city.

IZZY

That's something, huh? She comes to America in 1918—

JULES

1916.

IZZY

Finds out that she's got a brother that's born after she left. . . . He gets caught up in the war, in a concentration camp. They finally meet for the first time in thirty years, and in less than a year he decides to move on. So much for family reunions!

They walk back to the studio, followed by the PRODUCTION ASSISTANT. *As they walk away from the camera,* JULES *muses.*

JULES

"Guaranteed lowest sticker price," huh?

Cut to

179. Exterior. Trailways bus station. Day.

SAM, EVA, JULES, ANN, *and* MICHAEL *are at the bus station saying good-bye to* SIMKA, GITTLE, *and* ELKA *as they leave for New Jersey. We see* SIMKA *and* EVA *hug. He says something to her in Polish, and she reacts with a very warm, loving, sad look. It's a special moment between the two of them.* ANN *and* JULES *are talking with* GITTLE, *and* ELKA *is with* MICHAEL.

ELKA

Two, eleven, thirteen.

MICHAEL

There might be different channels where you're going.

As the luggage is being loaded onto the bus, GITTLE *and* ELKA *climb aboard.* SIMKA *follows. He turns around at the top of the steps of the bus and looks at* EVA *for one last moment. Then he goes into the bus. The hydraulic door to the bus closes.*

Cut to

180. Exterior. Kaye house. Day.

IZZY, JULES, TEDDY, *and* MICHAEL *come out of the house, followed by* ANN, *who is carrying* DAVID. IZZY *and* JULES *make their way down the steps toward the car*—ANN *follows with* DAVID. TEDDY *and* MICHAEL *linger on the porch.*

ANN

Good luck. I hope they show up.

JULES

Well, they came for the George Washington sale.

IZZY

It's one thing if they show up for a George Washington sale, but another thing if they don't show up on July Fourth with sixty thousand feet of merchandise.

IZZY *and* JULES *get into the car.* IZZY *calls to* MICHAEL *and* TEDDY.

IZZY

Come on, you boys . . . Time to go to work.

JULES (*to* ANN)

See you later.

TEDDY *and* MICHAEL *run down the steps toward the car.* TEDDY *gets into the rear seat.*

JULES *gives* ANN *and the* BABY *a kiss.* MICHAEL *is just about to get into the car and waves to his mother.*

MICHAEL

Bye, Mom.

(*remembering something*)

I forgot something. . . .

He runs back into the house.

ANN

Do you think he's going to be all right down there all day?

JULES

What? He's got Teddy to play with. He'll keep him busy. He'll be fine.

IZZY (*to* TEDDY)

Don't kick the seat.

TEDDY

I didn't.

MICHAEL *runs back to the car with a model plane kit.*

ANN

C'mon, Michael, hurry up, big day. Don't want to hold them up.

She gives him a kiss.

181. Interior. Izzy's car. Day.

TEDDY *looks at the model plane as* IZZY *puts the car in gear, and they drive off.*

MICHAEL

Take a look at that.

TEDDY

An SC-5A. This is gonna be good to build.

182. Interior. Izzy's car.

Angle on JULES *and* IZZY *in the front of the car*

JULES

You nervous?

IZZY

No, I'm not! . . . OK, I'm nervous.

JULES

What happens if we get there and eight or nine people show up!

IZZY

See this? Take a good look. You're not gonna see it again.

JULES

Back to the row houses.

IZZY

That's right.

They both laugh.

Cut to

183. Exterior. Warehouse and surroundings. Day.

Helicopter aerial shot of K & K Discount Warehouse. The whole building is decorated for July Fourth with American flags and banners. It is very festive.

Camera on lines of PEOPLE *around and in front of the warehouse, which is cordoned off with barricades for crowd control. At the door are a couple of* FIRE MARSHALLS, *who monitor the* SHOPPERS' *coming and going.*

Cut to

184. Exterior. Country-club pool area. Day.

Angle on blue, shiny water splashing in a pool. The MEN, WOMEN, *and* CHILDREN *are swimming and playing in the pool. The camera pulls back to reveal more of the pool area surrounded by chaise longues and tables, where* PEOPLE *are sitting and lounging and enjoying the July Fourth holiday.*

The camera closes in on ANN *lying near the pool on a chaise longue sunning herself. A baby carriage is next to her, covered with a shade.* DOTTIE *approaches, sits next to her, and starts to put on suntan lotion.* MINDY *sits on a chaise longue on* DOTTIE*'s other side. They're both in bathing suits.*

DOTTIE

Finally got through to the store. They say it's a madhouse there.

ANN

What a relief.

MINDY

Mom, can I—

DOTTIE (*to* MINDY)

Just a second, honey.

DOTTIE (*to* ANN)

I didn't get a chance to talk to Izzy, but Joe says that they've got the fire marshall there keeping people out. They've got more people than they know what to do with.

ANN

That's amazing.

DOTTIE

They did it.

MINDY

Mom, can I go—

DOTTIE (*to* MINDY)

Just a second, honey.

ANN

How are the kids?

DOTTIE

They're doing fine. They're playing down in the basement, . . . away from the craziness. The last time they checked, they were building a model airplane.

MINDY

Mom, can I go in the—

DOTTIE (*to* MINDY)

Just a second, honey.

ANN

They could be out here in the sun and fresh air playing with the other kids, but instead they have to be in a hot basement on July Fourth. Beats me.

DOTTIE

I blame Teddy.

(*to* MINDY)

What do you want, sweetie?

MINDY

Is it time to go back in the water?

DOTTIE

Ten minutes until you digest.

Cut to

185. Interior. K & K Discount Warehouse basement. Day.

Tight shot of the completed biplane sitting on a concrete floor. The camera slowly moves around it and examines it. It's very well put together. It has been painted and has its insignias. The camera continues to circle the plane and pulls back to reveal TEDDY *and* MICHAEL *staring at it.*

MICHAEL

So, what do you think?

TEDDY

It's a beauty!

MICHAEL

Should we burn it?

TEDDY

Yeah, OK. . . . Looks good enough for burning to me.

MICHAEL *takes the tube of glue he'd been using to make the plane and starts making a trail from the fuselage across the basement floor, around an old crate, and in between several other scrap objects that are lying in the basement. He makes an elaborate trail over a large area until he's used up all the glue.*

MICHAEL

You bring the matches?

TEDDY

Yup.

TEDDY *puts his hand in his pocket, pulls out a box of matches, and hands it to* MICHAEL. MICHAEL *strikes a match and sets the glue on fire. The flame makes its way along the trail of glue, around an old chair, and between two cardboard cartons on its way to the plane. The* BOYS *watch with glee. The flame reaches the plane, setting off firecrackers that the* BOYS *had tied to the wings, and the plane explodes.*

MICHAEL

You put too many in there!

We see little particles of the flame from the exploded plane lightly floating up in the air. The wings of the plane catch on fire and fall to pieces. Little particles of flame continue to float in the air. Suddenly a piece of a cardboard box catches fire.

MICHAEL

Oh my God! A fire is starting!

MICHAEL *dashes over and starts to swing at the box with his hand in an attempt to put out the fire. This causes it to flame more.* TEDDY *sees another box starting to smolder.*

MICHAEL

Everything's catching fire!

The BOYS *run from one small fire to another frantically stamping out and beating flames with the cloth. Finally everything seems to be under control. They stand nervously looking to see whether any more fires are starting. They move the scrap objects, look behind boxes, etc., until they're satisfied that there's no sign of more fires.*

MICHAEL

Nothin'. I think that's it. That was close, huh?

TEDDY

Just what we need . . . burn our fathers' store down the first day it opens! That's just what we need.

186. Interior. K & K Discount Warehouse. Day.

The last of the CUSTOMERS *are leaving the store after the big July Fourth sale. One of the store* EMPLOYEES *shows the last* CUSTOMER *out the front door and locks it.*

187. Interior. K & K Discount Warehouse.

Angle on IZZY *relaxing with a few of the* SALESMEN *in folding chairs surrounded by boxes and some merchandise.* JULES *is sitting at a desk hitting keys on an adding machine as he goes over receipts. A* SALESMAN *throws the day's cash in the air.*

IZZY (*to* JULES)

Well, it don't get much better than that.

JULES

Nineteen thousand six hundred and twenty-eight dollars! You were right! We're rich!

IZZY

Five-hour sale . . . Nineteen thousand six hundred and twenty-eight dollars?!!

We hear a champagne cork popping, and one of the salesmen, JOE, *comes forward with champagne flowing from a large bottle.*

JOE

To K & K's biggest and most successful sale!

Everyone applauds and takes a paper cup from JOE, *who pours champagne into the cups.*

188. Interior. K & K Discount Warehouse.

Angle on door leading to the basement. It opens, and MICHAEL *and* TEDDY *come up into the store, where everyone is congregated.*

JULES (*seeing the* BOYS)

What you boys been doing?

MICHAEL

Oh, just playing.

JULES

We're leaving in a minute. . . . Just gonna have a little champagne to celebrate, and then we're gone.

TEDDY

Can we have some?

IZZY

Sure.

(*to* JOE)

Give 'em a little drop, Joe.

JOE *fills a couple of paper cups with champagne and hands them to* MICHAEL *and* TEDDY.

JULES (*raising his cup*)

To everyone, . . . thank you, and I hope this is the first of many successful days.

IZZY

We're just a couple a Yankee Doodle Dandies!

Everyone drinks his champagne. MICHAEL *takes a sip from his cup, pulls a face, and spits out the champagne.*

MICHAEL

Ugh! What a taste. . . . Ugh!!

TEDDY *is not thrilled with it either, and after he's taken a gulp, he shudders.*

The SALESMEN, IZZY, *and* JULES *laugh at the* BOYS.

Cut to

189. Exterior. Street. Dusk.

IZZY'*s car drives along a tree-lined country road and through a large gate on which a sign reads* BONNIEVIEW COUNTRY CLUB. *The camera follows the car along the driveway leading to the country club, which is surrounded by rolling hills and is very lush.*

Cut to

190. Exterior. Country-club patio. Night.

Angle on steaks being thrown onto a barbecue grill

191. Exterior. Country-club patio.

The patio is resplendent with July Fourth decorations—fairy lights, flags, and lanterns adorn all areas of the patio and an outside dance area, where a BAND *is playing cha-cha music.* JULES *and* ANN *are dancing the cha-cha and are very good, using great precision in their steps.* DOTTIE *sits at a table on the patio holding* ANN'*s* BABY *on her lap.* IZZY *is standing and dancing by himself near the table where* DOTTIE *sits. He sings to the music that the* BAND *is playing.* MINDY, TEDDY, *and* MICHAEL *sit next to* DOTTIE *sipping cold drinks.*

IZZY (*singing*)

"Cherry pink and apple blossom time. . . . It is the time to dah, dah, dah, dah, dah. . . . Because it's cherry pink and apple blossom time. . . . It's the time to dah, dah, dah, dah, dah."

MINDY

Dad, that sounds horrible!

IZZY

Are you kidding me? I used to sing on radio.

MINDY

You did?

DOTTIE

What are you talking about? You used to sing *to* a radio.

A country-club EMPLOYEE *approaches* IZZY.

CLUB EMPLOYEE

Mr. Kirk? I'm sorry to bother you, sir, but you have a telephone call.

DOTTIE

What is it?

IZZY

I don't know. I haven't gotten the call yet. What, is it at the main house?

CLUB EMPLOYEE

Yes, you can get it right over there at the snack bar.

IZZY

All right.

IZZY *tips the* MAN.

CLUB EMPLOYEE

Thank you, sir.

IZZY

I'll be right back.

Camera follows IZZY *as he makes his way to the phone at the snack bar, situated in an outside area. He picks up the phone, which is dangling off the hook.*

IZZY

Hello.

(*he listens*)

Yeah.

(*listens some more*)

Oh! My God!!

Cut to

192. Exterior. Country-club patio. Night.

Close-up on a trumpet that bursts forth with a blast of the "Cherry Pink and Apple Blossom" tune.

193. Exterior. Country-club patio.

The camera swings over to JULES *and* ANN *as* IZZY *approaches them.*

IZZY

I just got a call. The new store's on fire.

JULES (*shocked*)

What happened?

IZZY

They don't know yet. . . . It's already a four-alarm fire. . . . Let's go.

IZZY *moves through the dancers toward the table where* DOTTIE *and the* CHILDREN *are sitting.* JULES *and* ANN *follow. The camera stays with them.*

IZZY (*to* DOTTIE)

I gotta go. . . . The store's on fire!

DOTTIE

Oh, nooo!

194. Exterior. Country-club patio.

Angle on MICHAEL *as he looks at* TEDDY.

Cut to

195. Exterior. Country-club pool area. Night.

MICHAEL *and* TEDDY *walk around the pool. The patio and music are in the background.*

TEDDY

Just don't ever say anything, . . . ever.

MICHAEL

We did it! We burned the whole thing down with glue! My grandmother always told me I was gonna burn the house down. . . . now I burned a whole store down!

TEDDY

Just don't say nothing to nobody.

We hear ANN*'s voice calling.*

ANN (*voice-over*)

Michael! Teddy! Come on boys, . . . we're going to go!

TEDDY

Remember, nothing to nobody.

Cut to

196. Interior. Ann's car. Night.

ANN *is driving.* DOTTIE *sits in the passenger seat holding the* BABY *in her lap.* MICHAEL, TEDDY, *and* MINDY *sit in the back.*

ANN

Izzy didn't know anything more. Didn't know how it started.

DOTTIE

I don't know. . . . I just don't know.

TEDDY *and* MICHAEL *glance at one another.*

ANN

I don't know about you, but I'm gonna be a basket case just sitting home waiting to hear what happened.

Cut to

197. Exterior. K & K Discount Warehouse. Night.

IZZY *and* JULES *drive into the alley and stop the car as we hear the sound of sirens wailing in the background and the faint sounds of* FIRE CREWS *and* POLICE *in the distance. The sky is red from the fire, and the whole area is smoke filled.* IZZY *and* JULES *get out of the car and begin to run up the alley in the direction of their burning store. The camera moves with them through the alley into the pockets of darkness and light. They reach the top of the alley and stop. The camera moves slowly to their faces as the sounds of the fire, sirens,* POLICE, *etc., grow louder and louder.*

198. Exterior. K & K Discount Warehouse. Night.

Angle on JULES *and* IZZY *as they move around the fire apparatus, helpless to do anything. From their point of view we see that the fire seems to be somewhat concentrated in the middle section of the building, up four stories. The top floor seems OK at this point.* JULES *and* IZZY *spot the* FIRE CHIEF *and run over to him.*

JULES (*yelling to the* FIRE CHIEF *over the noise*)

We're the owners.

FIRE CHIEF

Sorry. It doesn't look good.

JULES

What do you mean it doesn't look good?

FIRE CHIEF

What we're trying to do is contain it at this time.

IZZY

So you're saying there's nothing you can do?

The FIRE CHIEF *moves off to say something to one of his* FIREMEN.

FIRE CHIEF (*to* IZZY *and* JULES)

We're doing all we can. The fire boats are coming into service now.

The fire boats pull up to the dock as IZZY *and* JULES *watch the cascading water from the* FIREMEN*'s hoses spraying the old structure. We hear four or five loud popping sounds, and we see the beginning of July Fourth fireworks high in the sky above the blaze and smoke of the warehouse fire.* JULES *stares as he sees burning furniture being hurled out a window and into the water below.*

199. Exterior. Kaye house. Night.

The screen door opens, and MICHAEL *bolts out, runs down the steps of the house, and starts to run up the street at full speed.* ANN *comes running out of the house after him.*

ANN (*yelling*)

Michael! Michael!

She runs down the steps and begins to run a little way up the street after him. She stops, out of breath, turns, and goes back toward the house. As she walks up the steps, DOTTIE *comes out of the house onto the porch.*

DOTTIE

What's going on?

ANN

I don't know what's wrong.

TEDDY *comes to the door.*

DOTTIE (*to* TEDDY)

Did you two have a fight?

TEDDY

No.

ANN

I'm gonna get the keys to the car and drive after him. You'll stay here?

DOTTIE

Of course.

200. Interior. Kaye house. Night.

DOTTIE *and* ANN *go back into the house with* TEDDY.

DOTTIE (*to* TEDDY)

Are you sure the two of you didn't have a fight about something?

ANN *takes the car keys from a hook in the hallway.*

ANN

I don't know whether he's going to try and go to the store. . . . I don't know.

Cut to

201. Exterior. Street. Night.

Angle on the headlights of ANN*'s car as it moves slowly along a street*

202. Interior. Ann's car. Night.

Angle on ANN *searching for* MICHAEL

Cut to

203. Interior. Streetcar. Night.

MICHAEL *sits in the moving streetcar looking very glum.*

Cut to

204. Exterior. Street. Night.

MICHAEL *is running as fast as he can down one street and then crossing another.*

205. Exterior. Street. Night.

Another shot of ANN's *car moving through the neighborhood. She drives alongside a moving streetcar and looks up to see if* MICHAEL *is inside. There are only a few* PEOPLE *on board. There is no sign of* MICHAEL.

Cut to

206. Interior. Sam's house. Night.

SAM *is in the living room watching television. The horizontal hold is off, and the picture is rolling over.* EVA *comes into the room carrying snacks.*

EVA

How can you watch with a picture like that?

SAM

Ah! To hell with it. You're up; you fix it.

EVA *puts the snacks on a table in front of* SAM.

EVA

I'm not touching that thing.

SAM

It's one of those knobs. . . . you touch a few of them, and it'll be all right.

EVA *goes over to the television and starts to fiddle with the knobs. The vertical hold goes out.*

SAM

That's good. . . . You just got to play with it.

EVA *continues to play with the knobs, but the condition of the picture remains the same.*

EVA

I hate this thing. A radio, you put it on a station, it's there. Here the picture can go this way and that way. . . .

As she turns the knobs, the picture goes to black, and only the sound is heard.

SAM

That's it! You got radio!

She sits down next to SAM, *and the two of them sit listening to the sound of the television.*

Cut to

207. Exterior. Street. Night.

MICHAEL *hurries along a street lined with row houses. We hear explosions and see a number of fireworks displays—a beautiful array of color.* MICHAEL *stops and looks at the fireworks. No emotion is visible on his face.*

Cut to

208. Exterior. Street.

MICHAEL *continues down another street. He stops and looks at a couple of row houses for a second, then seems to recognize the house he's looking for. He goes up the steps of the house and knocks on the door.*

Cut to

209. Interior. Sam's house. Night.

SAM *hears a knock at the front door. He gets up and moves toward the door.*

EVA

Who's knocking?

210. Interior. Sam's house.

Angle on SAM *opening the front door to reveal* MICHAEL *standing there*

SAM (*surprised*)

Michael! What are you doing here?

EVA

Michael? Michael is here?

MICHAEL *comes into the house. He is slightly out of breath. He tries to catch his breath so that he can speak.*

MICHAEL

I did a terrible thing. . . . Terrible.

SAM

What happened?

EVA *comes out of the living room and into the hall, where* SAM *and* MICHAEL *are.*

MICHAEL

I burned the store down.

SAM

What are you talking about?

MICHAEL

Me and Teddy were playing with the model airplane and the glue, and something must have happened.

EVA

I told you! I told you not to play with that, . . . you'd burn something down. Now it's happened. Oh my God!

SAM

Eva, please!

MICHAEL

We put it out. It was just a little fire. . . . We put it out. I don't know what happened.

He starts to cry, and SAM *puts his arm around him.* EVA *makes her way to the kitchen.*

EVA

I'll get you a cold drink. You'll feel better.

Cut to

211. Interior. Sam's house. Night.

EVA *is in the hall on the telephone.*

EVA

Dottie, where is she? . . . She went looking for Michael? Michael is here with us. Just tell Ann. . . . Did you get any more news from Jules and Izzy? . . . Yes, I don't want to tie up the lines either. . . . OK, good-bye.

Cut to

212. Exterior. K & K Discount Warehouse. Night.

ANN *is at the scene of the fire talking to* JULES.

ANN

I don't know. . . . I have no idea. . . . He just ran out of the house. I drove through the neighborhood and couldn't see him. . . . I thought he might have come down here. . . . I don't know where he is.

JULES

Jesus Christ. All right, don't yell at me.

ANN

I'm not yelling. I'm worried about him.

FIRE CHIEF

Mr. Kaye, can we see you for a minute? I'd like to go over something.

JULES *makes his way over to the* FIRE CHIEF.

Jules *(calling back to* ANN)

Call my parents; maybe he went there.

ANN

All right, I'll go look for a phone. I'll be right back.

JULES

Let me know, all right?

The blaze is now being contained, but it is obvious that the building has been lost.

213. Exterior. K & K Discount Warehouse.

Angle on JULES *and the* FIRE CHIEF *talking. The* FIRE CHIEF *is pointing up to a section of the building that's no longer burning. The fireworks continue in the distance.*

Cut to

214. Exterior. Sam's house. Night.

We see SAM *looking through the window of his house. From his point of view we see* JULES *drive up and park in front of the house.*

Cut to

215. Interior. Sam's house. Night.

MICHAEL *is sitting on a chair sipping his cold drink.*

SAM *(to* MICHAEL)

Here he is.

(a beat)

You're gonna have to tell him.

MICHAEL

How am I gonna do that?

SAM

I told your mother to have your father come and get you because you had something very important to say. Let's go.

MICHAEL *gets up.* SAM *puts his arm around* MICHAEL*'s shoulders, and they walk to the front door, open it, and step out onto the porch together.*

216. Exterior. Sam's house. Night.

Angle on JULES *getting out of his car. He stands at the curb and calls to* MICHAEL.

JULES

So, what's all the mystery?

SAM (*calling from the porch*)

Michael has something he has to tell you. Go, Michael.

(*to* MICHAEL, *gently*)

I'll leave you two alone.

MICHAEL *looks up at his* GRANDFATHER *with foreboding.* SAM *gives* MICHAEL *a reassuring squeeze on his shoulder and then turns and goes back into the house.*

JULES *moves toward the steps of the house but remains on the sidewalk while* MICHAEL *stays on the porch.*

MICHAEL

Daddy, it's my fault.

JULES

What?

MICHAEL

I burned the store down.

JULES

You what?

MICHAEL

Me and Teddy were playing with the model airplane, and we finished, put glue all around the basement. And Teddy had some firecrackers, and we added those. And it caught fire, but we thought we put it out, but we didn't I guess.

JULES (*a beat*)

Sit down.

JULES *and* MICHAEL *sit on the porch.*

JULES

How many times have you been told not to play with fire?

MICHAEL

Lots.

JULES

Lots. A lot. You think maybe it's about time you started listening?

MICHAEL

Yeah.

JULES

I'm glad you told me, Michael. It was very brave of you, . . . but it's not your fault. I was just talking to the fire marshall. The fire started on the fourth floor.

MICHAEL (*a beat*)

It started on the fourth floor?

JULES

They're not one hundred percent sure, but it seems to have been some kind of an electrical fire.

MICHAEL

It started on the fourth floor, huh? Not in the basement?

JULES

No. You didn't do it, Michael.

(*a beat*)

Come on, let's go.

JULES *puts his hand out to* MICHAEL, *and* MICHAEL *comes down the steps of the house. His* FATHER *puts his arm around his shoulder, and they walk toward the car.*

217. Exterior. Sam's house.

Angle on SAM *standing at the screen door. He steps out onto the porch and calls to* JULES.

SAM

Jules! So, what's with the store?

JULES

It's gone, Dad. . . . It's all gone.

JULES *and* MICHAEL *get into the car, and as* SAM *watches them drive off, fireworks explode in the sky, and the street turns into a burst of colorful light.*

218. Exterior. Street. Night.

Long shot of the car driving down the street with the burst of light from the fireworks glowing above it.

Slow dissolve to

219. Exterior. Burned-out warehouse. Day.

The now-extinct warehouse resembles bomb-site ruins. Smoke drifts into the air from the burned-out building. In the distance JULES *and* IZZY *walk among the ruins and assess the damage. We see them ducking inside part of the building that remains, which is merely a shell.*

220. Interior. Burned-out warehouse. Day.

Angle on JULES *and* IZZY

JULES

And the televisions will go here. . . .

He moves his arm to indicate a nonexistent wall on the right.

JULES (*continuing*)

The appliances will go through this section. . . .

He points to the opposite wall and shakes his head.

JULES (*continuing*)

Whew!

He is quiet as he looks at the damage.

JULES (*continuing*)

Open for five hours, and that's it!

They move among the rubble as smoke continues to rise gently from the smoldering embers. IZZY *is unusually pensive.*

IZZY

You want to hear the worse part?

JULES (*caught off guard*)

What?

IZZY

You want to hear the worse part?

JULES

What's that mean?

IZZY

Well what it means is we don't have the insurance to cover this.

JULES

What the hell are you talking about? You take care of this stuff.

(*a beat*)

You're telling me we don't have any insurance?!

IZZY

We had it. . . . I canceled it.

JULES

You canceled it?!! There's no insurance for this whole goddamn thing?! How's that possible? What the hell did you do?!!

IZZY

I told you when we were doing the television commercials that we didn't have enough money. You didn't seem to care when I told you I'd have to move money around. Borrow a little from here and a little from there, . . . bub, bub, bub . . .

JULES *walks among the rubble, kicking at the embers, hardly believing what he's hearing.*

IZZY

It's always been borrowing from Peter to pay Paul. . . . It's like a gamble. I borrowed from the insurance. . . . thought we'd save a little money from there while we handled the advertising budget, . . . get this place on its feet.

JULES

There's no insurance for this whole goddamn thing—

IZZY

No, there isn't. This is like a fluke, Jules, you know? A fluke.

JULES *laughs ironically.*

JULES

Yeah, . . . it's a fluke all right.

IZZY

These things don't happen. What are the odds on something like this happening?

JULES

Something like this?

IZZY

Yeah.

JULES

Gotta be a million to one.

IZZY

Exactly. A million to one. Maybe I should have told you more, but you didn't want to hear it, right?

JULES

No, no. I didn't mean to yell. It's not your fault. It's one . . . .

His voice trails off.

IZZY

You want to hear some worse news?

JULES

Worse news?

IZZY

It's one thing that this building burns down and we're back to square one, but this thing puts us about two and a half million in the hole.

JULES

How much?

IZZY

Don't hold me to it. . . . Might be three; could be two. Probably closer to two.

JULES

Two, three million dollars in the hole. Not a bad day's work. So what do we do?

IZZY

File bankruptcy and then regroup. We'll lose some of the distributors because they're not gonna want to do business with us anymore, but we'll pick up some new lines. With a little luck, we can get back..

JULES *looks around at the burned-out building.*

JULES

Nah! I think that's it for me. This is too much of a roller-coaster ride for me.

IZZY

The Krichinsky cousins, Kirk and Kaye.

JULES

No, I think this is the end of the road for me.

He walks among the debris.

IZZY (*a long beat*)

What are you gonna do?

JULES

A salesman can always sell. It's not the product; it's the salesman. That's what my father always said.

Dissolve to

221. Exterior. Street. Day.

SAM*'s Coffee Grinder is moving along a country road.*

EVA (*voice-over*)

Sam, don't run with the machine.

SAM (*voice-over*)

I'm not running. . . . I'm not running!

The car approaches a set of large gates with a sign that reads WELCOME TO FROCK'S FARM—PICNIC & BARBECUE AREAS, SWIMMING, BOATING, RESTAURANT, SUNBATHING DECKS, HOLIDAY CABINS—FUN FOR ALL. *We see* SAM*'s car drive past the gates.*

EVA (*voice-over*)

You missed the gate. . . . You missed the gate! Thirty years we've been coming here, and you missed the gate!

SAM (*voice-over*)

I didn't see it.

EVA (*voice-over*)

It's because you're running with the machine. How can you not see the entrance?

SAM *backs up the car, and they drive through the gate to Frock's Farm.*

Cut to

222. Exterior. Frock's Farm. Day.

We see a lot of FAMILIES *scattered over the picnic area.* ADULTS *are sitting at tables, lying on deck chairs sunbathing.* CHILDREN *are playing on the grassy area and swimming in the lake.*

223. Exterior. Frock's Farm.

Angle on SAM, EVA, HYMIE, *and* ALICE *at a picnic table that is cluttered with food and beverages. In the water, in front of the picnic table, we see* TEDDY *and* MICHAEL *swimming.*

HYMIE (*to* SAM)

Why don't you speak to Gabriel, Sam?

SAM

I'll never speak to him.

HYMIE

Yeah, . . . but you don't speak to Gabriel, and then Nathan doesn't want to speak to you because he doesn't like the idea that you don't speak to Gabriel. So now we've got four brothers, and two don't speak to one another.

SAM

How come Nathan speaks to you when you speak to me?

HYMIE

I can talk to you. . . . This he can tolerate, . . . but he won't talk to you unless you speak personally to Gabriel.

EVA *makes a loud burping noise.*

EVA

Whew! I've got an indigestion.

ALICE

You've been having indigestion a lot.

EVA

It lays on me. Whatever I eat.

HYMIE (*looking out at the water*)

Look at the kids. . . . Look at 'em play.

ALICE

How come they don't go out to this country club?

EVA

I don't know. They don't seem to like it there. They like it better here, with us.

HYMIE

Well, they'd better like going to the club, because they're gonna get rid of this.

SAM

What are you talking about?

HYMIE

I was talking to the old man. He's gonna sell the place. They want to build homes here.

EVA

Homes? Too far for homes. Gotta be a pioneer to live out here.

ALICE

You couldn't get here with a streetcar.

SAM

If they can build homes, they can put more streetcar tracks down.

HYMIE (*to* SAM)

Let me ask you. Jules can still afford the club?

SAM

Well, he's paid up for now, and we'll see what turns up with some work.

HYMIE

Ha! He can always get a job.

SAM

Of course. The boy could always sell.

HYMIE

And Izzy?

SAM

Still looking to get money to open another store.

EVA *burps again.*

Cut to

224. Exterior. Frock's Farm cabin. Day.

SAM, EVA, HYMIE, *and* ALICE *are playing cards at a table on the porch, and* TEDDY *and* MICHAEL *are sitting close by at a table that is covered with sunflower seeds.* MICHAEL *is filling his mouth with the seeds.* TEDDY *watches him as he starts to do the Stuart Baum Sunflower-Seed Classroom Trick.*

TEDDY

If we get this worked out really well before we get back to school, then we'll be able to eat all year long.

MICHAEL, *with his cheeks full to capacity, is attempting to separate the shells from the seeds in his mouth.*

TEDDY

Too much mouth movement.

MICHAEL *adjusts his mouth slightly.*

TEDDY

That looks good.

Suddenly MICHAEL*'s eyes grow wide as he begins to choke on the seeds.*

EVA (*yelling over to him*)

Do you have to eat the whole bag at one time?! The boy'll choke to death.

As MICHAEL *continues to cough and spit out the seeds,* TEDDY *slaps him on the back.* EVA *gives a loud burp again, then starts to get up from the table, throwing her cards down.*

EVA (*patting her chest*)

Whew! I think I'll take a little walk. . . . It might help.

(*to* MICHAEL *and* TEDDY)

You boys wanna go for a walk?

TEDDY

Yeah.

MICHAEL *tries to speak, but he's still coughing and spitting out sunflower seeds*

EVA (*to* ALICE)

You wanna come?

ALICE

Nah, I'll stay and fix a sandwich.

EVA, MICHAEL, *and* TEDDY *start to walk away from the porch.* ALICE *gets up from the table as* SAM *and* HYMIE *continue to play cards.*

HYMIE

Fix me another sandwich, will ya?

ALICE

You already had two.

HYMIE

This'll make three.

ALICE

You want something, Sam?

SAM

Nothing for me, Alice.

Long shot of EVA, MICHAEL, *and* TEDDY *walking through a field where cows are grazing. All of a sudden in the distance we see* EVA *fall to her knees. The* BOYS *try to help her, and then* MICHAEL *turns and yells.*

MICHAEL

Sam! Sam!

Cut to

225. Exterior. Hospital parking lot. Day.

JULES *parks his car, gets out, and walks toward the front entrance of the hospital. He wears an overcoat, and it's obvious that we're now into the fall season.*

Cut to

226. Interior. Hospital corridor. Day.

SAM *is sitting on a bench in the corridor.* JULES *approaches.*

JULES

How she doing?

SAM

Same. . . . Every day's the same. She gets better; she comes out. . . . She gets worse; . . . she comes back to the hospital. . . . In and out, in and out of the hospital.

JULES

Listen, Dad, Ann is going to make a little Thanksgiving dinner. You want to come over?

SAM

No, I'd better stay here. I'll have a bite in the room with your mother.

JULES

Well, if you change your mind, you're welcome.

JULES *opens a door close to where* SAM *is sitting.*

227. Interior. Hospital room. Day.

JULES *goes in to see his* MOTHER, *who is lying in a hospital bed surrounded by an oxygen tent and the paraphernalia that goes along with it. It's obvious that she's seriously ill.*

JULES

Ma, how ya doin'?

EVA

I'm tired talking about it.

(*a beat*)

How's the new job?

JULES

It's good. . . . I like it. It's interesting, . . . challenging. I like it.

EVA

Selling time. I've never heard of such a thing.

JULES

It's not just time, Ma, it's time for television commercials. The companies buy the time for the television commercials so that they can sell their products.

EVA

I hate commercials, but I like the one where the cigarette packs dance. I like that. Did you sell them time?

JULES

No, Ma.

EVA

That's a shame, because I like that one.

She closes her eyes, and JULES *sits watching her.*

Cut to

228. Interior. Kaye kitchen. Early evening.

Close-up of a turkey being sliced

229. Interior. Kaye kitchen.

ANN *is putting slices of turkey onto three plates, then adding dressing, vegetables, and gravy. She puts the plates on a tray, and the camera follows her as she walks from the kitchen through the hall and into the living room, where* MICHAEL *and* JULES *are sitting in front of the television watching the evening news. TV trays are set out in front of them.* DAVID *sits in a high chair next to* JULES. ANN *sets the tray down on a table, then takes each plate of food and puts one down in front of* JULES *and the other in front of* MICHAEL. *She sits down with her plate.*

230. Interior. Kaye living room.

Another angle of JULES, ANN, *and* MICHAEL *as they sit and eat in silence while watching television*

231. The Screen

goes white. The camera glides across the white surface, and we realize that it is snow. The camera continues to move over the tops of a number of black umbrellas as snowflakes gently fall.

232. Exterior. Cemetery. Day.

MOURNERS *stand around a graveside. They are standing in snow. We see the* KRICHINSKY FAMILY MEMBERS *at the funeral of* EVA. *The* RABBI *is reciting a eulogy.*

RABBI

We have come here to pay our final respects to the late Eva Krichinsky, a woman of valor. She came to America in 1916. She married, raised a beautiful family, was a devoted wife and mother, one who was loved by her family and many friends. She lived a full and happy life, and she died peacefully.

The RABBI'*s voice trails off as the camera pans the* MOURNERS, *and we see that* GABRIEL *and* NATHAN *and their* FAMILIES *are missing from the group.*

Cut to

233. Exterior. Cemetery. Day.

JULES *and* SAM *walk together back to the funeral cars.* ANN *and* MICHAEL *walk behind them, and the other* FAMILY MEMBERS *follow behind them.*

SAM

Gabriel didn't come. . . . Nathan didn't come, . . . and what happened to Simka?

ANN

He called. . . . He couldn't get away, . . . couldn't get anyone to take care of the farm.

SAM

This is not a family. Not a family.

Cut to

234. Exterior. Kaye house. Dusk.

Establishing shot

235. Interior. Kaye house. Dusk.

SAM walks into the living room, where the television is on. He carries a newspaper and there's a somber feeling about him—the effects of losing his wife after so many years. He sits down in a chair near the window. Snow is falling outside.

The outside light slowly grows darker and darker until SAM is barely visible. JULES calls out.

JULES (*voice-over*)

Dad, come on for some dinner.

236. Interior. Kaye house. Night.

A hand reaches out and turns on a light at the side of the chair where SAM is sitting. We see that SAM now looks very much older and grayer. Ten years have gone by. The television is on and tuned to "The Cisco Kid." SAM gets up from the chair, and as he walks, we see that he has the walk of an old man and doesn't seem as sharp as he was.

The camera follows SAM into the kitchen, which has been modernized considerably since the last scene. There's a portable TV on a counter, and it, too, is tuned to "The Cisco Kid." SAM sits down at the kitchen table, where ANN, JULES, and DAVID, who is now ten years old, are already seated. ANN hands him a plate of macaroni and cheese.

SAM (*to* DAVID)

So, how was school today, Michael?

ANN

That's David, Dad. Michael's in college.

(*to* DAVID)

What's the madder with your corn?

DAVID

I don't like it.

ANN

Since when you don't like it? I've been making you corn since. . . .

SAM

Phew! It was yesterday I had to go up to the school; he was in trouble. . . . Something with *may* and *can.*

He carefully digs his fork into one piece of macaroni and puts it in his mouth and eats it. JULES watches with concern and exchanges a look with ANN.

SAM (*continuing*)

Those yesterdays I remember. . . . *Yesterday* . . . I don't remember.

Cut to

237. Interior. Jules and Ann's bedroom. Night.

JULES *watches television while* ANN *gets ready for bed.*

JULES

I don't know what to do. He doesn't walk well. . . . He's falling down. The idea of putting him into a home is so terrible to me, . . . but I don't know what to do.

ANN

It's hard, I know. I never had to confront it because my parents died so young.

ANN *gets into bed, and* JULES *climbs in next to her.*

JULES

He wets the bed. . . . I dunno. . . .

JULES *gives* ANN *a kiss and lies on his back staring up at the ceiling for a few moments. Then he leans over and turns off the light on the nightstand.*

The screen goes black.

Fade up.

238. Exterior. Driveway. Day.

Angle on a Mustang making its way up a long driveway toward a large, old building. The car pulls into a parking space in front of the building. A tall, thin man in his mid-twenties gets out of the car. He goes around the car and opens the passenger door. A small BOY, *four years old, gets out, and the two of them walk hand in hand toward the building, which has a sign above it* LEVINDALE RETIREMENT HOME.

Cut to

239. Interior. Levindale Retirement Home. Day.

Angle on a RECEPTIONIST *sitting at a desk just inside the entrance hall.*

RECEPTIONIST

You'd like to see Sam Krichinsky?

240. Interior. Levindale Retirement Home.

Another angle on the young MAN *and the* BOY. *They are standing across the desk from the* RECEPTIONIST.

MAN

Yes, I'm his grandson, Michael Kaye.

The camera pulls back to include the RECEPTIONIST.

RECEPTIONIST

All right, Mr. Kaye.

She hands him a visitor's pass.

MICHAEL

Does my son need one?

RECEPTIONIST

No, he's fine.

Cut to

241. Interior. Sam's room in Levindale. Day.

The room is fairly dark. SAM *is sitting in a chair, and* MICHAEL *sits across from him. His son stands by his side.*

SAM

In the end you spend everything you ever saved, sell everything you've ever owned just to exist in a place like this.

There's a long, awkward pause.

SAM

So, are you dating?

MICHAEL

I told you, Sam, I'm married.

SAM

You're married?

MICHAEL

Yes, and this is my son. I named him Sam.

SAM

Not supposed to name him after the living.

MICHAEL

I know.

SAM

You know? That's good. . . . That's good. . . . Carry on the family name . . . That's good.

(*a long pause*)

Couple of years ago I went to see the house on Avalon, and it was gone. Not just the house, but the whole neighborhood. I went to see the ballroom where me and my brothers used to play. Gone, . . . the whole place gone. Not just that, but the grocery store where we used to shop . . . gone, all gone. I went to see where Eva lived on Poplar Street; it isn't there, . . . not even the street. Then I went to see the nightclub I used to have, and thank God it was there, because for a minute I thought I never was.

(*a beat*)

If I knew things would no longer be, I would have tried to have remembered better.

MICHAEL

I miss you, Sam.

SAM

I came to America in 1914. . . .

Cut to

242. Exterior. Levindale Retirement Home. Day.

The camera follows MICHAEL *and* YOUNG SAM, *as they walk away from the camera.*

YOUNG SAM

Dad, that man talks funny.

They walk toward MICHAEL'*s car. The piano music begins.*

MICHAEL

He wasn't born here, Sam.

YOUNG SAM

You mean he wasn't born in Baltimore?

MICHAEL

He came to America in 1914. He said it was the most beautiful place he's ever seen.

Dissolve to

243. Exterior. Baltimore. Night.

We see SAM *walking through the streets of Baltimore as in the opening scene of the film, with lights strung across the street and fireworks exploding above. Then there's a burst of bright light, and as the piano music builds, we fade to black.*